Also by Emma Hinds

The Knowing

EMMA HINDS

THE
QUICK
AND THE
DEAD

Bedford
Square
Publishers

First published in the UK in 2025 by Bedford Square Publishers
London, UK

bedfordsquarepublishers.co.uk
@bedfordsq.publishers

ISBN
978-1-915798-87-9 (Hardback)
978-1-915798-88-6 (Trade Paperback)
978-1-915798-89-3 (eBook)

2 4 6 8 10 9 7 5 3 1

Typeset in Garamond MT Pro by Palimpsest Book Production Limited,
Falkirk, Stirlingshire

Printed in Great Britain by CPI Group (UK) Ltd, Croydon CR0 4YY

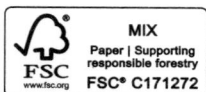

MIX
Paper | Supporting
responsible forestry
FSC
www.fsc.org FSC® C171272

For those of us still transforming

'The real test of knowledge is not whether it is true but whether it empowers us.'

—*Francis Bacon*

'Philosophy is odious and obscure;
Both law and physic are for petty wits;
Divinity is basest of the three,
Unpleasant, harsh, contemptible, and vile:
'Tis magic, magic that hath ravished me.'

—*Doctor Faustus, Christopher Marlowe*

SANGUIS

PART I

'Be careful not to take anything from the lion but the rose-coloured blood, and from the white eagle only the white gluten. Coagulate (corporify) it according to the directions given by the ancients, and you will have the *tincture physicorum* (The Elixir of the Red Lion). But if this is incomprehensible to you, remember that only he who desires with his whole heart will find and to him only who knocks strong enough the door shall be opened.'

—Tinctura Physica, *Paracelsus*

London, 1597

⟊ℰ⟊ ⟀ⴸⴸⵝⵝⴲ ⵝⴸⴴⵔⵔⵕⴸ⟊

He who cries aloud from desolation

Chapter One

K it is not afraid as he is tied to the whipping post at the Standard on Cheapside.

'For stealing, the cutpurse is to be whipped until bloody,' the sheriff calls over the assembled watchers.

Kit's audience is a smaller crowd than usual, unsurprising given the slow and steady spread of plague out from around Fleet Prison, not five minutes from the city walls. The watching crowd is reduced to bored fishwives, a few pious-looking types and the dog catcher, paused with his stick and hoop of rope over his shoulder. Kit wonders if the sheriff pays him per dog caught or dog killed. He could kill a dog. Surely it cannot be hard. The first lash lands. It tingles. He knows from the force that pushes his face against the blood-stained post that he should scream, so he does.

'One!' The sheriff's satisfied voice calls over the crowd.

The meagre crowd cheer – because why would they not? If he saw some frater or a jarkman tied to the post or pilloried, he would cheer just as much, and call them fools for being caught in their snatching and forging. There is not a spell or prayer in all of

5

Christendom that can take the crime out of criminals, and he has been thieving since he was a sprout. So he yells when the lashes come. He remembers how Ned Alleyn screamed as Faustus was dragged down to hell and gives it his best. He makes a good enough show of it, by his reckoning.

'A cutpurse!' someone shouts. 'Skin him alive!'

The sheriff seems to take that to heart. The pressure of blows across his naked back jolts his forehead into the post. Again. Again. Again. What makes other men piss themselves he just finds tedious, so to amuse himself, Kit considers how he can give the best performance of pain. Most people by this point in the process are less lusty of voice and give more whimpers, so he tries a bit of that. It is nothing to cry, really, just stare into the sun until the eyes are a little blind. At nearly twenty-one years old, he cannot grow a beard, and whilst it is certainly an annoyance, it is good at times like these, when he can squeeze out a few tears; with his young face, people might go easy on him. He ignores the thump of his head against the post and wonders what pie he might get Mariner to buy for him afterwards, if she has managed to filch a few purses during his performance. Or maybe Twentyman will take them to the Mermaid for a pint, if he is hidden in the back. Lads who take the brand for their master, they get pints.

'Have pity!' someone cries.

The lashes pause. The watchers are quieter now. He realises that, for a while, the only sound he has heard is the wet, gasping exertion from the round-bellied sheriff.

'Let the lad down!'

Now he notices that a few of the fishwives are covering their eyes and shaking their heads. Only one person stares at him with the greedy expression of a sadistic cosmopolitan. She stands out, even despite her dark cloak, because nothing in London can hide

Spanish satin from his thieving eye. It is strange that she is not pressing a nosegay to her face, like the finer ladies are want to do when passing down Cheapside. Those intent eyes linger upon him as he is untied and staggers. That surprises him. Perhaps his feet have gone dead standing so long in the same place. He surveys the crowd, looking for a thin face, perhaps a proud glower. He cannot see his master.

'Kit Skevy, for being a cutpurse you have been whipped with many lashes and now you are to be branded. God save the Queen!' The sheriff pushes him to his knees.

What a red-faced, sweaty man he is. It is a marvel really, that he is the one who has been delivering the punishment and not receiving it for surely he looks about to die with the effort. The blacksmith stands ready. A hand in Kit's hair, twisting his face down onto the block. He makes sure to watch carefully as the glowing brand is lowered to his temple, waiting until he hears the hiss and burn inside his own skull to scream pitifully and appropriately. Then it is done. Dragged up, tossed away, the smell of his own burnt flesh filling his nostrils as he stumbles into Mariner's waiting arms. She is a tall woman; she catches Kit easily and holds him steady under her armpit. Such height helps her daily deception along with her cropped brown curls and boy's clothes. Her young, rounded jawline has her frequently taken for a lad of one and twenty not the twenty-five-year-old woman she secretly is. Kit has always been envious of her dangerous face; a pink burn scar over her left eye, vivid against her light-brown skin, one eye queerly milky. When she wants to scare children she tells them she can see the devil with it and how the two of them laugh when the little ones scream, for there is delight in having a partner in perceived monstrosity. Mariner does not look like she is laughing today.

'Can you stand?' She appears oddly pale-faced for a Moorish girl out of Portugal, but she is probably hungry and twitching to get moving, especially if she is hiding snatched trinkets in her sleeves.

'Of course.' His feet do not seem to want to obey his desire to leave. 'I am only tired.'

Being whipped is more exhausting that he anticipated.

'Tired?' Mariner stares at him, incredulous. 'Kit, the fucker lashed you endlessly; Christ himself was not so whipped! You didn't faint or shout as you should have—'

'I did excellent cries, I thought.' His voice slurs. He has no notion why. 'Where is Twentyman? Are we for the pub?'

He watches as his best friend's face twists into a familiar mask of contained enraged disappointment.

'He's not here,' she says shortly.

Kit does not understand. What have I done this time, he thinks? 'I am here!'

He turns his head, hoping to see the man to whom he has given more than a decade of thieving, the man he was branded for, here to congratulate him, but it is only Griffin, sooty and sweaty as always.

'My sister sent me to help you home. I only have a few bells before rehearsal.'

Griffin manages stage craft for the Admiral's Men. At forty-one years, he retains the height and bearing of a man who was once considered a great beauty of the stage. These days, his long blond hair runs to ratty, a once-cherubic face a little jowly and speckled with blond-grey stubble. A transformation from top billing to the wings, using alchemy tricks and secrets sailed in from distant lands to make devil smoke seep up from under the boards of the Rose. It is Kit's favourite place to be when he is not brawling or stealing for Twentyman; crouched under the boards, helping Griffin spill magic from bottles and braziers.

'I see she was right to send me,' Griffin says, grasping Kit's other arm.

Griffin's hands are red and damp. Wet, he thinks, since he was taught to name these things, that will feel wet.

'I am bleeding,' he says. He cannot say he feels more because he does not. This is why he is never afraid.

The first time he spoke of it, Kit was burned. He'd been in England about three years by then; eight years old and Twentyman had sent him flying out of the door with a boot up his arse for a bad day's stealing. Fuck off, you little whorehouse shit, his chasing shout followed Kit scuttling down Bankside to the blacksmiths. He watched the smithy boys in fascination as cold, sturdy things became glowing and fluid. Why shouldn't he touch, when it was so bulbous and serpentine, red and writhing, pulsing with heat like a living thing? It was only after, in the sideways glances of the smith boys and Mariner's imperfectly concealed shock that he saw his mistake.

'Trying to broil yourself, Young Kit?' she said.

Everyone called him Young Kit, even Mariner, his newly arrived friend from sea who was only four years older than him, for he was still small for his age. He was in the habit of using it to see what he could get away with. Griffin called that canny and Kit liked the word, just as he liked the smells of London, his stable bed at the Silver Moon and the grand cavernous space inside the playhouse. At the pike ponds behind the Rose, Mariner dipped Kit's hand beneath the water.

'You must be careful around the Smithy.'

'I did not feel it.'

'No reason to pretend, it looks dreadful.' She touched the bubbly white skin hesitantly. It reminded Kit of the rind of fat that

9

sometimes gathered on the top of the stew at the Silver Moon when it was too cold. 'Does it not hurt?'

He concentrated on his senses, though sensation had never been something he was good at.

'The water is wetter than my skin, colder than my skin but warmer still than snow. What is hurt?' Kit put words to a truth he had known all of his short, confusing life. 'Is it... hot? It is a little hot, the wound itself. Does it make my skin tighter and harder? It is both. Is that hurt?'

Under the water, the fish nibbled at Kit's fingers with their smooth, enquiring mouths whilst Mariner stared at him, her one, stranger, lighter eye catching the sunlight from the water's surface.

'You say it does not burn or ache at all?' Her words were slow, disbelieving, and then suddenly, fast: 'Do you feel no pain?'

Kit did not know if it was true. Griffin had always watched him ever since he came with him from Antwerp, pulling his hands away from hot plates and thorn bushes. He had simply presumed that perhaps he had not yet done anything that qualified enough to hurt, but Mariner's face was incredulous and her tone urgent and Kit did not know how to placate her.

'What does pain feel like?' he asked.

'God's wounds. I will have to think about it.'

Kit waited. He knew he was different; he had known it for a while. He could stand in the sun for hours without fainting or retching. He could skate on the Thames endlessly and not complain like others did when his fingertips turned blue. He watched the pain of others with interest; he had seen Twentyman cut a man's ear off, seen the blood pour and thought it fascinating, the way men bellowed. Kit Skevy has made a study of screams but he has never screamed for anything.

'Pain feels as if there are warning bells inside your flesh,' she said, finally. 'As if a great hue and cry has been taken up inside you. You know that something is very wrong because you feel the pain. The pain makes your heartbeat fast, your brow sweat, makes time move differently.'

'How can time move differently?'

'It moves slower or faster, as it does when you are happy or sad. You know?'

Kit nodded but he did not know. Those words; pain, hurt, burn, ache, they were lands far away Kit always expected to arrive in but never yet had. Mariner, sitting beside him with her frown and disbelief, she somehow lived there.

'Perhaps you are made differently when it comes to pain,' she mused. 'Like a bear, maybe.'

They had watched bears fight, kill a dozen dogs and not go down. Kit was not certain he wanted to be a bear.

'None could hurt Achilles,' Kit said, nervously. 'Griff told me the story. He was dipped in the river Styx.'

It is a wondrous and wicked thing to be magical; even then Kit knew it could take you places. To the great courts of Europe or to burn at the stake. It kept him awake sometimes, those small nightmares of what he could be. Things that later they would call him behind his back, or shout at him in a fight: a witch child, a changeling, a demon, Satan's spawn, unholy. At the time, Kit could only think it was better than being a bear.

'They said the same about Goliath and look what happened to him,' Mariner said, drily. 'It is the Lord's doing, it is marvellous in our eyes, but no need to let it go to your head.'

Kit did not consider it marvellous. The world was full of people feeling; pain and time and sweat and heartbreak. Kit was burdened with being outside of all of it; curious, and alone. So Kit learned to play the part of pain, to hide the secret of his strangeness deep behind cries and moans and coughs. Sometimes he would test it, with things that caused great discomfort to others. He nearly drowned twice in the Thames, has fought many fevers and even more brawls. Nothing changes. His friends have kept his secret but his reputation as the oddest boy in Southwark has only grown. Even now, dripping blood through the city, he can sense it: those who saw him whipped watching him and the attention in their eyes curdling from sympathy to suspicion the longer he stays upright.

'Curse you, Skevy, you damned wretch!' a little boy yells to them as they press down through St Paul's square to the river. 'My master had a crown on you swooning!'

For the last four years he's been Twentyman's prize brawler. He's a whole head shorter than Twentyman's other lads and even Mariner but when he gets hit, he never stays down. There's always use for a lad who is as small as a robin and fights like a badger, so says Twentyman, and there are always people who scorn him for rising, over and over, as if all of Southwark waits for the day he does not. He cannot imagine it. Not even now, with slow steps that barely drag towards the bridge, Kit Skevy finds it hard to believe he can die, for surely, if he were to die, he might feel pain eventually?

'You need to be careful,' says Mariner, his arm slung over her shoulders as they weave their way through a flock of sheep crossing the bridge.

'Why should I?' Kit's words are a slurry of mumbles. He's been branded and whipped and he's still headed home for trouble. Mariner steps on his toe when he's looking down so that he'll see it. He looks up at her steadily.

'Ouch,' he says.

'Pushing yourself as close to your death as you can manage will not make you feel it,' she says curtly. 'All it will do is kill you eventually.'

Kit wonders how it is that a girl like Mariner, raised in the navy and coarse as fucking mud, always knows how to put words to the worst urges of his heart.

'We all die.' Kit's feet stumble underneath him. He does feel very, very sleepy. 'Better surely not to feel it. Better to feel nothing at all.'

'Despair is a sin.'

'So are all the delightful things,' Griffin says and Kit smiles. They say in the Silver Moon that Griffin had a famous atheist lover, the poet Marlowe, dead these four years. They say other things too, that Griffin picked up more than his vices, infected with Marlowe's deadly unbelief. If it's true, then it's an ague Kit seems to have been born with.

'Is hell?' Mariner glares at them both. She is the oddest confluence of things, a dark girl in a city of pale faces, a woman in boy's clothing, full of a sailor's superstitions but also raised a reformer. She amuses and exasperates him in equal measure every day.

'*Where we are is hell, and where hell is, there must we ever be,*' Griffin says.

'Southwark?' says she, and Griffin laughs. An awkward trio, they stumble under Traitor's Gate. All of Southwark is stretched out in front of them, cramped and sweaty under the summertime pall of Winchester House, its tall chimneys belching smoke out into the yellow air. These are the streets where the unwanted of London make their living; odd travellers from distant lands like Mariner, players born in the shadow of the tower like Griffin, or orphans from Belgian whorehouses, washed up in the city where anyone can be anything, like Kit. The great families of London, the Howards, the Sidneys, the Walsinghams, the Raleighs, they rotate distantly around the star of the crown, soar on each other's wings and plummet or rise on their names and fortune. In Southwark it is different. Here, you scrabble your way up from nothing; come from the country, come from the north, from wars and trades, with no family to catch you and a deadly fall below. Marlowe from Canterbury, Spenser from Smithfield, sons of cobblers and cloth makers rising up on rickety ladders made of grammar schools and English bibles. It is in Kit's bones, this impatient striving to make coin, to carve out a life, to leave something better than the little he started with in this patch of houses built on Thames mud. It's been sixteen years since Griffin brought him from Antwerp and when Kit once asked him who he was born to he only said this: It matters not who you are born to but where you are made. On days like these, bloody and beaten, he wonders what good it is to have this secret gift of painlessness if this is all he is? Kit Skevy is Southwark made, a brawler and a thief, and sometimes he worries that this is all he will ever be.

ᛩᛡᛣᛡᛚᛡᛏ

He who is in emptiness

Chapter Two

Bankside belongs to Will Twentyman. Kit's home has been anywhere he rules, the dusty road from the Silver Moon, Squire Kay's tavern where the bells of St Olaf ring over wherry men and wool traders east of the river, down along the Thames westward to the red painted whore's door of Twentyman's best brothel, the Cardinal's Hat. Then on to the bear-baiting pits where Kit fights bare-knuckled and bloody, and beyond it, his favourite place in the world, the Rose Theatre. Squire Kay (so called for a jest in her youth that no one now dares recount) is currently standing fierce and alert, in the doorway of the Silver Moon. Everyone in Southwark jokes she must be a royal bastard with all that milky skin, those robust curves and flaming Tudor hair. It is true that there is often less of landlady and more of monarch in the way she governs her tavern and the urchins that call it home but, at thirty-nine years old, Griffin assures Kit that his little sister has always been imperious.

'You're late,' she scowls. 'I worried.'

Squire Kay brushes the curls back from his new brand for

inspection. The close-to smell of her is reassuring; sweat and ale and the dandelion soap she uses on her ferocious red hair.

'Well, it won't make you any uglier.' She pets him fondly. He has always been odd to look at; gingery curls as tight as a sheep's, one blue eye, one green, and the darkest freckles all over that Squire Kay always says looks like he has stood next a cartwheel on a muddy day. Customers at the Moon make fun of him, saying his mother must have been a whore twenty times over to get a child so ugly. He does not mind, he is grown; he has no need of parents but a sweeter master would do.

'Skevy!'

The door is kicked open and there he is, Will Twentyman, with all the look of a man freshly dug out of the grave. Sallow, yellowing preserved skin, teeth too big for his mouth, muddy hair clasping the back of his head in thin drabs. He is barely forty but his unfortunate countenance suits his ominous moniker: the Grave Eorl of Southwark. It's a title earned by selling corpses, among other things. Kit's master is an Upright Man who sees a weakness or a need and meets it. He sees fat country purses in the city, he assembles an army of Southwark thieves to cut them. He hears of hot-blooded young gentry, looking for gritty amusement and saucy girls, he runs fist fights fights and the most lucrative whorehouse south of the river. Kit has been assured that there is an ugly iteration of his master in every city in the world, a king of rats in every rat pile, and even if it is risky to live under such a man, he is more likely to live under him than die under him. Yet Twentyman has no kindness for those he employs and only rewards those he finds useful. Now, with that cadaverous unforgiving gaze upon him, Kit has the discomforting feeling of not being useful.

'Twenty-nine lashes, they say. You could not endure for thirty?' his master snaps. 'There was money laid against you, lad!'

'If you had come and watched you might have told me so.' Kit wants to sound defiant but he is doleful and loathes it.

'What good does it do me to come and watch my prize brawler swoon for the whip?'

'What was he to do?' says Mariner. 'Politely ask to be tied back up?'

'Who asked you?' Twentyman glares at Mariner. The bitterest of contention simmers between them, as always. Twentyman thinks her a shrew, but Mariner steals her own weight in coin, so his distaste never brews too sour. He switches his glare back to Kit: 'Did you cry?'

'The sun was in my eyes.'

'Can't blame the lad for crying when flogged, Will' Griffin says, winking at Kit, who tries not to smile because Twentyman detests Griffin. Older lads swear up and down they were childhood friends, the only relic being that Griffin is the one person in all of Southwark who still calls Twentyman by his first name. Rumour is, not even his mother does. She calls him Twenny. When Kit is being humiliated by his master in front of other lads, it's this insipid, twittering nickname that he remembers.

'Can he fight?' Twentyman turns to Ezra, standing in the doorway behind him. Ezra Prophet should have been born a prince. His dark skin is smooth and he keeps his black hair and beard short, both heavy with speckled grey. He tells no one his true age, but Kit reckons him to be fifty at least. The stories around him are legend; he was Bishop Bonner's Worthy Moor, he was a Spanish general in the Armada who swam to England, he confirms or denies none of it but he is married to Squire Kay manages the brawls and ledgers of Twentyman and has the best handwriting on Bankside. He gives Kit a quick, reassuring smile whilst looking over his back.

'Sorry, Young Kit, it'll need stitching. You'll be no good for the next few days.'

'To the barber surgeon with you!' Twentyman aims a kick at Mariner and she glares at him, making a lewd gesture behind his back before walking down the street towards the butchers. 'I'll not pay for your stitches, Skevy, it's coming out of your takings.'

'I'll pay for it,' Griffin says.

'Oh, course you will,' Twentyman sneers. 'Which of your alchemists have you been sucking for it?'

'You don't object to my friends when they buy from you,' says Griffin.

The kind of men of science and alchemists who want to buy corpses from the Grave Eorl are the kind of people Griffin knows; buying his equipment and ingredients for stage craft from their odd little stalls up on the bridge. Consequently, Griffin is one of the few people in London who makes money off Twentyman, a compensatory cut for introducing clients, and the Grave Eorl despises nothing else more.

'I need brook no objection to their *coin*.' Twentyman spits at Griffin's feet. 'I'll not let a heretic use my arse for play, unlike your bloody Marlowe—'

'Griffin, you'll be needed.' Squire Kay's voice is sharp, cutting quickly through. 'At the Rose.'

Griffin and Twentyman stare at one another. There's a shiver of a moment when Kit thinks Griffin might punch him but then it is gone, a sail falling with no wind. Griffin's shoulders stay the same, mouth still clenched, but the vivid flash of violence behind the eyes retreats. Kit tries not to be annoyed for Griffin is a kind man and if Kit has family Griffin is part of it, but this flaccid slump in the face of a challenge makes the edges of his respect curdle. As soon as Griffin has strolled away, green cap jaunty and uncaring in the sunshine, Twentyman grabs Kit's collar, baring his blackened teeth. His breath smells of onions, raw and sharp.

'You were caught and branded and you cannot even do that right. You are useless, Skevy.'

Twenny, Kit thinks. At least I am not called Twenny. His master gives him a round slap, disappearing back inside and shouting over his shoulder:

'You'll fight two days hence or I'll send you back to fucking Antwerp, no matter whose bastard you are.'

'Am I a bastard? Twentyman says so,' Kit asks, later that day. He is stitched and watching Griffin roll a cannonball across the heavens of the Rose to create the effect of thunder. Griffin pauses, legs crouched around the iron, a frog with red hands splayed atop it.

'It is possible. When I found you, you were motherless and fatherless.'

This is the part of the story that never changes. Griffin found Kit in a whorehouse whilst he was living in Antwerp at barely twenty years old. For Kit, there are no memories of that house of women or his first four years. There is only the memory of Griffin, taking him aboard a ship and then, the sticky taste of the odorous London air.

'You know Will only talks to start fights,' says Griffin. 'Pay it no mind.'

Kit helps him lower the swevel down through the designated hole towards the stage floor below. Tonight, Griffin will set a firecracker off at the bottom of the wire and up, up, up it will shoot, illuminating the stage in a flash of lightning as hell is opened to swallow Faustus. It is Kit's favourite part.

'Why do you let him talk to you like that? Say that Marlowe used you so?' Kit watches the familiar flinch and retreat that happens every time Griffin's dead lover is mentioned. It is hard to look at him when his face crumples this way, so Kit turns to rolling fire-cracker papers into cones. He does not think there is a better smell than gunpowder, whispering of tricks and enchantment.

'Why not?' Griffin's mouth is soft, wry, but the lines around his eyes are sorrowful. 'Even when he lived, they said such things. It is a refrain without end.'

Kit says nothing. He has read every play Griffin has ever put in front of him, and Kit has an uncanny memory, so he is more than literate; he is learned. He's absorbed over and over the romantic notion of the agonising desire. It is curious to him, he who has never been in love nor felt pain, that the two things should be so regularly paired together. He's had dalliances, plenty of them, girls and boys, and they've mostly been pleasurable but Kit knows it is incomparable. There is a haunting to Griffin that Kit finds simultan-eously baffling and repellent.

'You met in Flanders?'

It's the kind thing to do, he knows, to let people speak of their losses. Kit's childhood was punctuated by Griffin's absence back overseas; taught to write by sending letters to Flushing.

'Aye, in eighty-five. When Walsingham died in ninety, I was cut loose like so many, but not Christopher. He was kept on for espio-nage.'

'You? A spirit?'

These are the things that are said of Marlowe: poet, player, atheist, sodomite, spy. Kit stares at Griffin, his long dirty-blond hair tied back behind his head in that same old green ribbon, his slowly receding hairline. He's never seen anyone who looks less the part.

'Everyone did.' Griffin shrugs away a dangerous past with a tip of his shoulders. Old Walsingham took advantage of every Englishman abroad, it seemed.

'Did you bring back secrets?'

'Only one.' Griffin reaches into his shirt and pulls out a small vial of black liquid on a length of leather string. 'It's a great alchemy formula, so they said. Everlasting fire. It was an important recipe, as it turns out, burned no more than five minutes. I've tried my hand at replicating it, over the years.'

'You could sell it to some puffer.' Kit rolls the glass between his fingers, watching the way the black liquid moves in the vial, sluggish and creeping against the sides.

Griffin drops the leather strap around Kit's neck.

'You have it. Hold it against your disappointment in me, that I did not knock Will's head off as you hoped.'

'There's always tomorrow,' Kit tries to joke but Griffin only shakes his head slowly, heavily.

'We are not all bred for defiance, Young Kit.'

Kit waits in the silence of this omission of Griffin's failure but nothing comes. He's been hoping for years that Griffin will put in a good word for him with Mister Henslowe so he can buy an apprenticeship into the Admiral's Men. Griffin has not done it. The older he grows, the more his disappointment in Griffin is a wet cloak, weighing him down.

'I want to be bred for stage craft,' Kit says. 'Like you.'

Perhaps Griffin senses something of Kit's true thoughts, because he reaches over and squeezes Kit's hand.

'Be better,' Griffin says.

Two days hence and Kit is fighting for Twentyman rather than being shipped back to Antwerp.

'They are holding, only just,' Ezra says, checking his stitches as Kit leans his arms on the fencing and spits blood and, unfortunately, a tooth chip onto his boots. Nearby, Kit watches as Twentyman gloats and bribes in a merry dance around the ring under the summer stars. There is nothing like the smell of a fist fight in June. 'Maybe punch less frequently and more effectively.'

'Do you not think I always try to do that?'

'Kit! Ezra!' He turns towards Mariner's voice. She is elbowing her way through men, indistinguishable from the other short-haired beardless lads around her except that her eyes are wide with fear. 'You must come, it's Griffin! There's fire!'

Fire. The most dreaded word in all of London. Kit runs, imagining the Rose ablaze, her boards and magic consumed into nothing, but it's Griffin's lodgings near the Cardinal's Hat they run to. Smoke is billowing out of Griffin's windows and in front of it, Squire Kay screams for water to be fetched, someone, do something! As rolls of thunderous black fog and smoke leech under the door. The smell is sharp and acrid, worse than the stink of sulphur and gunpowder. Others are coughing, unable to get near, but Kit is only struggling to *see* since it is so very dense. Yet as he blinks through it he realises there is no flame.

'It's not fire!' he yells.

'One of his experiments gone wrong?' Mariner shouts back.

'He's inside!' Squire Kay sobs, clinging to Ezra's arm. 'He must be hurt, the door is locked!'

'A backed-up chimney, I'll warrant! Come on, Young Kit!' Ezra shouts and whilst Mariner holds up Squire Kay, they set their boots to it. Again and again, again and again, other men may stop kicking but Kit does not need to stop and finally, the door splinters away from the lock. He cannot see anything; the blackness of the smoke immediately consumes them both and Ezra is turned back, coughing and retching. Kit pushes in, stumbling blindly into the two rooms, navigating by touch rather than sight but nothing seems to be dimming it and all the windows are shuttered. Flutterings of panic begin in his gut because Griffin only ever locks himself away for his most dangerous of experiments, the kind that kill a man.

'Griffin!' he shouts, fumbling his fingers on the latches, flinging the shutters open, charcoal-tasting urgency filming his mouth. The thunderous black clouds of smoke are starting to clear, revealing a truly devastated room, chairs upturned, papers rifled as if Griffin fought his way away from whatever horror he accidentally unleashed. Then there is a body on the floor. Kit's first thought is relief. This man laid out so haphazardly cannot be Griffin, he thinks, he is surely too small and crunched, frail and broken. Then Ezra steps into the room, bearing a pitch and tow torch.

'Oh, Griff,' he says.

The pitiless light illuminates that favourite forest green doublet, the worn velvet that thinned at the elbows, that long hair tied back just so, the same green ribbon. There is an ugly grey spittle around his mouth, evidence of lungs blackened, a throat grey with smoke, choking the breath away. Kit moves closer, all sound and voice lost to his ears as he crawls under the lingering smoke to touch Griffin's face. He has seen many dead people, but nothing like this, the extravagant absurdity of vacancy in such familiar lips and eyebrows. Come back, he thinks. Then he remembers that neither he nor Griffin believe that there is anywhere else to come back from. Still he thinks it, compulsively, mind so numb to all else: Come back to me.

'Away, Kit, the constables are here.' Mariner is pulling him to his feet.

For the first time Kit feels time stretch, for suddenly they are outside and Squire Kay is there, crumbling to pieces, a grasping, bellowing thing and Kit does not understand. How can he be out here when he is still on the floor with Griffin, his cheek absorbing the last warmth of his dead heart? Then it happens, thundering through him at last: pain.

No one said his body would become wrong, and small, that he would be sure he must be out of it, immediately, because there is an enormous yawning stretch of anguish inside his chest that he must outrun. He has seen the hearts of bulls on market day, lumpy and firm, with no secret places to hide, yet perhaps the heart of man is made differently to hold such hideous, invisible forces. He is fighting Mariner without noticing, her arms wrapped tight around him, and he hears a voice chanting; no, no, no, no! Is it him, his mouth? Is it his knees that buckle under him, uncaring of the horse shit, and his hands that dig into the mud, wanting to push down and back into the past? He has been a fool to be curious of pain, a fool his whole life, for he would rather be dead or buried alive or have his legs severed than this monstrous, drowning sensation. He knows he must find a way to breathe through it, fucking breathe, Skevy, but there is not enough air in the sky. As he wheezes at the indifferent stars above, there is the lightest flicker of something else, a distant robin's wing brushing against his mind. Despite thinking himself loveless and painless all this time, something inside reminds him: This is not the first time. I have felt this before.

ꡗꡘꡑꡋꡌ꡷ꡘ

She of many repetitions

Chapter Three

Mariner Elgin's world is pockets. When she was young it was wind, how it filled the sails, the speed at which it blew and how far it would take her. But she has lived in Southwark in the service of the worst man alive for thirteen years and the world is pockets. As Griffin's coffin is lowered into the damp earth she cannot help but eye the purses on display. Players are notoriously poor, but Mister Henslowe is here and his purse fair bulges. Beside her, Kit shifts, as the voice of the priest intones, the declarations of the holy gospel spoken over the plain board coffin:

'... And he shall come again in glory to judge both the quick and the dead. And I believe in the Holy Ghost, the lord and giver of life, who proceedeth from the Father and from the Son...'

These words are not for Griffin, the man she once heard describe the sacraments as having been better delivered in a tobacco pipe. Some of the players are sniffling, particularly the young lad who plays the heroines in the Admiral's Men. He has a face like a kicked dog but can cry like a virgin, so said Griffin. It seems to Mariner that those professing the least despair are the ones carrying it heaviest. There is Ezra, standing stoically with an arm around his wife, but Mariner knows all of Ezra's expressions. The way his face dimples under the left corner of his mouth is a repressed sob. Beside him, tucked under his arm is Squire Kay, eyes dry and hard. Her grief is turning her to a statue so brittle that one kind touch will break her, and in her hands she holds the items they pulled from Griffin's purse. Mariner is the one who cut it from the body, of course, thinking his sister would want it before the burial. A few shillings, a loose button, a folded letter so worn the creases were soft cuts in the paper. Mariner looked at it because who wouldn't, but it was written in a lilting script too elegant for her to easily read. A few couplets, an M at the bottom in lieu of signature. Marlowe, she presumed, some of his terrible poetry for Griffin to treasure. Mariner would rather be left nothing than verses, but looking at the way Squire Kay clutches the paper and the button, she might as well be gripping Griffin's own collar, holding him out of the grave, rather than cradling the banal remnants of his life. Mariner wonders what would be left of her. She fiddles in her pockets; a groat and a pie crust. The priest is finishing:

'... I look for the resurrection of the dead, and the life of the world to come, amen...'

Mariner doesn't mean to, but she thinks of her uncle Elgin's grave, somewhere deep at the bottom of the ocean. She has often thought that it is a long way to be resurrected from on the day of judgement. How much heavenly power will be needed to pluck Elgin from the deep, dark ocean floor with cockles on his eyes? She has been brought up under the teachings of Calvin to believe in the predestination of souls; Elgin's eternal path has been laid out before even the creation of the world; hers too. She knows it is supposed to be a comfort to the saved, the immutable justice of God, but Mariner only feels a discomforting prickle at the back of her neck, the sensation of being caught. To be known by God is only a relief to those who live unashamed and, besides, it is hard to believe anything south of the river is part of God's holy ordinance.

'Amen,' she still says, even after all these years. It's the hope, tender and flimsy, that gets her every time. Perhaps my little sinful life will be enough for paradise. Perhaps.

'Come on, enough praying.' Kit is dry-eyed but pale behind his absurd freckles. He is still weakened in the lungs from too much smoke and, on top of that, made stranger with grief. He is lopsided now; something has been cut off him. She has spent many long years watching Kit Skevy, fearing what his carelessness will do to his body. She has never before had to fear for his mind. 'Time for drinking.'

'What's on your face, lad? Jam?' There is a sailor leaning against the bar of the Silver Moon, watching Mariner as she collects pints. Griffin died at the very tail end of June. A week has passed since the funeral, the month has turned, but still Kit is wanting to drink as if Kent is running out of hops.

'A burn at sea.'

Mariner had been still a small child when a fire at sea had stolen away her parents, aunt and cousin to a terrible death on the journey between Lisbon and Edinburgh. Only she and her uncle Elgin had survived, both plucked from the flaming wreckage by a privateer. Uncle Elgin had been a ship's surgeon; he'd helped Mariner survive terrible burns over much of her body. Even though she had healed well everywhere visible, a patch of polished, hairless skin remains over her left eyebrow. Her sight is worse out of that eye, clouded, but she makes up for it with better hearing than most.

'Oh aye?' The sailor leans forward. 'You still in service, lad?'

'No.'

By the time Mariner was old enough to be breeched, Elgin decided she may as well live life as ship boy with him than be sent to her mother's family in Portugal. So Elgin had hidden her lack of a pecker with baggy clothes and called her a boy and she had been happy, content with Elgin and the wide, wild sea. Until everything went horribly wrong and Elgin left her with Twentyman, eight years later.

The sailor gives her an appraising look.

'You're dark for an Englishman, aren't you?'

'Been here thirteen years.'

'Aye, but been here from where?' he says and Mariner walks past him, but not before she hears him mutter: 'Spanish bastard.'

War with Spain has not made Mariner's life easy. In fact, she'd appreciate it if King Philip would fuck off back to Madrid and stop building his armada in Catalonia, which the sailors all rumour to be three hundred sails strong and set for England.

'All right, cock-less?' A shoulder bone, bumping her arm deliberately too hard, jostling ale onto her wrists. It's one of Twentyman's boys who always has a look halfway between derision and desire. 'Who's that for?'

'Not you.'

She jerks her head to where Kit is sitting, casually using a dinner knife to carve an apricot. It is helpful to have a best friend who can look so effortlessly threatening whilst eating. The boy grimaces and Mariner moves on, but she hears his voice following her as he comments to a friend: 'If Twentyman didn't favour her so, I'd make her feel her cunt all the way to her arse.'

Mariner doesn't turn back. It matters not what's between your legs if you can cut off what's between theirs, so Kit says. She pushes the ale towards him.

'To Griffin,' she says.

Kit's face crumbles in a way Mariner has never seen before. She presses a hand against his chest, because that was where it hurt most after Elgin was gone and Kit does take a steadying breath, looking down at her hand in slight curiosity.

'It is where the heart is,' Mariner says softly. 'It is broken.'

Kit shakes his head and frowns into his ale.

'It does not feel broken. Rather that everything is out of order, as if the world is... dislocated.'

Mariner remembers it well. When Elgin was killed in a skirmish a year after he left her at the Silver Moon, she felt that same sense of pure displacement Kit describes; the universe walking at a pace she could no longer match. Elgin had left a high debt with Twentyman, who, in payment, had 'apprenticed her' under him like the other lads.

'You look as a lad and you'll work as a lad, for no one else will have you, will they? Not unless you dress pretty and bend over. Will you do that?' When Mariner had shaken her head, Twentyman had looked victorious. 'So you are mine now. Forever.'

She has never relocated herself, not truly, or fallen back in step with the world. At least with Kit, she has someone walking in a similarly unique rhythm.

'It would be better if I left.' Kit looks sullenly around the tavern. 'Maybe I should go abroad. Learn more stage craft in Paris or Antwerp, like Griffin did.'

Mariner feels a twinge of fear. She does not like her life particularly, but Kit is the thing that makes it bearable.

'Have you been tupping a Lord you've not yet happened to mention?' She sips her ale. 'How else would you buy out?'

Like many of the poor young people of London, the only chance of advancement is apprenticeship, a master who provides a roof and vittels and a chance to learn a trade. Twentyman is technically a guildsman of the Innholders but he never pays to make any of his thieves, whores, brawlers, forgers and grave robbers free

29

guildsmen. Like Mariner, Kit was put under Twentyman's care against debt. The debt, as Mariner understands it, was simply that Griffin wanted him kept at the Silver Moon with his sister rather than kicked to the street and, in lieu of paying for a room, Kit was put to service. To be free, he needs to be bought out by another master. It happens now and again. Twentyman is a horror but he has no royal patron or great lord protecting him from the noose; he cannot afford to murder every young delinquent thinking about defecting to another master. Instead, Twentyman bets on their criminal pasts disinclining honourable merchants. A lad like Kit, branded a thief, doesn't stand a chance of a buyout, he would have to settle the debt himself to be free. Someone like Mariner has even less chance, for who, as Twentyman loves to remind her, has a use for a woman who runs around as a boy?

'I don't know,' Kit says glumly. 'I could go on the roads.'

Mariner pauses, her ale cup held against her teeth. A masterless man is a vagrant. Such people are worse off than they are, worse than the blind beggars; punished brutally by the law and given no charity.

'Aye, to get put in the Fleet or given another set of lashes, oh, you'd look fetching with a matching vagrant brand, right here.' She presses her thumb into his unblemished cheek. He bats her hand away.

'Only if I am caught. You could cut pretty purses in Paris. Or Venice.'

The notion of being out from Twentyman fills her with a warm, pleasant glow but bolting is an awful risk. Others have tried before. Someone usually drags them back. Fleeing lads get beaten, lasses get broken in again at the Hat. Examples, all. Have I not fed and watered you? Twentyman always preaches. What of loyalty? What of love? Still, if Kit runs, will she run with him?

'Do you have a cock?' The question interrupts her, a leering lad propping himself lopsided against their table.

'Why? Can you not find your own?' Mariner says. There's a gaggle of lads behind him; they all laugh loudly, clearly in their cups. They are city apprentices, over the river for a night of trouble.

'Show us your teats!' one of them shouts.

'Aye, show us.' The leering lad leans closer. His breath stinks, that unpleasant faecal quality of too much ale over too long a time. 'We hear it has pretty duckies under its boy clothes.'

It. A descriptor that irritates Mariner no end. She's never understood why she's less of a woman for wanting all the things a cock brings.

'Fuck off.' Mariner shoves the lad's forearm, a quick jab, that sends him sprawling clumsily to the floor. His friends laugh and slap their knees, enjoying their Southwark entertainment.

'Harpy, I'll show you!'

In a fluid movement, Mariner and Kit are on their feet; Mariner's whipped out her knife and set it against the boy's throat before he can reach into his pockets and make good on his threat. She enjoys the frightened widening of his eyes, his flinches as Kit deftly lays out one of his friends, rushing to help.

'Empty your pockets,' Mariner says. 'On the table there now, nice and quick.'

Out of the corner of her eye, Mariner sees Twentyman standing in the stairwell, watching with amusement.

'You can't do this!' the lad shouts. He looks around as if he expects help. The wherrymen don't even raise their eyes from their glasses and Twentyman's boys look on impassively, more interested in seeing if she'll falter than if he'll survive.

'Barely anything on him, drunk his pay away,' Kit says, dipping his hands into the pockets of the boy, stiff with fear

'Such a shame.' Mariner pulls her knife away and kicks him deftly in the balls. 'Look at that. You do have a cock.'

The boy staggers away. He's not made for this type of fight. His kind brawl in packs. He'll shuffle back across the river, tail between his legs.

'How much?' Twentyman saunters over. Kit hands it over and Twentyman counts it out. Three pence, a groat and a half groat, nine pence in all. Twentyman slips it into his purse. He nods at Mariner's knife. 'Could you not have got them all?'

'Thought you'd want some fun for yourself,' she says.

He snorts and walks away without even giving them a penny for their trouble. Others would grumble. Not Mariner. She lives for the indifference of this man. The punishment he holds over her, every day of her life, is much worse. The very first time she failed a job for him, lost a purse she'd cut at Smithfield's, he'd spoken words Mariner can never forget.

'You're the only lass I let run in the streets with my boys. That's because Elgin told me you were a boy sailor and you've a sharp eye and most of the time, you are worth it. For you have the softest tread and the quickest fingers in the city but when the sun sets, you're still a lass.' His eyes had drifted impassively over her legs in her hose, her body in her tunic, as if none of it mattered and she was naked in front of him. 'Maybe you would be better use to me elsewhere.'

Elsewhere was on her back in the Cardinal's Hat. She can talk back to Twentyman all she wants, she can act the part of the brash boy and bet on her own usefulness to him, but with each passing day, year on year, Mariner feels his eyes on her legs and hidden breasts. The scales are being weighed. She is still boyish enough to look at, thank Christ, but she is twenty-five years old now. She has no chance of another future, and one particularly vindictive day, Will

Twentyman will put her out for a whore. For this reason, amongst others, there is no one she hates more in the wide world.

'C'mon,' Kit says, and she follows him out the back of the pub and into the darkness. 'Look.'

Kit opens his hand. There, in the centre of his palm is a sixpence. Mariner stares at it, shining silver and swallowing moonlight, glorious and stolen.

'This is how we buy out,' Kit says quietly. 'You in?'

Mariner carefully picks up the coin, warm and sweaty and pilfered from a cut intended for Twentyman, turning it in her fingers as she looks at Kit's questioning face, that same curiosity he had on the day they first spoke. She had been down in the cellar of the Silver Moon, standing on a board laid on top of a broken barrel hoop, making it tilt from side to side. He stared at her for a few moments and then climbed up beside her, mirroring her quiet oscillation. At first, she thought it was a mean-spirited mockery, but then she saw the concentration in his odd eyes. After a few moments of silence, he spoke.

'Why are we doing this?'

She had not known what to do with Kit's soft inquisitiveness. After years of trusting boys, she had been launched into a world where she was suddenly other. A girl. Now boys were full of cruelty towards her.

'I feel odd when it's all steady.' The nausea was persistent in that first year. When she lay down at night, she felt as if the whole world was rocking on the high surf of the stars.

'You're a sailor?'

Mariner fought back sorrow and sickness and closed her eyes. If she swayed in just the right way, she could imagine the creak of timbers on the water and pretend that, yes, she was still a sailor.

'Not anymore.'

'Why not?'

'Because I'm a girl.' Mariner could not help the bile in her voice. The distaste. It was only one thing about her and yet it had made all the difference.

'Are you?' Kit looked at her with nothing but mild interest and then shrugged. Mariner still thinks it is the kindest response she has ever had. 'Does that make you bad at it?'

'No. It fucking doesn't.'

Kit looked at her, those odd, ugly eyes very bright.

'Then I guess they are idiots,' he said. His face split into a sharp, nasty smile but there was something victorious in it. At that moment, Mariner knew she wanted Kit Skevy on her side.

This is what she finds herself thinking as she looks at the coin stolen from her master. There is no path back to the wide open sea for her whilst she is tethered to the Grave Eorl and she wants no part of life in London without her best friend. Whatever the ordinance of God above, it is better to have Kit Skevy on her side than be without him. So she nods and slips the silver sixpence into her pocket.

He whose name is Flame

Chapter Four

'That's the signal,' Kit says. A lamp turns off in the window of a small hut across the way. It's where the grave keeper stays and his boy has been bribed handsomely, both to give signal and dig shallow. Tonight, Twentyman has them robbing graves and making delivery of the unfortunate corpse to the medicine man, apothecary or alchemist on the Southwark wharf. Such men will pay good coin for bodies that aren't criminals, since that is all the law allows, and it doesn't seem that the loss of Griffin and his connections has slowed the Grave Eorl's trade. It's been six weeks since Griffin's death and Kit has bent his will to one thing and one thing only: getting out.

He's won every fight, he's nearly cut as many purses as Mariner and whenever he can, he's been quietly skimming from the top. He knows it's a risky game, but he doesn't care. Twentyman is glorying in Griffin's death and their grief, never wasting a moment to tell Squire Kay of her feckless brother or taunt Kit of his worthlessness: You're nothing, you're nobody, Griffin was a fool to ever put bread in your hand and clothes on your back, you're just a whore's son, a bastard brought from Antwerp—

'I'm the best you've fucking got,' Kit said the other day, and Twentyman pinned his ear to the wall with a knife. That's the thing about Twentyman, he never fights fair.

'Your pervert of a protector's dead, you little arsehole,' he said. 'You're nothing but a freakish means to a richer end. I bet he fucked you too.'

He notices the looks from the lads more, the sideways sneers and lingering, hateful glances when they eat supper in the corner of the Silver Moon each night. London is getting worse for Mariner by the day as the British fleet prepares to intercept the Spanish at Ferrol. She's a Spanish defector, they say, she deserves to be strung up; he was the fuck toy of a player, nothing better than a whore. No amount of casual fist fights in the alleyways keep their names out of everyone's mouths.

'Well, which one?' Mariner picks up the shovels they have hidden under potato sacking by the gate.

'Freshly dug by the back wall, facing south.'

They move quietly across the pauper's field of Crossbones cemetery, the place where the poor of Southwark, the dead and diseased and the Winchester geese plucked and buried, lie. The turn from July to August has brought with it wet weather and the earth is boggy, the grave markers sliding and the poor souls buried too shallow rising. Paintings of the last judgement are brought to life in the thick mud; a rotted elbow or row of teeth.

'Don't you find it strange that the client desires a specific body?' Mariner whispers. 'What unholy things could they be doing with it?'

'They can have the corpse of Anne Boleyn as long as I get paid.'

Kit finds it difficult to care. After over a decade of wondering if he would feel death at all, he believes he is suffocating in Southwark. Kit's own body is rejecting the air in it, refusing to settle into a safety that used to be easy. In the choice between rotting forever under Twentyman and the noose, he knows what he would take. Mariner gives him an exasperated look.

'Why can you not fear hell, like other men?' she says. 'They are much easier to deter.'

'Everyone goes to hell these days. At least it is bound to be interesting.'

Kit has already dug his shovel into the wet ground, dislodging fresh dirt and stones on his way to the coffin. Mariner stares anxiously down at the grave. Kit stops and gives her a look.

'Where in the gospels does it say not to? For if you are going to hold tight to the eighth commandment you need to consider a different trade.'

'Give me the eighth commandment and I'll give you a shovel to the head,' says she. She hates to be reminded of her sins. Like all followers of Calvin, she views them as hints of her own fiery destruction. Kit has never understood why, if one is so sure they could be damned, they do not enjoy all earthly and devilish pleasures with the time allotted to them? If it is a fifty per cent chance, he would rather gamble and revel in the present than abstain for an eternity of further abstinence. 'Do you even know who the poor whelp is?'

She points to the small marker above the mound of earth. A wooden cross with a name etched into it and darkened with ash, perhaps by a well-wisher or a sensitive priest, the letters crude. *Edward Kelley.* Kit frowns.

'Edward Kelley,' he says. 'There's an alchemist by that name, Griffin told me. A proper puffer, convinced the Emperor he could make gold and was imprisoned in Prague, they tell. Some say he's dead but no one's seen him in years.'

'A coincidence,' Mariner says.

Kit scrapes his shovel against the pauper's coffin and thinks. It's been buried quickly and just as quickly, an alchemist or a medical man or an apothecary is paying Will Twentyman for the pleasure of having it dug back up. There is no worth in bones, Kit knows, but perhaps there is something else inside. What kind of person wants to dig up a nobody from a pauper's graveyard for their secrets? The answer is easy: someone who knew he was not a nobody.

'We should open it up.'

'Should we fuck!' Mariner blanches. 'Why would we—?'

'Because maybe it is Kelley.'

'What, flown from Prague on magic wings?' Mariner glares at him. 'It is not Kelley, and even if it *were,* why should we care for a dead puffer?'

Kit pulls the vial of alchemist's formula that Griffin gifted him out from his jerkin. 'Griffin gave it to me, said it was not worth much but other alchemists, they have secrets worth a lot more. The kind emperors want.'

'The Emperor of fucking Prague does not want this poor shit; he's likely just a dead wherryman with the same name.' Mariner shakes her head.

'If he is, we've lost nothing, and if he's not then perhaps he's got something valuable in there, puffers are often buried with secrets and Twentyman's client is paying heavy in sovereigns for his.' Kit digs around the edges to loosen the suction of the earth's grip. 'If he is no use to anyone dead then why pay so much? What's the harm in looking?'

'Oh, let me think on it, you know the bloody harm!' Mariner shakes her head and folds her arms defiantly. 'I'll not go down the Hat for you, Kit; not for anybody.'

Mariner lives in fear of being sent to lie on her back in Twentyman's brothel. Twentyman can whip Kit until he bleeds to death for skimming coin and he will not shrug but he knows he would feel every moment of Mariner's despair in that place.

'Twentyman will get his gold, I promise you,' says Kit. 'We will still deliver, let us only look inside first. You will not be sent to the Hat. I swear, and if it's a little trinket that takes us closer to getting away from the Hat forever, isn't it worth it?'

Mariner gives him a long, anguished look and then clicks her teeth. She puts her shovel back in the earth, helping him pry out the coffin.

'God's wounds, this is the worst thing we've ever done,' she says.

'Christ opened his own grave. Allegedly.'

'Do not *allegedly* me!' Mariner's shovel hits a rock with an emphatic zing of steel. 'It's a sin and if it's not, it's an ill wish if ever there was one.'

'Griffin said there is no sin but ignorance.'

Mariner glares at him, her hot breath a cloud of steam in the dark, cold moonlight.

'Perhaps that is why he is dead.'

Before he can answer, her shovel brings up the wood and the casket is free, a sucking sound of damp earth. She grabs the edges of the coffin and swearing and praying and cursing to high heaven, they manoeuvre the wooden box across the empty graveyard. Kit is very glad of the mist from the rain that is rolling in and the extra cover it will provide. The cart is on the edge of Blackman Street that runs from Crossbones graveyard back up to Long Southwark street and, from there, the river and the wharf at St Mary Overie Stairs, where the client's boat will be waiting. It is not a long journey, but any journey with a stolen dead body is too long for comfort.

'Christ, was he buried with everything he owned?' Mariner huffs. 'Let us see.'

Hidden behind the crumbling cemetery wall, they hoist the casket onto the cart, a simple thing they can pull between them, and Mariner sets her knife to dislodging the nails. With a great, groaning creak, the lid comes forth and a deep stench of rot and death engulfs them. Kit pulls up his collar to cover his face and Mariner steps back, fearfully.

'If it was a plague death I'll be the end of you, Skevy,' Mariner coughs.

'If it was plague then I'll be grateful. Quickly, come on.'

She fumbles on the flat of the cart for the pitch and tow and uses her pocket flint to light it. The pitch is damp in the misting rain and the wood hisses, but the smoking glow is enough to see by. Kit steels himself and looks down at the bloated body. Yellow, blotchy flesh underneath stubble. His dirty shirt is stretching unpleasantly across the chest and the ties of his greying coif are cutting into the bloating skin of his neck; a body still swelling, even in death.

'Shoddiest looking alchemist I ever saw,' Mariner whispers, his dead presence compelling soft voices. She's right; it's a simple wool jerkin, nothing fine enough to be worth pinching.

'Perhaps he was not buried in his alchemist robes.'

'Or perhaps he's just some poor dead bastard and Twentyman is making money off puffer's hopes.'

'Even then, maybe he was buried with coin in his pocket.'

Kit glances over his shoulder at the empty street. Bracing himself, he begins to pat the doublet down, wincing at the way his touch encourages a pinkish foam to leak from the dead man's nose.

'Anything?' she asks. 'Philosopher's stone? Elixir of life? Staff of Merlin?'

Kit fumbles his hand down the dead man's sleeve, grimacing when he touches damp flesh but then, something colder and firmer. It is not a vial or a locket with secret papers inside, only a coin, catching the amber light of the torch. A gold angel.

'Better,' he says.

'Check the other side,' Mariner says as Kit slips it in to his purse, all reluctance gone in the presence of good coin. Before Kit can move, there is the ominous sound of a boot on the cobblestones behind them. Both of them twist, Mariner's knife in her hand and Kit's fists up in case it is a group of lads, looking to take what is theirs and sell on, but it isn't. The figure is too tall. There is a feeling inside him that he doesn't immediately understand, something between anticipation and excitement, and then he notices other figures in the shadows at the corners of his eyes. He recognises it: the sharp bitter copper taste in his mouth before a fight.

'Can we help you, good sirs?' he calls to the shadowed person in front of him.

'The coffin. Give it to us, thief,' a strong, rich baritone of a voice calls back. That is not a Southwark voice. It is tinged with Whitehall, gold plate and hunting dogs, but has an accent too, a slight burr. It is the kind of voice that gets men hanged.

'Give up my dear Aunt Constance as I take her to her final rest?' Kit says. 'For shame, milord.'

'Do not lie for me. I am come to see if my friend, Edward Kelley, is truly buried here in Southwark.'

'This man?' Mariner lifts the dead man's rough sleeve. 'Nothing but a pauper, milord.'

'Hand him over and we will let you go.'

Kit sees Mariner stiffen. It is no good in being promised freedom if it will simply send them back to Twentyman empty-handed, owing him three gold sovereigns. They cannot give up the body but they cannot run and leave it either.

'Sorry, gentlemen, we've got our orders,' Kit says. In the shadows of doorsteps and leaning houses, figures move closer, as if the man standing facing them is wordlessly commanding them to advance.

'Mr Kelley was one of my friends, his secrets are mine.'

41

Kit realises it must be an alchemist. He thinks of the vial hanging around his neck and wonders exactly what this body – whether he is truly Edward Kelley or not – is worth to them. If it's worth enough to get out from under Twentyman.

'We'll hand him over for five sovereigns,' he says.

Mariner sucks in her breath. Maybe she thinks this is too large a gamble but Kit doesn't care. The air around him is damp, the night is shadowed and starless and inside him there is a gnawing emptiness that nothing in Southwark will cleanse. Here he is nothing but a freakish means to a richer end. If gold is the way to be something more, if selling bodies and betraying Twentyman and fleeing the country is the only way to get it, that is what he will do.

'You will hand him over for your lives.'

One of the shadowed men moves, launching himself towards Mariner who, with every instinct of a girl taught to fight by sailors, twists with knife outstretched to face him.

'I fucking told you it was an ill-wish!' Mariner's furious voice is muffled by the sound of her thoroughly kicking someone in the darkness. The pitch and tow has been dropped and casts damply flickering light along the wet road and, before he can answer, he sees her slip on the wet stone, the coffin she had been steadying going down with her.

Kit tries to catch the damp wood as it falls but he is too late. He stumbles instead to grab at the horrible, bloated body spilling out and, in the fumbling mess of it, his feet slide out from underneath him too. His body is against the dead man's; the sweet sickly scent of rot surges in his nostrils. He twists away, desperate, thinking of the pink foam bubbling out of the dead man's mouth and how it could explode all over him. He falls, heavy and fast on his chest, hears the clicking snap of glass breaking underneath him. Griffin's keepsake, smashed into the cobblestones, black liquid seeping towards the pitch and tow. He curses, thinks to gather it up, sees in the dim light he is cut and his blood mingled with black liquid on his palm, but the spluttering fire has caught the spilt secretion. It lights, a sharp whoosh of growing flame that gushes over the cobblestones, just like Griffin said, running faster than normal fire, chasing the substance onto Kit's damp palms.

Then something impossible begins.

Kit knows the impact needed to break bones, the dizziness that comes in fever, but this is not like that. It is more. Perhaps this is what it feels like to be pressed. Whatever was in Griffin's trinket is forcing its way through the cut in his hand and down into his bloodstream. Kit sways on his knees, stifled under the weight of an invisible mountain and then, deliriously, the mist around him is alight, the air turned to orange flame, pulsing with the screams of angels and scales of dragons and hounds of hell.

'Greek Fire!' someone screams. 'Kelley's coffin had Greek Fire in it!'

The only people he has ever heard mutter about such things are alchemists. Is it possible that Griffin's trinket was more powerful than he imagined, or he missed some key component for its success? Surely it must be, for there is fire on the cobbles, bouncing off their wet surface, fire that is repelled by water, and he does not understand where else it has come from. Then he looks down. His hand is on fire. Kit has been accidentally lit aflame before, and it is nothing like this. Fire is leaping *from* his hand, coming from inside him. This is not logical, Kit thinks dazedly. This is not real. Fire without smoke, Fire without wood, Fire burning air and nothing and only Kit's skin. He thinks of the firecrackers he made with Griffin, he thinks of the swevel and all the other tricks they used to make hell burn Faustus onstage. Puffers tricks, Griffin always said, but Kit does not understand this new trick, and suddenly, he is afraid. Since his body is too heavy to move he screams for Mariner.

'Run, you fucking idiot! Run!'

In the haze and the heat he thinks he might hear footsteps pounding away and is glad, but then arms are enclosing him, not Mariner's arms, a stranger's arms.

'Do not fight,' says an oddly polite voice, again tinged with a gentle, fluid accent. Fight with what? His hand is still aflame and surely soon it will devour him. He slips, an eel through the polite arms, and closes his eyes. This is like the dream when I am running so fast and so full of fire that I can fly, he thinks. This is like that dream. I will wake up soon.

ⲛⲭⲃⲭⲧⲟⲭ

She who is unchanged by time

Chapter Five

Kit tells her to run so she runs. It is fire that dances on water, that can eat boats alive, burn up souls, and Mariner has a sailor's fear of everything that means. So she runs, tasting ash on her tongue, and smelling singed fabric, imagining it chasing just behind. This is not normal puffery; this is something else entirely and she is terrified because it is nothing good. When she is far enough away that she cares to look over her shoulder and sees only summer mist, she has the presence of mind to consider how terribly not good it is. Mariner Elgin has to be the one to tell Twentyman that she's lost his three sovereigns, his sold goods and his best brawler to some puffers. Fuck me, she thinks. He will send me down the Hat. She immediately hurries back to Crossbones, creeping up to the corner where their cart had been. It is gone, so is the charred corpse and so are the alchemists. There are scorch marks on the cobbles; just the sight of them gives her a terror that trembles all the way from her knees to her neck, but there is nothing she can do but trudge back to Twentyman.

*

'He was taken, down at Crossbones, we were on a job. I lost him.' Mariner braces herself, but Squire Kay is an easier hand to start with than Twentyman's. Standing in the back door of the Silver Moon and facing Kay behind the bar, she watches her wipe her hands in a slow, thoughtful motion.

'Is he alive?' she asks. This is a good start. She has not been yelled at yet.

'He was,' Mariner lowers her voice and steps closer. 'But there was fire. Alchemist's fire. It… it bounced on the water. Like in the stories.'

Greek Fire, they had yelled, but Mariner knows it as Dark Fire said to be lost in ancient times, a weapon of terror. When it is mentioned aboard, sailors cross themselves to ward off the destruction that the ocean around them cannot save them from. When she saw it, bouncing off the cobblestones, God help her, she had wanted to run, and she did.

'Who set the fire? The alchemists?' she asks.

Squire Kay loves Kit in her own brusque way; he brings a tenderness out of her that no other urchins do. She is a sound choice of confidante for this and yet still, the words are reluctant to leave Mariner's lips.

'Kit was on fire. They took him away.'

It's not entirely the truth, but the further away Mariner gets from the impossible moment of it happening, the less certain she is of the reality. She saw fire pouring from Kit's own flesh, yet how can that be? Mariner has travelled far and was raised on the good book; she knows there are things formed of the devil for destruction and a man who produces fire must be, but Kit cannot be a devil. So this much she can say: that Kit is burnt and was alive when taken, for these facts she can at least reconcile.

'You'll keep the fire to yourself then, Mariner.' Squire Kay shoots a sharp look over the bar to see if anyone is listening but it's after midnight and quiet. Mariner realises that Squire Kay suspects worse. Maybe she's been anticipating it since her brother died in one of his ill-advised puffer's experiments. Has Griffin's poor judgement come back to rain down on Kit? Kay's eyes are as bleak as the day he died as she jerks her head towards the stairs.

'Now go tell him before someone else does.'

The Grave Eorl of Southwark never sleeps. As Mariner apprehensively climbs the stairs, she imagines him returning to the Cardinal's Hat in the daylight hours, like a bat to roost. He probably slumbers hanging up by his boots. She tries to school her face to reveal none of her fears and secrets, knees jiggling with nerves. She and Kit have been stealing from their master for six weeks and although he cannot know, for they both still have all of their fingers, she has been trying to stay out of Twentyman's way as much as possible. Her fist hovers over the door, shaking. She forces herself to knock.

'In!'

The upstairs room Twentyman uses as his office is baking. With only two high windows that let in the heavy stench of the river rather than air, it is made hotter by the fire burning low in the grate for the light. Twentyman looks up from where he is seated at his desk, jaw tight with annoyance, face and balding head filmed in sweat.

'The client's expecting you at two bells. You'll be late.'

'There was trouble. The casket was taken from us.' She speaks fast, her words tripping over themselves in eagerness to be spoken, to be past it. Perhaps it will be better on the other side. 'They took Kit too.'

Twentyman's quill stills on the page. Mariner's seen that face before, once, he took a lad's ear off for skimming profit. With sweating palms she takes off her cap to twist it with trembling fingers, the rules of Her Majesty's navy still in her blood. She wants to speak, to give Twentyman the usual impassivity she reserves especially for him, but she cannot find it. Her armour, her sharp nerve and quick words have all been burned away, like Kit's fingerprints. Fear tastes like vomit and pennies behind her tongue, but she clamps her lips closed. Other boys quail under his gaze, begging and spilling excuses, but she won't let herself do it, not now, not ever, no matter how much terrible fury mounts in his knitted brows. She holds her breath and stares at his ear impassively until she is nearly dizzy, counting inside her head to control the terror – five, four, three, two – until finally he shakes his head with a snort and looks down.

'Say more.'

'They were waiting, they wanted that particular body, said it was Edward Kelley, though Kit says he's in prison in Prague.' She watches him carefully to see he is surprised by that. He is not. If she had to guess, she'd suspect he's been putting the rumour about himself – here's Edward Kelley's corpse, back in London, no one knows how, worth ten sovereigns! – to drive up interest and the price. She wouldn't put it past Twentyman to even find some poor London sod with the same name and chivvy him to his death with an unfortunate fall or blind beating. 'They were alchemists, they said they were Kelley's friends. There was a struggle. Kit was taken.'

She will not admit to Twentyman that she ran. There is already guilt, sharp and poisonous, beginning to seep into her bones. His glare is ferocious. He's made a great deal of coin off being the only criminal lord in London with balls enough to risk stealing bodies. If someone is cutting into his business, he'll be ready to murder.

'Ezra!' Twentyman bellows.

'Aye?' Ezra pops his head around the door, dark eyes flickering to Mariner curiously.

'Mariner has lost Skevy, nicked by some alchemists who have made off with my goods, worth three sovereigns.'

Ezra's face doesn't change. Undoubtedly, his wife has already told him Kit is lost or he would look more troubled.

'You're to go to Crossbones to see what you can find of these bastards and you—' Twentyman glares at Mariner '—you're to go to the wharf and explain to the client why you don't have what they paid for. Let their dissatisfaction pour on your fucking head for losing the corpse of such a great man.'

He gives her a nasty grin and Mariner's stomach clenches with familiar hatred. Of course Twentyman will make this her fault, no matter what she says. She is actually relieved for it, some of her fear and worry is flushed away in the wake of this normal, righteous indignation. Still, she waits for the worst blow, her spine tense against it.

'Go,' says he.

Nothing more is said. Mariner doesn't dare question, desperate to be out of the room before her sentence is adjusted. She scampers to the door, wrenching it open in relief, thinking she's got away with it—

'And I'll tell Plenty to expect you at the Hat on the morrow.'

She was a fool, of course she was, to ever imagine Twentyman would let such a failure go unpunished and now, she is for the Hat. The pain of the thought burns through her like a surgeon's lance. She bites her lip, tastes blood, but will not turn back to see his greedy satisfaction. All she can do is walk away, Ezra by her side.

'He might change his mind on the morrow, want you back at cutting purses,' Ezra says. He's a good friend, attempting to be both comfort and hope at a time like this, but Mariner cannot bear them. It is too bitter, so she merely smirks at him.

'Or he might take holy orders.' Outside, the rising mist from an hour ago is now a persistent grey summer drizzle, warm and damp. 'It was a scheme, wasn't it? The corpse of Kelley?'

'Aye. I don't know what's bought it but it's probably some kind of alchemist. Do you think if the Grave Eorl of Southwark had the real remains of Edward Kelley, he'd be selling them so cheaply?'

He's right, of course. Twentyman knows the worth of everything in London. Inside her mind, Mariner sees Kit's hands, dancing with flame.

'Don't tell him about the scorch marks,' she warns Ezra and then gladly disappears into the dark. Tonight every lamp she passes could be the start of a fire and Kit's fingers burn inside her mind. Thoughts turn to prayers with the rapid beat of her heart. She knows it is holier to pray God's will be done, but she cannot help it: Let him not be gone. Jesu, save him. This is fear, she realises not that the fire will have killed him or could have killed her, but that it will scorch their memories away just as her early childhood and parents had been scalded out of her. If such a brutal searing of the mind was possible once, it stands to logic it could reoccur. She touches her fingers to the scarring around her eye, thinks, I will not be burnt out of him, Kit will not be burnt out of me. He is a part of me as much as the endless sea and Elgin's kind eyes. I will not lose myself again.

The worst loss of Mariner's life was not the loss of her parents or the fire that nearly took her sight, it was the day she became a woman. It began with blood. Her first thought was that she had the most terrible runs. Her stomach cramped so badly she screamed, a terrible, wrenching tug out of her abdomen. Some poor sailors had been sent up the jakes with bloody shits before, but the smell was all wrong. Meaty and metallic, coin and beef, and before she could wonder if she was dying, she was dragged from her bunk. Woman, they had screamed. Woman aboard! Later, after staring at the bars of the brig with blood in her breeches, Elgin came down. He told her Captain Drake would not maroon her, for it would be an ill omen to cast off a woman alone with the natives. She would be imprisoned until Portsmouth, and then set free in England.

'He will not turn me over to the constables?' Mariner had spent all day with a noose swinging inside her mind.

'He fears the Queen's response to the news that he has harboured a woman aboard for so long, that perhaps she will use it to blame him if any of his battles with the Spanish go ill. I know someone in London, a businessman in Southwark. He doesn't mind odd boys and girls. He'll make use of your skills although—' Elgin sucked his teeth regretfully '—it shall not always be honest work.'

But I will live, Mariner thought. Elgin might have taught her to memorise the book of James and she knew that liars go to hell, but she also knew, from a very young age, she did not have the purity or patience of the martyrs. She had not the charity to go to her father's Scottish family to be scolded for her boyish ways and made a spinster and she had not enough piety to go and starve with her grandmother in Portugal. She was only thirteen years old and in Southwark she would live.

'Willow bark and whisky.' Elgin handed her a small flask through the bars as well as some rolled up rags. 'It'll help with the pain. The rags go in your breeches, staunch the blood.'

'Is it forever?'

'No, lass, monthly blood is just that.' Elgin's smile was tender. 'Until you get with child.'

'But I don't want to get with child,' she whispered, as if it would make a difference. 'I don't want to be a woman. I'm a sailor.'

'I'm afraid you are a woman indeed.' Elgin's eyes were wet. She had been enough of a son for him those eight years and now he would be childless again. 'Better get used to it.'

She could not get used to it. The abrupt withdrawal of kindness of those around her, lads she had slept beside for months, with whom she had mourned friends lost to plague or battle, was unbearable. In the long, lonely journey back to Portsmouth she had laid her head down each night and prayed for their familiarity, their jokes and love to return to her. Now, Mariner knows better. She could have started a mutiny, she could have missed a doff of cap, she could have been a Jonah, but as long as she had a cock they would have still looked at her like she was a person.

'You are late, boy. Where is my prize?' A cloaked figure stands by a barge in the darkness at St Mary's Overie stairs with a voice that jerks Mariner out of her melancholy musings. The voice is female with the sharp elocution of someone who has been educated in a gentleman's house. Mariner has seen puffers on the bridge; they fashion themselves after Doctor Dee and other star seers, wearing capes and caps and growing their beards long. This lady's hem is spun with gold thread, glinting through the muddy residue of the city. Alchemists do not look like her. Mariner ducks her head respectfully, whilst thinking: Dig your own damn corpses.

'Forgive me, Mistress. We do not have it. We were intercepted. Your cargo was taken.'

'By whom?' The lady steps closer. There is a sudden strong smell of rosewater, almost overpowering the sewage stink of the river under the wharf. Nothing smells more like money more than rosewater. She is clearly a courtier. Why did you want him? Mariner thinks to her feet. Was it a trick for your fine parlour, to have the secrets of Edward Kelley? Or did you know him, as courtiers know such things; were you his foolish lover?

'Other alchemists, friends of his, they say, Mistress. Maybe friends of yours, too.'

She expects a rebuke, maybe a sharp cuff to the back of the head. She does not expect a gloved hand against her cheek. Mariner jerks back, unable to stop her head from snapping up and looking into the lady's eyes. They are warm and brown, the torches on the wherry stairs making them glow with the predatory watchfulness of a cat.

'Curious.' The lady rubs her gloved fingertips together. Mariner realises that her face must be covered in soot. 'What fire was this?'

'I am a smith lad,' she lies.

'You're not a lad at all,' the lady says, mouth twisting into a wry smile. Mariner stiffens. It is not often she's caught out. Fine folk see a scuffed cap and cropped hair and assume an impoverished lad. 'You tell Twentyman if he finds the so-called corpse of Edward Kelley, I'll pay him double.'

So not so foolish, perhaps. A woman who knows she might be taken in but is willing to pay for peace of mind. Mariner struggles to slot this feline perceptive woman into the neat shelves of London society and finds she will not fit.

'What is your name?' she asks.

'Mariner Patience Elgin.'

She wonders why she has given her name entire. Very few know it.

'I hope to see you again, Mariner Patience Elgin.' The lady steps into her barge. 'I am at Hart House on Lime Street.'

Mariner watches as they push off to catch the current. What would Kit make of her, so finely dressed and well spoken, paying a fortune for the body of a nobody? Then she wonders what the lady of Lime Street would think if she saw the dead man's body burned to a crisp by Kit. Or perhaps it only looked like Kit. Maybe there was something in the coffin they had not seen, or the alchemists did some kind of trick, but Mariner cannot set it straight in her mind. She watches the water, the mist and breeze cooling her skin, calming the itching that has started underneath her scar since she first saw Kit's hand aflame. A colder, harder part of her knows people die in London every day for all sorts of reasons and being set on fire and stolen by alchemists could easily be one of them. Maybe she should take the money they've skimmed and hope the events of the night are enough to distract Twentyman from her flight. Kit's been keeping count of it, but she imagines it's enough for passage to Dover and she cannot be sent down the Hat if she's not here. Then she hears Kit's voice in her head; Run, you fucking idiot! Run! She has no one in the wide world who loves her enough to save her but Kit Skevy. She will have to work out a way to get him back, fingers full of fire or no.

She scratches her itchy brow absent-mindedly as her eyes turn towards the Cardinal's Hat. It's easy to spot out here on the wherry, the red glow of the red silk hung over the windows are peeping eyes out towards the great city, always watching. She imagines fire leaping from Kit's fingers, shooting along the Thames and eating up the whorehouse, turning Twentyman's crown jewel of Southwark to ash. Mariner cannot help it. She smiles.

CXLXΓƐΩ

He who is first in arrogance

Chapter Six

Kit is surprised to find he is not dead. When he tries to move, there is heavy weight on his wrist. A manacle. A prisoner, then. Jesus Christ, let it not be the Tower, he thinks. The place no one comes out of the same; either their minds or bodies broken beyond repair, or in a coffin. Then he remembers. He scrambles to stare at his hand, now quiet and invisible in the thick darkness. You were on fire, he thinks to it, as if it will respond to him. Fire poured out of you and I had nothing to do with it.

'Tell me who you work for,' asks someone nearby. Kit jumps, tries to stand, but there is an iron heaviness against his ankles too. He recognises the voice, that slight burr on the r's, a Scottish ring to it. Here is the man with the Lordly countenance who made demands of him and Mariner on the road and would not entertain a sale. He blinks furiously, eyes beginning to adjust to the impenetrable blackness, softening it into dark blues and pitch greens, details caught from the impossibly thin slice of light coming from perhaps a door jamb or a covered window. Italian lace cuffs, the shine of leather shoes, light swallowed by velvet. Most alchemists are shabbier than apothecaries. This man wears his wealth. That is not good. Wealthy men get you sent to the Tower.

'Where am I?' he asks, trying to keep his voice dazed, to buy for some time.

'In my care.'

Suddenly, Kit's hands are both pulled upward and he realises that the shackles are attached to a bolt on the ceiling. He is cranked up, his toes barely touching the floor of the cell and his arms above his head, pressed to his ears.

'For the time is come that judgement must begin at the house of God.'

Kit thinks frantically of the times Ezra has told him of the great torturers, of Bishop Bonner and Lord Cromwell: The only difference, Young Kit, is the reformers speak the scripture in English, not Latin. He must be in the Tower then. Wildly, he imagines they know him for an atheist, as doomed as Griffin's Marlowe. Like all criminals, Kit has considered his potential death many times – a hanging, quick, a burning, terrible, a sword in the back, probably the kindest – but this one leaves him breathless, because how long will it take them when he cannot feel pain?

'So tell me, thief. Who is it that you serve?'

Kit tries to look pained as he scrambles to utilise his relative elevation, searching his new prison for clues; blocked windows hiding views of Tower Green or the river, instruments of dire torture, he finds none. There's a smell, certainly, but it is fishy and musty, like a food cellar. Unless they've run out of torture chambers in the Tower, it seems unlikely he is there. Relief loosens his arms a little, sagging his body down and shoulders up with a crunch. If it's not the Tower, he can probably get out. He decides to give a very good performance of agony, tell this bastard whatever he wants and get back to Mariner by dinner.

'The Grave Eorl of Southwark,' he says. 'I was only doing my job, I must eat.'

He makes himself breathe heavily, since it usually convinces people he is suffering.

'Then how did you come to produce the fire?' The rich alchemist leans closer. He has a burnt scent, like a founder. 'What did you find in the coffin?'

Clearly, he thinks that the flames at Kit's fingertips came from something in the coffin, rather than from inside Griffin's trinket. Kit immediately thinks of the vial of dark substance that broke in his hand when he fell. He remembers the sudden, extreme pressure on every part of him and then, the fire. All Kit knows of alchemy is what Griffin has taught him, how compounds can be mixed to create surprising things, and he has a feeling that whatever was inside the vial is what this man seeks. It was poured out, onto, or inside Kit and if the alchemists were not responsible for the lighting of it, then something inexplicable took place, and how can Kit give this man what he wants if it is lost under his skin? These facts clunk inside him and with slow dismay, Kit realises he must change his plan. If he confesses all now, he will be powerless at best. Dead, more likely, if this man cuts his skin open to pull the fire back out. Survival first, thinks Kit. Schemes later.

'What is often found in coffins, milord. A dead man.'

'You are cursed with a literal mind, I fear.' The alchemist turns the crank again. Kit's read catholic accounts of this particular tool; he knows the level of pain expected. He gasps readily and does a little yelping scream which is a good imitation of a dog with a trodden tail. 'I think you took something.'

'Never, milord, never! Have pity, I am not yet one and eight!' Kit lies.

'Have pity?'

There is suddenly light in the room, and Kit's eyes adjust slowly, a dark form against the wall, twisted low like an animal, but slippery, reflecting gold candlelight. Something white and set in rows, small pearls grinning from a melted bulbous thing. Kit realises he is looking at the crisped remains of the dead man. He tries to scramble back, but he merely peddles on the air, swinging perilously close to the corpse, slumped awkwardly against the wall, all charred flesh and red muscles.

'What pity did you have?' The man behind him stops him swinging, pushes his hips forward so his bare toes brush against soft, dead flesh. The air smells of overcooked meat and something sharper, more astringent, hitting the back of his throat. How long can he hang before his captor realises he does not feel pain? The Catholic priest swooned, but Kit cannot swoon. So he twists, violently, and sews panic into his voice.

'I know nothing of it, milord! Rumours tell Kelley is locked up for the Emperor, this is nothing but a fluke encounter, the coffin fell, the fire began! It was someone else's mischief, milord, I know nothing of it!' Thankfully, his shoulder pops. His right side sags. He knows the cry he needs to make for this type of wound, a shot stag, going down. 'Let me down for pity's sake! I know nothing else!'

His feet meet the floor, followed by the rest of him. His sigh of relief is genuine. Time is what he needs, time for assessment and preparation and escape. By the thrice beshitten shroud of Christ, Griffin, he thinks. What the fuck has your little keepsake mixed me up in?

'If Kelley is still imprisoned, we will find it out. Then we shall know how you lie, for either it is Kelley's coffin and you have stolen the formula from it, or it is not and you are a liar.'

Or I am the most unlucky of bastards, Kit thinks. The alchemist's face is cloaked in darkness, the one small candle set beside the dead man not reaching his features, but Kit can make out the cruel lift of his lip as he leans forward, and twists Kit's head, forcing him to look at the dead man's bubbled and burst eyes.

'All liars shall have their part in the lake which burneth with fire and brimstone which is the second death.'

Kit swallows drily. He knows he would not feel the pain of his eye popping from heat, eye juice sliding down his cheek, but he cannot imagine the sensation is pleasant. He has spent the better part of his life learning how to hide fear from Twentyman. That daunting dread from the first time he stepped into a ring, the opponent two heads taller than him and the sudden breathlessness that accompanied his own imagined vanishing from this earth. He will not give this stranger fear he has not earned.

'If that is to be so, might I trouble you for a drink, milord?' he says, forcing lightness into his tone. 'If I am for hell, I would hate to arrive thirsty.'

The alchemist does not answer and moves away. A loud knock, the clang of an opened door, a looming figure illuminated in dim orange light, features utterly obscured in a solid silhouette of darkness.

'Just a small ale?' Kit calls.

The door slams. A metal bar scraping against a latch is his answer and then he is left in the dark. Kit breathes, or tries to. His mind slides insidiously to dead hands pushed through churned earth at Crossbones, to screams hidden away under the stones of London, to the clods falling in a deathly beat on Griffin's coffin. Each thought brings his breath more rapid, sharper through his nose. It will not do, so he clicks his teeth and decides instead to be irritated by the heavy weight of the darkness around him or how, if he stretches his foot too far, he will touch the exposed, charred toe bones of a dead man. Then he thinks about the fire. He licks the skin on his hand, tastes for blood, feels the texture of it on his tongue. It is greasy and smelling of herbs but otherwise normal. He is sure it should be crisped and bloody like the poor sod in the corner but he remembers how the flame seems to come from inside the skin. It reminds him of oozing things; sweat out of armpits or sap from bark. Kit prides himself in being a fairly logical lad. What he can see and steal, that he believes in, but it was easier to do that when fire wasn't jumping out of his fingers and strange alchemists were not talking to him like he should know how he did it. Some could call it a miracle; others will call it witchcraft but Kit cares as little for the holy fathers as he does for ill-wishes from crones. He was on fire and lived and he does not know how or why. That is troublesome, to say the least.

The door opens and Kit rouses to blink in the shaft of unexpected light before it closes. A solemn-looking man with dark hair is standing in front of it. He has a candle in one hand, a wooden cup in the other and a length of bandages courteously draped over his arm.

'My lord wants me to see to your wounds,' he hesitates. 'I brought you wine, too.'

He has remarkable eyes, very silver, and the tone of his voice is familiar. This is the person who held Kit up when the fire started, with a polite whisper and strong arms. He does not look like he has secret intentions to hang Kit up by his ankles.

'And here I only asked for small ale.' Kit licks his lips and gestures to the corpse. 'Do not mind my friend here, he is only shy.'

The man does not laugh, a frown between his dark brows, but he steps forward, cup outstretched. Kit notices then the awkwardness of his gait, the slope of his shoulder. He has a crooked back under his fine doublet. There is a nervousness in the flicker of his eyes, perhaps shame of his twisted spine has given him no sense of his own stature for he does not approach Kit like a superior even though he clearly must be. Kit muses on his tall, stocky build wrapped in crimson, the embroidery on his doublet must be worth a couple of sovereigns. Spanish silk, Kit thinks, or I am a turnip.

'I'm obliged.' Kit takes the cup, drinks slowly, and makes a study of the man in front of him. His eyes dart constantly, and though he has the bearing of a meeker, younger boy, Kit reckons him to be around Mariner's age. He has a neat, handsome dark beard at least, which Kit is envious of. His accent matches his Lord's, perhaps he has been brought from Scotland too. The lace on his cuffs and his clean, pale hands say here is a person with wealth and yet clearly has no control over his own destiny. Then there is the way he is trying not to look at Kit's throat as he drinks. Kit is used to stares for his persistent freckles that some mistake for pockmarks, but a glance that won't leave his throat is something else entirely. This is a person I can use, he thinks.

'You have my thanks, Silver,' he says.

'Silver?'

'You have silver eyes.'

Kit dares him to hold his gaze. He manages it only for a moment, blushing as dark as his doublet. He coughs, bringing a pale hand to his mouth, either out of awkwardness or Kit has flustered him too much to speak. He has the kind of white skin that reminds Kit of snow and blood; those pale, yellowish cheeks, spilled with pink.

'I must dress your wounds.' He kneels in front of Kit, unrolling a bandage, transformed into a genteel squire. 'I already applied a healing balm, but I should cover it to protect the skin.'

'Thank you,' Kit says, remembering to wince as his wounds are wrapped. 'I do not suppose there is anything to be done for my cellmate. He is rather past his best.'

Kit thinks he detects the small lift of amusement in his cheeks. His interest is tension on a fishing line. It is often slow at the beginning, the drawing of a man, then rapid once understandings have been reached. With lasses, Kit's often found it reversed, but he has never tried to catch a person so finely robed, man or woman.

'Are you an apothecary, Silver?' He keeps his voice soft as that dark head is bent over his hands. Kit can smell the rosy soap in his hair.

'Do you always choose names for your captors?'

'This is my first time,' says Kit. 'You could tell me who you are instead.'

His ears flush. It is both funny and endearing.

'I have a physician's training, I am an explorer of the alchemical arts. I serve Lord Isherwood,' he says eventually. Kit knows this can only be partly true. If he is a mere servant, Kit is the King of fucking France.

'Who is that?'

'The gentlemen you just made the acquaintance of, in whose cellar you find yourself.'

'Ah yes, a kindly fellow, stringing lads up for amusement.' Kit shrugs his loose shoulder and performs a deliberate grimace. He has never heard of a Lord Isherwood but Kit does not know the Scottish Lords. Either way, it does not bode well. These are the kinds of people who can get you hanged. If they do not kill you in their cellars first.

'I will re-set it.'

He moves Kit's arm confidently, despite his crooked shoulders. Kit nods, watching him carefully. He must gasp appropriately. He's seen it done to Mariner before, when she tumbled under a cart a year or two ago. Twentyman did it with a blank, hard face, furious that she didn't even scream. The arm is moved slowly into position and Kit sucks air through his teeth, mimicking Ezra when he pulls splinters out of his thumb.

'This realigns the bones,' he says, 'and this—'

Kit is ready for the jerk and knows to yelp then, not at the pop. The pop, Mariner has explained, is the relief of the bone back in joint. So Kit closes his eyes and breathes deeply, pretending to be soothed.

'Well done, Silver, very good,' he mutters. When he opens his eyes again, the strange physician is looking at him out of those steady, silver eyes. They remind Kit of the way water looks under ice. He uses the closeness to risk a question. 'What does he intend to do with me? I only wish to please him and be done, you see.'

The physician frowns for a long moment, deep dimples in his otherwise clear forehead and then shrugs.

'Make you produce Greek Fire again,' he says. 'We have the formula for something similar, we recognise it, but no one can make it do what you did — make it leap and pounce. Either you have a new alchemical secret or you stole it from the coffin and gave it to your friend. He will find out which is true.'

Here is the problem, then. If Kit has an alchemical secret to trade it has sunk in his skin, so he has nothing to offer for his freedom and no reason to be kept alive unless he thinks of something very fast. Or he gains an ally, quickly. Slowness be damned, he risks pellucidity.

'Thank you for your kindness.' He smiles his most charming smile as the physician rises, folding the spare bandages and sliding them into his doublet. 'I am Kit Skevy. What do you call yourself, Silver?'

'I call myself Laz.' He smiles. A smile from a captor is worth a hundred sovereigns and it pushes Kit on, because people can always be worked around to what he wants, if he can be quick enough.

'Laz.' Kit tests it on his tongue. 'Shortened from?'

The smile becomes something bitter and sardonic.

'I am Lazarus Isherwood. I am the son of the man to whom you now belong.'

Kit watches Lazarus Isherwood walking back towards the door. He is so close, he can feel it, the thin stretch of fragile goodwill between them but he must do something now, something to secure this son of a Lord. He has never shot so high or for someone so beautiful and his mind is turning; quick, Young Kit, what is the next line?

'Then I hope I am in safe hands with you, Silver.' His words are bold, too presumptuous, but Lazarus pauses with the door open an inch, a slither of dusky light creeping across Kit's knees. For a second, the look he gives Kit is eerily blank, incomprehensible, but then he shrugs his uneven shoulders.

'You could be.'

That delicious flush again, this time high in his cheekbones, and Kit keeps his face schooled of victory as the door closes, but Kit knows. He has caught him.

ᛁᛗᛚᛁᚷᛈᚥ

She whose visits brings victory

Chapter Seven

'Not you,' Mother Plenty sighs, looking up from where she is serving ale to patrons in the Cardinal's Hat. Mariner hates Mother Plenty nearly as much as she hates the chipped red paint on the front door, the stench of the place, sweaty bodies and men's sour seed, nearly as much as she hates Twentyman. She is a sturdy woman, her face could probably be charming – at approaching fifty she still has smooth, light olive skin unblemished aside from the dark, scarred W pressed into her cheek (a whore's branding) and comely dark hair with canny eyes to match – but Mariner has never seen it. Mother Plenty never looks at Mariner with anything other than a rigorous scowl. Today, her stubby finger points towards the stairs. 'Dirty linens.'

Mariner tramps upstairs. Just as she predicted last night, Twentyman has not changed his mind, and Mother Plenty will have her for laundry and bar work until he does. The mistress of the house makes no bones that her customers don't want to fuck a brown boy without a cock, at least not yet. Any time Mariner passes through the doors, she hopes that today is not the day that is inevitably careening towards her; when somebody does.

'Linen!' Mariner calls, knocking on the third door.

It springs open and a lad rushes by, shoving his feathered cap back on as he clatters downstairs and a musical voice calls for Mariner.

'In you come, sailor!'

If Mariner hates the Cardinal's Hat, she hates it most for the people it has taken away from her. Girls who originally started at the Silver Moon, running errands for Squire Kay down the backstreets in bare feet, have ended up here as soon as their blood came. She has mourned them all, but none as much as Daisy. As Mariner steps in, she is sitting on the bed, as bare as the day she was born, flushed and beautiful as always. Daisy is the same age as Kit and if she had been high born would have fetched a dowry the size of a castle, with her peaches and cream skin, her silky, buttery hair and tranquil disposition. Instead, she is Will Twentyman's best girl, which is just one more reason to hate him.

'How are you?' Mariner asks, closing the door behind her.

'Well enough.' She's held on to the childhood country lilt of her voice that always makes Mariner think she must have been born in a field of clover. As she leans up on her elbows, Mariner spies a round, red bite mark on her shoulder. Daisy sees her looking and rolls her eyes. 'Some like to go like a mule, you know? No interest in my face.'

'That cannot be true,' Mariner says, without thinking. Daisy smiles at her sweetly, batting the compliment away like a dandelion seed on the breeze and Mariner flushes. Not for the first time, she wishes she could step into this room and meet Daisy face to face, like so many other boys.

'What did you do this time?' Daisy asks.

'I lost Young Kit at Crossbones. Taken by a client.'

Daisy crosses herself, a futile whore's gesture to protect against a sudden death that ends at that accursed graveyard. The working girls in Southwark are called Winchester Geese and so often, are buried there, part of a sad flock.

'Young Kit is grown; it's not your responsibility to keep him safe.'

Daisy pats the bed and Mariner sits down beside her, relishing the warmth of her little feet pressed against her thighs for a moment. She remembers Kit screaming at her to run. I did exactly what I was told, she thinks, I left him and he would never have left me. As much as Twentyman's punishment chafes her, Mariner can't stop the bitter taste of guilt rising in her throat because if she is not responsible for Kit then she is responsible for no one in this wide, horrid world and that is too maudlin a thought to bear.

'Don't look so sad, he's not dead, is he?' Daisy presses her little toes into Mariner's leg playfully. 'There's none so savvy as Kit Skevy. It's not your fault.'

Mariner swallows hard and nods. This is what Daisy does, her sweetness is an absolution for Mariner's soul. If you were my wife I'd drown you in pearls, she thinks. I'd plant a garden just to have flowers to cover you in. Saccharine thoughts inevitably sour when she imagines hellfire and her dead uncle's crushing disappointment in her lewd impurity. Before Mariner can truly wallow in it, however, she is interrupted by the door banged open, Mother Plenty's glower, a callow youth at her side. A fine doublet, well dressed, bright-green hose. A courtier, no doubt due back at Whitehall before the bell tolls.

'Next customer, Daisy.' Mother Plenty grabs Mariner's arm and tosses her back out into the hallway, slamming the door on the couple.

'If you're going to look at my lasses like that, you're going to have to start paying, but since you've not a penny on you, go downstairs and serve ale.'

'I'm not looking,' Mariner lies but Plenty kicks her downstairs all the same. Away from the goodness of Daisy, there is nothing to calm the persistently low itching panic inside her, the knowledge that Kit is lost somewhere and she has no idea how to get him back. The hours crawl by behind the bar, the working boys jibe and jostle her, and Mariner wastes the morning holding her elbows sharp, stopping these lads from getting any notions with firmly placed jabs.

'Ahoy, fair sailor,' a voice giggles. Daisy is lolling casually against the bar, skin puckered against the damp spill of ale across the wooden surface. It is noon bells, the stew is busy with customers, the sun stinking up the river waste as the tide slips back. 'I've got a treat for you.'

'I'm not allowed upstairs, Daisy,' Mariner says without thinking.

'No, you daft thing,' Daisy laughs.

Mariner looks down at the glass she is cleaning. She wonders painfully what is worse, to be treated like her desires are shameful or laughable.

'I've got a name for you. Of whom took Young Kit. The lad I tupped; he works at Whitehall. He's in service to a Lord down there, said they took back from over the bridge yesterday a very odd-looking boy. Mismatched eyes. There's only one boy I know with silly eyes.'

'It's Kit.' Mariner leans forward eagerly. 'What's the name of the Lord?'

'Isherwood?' Twentyman leans back in his chair and frowns at Mariner the next morning. She worked all day and night behind Mother Plenty's bar with the name chanting in her impatient mind, and now she has carried it on her lips like a prize all the way up Bankside. She is sleepless and urgent. Twentyman is gnawing a turkey leg. 'Scottish bastard. Lord warden or something, a mathematician. He's not one of Griffin's sloppy lot, a sorcerer for the King of Scotland.'

'I asked on the Overie stairs on my way up,' Mariner says. 'There's an Isherwood House down west of Durham House on the Strand, there's a wharf at Ivy Bridge Lane. Shall I go and take a peek?'

She can't shake the sensation that if she does, Kit will be waiting there, arms folded: what took you so fucking long?

'No, you shall not.' Twentyman glares at her, grease making his lips shiny and plump. 'You'll go up to Lime Street. She wrote and told me to send you.'

Mariner feels a thrill of disquiet when she thinks of the fine lady with her unflappable eyes. She also uncomfortably wonders what gold and transactions have passed between that lady and her master, treating her like a dog to be sent and called for.

'And Kit?' Mariner dares to ask.

'I'm not risking my neck for Kit bloody Skevy, not with someone in Bonny James' pocket,' Twentyman grumbles. No matter how appallingly uncaring Twentyman is, he yet somehow has this ability to be spectacularly disappointing. Still, Mariner tries.

'He's your prize brawler.'

'There's always another brawler.' Twentyman throws the turkey bone at her head. She ducks. 'Off to Lime Street with you.'

Mariner does not like the Lime Street Ward. The sounds are unsettling; the snatches of language she catches. French, Flemish, Italian, even some Portuguese that has her turning her head without meaning to, following hints of words she cannot forget. Her thoughts churn inside her as she is bustled by founders and glaziers around her, puzzling for an easy way to release Kit from the clutches of Isherwood but nothing comes to her. Twentyman is the most powerful person she knows and he has abandoned them. Despite expecting it, the sting is still piercing. What of loyalty? she thinks bitterly. What of love?

She is surprised when she knocks at Hart House and is ushered in. She expected a guildsman's home, but the house is too grand. The diamond-stained glass windows behind high walls covered in ivy, hints of perhaps a neat, dry tennis court beyond.

'Who lives here?' Mariner asks the servant anxiously as she is led upstairs.

'I am Lady Elody Blackwater.'

She waits atop the stairs, standing by a door ajar. No longer concealed in the darkness of Southwark night, Mariner can see the full of her — she cannot yet be thirty, tall, and wearing her wealth as well as any courtier Mariner has pickpocketed. Coventry silk ribbons, ropes of gold chains around her waist and wrists, sapphires sewn into her hood. Mariner is used to seeing women as walking purses, but today her eyes snag on the less profitable things. The pointed chin and muddy brown eyes, the skin with its bluish under-tone which, along with the coils of her dark-brown hair, reminds Mariner of things pulled out of the deep water, the colours of another world. It is not beauty, precisely, but a presence that demands attention, deference, and Mariner is welded to the floor by it, for a moment.

'Milady,' she says when she remembers herself. She pulls her cap from her head and scrabbles her fringe forward.

'Welcome to Hart House, Mariner Patience Elgin,' says the lady of the house, that arresting wide mouth pulling into a curious quirk. Mariner flushes and dips her eyes away. Why she ever gave her full name she'll never know. 'You are less sooty today.'

Mariner glances upward, searching for sarcasm, but there is none. Her eyes still rest entirely on Mariner's face so that it itches, flames in her cheeks and sweat behind her ears. Women do not usually like to look at her so long. In the past the ones that do have been a little drunk, a little bold, sure she is a lad and dragging her into the dark corners of the Silver Moon for a 'Spanish kiss' to dream about later. Lady Elody knows she is not a lad. Mariner has no idea how to respond so she only nods, mechanically. She's surprised when Lady Elody smiles and opens the door wider.

'Come in,' she says.

The room is boiling hot, as hot as a smithy, with a fire blazing despite the sun outside and an apparatus over the fireplace, holding a flask over the flame that is bubbling violently and spitting. Star charts are pinned on the wall, an altar with a cross and a tapestry of what looks to be a man and a woman fused together behind it. Mariner has never seen such a room like it in real life, but she has seen it on the stage. This is exactly the collection of props and items Mister Henslowe pulls together for Faustus' chamber.

'What think you?' Lady Elody asks, leaning against the closed door.

'I think your husband must be an alchemist,' says Mariner. 'Or a singular obsessive.'

Was that rude? Mariner wonders. She has slept too little and worried too much to truly tell, but Lady Elody does not look affronted. Her lips have quirked in amusement.

'The singular obsession is mine. God rest my husband, but he did not dabble in such things. It is the Blackwater women who explore the mystical arts.' Today when she speaks, Mariner hears a curious lilt to the cadence of her speech. French perhaps, or a Gaul education, not immediately noticeable under those neat Whitehall vowels. Lady Elody pours two glasses of wine and hands one to Mariner. Charity usually chafes, but it is a hot day and Mariner is glad of the chilled liquid, soothing and berry-tasting in her weary mouth.

'Though you must know something of that.' Mariner stares quizzically at Lady Elody with a sweet mouthful until she says, 'The alchemist's fire you witnessed two nights ago, ah—' Lady Elody raises her hand and shakes her head as Mariner swallows hard and opens her mouth to lie. 'It is my business to know such things. It does not surprise me, if Mr Kelley did indeed meet his end, such wonders followed him. We alchemists live and die by our secrets.'

Mariner does not understand. Alchemists are puffers, charlatans, men selling powdered unicorn horn for harder members in amongst the ironmongers and barber surgeons in the stacked shopfronts of London Bridge. They are the type of person who will do anything for a crown, even sell Griffin some deadly powder that would kill him in his own house without a care. The bible says sorcery is a sin even if the spell maker never breaks the law and kills a person or a pig. Yet the woman in front of her is well made, well moneyed. She certainly doesn't look like she can kill a pig, witchcraft or otherwise.

'You do not think a woman can be a worthy alchemist?' Lady Elody asks, clearly interpreting her doubtful silence as incredulity.

'Does it matter what I think, my lady?'

'I am interested.'

'Then I think a woman of your wealth can be anything she fucking wants.' She hears herself, those surprising sharp words, feels the echo in them. She looks down at the wine goblet in her hand and wonders: have I eaten today? She is sure that she will be kicked out, but the lady does not look shocked, rather, Lady Elody is laughing. It is magnificent, that is the only right word. Mariner makes no one truly laugh but Kit and so she stares at those rosy lips, stretched in an impossible smile.

'How charming you are,' says she. Mariner scrutinises her face but finds no hint of pitying altruism.

'I do not aim to be,' she says, because it is true. She has only ever been called charming once, and that was after winning a belching contest aged nine. She suspects it was sarcasm.

'That is why you are.' Lady Elody's voice is soft, earnest. She moves gently, so they are both leaning against the long alchemy table, a foot apart. 'Has no one told you?'

'None.'

It is disarming, this quiet truth-telling, but there is a strange tranquillity to it; having spoken so frankly and not been rejected or batted away as a mere curiosity. Lady Elody smiles and Mariner has the uncanny but not unpleasant sensation of her own mind being read. She sips her wine, basking momentarily in the need to say nothing. The muscles in her shoulders relax for the first time in two days, the tightness in her limbs where Kit's absence resides lessens.

'Where do you hail from?' asks Lady Elody. 'Spain?'

Dark-skinned and Spanish go hand in hand in this city, but why should Mariner not give the truth? It was asked for.

'My mother's family are in Lisbon. My father's family in Inverness. Both of my parents are dead, as is the uncle who had the raising of me.'

'And raised you a lad?'

The soft bubble of congeniality Mariner had been floating weightlessly in is violently popped. All of her words are lost except one. Her mind fixates upon it: Please. A plea not to be seen, not to be known, not to be thought of and since she cannot speak, she stares into her goblet, the seconds stretching painfully. Then Lady Elody sighs, a disappointed sound.

'I was married at fourteen to Lord Blackwater, a Lord twice my age who had lost his lands and all but his name. That was fifteen years ago. I always had a good head for figures; my father did not shun my education. I made my husband a rich man. Now he is dead these two years and I am alone for courtly ladies and gentlemen alike say I am too high-minded for my sex. I tell you this so you will see you do not need to fear me. I care not that you are a girl who takes a boy's name and boy's garb.' She nudges Mariner's foot softly with her own shoe; unexpected myrtle green stockings. 'We all do what we must to survive.'

Mariner feels a rush of dislike towards this lady, in her fine stockings, speaking about survival. Growing a husband's fortune from reasonable to bursting is not the same as running each day from the noose.

'Like your young friend, stolen away by Lord Isherwood. He must have done something fascinating. Lord Isherwood is a very particular breed of alchemist.' Mariner wonders how Lady Elody knows this but the gentry can afford to have eyes everywhere. 'Tell me, does the Grave Eorl intend to retrieve your friend?'

To Mariner's ears, it is a mocking reminder of how she left Kit behind. She stares around the room of strange and unholy objects and suddenly hates every inch of it, every patch of Lady Elody's skin. I should not be here, she thinks, I am on the wrong path and so is Kit. Somewhere, we have gone horribly wrong. Yet Twentyman bade her here, so here she is. The futility of her own will loosens her tongue.

'Perhaps you can ask him yourself. Your gold is in his pocket.'

Her voice is more contemptuous than it should be. She wonders if this is the moment when Lady Elody's benevolence wears thin, but she only leans closer, pressing her shoulder against Mariner's. She smells of rose petals, of wealth and warm water.

'You seek to protect your friend,' she says, and then, with a smile, she drops her voice to a whisper, as if it is a secret, words in confidence breathed over Mariner's nose and lips. 'I only wish you to know that I would be your friend also.'

Mariner's pulse thunders through her, right up to her tongue, silencing it. This is not like those tavern girls, with their grabbing advances and sloppy, selfish lips. This is considered and anticipatory and entirely new. She huffs out stiffly through her nose and nods, too worried to speak, to accidentally breathe on this fine woman's skin, so very close to her mouth. Lady Elody pulls back, her face neutral, closed. It is like the moment was nothing more than a mirage, a spell imagined or broken, if not for the fact Mariner can still feel those words against her cheek. They tingle. Perhaps, Mariner thinks, Twentyman is not the most powerful person she knows.

'Call again soon,' says Lady Elody. 'You are always welcome at Hart House.'

ᴄʜᴀᴘᴛᴇʀ

He who is from the Waters of Torment

Chapter Eight

'Could I trouble you to know what day it is?' Kit asks as Lazarus wraps his burnt arms in bandages soaked with lavender oil. The smell is much more pleasant than the pervasive scent of the damp straw around him. He has no idea what time or day it is. The darkness is pitiless and endless but at least the dead man has been taken away. He was shovelled into a coffin, leaving his stink in the air: a damp, meaty taste of wet leather. It is not conducive to Kit's goals of charming Lazarus Isherwood. Getting Lazarus to move beyond blushing and fumbling at Kit's flirtatious comments as he tends to the various wounds Lord Isherwood inflicts (the man has a penchant for a hot brand) is proving troublesome enough without the disgusting setting. Kit must make headway, before Lord Isherwood burns off all of his fingers and toes in his quest to know how the Greek Fire was produced.

'It is only two days gone.' Lazarus tightens the bandage and Kit makes a point to wince through his clenched teeth in a display of false bravery that he's seen other lads do to impress lasses. He notices the corners of Lazarus' mouth turn up, as if this is endearing.

'Truly? Only two?'

'Lord Isherwood likes to disrupt the clock inside a man,' Lazarus says. 'A man who despairs in a hole is more likely to give him what he wants.'

'I cannot give him what I do not have.'

'Then you will suffer.' Lazarus is pitiless as he rises with his candle, preparing to leave. Perhaps his father has chided him from talking too much with the prisoner, but all of Kit's hopes depend on it.

'Stay awhile, Silver,' Kit pleads, keeping his mouth soft and wry, prepared for flattery. 'I appreciate the company. And the light, of course.'

'You can make your own.' Lazarus looks significantly at Kit's burnt fingers.

'Not to my own knowledge.'

The more time that stretches from the moment the flame first caught, the more laughable the notion seems that Kit could ever command fire from his fingertips.

'But the flame came from you.'

'And I am supposed to know how?' Kit shakes his head. He has given up trying to puzzle out Griffin's daft trinket, settling instead on more practical quandaries: how to escape Lord Isherwood, how to piss with manacled feet, how to flirt effectively when he is dirty and smelly and chained to the wall. 'You are the son of an alchemist. You tell me how it is possible.'

Lazarus gives him a long look and then sits hesitantly on a small stool that Isherwood used to stand his bible on whilst he delivered his edicts.

'What do you know of alchemists?'

'What the poets say, they are magicians and puffers and full of useful tricks for the stage. *He that is grounded in astrology, enriched with tongues, well seen in miracles, hath all the principles magic doth require,*' Kit quotes.

'What is that?' Lazarus frowns.

'*Doctor Faustus.*'

'By Marlowe?' Lazarus wrinkles his nose. 'I thought it far-fetched.'

'Did you? I am surprised that no one in your father's house sued for libel.'

'Lord Isherwood does not enjoy poetry.'

'You do not call him your father. Is he not proud of you?'

'Proud of a first-born son who cannot stand with shoulders straight before the King or before the English Queen, and the only heir to the Isherwood name?' Lazarus shakes his head. His face is desolate. Kit tries not to rejoice, but desolate people are easy to navigate. 'He will not accept my contributions to his alchemical work; he fears my cursed shape will defile his purposes. He sends me to Flanders for Walsingham, doing physician's work and sending reports. He would rather I were made different, he would rather I were…'

Lazarus cuts himself off, may as well have bitten his own tongue. Kit does not care that Lazarus has admitted to being a lowly spy, he sees a wounding in his eyes that he's seen many times before. Lazarus might be the heir to a powerful Lord but he has been beaten down by his father, just like blacksmith and butcher boys all along the river.

'I think I have the measure of your father, Silver, for all his fine aspirations.'

Kit leans forward, pulling gently on Lazarus' arm, guiding their faces dangerously close together, not caring that he must stink.

'He is a dismal cunt.'

Lazarus laughs and pulls back, Kit's irreverence making him blush. Still, he is not offended. He does not leave.

'What of your father? We hear you could be the bastard of the stage-crafter for the Admiral's Men, Griffin. He was… known.'

It is unsettling to think that Lord Isherwood has been looking into him. Kit reminds himself that even if Lazarus despises his own father perhaps enough to engage in idle talk with his prisoner, it does not mean he will easily be persuaded to turn coat to Kit's cause.

'Aye, his firecrackers were the best in London.'

'No. He was Marlowe's lover, the atheist, in Raleigh's set.' Lazarus' gaze is sharp. 'He was known.'

Kit understands. To be Griffin, to believe nothing and to say it aloud in laughing jest like Marlowe, to gather with Walter Raleigh and Thomas Walsingham and other great lords of state to drink and disparage the bible, is to be known for all the wrong reasons.

'Well, it is not how he was known to me.'

Lazarus pauses. His eyes are furtive and when he speaks, for the first time, his words are staggered and unsure.

'I see. If not his bastard then perhaps... a replacement for Marlowe?'

Kit wonders if this is Twentyman's bile, spat out all over Southwark, that Griffin had Kit and was a perverse sinner who deserved to die worse than he did, and if it has followed him all the way to the house of Lord Isherwood. Kit tucks his rage behind his smile.

'He found replacements elsewhere. He and I only made stage craft together.' Kit pauses. 'Not that I judge a man for that.'

'Nor I,' says he.

These are dangerous conversations to have, but there is no hint of reproach in Lazarus' nervous glance. Usually, Kit relies entirely on the language of bodies. A lad who follows him into the stables with hungry eyes does not want words about proclivities only silence and lips, but what does a man like Lazarus Isherwood have to fear from speaking as he finds? If the King of Scotland can take men to bed and no one says a word to him, not even his wife, Kit doesn't think it's above the son of Lord Isherwood. He wonders, perhaps, if Lazarus Isherwood is 'known' to that monarch. After all, he would be the right age for a man who likes pretty men. If so, the question is whether Kit is tempting enough for a man who will have finer, cleaner tastes. Kit wants to be appealing, and the thought plants a poppy seed of disquiet inside him. Is it a desire to be entrancing for his own gain, or to merely know what it feels like, to be touched by softer, richer hands? Kit cannot tell but Lazarus has not looked away. Very slowly, he offers Lazarus his cup of wine. Silver eyes flick between the cup in Kit's grubby hand and Kit's face. A shimmer of indecision and then he takes it, clean fingers with nails cut so short and neat, brushing against Kit's own. Kit smiles again. Desire is so useful.

'You were telling me of alchemy.'

'Yes. You must know that all the things on earth are made of a composition of elements, of fire, water, earth and air.'

Kit nods. He has seen the grand diagrams relating to Galen's theories of the four humours in the apothecary.

'In alchemy, we seek the secrets of the balance of those things. For if all of creation is simply a matter of finding the right balance of the four, then what else can we create? Can we not draw gold from that which is mere lead? Can we not make unquenchable fire?'

'Can you?'

'I cannot, and I have studied alchemy since I was a youth. It has been the endeavour of my life.' Lazarus traces a shape in the ash from the brazier on the floor. It is a triangle. He taps the base of it. 'There are levels in alchemy; your puffers on the bridge, we can all do as they do; art for the stage and recipes for sore stomachs. This is where your Griffin likely played.'

Kit looks at the base of the triangle and wonders what horrible deaths are possible in the higher levels.

'With the right money, the right connections, a good enough

education, the level above can be achieved too. Deeper experiments, the mathematics of the universe, truth-telling from the stars and map making,' Lazarus says. 'Many of us dance in this sphere; the greats of our time. Doctor Dee, Lady Sidney, my father.'

'And here?' Kit points to the tip of the triangle.

'Here sits everything we aspire to.' Lazarus' voice is almost deferential. 'The truest alchemists, capable of unlocking the secrets of the universe. Agrippa was one, Paracelsus another, the kind of men who can produce Greek fire, the philosopher's stone, the red lion elixir—'

'And what is that?'

'An ethereal liquid, as red as Mars, capable of transmuting all inferior metals into gold. Some say it will produce the philosopher's stone, some say it must be formed of Greek Fire—'

'Your father wants fire out of me so he can make gold?'

Kit looks at Lazarus' fine doublet. He doubts Lord Isherwood is impoverished and if he is, it seems like a foolish gamble to put all his existing gold into the far-fetched possibility of drawing gold out of horseshoes.

'The promises of perfect balance are not simply the wilful production of gold, though what prince in Christendom would shun the hope of having their coffers eternally replenished? The Red Lion elixir is also the elixir of life, it purifies any formula it touches, purifies base metal to gold, could purify man's illness, even. Perhaps all sin.' Lazarus traces the pinnacle respectfully. 'Man made perfect, that is Lord Isherwood's only goal.'

'So lofty.'

Lazarus seems to pull out of a trance, brushing ash from his hand, voice becoming more factual.

'Where else is there more glory, more power? All over Europe, there are always rumours of someone who has climbed one more step on the ladder, a blessed alchemist who has achieved what none of us can and imitated the great masters on whom we base our art. Until your fire at Crossbones, Kelley was the furthest ahead, and with him King Rudolf. What boons will an Englishman receive if he takes the Queen of England to this pinnacle?' Lazarus counts them off upon his fingertips. 'Gold to fund his work until he dies, at the least. The finest tools. The best literature. To be the artist of man; incarnate.'

'Are you so taken in, Silver?' Kit can't help his disparaging tone, despite his attempts to keep Lazarus talking. 'Have you read no Chaucer in your fine education? Such things make better stories than facts.'

'You can tell me these things are beyond the pale of your imagination when two days ago you produced fire from your fingertips?'

'I produced nothing, something happened to me,' Kit says firmly. Just because he can't currently understand why doesn't mean Kit will be drawn into believing in far-fetched nonsense. Griffin said it was a penny trick and a part of him is pushing his mind hard to believe it. There must be a catch, a hidden figure in the wing, somewhere.

'So it did.'

Lazarus reaches forward, taking one of Kit's bandaged hands and turning it, thoughtfully. Kit holds his breath. He is used to Lord Isherwood's cruel grabs, not this.

'Show me something,' Kit demands. 'If it is true.'

Lazarus smiles as if he expected this and withdraws a small vial from his doublet.

'This is a formula like the one that you produced, but it has nowhere near as strong an impact. Merely lights a flame.'

Lazarus pours a little of the liquid onto the stone and then sets the tip of the candle to it. The spark catches the liquid and it burns, but burns blue, unlike anything Kit has ever seen. Then the flame is gone, vanished, left with nothing but an alcoholic smelling smoke. He can only think of what a wonderful trick it would make on the stage but he must not be distracted.

'You are more than physician, you are chemist and apothecary both—' Kit tries to flatter '—or is that all an alchemist truly is? A chemist with a star chart?'

'A weaver who manufactures cloth is like a chemist; the man who makes the coat is like the alchemist, for he has done more than imitate nature.' Lazarus pours a little more but this time, adds a small powder from another vial. This time, the fire ignites all by itself, small and white and fizzing. Kit laughs without meaning to, because it is marvellous to look at really, and Lazarus smiles, grudgingly. Without thinking, Kit touches it with his forefinger, not giving thought that it might be hot, and for a second, it leaps higher, like a star falling upwards and Lazarus leans back, his eyes eager.

'What would Chaucer make of that?' he asks softly, looking at Kit's hand. Kit looks at it too, trying to make a show of shaking it, as if is it uncomfortable but he does not know what kind of pain white fire that lights itself might produce. He also does not know why it grew taller with his touch. Perhaps there was something of the other formula from Crossbones still there.

'Perhaps I am a natural coat maker,' Kit tries to joke but Lazarus only nods, steadily, and Kit senses he is in danger here. It does no good to suggest, in any way, that he's capable of grand feats of magic or alchemy. Then Lord Isherwood will never release him.

'I spilled something on my hands that night,' he admits wildly, grateful when Lazarus' eyes finally pull away from his hands. 'Something in a trinket from Griffin's workroom. I don't know what it is. Perhaps it is some kind of accelerant.'

'Perhaps.'

Lazarus does not look convinced and Kit thinks, I was a fool to let my guard down, I was a fool to touch the rising star and now I am trapped. He takes an even wilder swing.

'Will you tell him?'

Kit sits bare under Lazarus' silent assessment, waiting for the moment Lazarus admits he will. That all Kit's clumsy seduction has been for nothing. Then, gently, Lazarus shakes his head. To speak the dissent is clearly too much and Kit knows that if he voices exorbitant gratitude, Lazarus might renege. So Kit leans dangerously close — tilts his head, sees dark pupils, feels ragged breath — and presses his lips, maddeningly close, against the corner of Lazarus' mouth. This is usually enough, this teasing of a man, it breaks a dam inside them and then they are unceasing, but Lazarus does not close his eyes in pretty surrender or crowd Kit down to the floor, tongue first. His expression is indecipherable. Kit is unnerved by it, unsure if he will be fucked or slapped. Then, moving slowly, so slowly Kit could name all the saints, Lazarus presses a thumb against that same corner of Kit's own mouth. Follows with his lips.

Kit has kissed many people for all sorts of reasons; for bets and dares and for money and to prove a point, occasionally for fun and never for anything beyond lust. Always with a present intentionality, a voice inside himself giving stage directions, commentary, unsilenced by pleasure. Uncertainty quietens him. He's trapped under this man's lips and sharp thumb still dug into his flesh, held in a muted ambiguity.

'I cannot save you.' Lazarus' voice is urgent, his other hand entangled in Kit's hair, tugging firm enough to be pleasant. 'I cannot, but... if I were to help you, if I were to tell someone where you were, who should I go to?'

Kit is victorious and absolutely must not show it. He swallows it down, trying to appear distracted in a cloud of lust and it is easy to do with his body so suddenly heavy with relief that unexpected hunger pulses through him.

'Mariner Elgin at the Silver Moon in Southwark. She will give you all the aid you need.'

Kit begins to unlace his shirt. Lazarus' eyes widen but they do not flicker away.

'I am not… well formed.' Lazarus' face is full of the pain of potential rejection.

'Different forms are not unpleasant. Trust me, I know.' Kit moves a practised hand to the points of Lazarus' doublet and watches the silver eyes of the son of his captor flutter closed with lazy, common lust. 'All that matters is what we do with them.'

＊ᛏᛚ♭ᚲ♪ᛉᚷ

He who visits the darkness

Chapter Nine

'How did you fare with that tip from my Whitehall lad?' Daisy asks, leaning against the bar of the Cardinal's Hat. Mariner has gained no reward from Twentyman for her good service in Lime Street and Mother Plenty has put her to work serving ale. A ship has come in from a long-haul voyage and the house is filled with the raucous laugh and songs of sailors. It is a sound that Mariner finds nostalgic and worrying.

'It was a sound tip. Not that Twentyman cares to retrieve Kit.'

Mariner had, just for her own sake, taken a wherry down to Whitehall to stare at the walled garden of the Isherwood estate. She could not scale it without help.

Daisy sighs. 'The girls always say Twentyman's heart is in his purse.'

'Small ale, if you please.' A young man interrupts, tapping a gold angel against the bar with a dull ring. Daisy's eyes widen. Gold like that is a sign to all and sundry that here is a man who wants to be treated richly. He cannot be more than twenty-five and blessed with handsome enough features, a bow lip and a clean jaw, a sloped shoulder draped in the finest doublet. Yet something in the symmetry of his face and the stillness of his bearing reminds Mariner of the sharks she used to see in the clear water of the Indies; elegant, blank-eyed, dangerous. She does not like him.

'Come, Mariner!' Daisy pulls the yellow fabric of her gown lower over her pale breasts. 'Serve the gentleman.'

'Mariner Elgin?' he asks.

It does not bode well but Mariner only nods, filling a cup. He pushes the angel across the counter towards her.

'For the pleasure of your company,' says he. Mariner's body clenches against the long-awaited, devastating blow.

'No, I'm not—' she stammers, trying even now to dodge it, but like a devil summoned by ill tidings, Mother Plenty is suddenly there, simpering.

'All of my women folk are for sale. Daisy, take this one upstairs, make her presentable.'

'As she is will suit me,' he says. Mother Plenty looks thoroughly put out that she cannot take this opportunity to dress Mariner up like a true Winchester goose, but it doesn't stop her from tucking the golden angel into her purse. Mother Plenty's grip on her arm is violent, nails digging skin, her whisper vicious.

'If you make trouble for me, I'll have Twentyman cave your skull in.'

Mariner wonders if it would be worth it but she is shoved towards the stairs and Daisy tugs her up, into her room. It stinks of tangled bodies on a hot day next to a filthy river; sweat and men.

'Sit,' says Daisy, and Mariner drops onto the damp, warm linens. 'Now he likes your lad's garb well enough so no need to change, but let's do your feet.'

Daisy's voice is horribly matter of fact as she bends in front of Mariner to slip off her shoes. She begins to rub her feet briskly with an oil that smells strongly of fennel. When she glances up and finds Mariner staring, she smiles.

'Oh, I know it seems odd but, in my experience, nothing stinks on a body like the feet. It goes a long way, trust me.'

Mariner cannot stop herself from placing a hand on the crown of Daisy's head; a strange, pastoral and benevolent blessing, Christ and the sinner woman, but Mariner only wishes to stop her words, to stop this moment. Her fingers move without thought, the dry, chapped hands of a thief covering Daisy's small mouth. How warm her breath is, how wide her eyes are, full of questions and her hands dripping with fennel oil.

'Leave with me,' Mariner whispers, her voice quelling the muffled surprise of Daisy's lips against her palm. 'Please. We'll leave London, we'll go anywhere. You would want for nothing and you'd be free of Twentyman. I'd be good to you, Daisy, I swear.'

Daisy twists her head. There's a slick second where Mariner thinks she might keep her hand over Daisy's mouth, force her silence so Mariner does not have to hear whatever comes next, but Daisy's face easily slips from her touch and her lips are smiling ruefully, unstoppable.

'You've been around lads too long, sailor. You sound like you're making me an offer!'

Mariner's juttering, disappointed heart weighs down her voice. Daisy's laughter dies in her silence and she gives Mariner a pitying look.

'Will loves me,' says Daisy in the hideous tradition of all the women Mariner has ever seen make excuses for horrible men, but she may as well have slapped Mariner with the back of her hand.

'And love makes people fools.' Mariner shakes her head, dazed by her own stupidity. 'Maybe I have been a fool since I met you.'

It's a clumsy declaration but it is all she can bear to manage with her worst fear climbing the stairs. Daisy's face is transformed, surprise making her younger, but, before she can speak, the door opens and

Mother Plenty is leading the young man in. Daisy rises but Mariner doesn't let go of her hand.

'Please,' she says. One last plea to God and Daisy to keep her from it, but Daisy is a saint pulling away from a desperate acolyte, and the door is closed, her fate sealed. Mariner can do nothing but stare at him. Plenty has clearly dug deep in her cellar and found a bottle of wine, for he is leaning against the door and drinking slowly, watching her as if she might suddenly perform a dance. She cannot help herself from scanning his pockets, spotting a fine ring or two, as if she had seen him across a market and was not locked in with him. Christ save me from this, she prays, sweet Jesu save me from this... She's been taught that the Lord listens and will be her salvation in times of need but when he steps towards her she cannot wait for the Lord. She pulls her knife from her pocket. He stops, a wry smile breaking across his features.

'You will not be needing that. I have no desire to touch you.' His expression loosens some of the fear in her chest until her frantic imagination wonders what the pissing hell he might want to do instead. He simply sips his wine and nods to the door. 'You lust after that fair whore, don't you?'

Mariner stares at him. He speaks so normally that she feels utterly wrong-footed. As if he has merely mentioned the weather and not the darkest secret sin of her life. No one, apart from Kit, has ever asked her about this. It was one of their sleepy bedtime conversations in the dead of winter when Kit was no more than twelve, huddled so close for warmth that their words were damp on each other's cheeks.

'The baker's girl, Alice, gave me a bun for a kiss,' Kit whispered.

'You sell your kisses cheap, Young Kit.'

'That is true. I let Godfrey from the Pike Ponds kiss me for free.'

Kit was silent for a long moment, pressing the cold soles of his feet against her warm calves. 'I do not think I liked one better than the other.'

Mariner could feel the heaviness of Kit's heartbeat where it was pressed against her own chest. Lads in Southwark didn't have to fear the noose for sodomy, not like the great men of court with their showman's trials, as long as no one ever said it aloud. Some men, players like Griffin, seemed to only like other men, and there were distasteful mutters about them. At the time, Mariner knew she should be dismayed but the only thing she felt was relief. She nestled even closer, her sinful words travelling through their shared skin.

'I would have liked Alice better,' said she.

Men can be hanged for sodomites, their sin is in the bible, but there is no law against a woman tupping a woman because such thing is insanity. How would it even be done? She thinks of Lady Elody's breath against her cheek, starting a burn from the inside out. Mariner knows her own desires are a sin so unnatural they are not even thought of by lawmakers, that priests do not have penance for them. Now this strange man standing in front of her in the Cardinal's Hat has given word to it. She starts to tremble.

'You speak of sin, sir,' she whispers. 'Great sin.'

'We are in a whorehouse.'

In the way he says it, she hears the Scottish lilt on his tongue. That cadence of speech reminds her painfully of Elgin, but this priggish man is infuriating.

'If you do not want to bed me then why ask for me?'

He looks pleased at her question and sets down his wine glass.

'Kit Skevy. He is held in the house where I stay. I would enable him out of it, if you are willing to be an accomplice.'

'Kit?' A million questions immediately jump into her mind but when she looks at his cold, waiting expression, the large ring on his

finger and the rapier at his belt, she bites them all down. 'I don't
believe you.'

'You were there when the coffin fell.' His silver eyes fix on hers
for the first time. Whilst he looks at her constantly, almost without
blinking, their eyes have not yet met. 'Do you not know me?'

Mariner realises she does. He was one of the men who grabbed
Kit when flames poured out of him. He was the reason Kit told
Mariner to run. Her neck tickles where the burnt skin from that
night is still healing. Yet having played witness to that monstrosity
and still having access to Kit are two different things.

'You do not believe I have him?'

Mariner shrugs. After all, if her journey to Hart House has taught
her anything it is that there are more players in this shadowy game
than she ever anticipated.

'He sent me to you. He has an uncommon memory for poetry.
There is a scar like a star, here.' The man gestures to the back of
his left thigh. 'It is a burn; now the skin is white and raised to the
touch.'

Mariner stares at him. It is an old scar from a time Kit in his
ignorance at the smithy leaned against a heated cattle brand and did
not know it. He has always thought it ugly, for he only likes the scars
he has from fights, and he never shows it to anyone willingly.

'You have tupped him.' The young man's eyebrows shoot up. 'Well,
you've either tortured him or bedded him and a torturer probably
would not take much time to stroke a scar to feel its texture...'

He says nothing, silent and appraising, but all the lads who have
tumbled Kit Skevy have this same look when they are found out: a
smug smile or proud eyes, as if drunk on the charm of thrusting
too hard and pulling too tight. She's told Kit many times that he can
get caught out in bed as much as being whipped at the Standard but
Kit Skevy is not blessed with discretion. She inwardly curses him

for his audacity in tupping one of his captors but also looks at the man in front of her with new assessment. Kit would not risk it for nothing. He must think this rich lad can be useful. Maybe this is how.

'What is in it for you?' she demands abruptly. 'We've no coin between us and Twentyman will give no favours on our account. Or has he caught your affections?'

Mariner would not put it past Kit's ability. He smiles but doesn't answer.

'I can get him out and to our wherry stairs. He will need to be picked up from there. A private barge.'

'And you think I can provide one?'

'You have friends in high places. In Lime Street.'

It seems all alchemists have eyes in unexpected places. It is a discomforting itch to the scalp to realise that whilst she has been sneaking around Southwark on Twentyman's orders and gazing at Daisy, strange eyes have been following her. The gentleman smiles sardonically and sets a piece of paper down on the nightstand.

'What is that?'

He drains his glass and then walks to the door.

'Tell the good lady at Lime Street that Lazarus Isherwood will sell. See how quickly she jumps at the offer to help you then,' says the gentlemen, Lazarus Isherwood, surely the son of his Lordship, as he opens the door. 'Tomorrow night. Midnight bells at our wharf. No lamps.'

'Tomorrow night? Must it be then?'

He gives her a cold look, deadly eyes.

'For his sake, yes.'

Mariner understands, a numbing chill spreading through her. Whatever these alchemists are doing to Kit, it is not benign. Young Isherwood leaves. Mariner scrambles to look at the paper on the nightstand, unfolding the thick parchment to see an elegant scrawl in a language she cannot read. Yet she's seen these characters before, hung over puffer stands on the bridge and scrawled across the covers of the books in Hart House. Alchemist secrets it is then. Mariner only hopes they are worth buying.

'What can I do for you back so soon, Mariner Elgin?'

Lady Elody leans back on her great, carved wooden chair in Hart House the next morning. Mariner has managed to sneak out of the Cardinal's Hat and rush over the river to be showed into the library, where the walls are lined with books, their spines facing outwards on many, many shelves and in stacked piles on the rushes. The air tastes papery.

'I...' Mariner sets her feet apart, holds her cap between her hands, hopes her posture conveys a confidence she does not feel. Words elude her when faced with this woman, the deep scarlet of her gown robing her like a cardinal, bloody and regal. Still, she must speak, for Kit, she finds the words.

'Did you mean it?' she blurts out. 'You are my friend?'

'I am not in the habit of saying what I do not mean.'

Mariner is not comforted. This is a woman who writes to Twentyman. She could tell him that Mariner has come here, pleading, she could tumble down the precarious bricks of Mariner's little life if she wanted. Perhaps Lady Elody sees it in her face because she sighs and Mariner watches in surprise as she slumps in her grand chair like a slovenly secretary and uses her finely shod foot to kick the opposite chair out from the desk. It scrapes across the floor, a strange and almost comedic invitation. Mariner stares between the chair and Lady Elody's playful expression. It is a long moment before she sits.

'I told you I am not liked at court. It is not only because of my widowhood, my ambition. It is because I never bred with my husband. I am barren.' She speaks brusquely but her lips are tight and flat, momentary grief suppressed, then they turn into a wry smile. 'Though I suppose you know something of finding your God-given body unfit for purpose?'

Mariner doesn't respond and Lady Elody goes on.

'Perhaps because the Queen is herself such a hard, uncompromising woman, you might think she likes that in her own sex. She does not. Her favour is not for me. She does not find me charming.'

'That cannot be true,' Mariner says. Lady Elody laughs. As she chortles, she tips her head back and Mariner wonders at the pieces of hair that are not swept up into her pearled caul, stuck sweatily under her ear like seaweed. This is a woman who laughs and the sun rises and Mariner is filled with unsteady warmth.

'Sadly, the Queen is not as forgiving to her sex as her nephew Scotland is.'

Mariner imagines it is some kind of courtly brashness, to make lewd insinuations about the cockstruck King of Scotland. It is what Griffin and Kit would do, but after the comments of Isherwood last night these words make her jaw clench up, her back teeth grinding anxiously.

'Consequently, I am forced to scuffle and flirt with Earls and Dukes, begging for their ear so they will tell the Queen I am a worthy investment; that my alchemical work will bring fame to England as Edward Kelley has done in Prague. It is a grubby task. Now you know the truth of me, of my own reduced circumstances, perhaps you are less afraid.' Her smile is twisted now, devoid of humour. 'So, ask what you came here to ask.'

'Your barge,' Mariner blurts out and then winces but she must plough on. Time is marching, the tides are turning and if this woman denies her, Mariner only has twelve hours to figure something else out. 'What I mean, my lady, is that if you would be so generous to give me the loan of your private barge tonight at eleven bells then it would do me a great service. I will only need the loan of it for an hour, two at most, as far as Whitehall and back.'

'And this I do out of the kindness of my heart?'

Mariner takes the folded note out of her pocket and sets it on the desk, feeling like a hound bringing back a fat pigeon.

'He says he will sell,' she says. She watches Lady Elody's face. She needs no tool, no dictionary, does not mouth or sound words or frown. Still, her fingers skim over the letters as if she expects them to rise up and greet her. Mariner finds her breath caught at the top of her lungs, desperate for a clue. Then, with a flourish, the curious note is tucked away in a drawer.

'You are all grim news and formality today, Mariner.' Her voice is light and Mariner's hands clench. She curses her own coarseness. She has been too direct, yesterday this woman found her charming and now Mariner's inelegance has chased away her interest. She knows she must do better, but Mariner cannot summon any agreeable words to relight her curiosity, so in her desperation, the truth spills out.

'I need it for my friend, the one taken,' she says. 'Please. I have no other friend to ask.'

Lady Elody cocks her head to one side, that mouth twisting slightly and Mariner has the uncomfortable sensation that her deficiency has been found amusing.

'You may have the barge—' Lady Elody taps her fingers against the grand desk '—but I will have something from you.'

'What, my lady?'

She can think of nothing of value she could give.

'When you recover your friend, come to Hart House. You will

need a safe port and you cannot hide from Isherwood in Southwark. He will not come knocking on my door.'

Come to Hart House. A command, an offer, words Mariner wants to say yes and no to, at the same time.

'We belong to the Grave Eorl,' she stammers. 'We are bought.'

'I owe the Grave Eorl a fee. I am sure he will consider it settled.' Lady Elody shrugs. 'I can sponsor your friend an alchemist's apprenticeship here at Hart House.'

Kit hoped to apprentice under Griffin, who had alchemist tricks if not alchemy. Perhaps it will be close enough. Besides, a woman with a fortune and a barge is offering to help her, and it is not as if Twentyman will extend any protection for Kit if Lord Isherwood offers him a shilling for him back and time is wasting. Mariner is not sure if she trusts the woman in front of her, but in the choice between a torturer, Twentyman and a lady alchemist, is not Lime Street the better one? Or will Kit think she has betrayed him and their dreams by selling him elsewhere? She does not know, and the choices are cannonballs, strapped to her knees. Any one of them could drown her.

'I can shelter your friend, Mariner Elgin.' Underneath the desk, Lady Elody presses her soft, red shoe against Mariner's tattered leather one. 'Say yes.'

The pressure is a finger upon a trigger, a reverberation of impact in Mariner's flesh. Want shimmers through her and, as so commanded, so she speaks.

'Yes,' she says. She hopes Kit will not hate her for it.

ᗉ𓊿ᑎᒐ𛱁ᕼᕽ

He who is like nothing else

Chapter Ten

When Isherwood walks into his dank little prison, Kit cannot help but smile. Even when he pulls the crank and Kit's shackled form is wrenched, hanging, into the air. There is something about having had his torturer's heir on his knees last night that brightens Kit's mood, but the man's stance is different today. Kit notices the wide plant of his legs, straddling the earth. Here is a man who believes he has the upper hand. A quiet, creeping unease starts in Kit's stomach, the nauseous tightening of the gut that occurs when someone follows him and Mariner down a dark alley, looking for trouble.

'*And God created man after his likeness after the likeness of God created he him: male and female created he them.*' Isherwood's voice is soft. 'You have kept many secrets from me.'

There are moments when danger announces itself; the moment before a fist collides with a jaw, the stomp of boots at his back. They are unpleasant but bearable, they are Mephistopheles conjured from the blood of Faustus, they follow a logic of the world that is at least predictable and therefore comforting. Then there are moments when danger roars up, a corpse rising, its deadly breath against the ear, and there is no warning or occult chanting to herald it. As Isherwood knocks on the closed door, as it is opened and Lazarus enters followed by a physician, cloaked in black and wearing a cap, Kit hears it. Here I am, danger whispers. You did not see me coming.

Kit looks at Lazarus for an explanation. Did you not have enough time? he thinks, expecting to see some pleading in his downcast eyes, evidence that his father took a rod to his already pained back and beat it out of him, any small hint of subjugation or humiliation but there is none. Lazarus' eyes are cold and vacant, a dead fish on a silver platter. There is no sign there of the man Kit laid with mere hours ago.

This is not happening; Kit thinks to himself.

'Strip him,' Lord Isherwood commands.

The physician must be well paid for he immediately moves forward, gently peeling Kit's shirt and breeches from him even as Kit twists from his invading hands, spinning almost comically on his suspended wrists. He nearly forgets to grunt with pretend pain, he is too focused on trying to evade the physician but it is useless. Kit is hung and naked; a carcass at market.

This is not happening, he thinks. Inside his mind he sees the boards of the theatre, the crowd beyond them. This is a play. It is not really happening to me.

'A member, a scrotum,' the physician reports, his head bent to Kit's groin. He wishes, more than anything, he was less fair skinned, less freckled from head to fucking toe, for he cannot stop the shameful blush spreading over every inch of him. 'Smooth skinned and lithe boned as a woman, no Adam's apple—'

'Yet.' Kit scowls at the physician and remembers the only advice Griffin ever gave him about this: You are not yet grown; they do not get to decide what you are. It is what has kept him alive in

Southwark; when other boys have teased him about his youthful face and member it has been easy to snap back: if this is how hard I can beat you now, think how much you will suffer when I finally have hair on my chin.

'Where does he hail from?' asks the physician.

'Found by a player in a whorehouse in Antwerp, at least that is the story from Southwark,' Isherwood says.

'He could be castrati.' The physician's thoughtful fondling is making Kit stiffen, a petrified rabbit in the wet mouth of a dog. A memory assaults him, Lazarus' beautiful clean hair tangled in his burnt fingers, the coronet of his manacled hands adorning his head as he knelt before Kit. 'It is small, after all, perhaps underdeveloped. Does it function? Spill seed?'

The physician isn't addressing anyone particularly and Kit, blood full of vengeance, glares at Lazarus.

'Well, you would know.'

If Kit expects more outrage from Lord Isherwood, the man holding Tyndale's bible against his chest, with the revelation that his son has buggered his prisoner, he is bitterly disappointed. Isherwood and the physician simply look at Lazarus for confirmation, as if they expected it. They knew it was coming, and with that realisation comes an unrolling of cringing horror. Every aspect of their encounter flitters through his mind, every suck and lick and grunt recounted to Lord Isherwood and his physician. Lazarus nods.

'And you are sure about the other?' Isherwood asks his son.

Kit's breath catches in the back of his throat. He remembers how it felt to nearly drown in the Thames, the blockage of mud in the back of his windpipe. Kit looks at Lazarus and foolishly dares to hope that the limits of Lazarus' intimate betrayal have already been reached, but he does not hesitate. Lazarus nods again. Such a small movement, a jerking incline, but Kit feels it run through his body, the ignominy of his calamitous miscalculation. Isherwood turns back to the physician.

'Check it thoroughly.'

It. A tiny word but Kit is transformed, a secret that until now only he and Griffin and Mariner have carried moving from his innermost self to settle on the outside of his skin for all to see. *It.* With the word comes a familiar despair wide and deep enough to sink an armada, an old darkness to plummet through, as old as himself. Yet Kit is hanging and there is nowhere to go and the physician's nimble fingers are opening him. His mind is empty, Mariner is gone, Griffin is dead, there are no quick verses or fast remarks on his tongue. He forces himself to think, not to wince at the strangeness of this uninvited impalement, I am, I am, I am Kit Skevy and I can be anything I want to be. He forces eyes open he had not realised were closed, blinks away tears he refuses to shed. He stares at Lazarus, the betrayer, but he leans against the wall, arms folded, brutally composed. The weight of Kit's own idiocy makes him breathless; of course lovers lie, he has seen it over and over and he hates himself for his forgetfulness, for being so certain of Lazarus' want that he had succumbed to the delight of wanting. When Lazarus had laid his doublet on the damp straw and let Kit rest his head against his heaving chest for a blissful moment after they were both spent, Kit had congratulated himself on such a successful seduction. He'd allowed himself to linger in the luxurious quiet of his mind, for Lazarus' fingers to tenderly pick straw from out of his hair. He is a fucking fool. He has misjudged Lazarus Isherwood and it is costing him everything.

'I can confirm a maid's entrance,' the physician says. Isherwood's eyes ignite with something awful. This is flesh, this is skin, this is hair and blood and nothing to do with me, Kit tells himself, hoping for that same loose ascension of mind he achieved whilst being flogged. It's enough for him to swallow the terror of the worst secret spoken aloud by snorting with disdain.

'Thanks to your fingers, Master Physician, I think you will find I am a maid no more.'

He's roaringly gratified at least to make the man blush but the Isherwoods, however, are devastatingly immovable, statues at the gates of hell. I am flesh, I am not here, he thinks, more frantically.

'You are no maid or man. You are *Hermaphródito*, the child of Hermes and Aphrodite, merged in the form of female and male, a perfect union of opposites and the answer to my prayers.' Isherwood stands in front of Kit, eyes raking him over with wild, excruciating relish. 'This is why you produce Greek Fire. There is holiness in your blood, and with it, we will unlock the miracles of nature.'

Kit's ears ring. He cannot stop the way he trembles, despite never feeling cold, but he can stop whatever hideous, screeching panic is rising up inside him as the words are spoken. You are useless, Skevy, Twentyman's voice echoes inside his mind. He would rather be useless than whatever this puffer shit stain thinks of him.

'I am nothing and I produced nothing. It was all in a trinket from Griffin, a touch of fire, and it was smashed and is all gone so there is nothing to be done with it.' Kit keeps his voice flat, holding it on the tightest rein; he will not show these men fear. 'I am useless to you.'

'Is there a way to know if it is fruitful?' Isherwood only has eyes for Kit's narrow belly.

'Not without vivisection. Though I suppose you could plant a seed and see if it grows in whatever fertile earth might lie within.'

Kit wishes his heart would stop. There have been times in the past when he and Mariner have discussed their worst fears. Kit said disappearing into the tower, for every Londoner fears it more than the noose. Mariner whispered words up to the leaky roof above their bed: to be taken by a man, to be seeded by him, to grow big in my belly with a thing I did not want, to die trying to lose it or in birthing it or worse, to survive it and live tethered to the man who stole my life from me for all time. You don't know, Kit, the fear of being a woman. Kit had stared up at the stars peeking between the loose rafters and did not say the truth. That her worst fear lived inside him too, a malignant speck of a curse he tried to ignore.

'I choose vivisection.' He hates that his voice is trembling along with his toes, but he will do anything. 'Vivisection, please.'

He thinks he might see Lazarus shifting out of the corner of his eye but Kit will not look at him.

'I may be able to ascertain if there is a womb to be fertilised. With further examination. It will need to be...'

The physician makes a series of gestures that Kit takes to mean laid out, splayed, held down, a sacrificial lamb. Isherwood waves a hand in assent. How quickly these people flick away your whole life with a fingertip. On the stage, gestures must be pronounced, large enough for the cushions and yet all of Isherwood's are small, inconsequential and catastrophic. This one is a blow to the back of the head; Kit is seeing spinning stars in front of his eyes as the ominous lowering of his chains rattles through him, the realisation of the hellish descent, the scent of rotten straw rising to consume him, and his scream rips out.

'Wait, just fucking wait! I am just an odd boy! I am just a lad and a thief!' Kit is fighting the urge to vomit, on the precipice of paralysing humiliation, desperation making the words stagger out. 'Perhaps I am queerly formed but I am nothing else! Nothing at all!'

He is ignored. His words are ash in the wind, and he is a pig trussed and hung for butchering, voiceless.

'How the Lord works in mysterious ways. You are everything, child of Hermes. I have explored the realms of my art, I have created much that has been impure and doomed to failure, but I have never met a thing like you. Your blood will create rivers of truth, your womb will grow the philosopher's stone, you are garden and soil and rain and sunshine all in one.' Isherwood's voice is thick, coarse with rapture as he touches Kit's abdomen reverently. Kit squirms, not caring how Lazarus frowns when he does not squeal with the pressure on his wrists. Isherwood is too eager to notice. 'The Lord in heaven sent you to me for his good work and I shall make such good use of you.'

Kit turns away from Lord Isherwood's feverish face. Beside his bare hips, the physician is unwrapping his tools. He recognises one from birthing days at the Cardinal's Hat. A heron's beak of iron, three wicked teeth attached to a hand crank.

'Drink.' Lazarus is there, bending over him, presenting a bottle, and Kit hopes it is poison, a last mercy delivered from the hand of a Judas. He drinks it eagerly, it is sharply bitter, with a strange, tobacco taste. Kit gulps and waits to die, but it is not working quick enough, the physician is settled between his knees, and then Kit feels an untethering from himself. That moment of a dream, when the sky is rising and he is soaring through it and then plummeting down.

'It will be done soon,' Isherwood is saying, hideously stroking Kit's hair. 'The henbane shall soften your journey.'

Rage is useful, Kit thinks, as the henbane floats his mind away. It does not make the physician's forced, uninvited touch bearable, or the sensation of being winched open, bloody and animal, any less crucifying, but rage is nourishment. He never takes his eyes off the quiet, disinterested figure leaning back against the wall who has done this to him. The man who fucked him and lied to him, outperformed him so thoroughly in this deception and did not even have the grace to poison him. Kit will burn Lazarus Isherwood, if he can.

'You sent him to me,' Kit croaks out.

'Do not take it harshly,' says Isherwood, voice sickeningly kind. 'Lazarus has travelled far and gleaned much for me.'

'You are a man of Tyndale's sweet and holy words, so you should know, my lord, your son enjoyed me.' Isherwood's hands pause in Kit's hair as he takes words and fashions knives with them, stabs until he is breathless, his eyes fixed all the while on Lazarus. 'He enjoyed me as a man who knows how to please them, who takes them frequently and without shame. Yes, he enjoyed me very much.'

Kit sees something flicker in Lazarus' eyes. His victory is small but delicious. Lazarus is wounded and at last, Kit is glad of something. Then the henbane truly takes him.

Kit does not know how long he flies. He is spirit, he is air, his body is lonely and bruised and bloody below him for endless days or years on the soiled straw. Then flight becomes dream and the walls are vanished, replaced with an open window. Snow drifts through it and Kit's hands are no longer free, but blue. When he sucks on them, he can taste ice.

'How long has he sat there?' A voice speaks that immediately makes Kit shrink into shadows. He wishes to be small, so small that he is no longer of notice.

'I do not know! He never said he was hurting.'

'Fascinating,' the voice says. 'I will write it in the ledger. So very fascinating.'

He does not want to be fascinating, he does not want to be seen, but he feels eyes that always bear down upon him, eyes that are always looking to catch, to examine, to measure. Do not look at me, Kit thinks, gazing down at his blue hands. They are rigid and ugly and he could pull off a finger like a stiff branch. He reaches for it, the smallest one, the crunch of bone, the twisting of the join in the socket.

'Wake, Skevy.' Kit opens his eyes. Lazarus stands above him, a bowl in his hand, a towel over one arm. 'Lord Isherwood requires some of your blood.'

First the blood, then the nails, then the hair, then the eyes, Kit sees it stretch before him. His slow dismemberment: a saint chopped apart for relics.

'Slit my throat, Silver, I beg you.' Kit's voice is hoarse. He does not feel his own mouth. 'It is the least you can do.'

Lazarus sits beside him, setting the bleeding bowl under his arm. With no ceremony, he cuts the inside of Kit's elbow. Kit watches the blood run, his mouth dry. Lazarus lifts the wrist to encourage the flow.

'Give me time,' says he.

Kit's laugh is wild, a banner caught on high breeze.

'What more could I give you?'

He wishes he could move, he wishes he could run, but he is sluggish, his mind still flying. Come back, he thinks, come back and let me punch this motherfucker, let me feel the crunch of his bones, let me just.

'I see you do not consider what I did not tell him.' Lazarus pinches Kit's thigh and Kit sees it, the way the flesh pulls, so he winces, too slow. Lazarus shakes his head in amusement.

'Do not waste your breath on a lie. I have had you. You flinch the wrong way.' Lazarus whispers over Kit's face, and he remembers kisses, soft and warm, delivered just this way. 'You do not feel pain. You are rarer than he imagines.'

'I am rare? You liar, you *turncoat*—'

'Better to turn a coat than burn in it.'

'Speak to me of burning.' His mouth is parched, fighting to form the words, but no matter how much his mind unravels, the scorch of this betrayal is eternal. 'You *burned me,* spirit, you spy, you disgust me, you crawl across Europe using your bent back to garner pity and your physician's cloak to steal secrets for your monster of a father, gorgons together. Do you think it will make him love you, Laz? He loves Luther too much to see you as anything but a broken buggerist, destined to burn, and all I see is a pitiful boy, chasing his cloak.'

'You are too much a storyteller.' Lazarus presses the towel to Kit's elbow, his silver eyes flinty and raw. 'You think I am Odysseus, the broken man with a broken form and a tale of woe, that I am hurt and lacking. I am not. You looked at my back and heard my words and believed so quickly the tale of the lonely, crippled son. You do it still. You do not imagine I have chosen my life and chosen to bed you because it served me best at the time, even as you calculated just the same, luring me with your touches and jokes.' Lazarus brushes a piece of straw out of Kit's hair and smiles. His lips are bitter, full of secrets. 'Your rage, Skevy, is not from the fact that I chose to use you. It is that you did not have the chance to use me first.'

Kit closes his eyes again as another shift of soaring echoes through his blood, henbane shaking him free, wafting him away from this man who he got so utterly wrong. Yet there is truth too, seeds of it, blooming softly as he drifts.

'But you did want me, very much,' he hears his voice say. 'I was not wrong in everything.'

If Lazarus responds, Kit doesn't hear it. He is sailing again on buffets of air, rising, still rising, up into the unending sky and further to those terrifying stars so far away. The earth in its petty smallness is lost before the inimitable weight of infinity and with it, the fleshy cage he lives in, those protruding physician's fingers inside him. He is so far away that it is nothing at all. So far away. So safe.

ᚱᚢᛈᚱᚢᛉᛉᚱ

He who has true power

Chapter Eleven

'Wake, Skevy.'

He hears the clanking of metal against stone and feels the relief of a weighted irritation around his ankles.

'He has gone, he has taken the barge and your blood upriver for further experiments. It must be now.'

Kit does not understand, his mind flittering. He hopes this is the moment Lazarus kills him. Despite everything, he would be grateful, but when he looks down, Lazarus is unthreading a rattling chain from the manacles on his wrists.

'I do not have the key for these, but you only need your legs to run.'

Kit is launched to his feet; legs unsteady from so little use, and Lazarus wraps an arm around his waist, hoisting him up. He smells so sweet, especially in this damp, dank place. There must be roses hidden inside him, growing out of his buttonholes with their green, ripe leaves pushing from his seams. Kit follows the fragrance out of the door. Outside, they move cautiously through a grey passage full of barrels, Lazarus' boots clicking and Kit's bare feet slapping on the chilled stone and marble. There are steps that Kit is walking up, there are doors that Lazarus is opening, and now there is a corridor, dark and richly panelled with tapestries.

'Lean here.' Lazarus props Kit against a hung carpet. It is beautifully soft and dusty against his head, smelling of the lavender the servants have woven into the back to keep away moths. As Kit turns his head to the side he can see at the end of the corridor of burnished wood, a window that overlooks the river. The blessed moon is ripe and high and Kit's eyes sting to look at her blue face. He thought never to see her again. Lazarus sets flame to the corner of the hanging carpet and it lights, far too quickly.

'Jesus.' Kit staggers to stop the fire catching his breeches but it has little interest, shooting up the carpet's edge.

'I soaked it in something earlier.'

Kit instantly imagines Lazarus, painting pig fat on the Turkish carpet, and snorts, but Lazarus is pulling him along the corridor, taking the candle and setting it to tapestries and hanging carpets. Kit wonders if he has soaked every one in pig fat and what his father might say when he finds out the extent of his son's vandalism. Running unsteadily down the stairs, Kit thinks he will take off, the dark spiral tilting away from him as the henbane continues to twist inside him.

'Fire!' Lazarus is shouting over his shoulder. 'Fetch water!'

Distantly, Kit hears the call taken up throughout the house, servants bellowing for water as Lazarus Isherwood kicks open a back door and they stumble out into the garden. Beyond the towering, ivy-covered wall, Kit can smell the river, high with the tide, pungent with summer heat, and as they stagger towards it, Lazarus sets his candle to something in his palm. He thinks it is a piece of horse dung, but Lazarus throws it. Kit watches it soar through the black air, barely glowing, and then, he is pushed back by the force of noise.

An explosion feels nothing like he thought it might; he is assaulted by brick thrown at him, clumps of mud and clay bashing his face and forearms and sound, pounding in his eardrums. This is a type of burial, Kit is sure, under a rain of upturned earth that will suffocate him, but Lazarus drags him on, through the ringing of his ears, staggering over a mountain of rubble.

'Only gunpowder,' says he, and there is the river. How black it is, spilled with the saffron glow of the city. Kit could weep with the beauty of it and he sucks more air into his lungs and holds it there. This is real, he tells himself. This is not the henbane, I am free, I am Kit Skevy again. So he twists, shoving Lazarus up against the wall. Lazarus' eyes immediately widen. He seems to have forgotten they have never met in a fair fight.

'You told him, you *watched.*' Using a deft knee, he kicks Lazarus in the balls and, whilst he is groaning and gasping, Kit presses his shackled wrists against his pale throat, using the chain between the manacles to bruise Lazarus' windpipe. 'Why shouldn't I kill you?'

'Because she's there, at the end of the wharf, your Mariner.' Lazarus' eyes dart into the darkness. 'No lamps, in a barge, but they need me to get away and you need me too.'

'Why do I need you?'

'I will show you but I can do nothing if I cannot breathe!' Lazarus gasps and scrabbles but Kit's arms are iron. There is nothing like the power of someone else's fear to make him feel like himself and he watches Lazarus curiously, his genuine terror and desperation to avoid pain. Would it not make him feel better to choke the life out of this man? Would it not strengthen the part of him that has been shivering inside since it was laid out on the stinking floor?

'Kit?' a soft voice calls from near the water. 'Is that you? Did you blow up a fucking wall?'

He knows that voice. He lets Lazarus go and he slumps with

freedom, staggering urgently back from Kit with terrified, relieved eyes but Kit doesn't care. He is turning on lurching legs to follow that voice down onto the wooden boards of the wharf. Mariner is in front of him, she's grabbing him into her arms, his own trapped awkwardly between them, but she smells of tobacco and ale and sweat, the stink of the Silver Moon on his tongue. Tears prick in his eyes and he squeezes them tightly shut.

'Are you real?' he mumbles, clenching her to him so she cannot slither away, the way light and sound all seem to be doing.

'I am.' Mariner pulls back, her eyes reflecting the glow of the fire starting over the wall so, for a moment, Kit panics she is made of fire about to consume him. 'Christ but your eyes look like you've been on the belladonna.'

'Henbane.' He digs his nails into her arms but no fire leaks out from her skin. 'The world is slippery.'

'Let's get you cleaned up then.' She looks over Kit's shoulder. 'Come, Isherwood.'

'Why is he coming back to Southwark?' Kit stares, the world tilting wildly as Lazarus Isherwood climbs into the boat.

'Do you not think it is the first place Lord Isherwood will look for us?' Lazarus' voice is nothing more than darkness from the black water, chiming with its laps and sloshes. 'Can we be away? I just blasted a hole in the garden wall. It is rather conspicuous.'

'No, no, no, no—' His feet are staggering back but the planks of the wharf are tipping him down towards the boat and he will not fall in.

'Kit, Kit, what happened?' Mariner twists him around urgently so his back is to the river. 'He came to the Hat, he told me he would help you if I got a barge and if Lady Elody, the alchemist I borrowed from, bought his formulas. You bedded him, didn't you? I assumed you were using him, making an ally of him—'

'No. Christ, no.'

Kit's throat is thick with the taste of bile, the scent of the burning house battling its way down as his stomach churns. How his ears still ring. He shakes his head to dislodge it.

'He's selling a formula to settle our debt.' Mariner clenches his hands. 'Please, Kit, just get in the boat.'

'This is a bad choice. He is a bad choice!'

'There are no good ones!' Mariner pulls him close and he can smell her breath, can scent out her desperation and anxiety amongst the sour tinge of it. 'Please, for the love of God, I have risked too much, I am supposed to be down the Hat at this minute so please, just do it for me! Just get in the boat.'

Mariner is panting. The orange glow above the wall is getting stronger, the smoke starting to become grey and hefty. Kit wonders if it would have been better to have been left in there, hung in the cellar, slowly choking to death on smoke, but here he has Mariner again. She is real and alive and he fancies that if he set his mouth against the side of her throat he would taste the beat of her heart. If the cost of having his best friend back is enduring more time with the person who stood by and let the worst things happen to him, is it truly too high?

'For you.'

He climbs into the barge and sits abruptly in a soft, cushioned seat under a small canopy, facing the back of the small barge and the water as Mariner takes up oars behind him. He realises that this is not the barge of a merchant. He reaches up and strokes the cold tassels. This is the barge of gentry. He hears footsteps and yelling from the other side of the garden wall. Someone is chasing them.

'Shit,' Mariner says. 'They'll see us.'

Lazarus produces a bottle from inside his doublet. Another incendiary, perhaps, and when he grabs Kit's hands, pulling them closer,

Kit tries to twist away, fearful of another explosion, this time a burial of river water cascading over them all.

'No, I don't want to—'

Lazarus unstoppers the bottle. Smoke pours out of it, whiter and thicker than Kit expects but without heat. Kit gasps. For a moment, he is stumbling through the black smoke in Griffin's room, but this smoke has no scent, no harsh invasive humours that push into the nostrils and make the eyes stream.

'Time to make a coat, Skevy,' Lazarus says, and he tips the bottle out over Kit's hand.

When the smoke slips over his skin, it becomes whiter, pulsing, vibrant. The skin on his hand tingles with a specific pressure, the same way it does when he accidentally catches it on a nail or a splinter, but the tingling feeling spreads, as it has never done before, crawling up his arm, a pox, a burn. He has the horrifying sense then, that there is a liveliness in the smoke, if not a mind then an animal sense of response and is that not worse? For a mind can be reasoned with but he cannot stop this hunting, questing thing reaching inside of him, burrowing and digging into his flesh and churning out more smoke.

What trickery? He wants to demand, but this is no vial in a bottle crushed against his fingers, there is something inside him, inexplicable and dangerously demanding, and Kit tries not to breathe. For if he breathes it in, what will happen? He will breathe in a living creature, its smoky scales coiling around his lungs, squeezing the life from him, but it comes anyway.

Sinking into his skin, just as the black liquid from Griffin's trinket did, and then, the sensation is the same, just the same as the flame. He is being crushed under an invisible pressing stone, there are rivers of something fast flowing and unstoppable inside his veins and in the buffeting smoke he sees teeth and tongues and ravenous beasts cantering and snarling away from him.

'Jesus Christ!' Mariner cries behind him but Kit cannot turn; Lazarus is holding him in place.

'Better she thinks it comes from me,' he says. It cannot be real, Kit thinks madly, it is a dream, it is henbane, I will wake up soon, but Lazarus pushes Kit's hands forward, over the back of the boat. The smoke billows behind them, a mist spilling across the dark surface, obscuring the width of the river. Kit watches in gasping terror as the figures on the banks of Isherwood House who are sprinting down towards the wharf, perhaps searching for them, are eaten up inside it. As Mariner drives them further down river, the clouds of mist follow them, still pouring from Kit's hands and inside him, the tightness goes on and on, and he has not even the words to command it to stop. Will every particle of air inside him, everything sustaining him, be pushed out to cover the river in fog? Will he be a spent husk, nothing but wrinkled skin and dry bones that turn to dust when touched?

'Enough,' says Lazarus.

Kit scrambles blindly forward, ignoring Lazarus' grip on the back of his shirt, to plunge his hands into the water, careless of the turds and rubbish that float in it. He coughs frantically, the dousing of his hands releasing his lungs, and he is amazed he even has the air in his chest to do this. He is drowsy, slumping forward, thinking of the deep riverbed with its silt and mermaids he could sink into, but Lazarus is pulling him back up, grabbing at his hands.

'Let me see,' says he.

The skin, which had been red and shiny from recovering burns, is now white and dusty, peeling and crinkly. Kit has never seen anything like it, but the closest he can imagine is how skin becomes almost webbed and textured when exposed too long in water.

I poured fire from my fingertips, he thinks, and then I poured forth clouds and air, as if the whole sky were inside of me and clamouring to get out.

113

His hands will not stop shaking. This is terror, deeper than the pain of Griffin's death or the fear of Isherwood's cellar. I am, I am, I am, he tries to tell himself, but no, the sentence will not complete. Nothing will come, no words, no explanations, no verses, just an uncanny dream that he keeps falling through, waiting for the ground to meet him.

'Just henbane, just henbane,' he chants, rocking slowly and holding his hands against his chest. He is grateful Mariner cannot hear his sniffling, plaintive voice over the splash of oars and the dismayed cries of the Thames wherry men, suddenly navigating through a celestial fog.

'It is not.' Kit looks at him, the man with the henbane, the man with the secrets, the man whose eyes are just as foggy as the river. 'It is you.'

'It is *you,* your bottle—'

'Lord Isherwood thinks you are alchemically valuable, that your holy blood or holy womb could produce the elixir of life or bear an alchemical child,' Lazarus interrupts. 'I think he was wrong. It is not your blood or your skin or your teeth that will make or perfect a formula. You do not make the thing, you are the thing. You are the holy union of opposites, both male and female—'

'You talk out of your fucking arse,' Kit's teeth are starting to chatter. 'I have been this way my entire life and I have never done anything like this.'

'But now you are, you cannot deny it.' Lazarus narrows his eyes. 'Have you never wondered why you are this way? This middle sex, why you feel no pain?'

'No,' he lies. He wraps his own arms tight around himself. If he does not, he will topple into the water. He is made of nothing but air, nothing but wind and steam and the faintest of clouds. They are skimming through the sky, the stars are in the water, the moon is cleaved with the prow of their boat.

'It is like you said, you are a natural coat maker. You are beyond the course of human, Kit Skevy. You do not know your providence but I would swear on my life you have been made by alchemy as much as a philosopher's stone. You are the pinnacle. You are an alchemical child.'

Kit stares at him, this creature from another world, eyes full of moonlight, telling a story in a language Kit does not understand. He thinks of the triangle drawn in the ash on the cellar floor, of the courts and kings of Europe reduced into three lines. It has nothing to do with him. So he closes his eyes and reaches down to grip the wood of the boat. This is skin, he thinks fiercely, this is wood, this is the Thames, this is London where witchcraft is for the illiterate and alchemy for the gullible and all that matters in this life is gold. He is a freakish means to a richer end, so says Will Twentyman, and every time Kit has considered his own oddness, he never imagined that this reality, the one where his hands are full of power he does not recognise, was a possibility. If he had known, would he have wanted it? Would it not have been better to have snuffed the life from Lazarus Isherwood at the wall and fled under the cover of darkness back to Southwark? To have been nothing again but Kit Skevy, Southwark made? He has no answers but if he does not open his eyes, if he does not see himself skimming through mercury, he will not feel the nasty, staggering terror of unknowing. So he keeps his eyes closed and thinks: this is just the henbane.

ARGENTUM VIVUM

PART II

The *electrum magicum* is prepared as follows:– Take ten parts of pure gold, ten of silver, five of copper, two of tin, two of lead, one part of powdered iron and five of mercury. All these metals must be pure. Now wait for the hour when the planets Saturn and Mercury come into conjunction, and have all your preparations ready for that occasion […] Many wonderful things can be made of this electrum, such as amulets, charms, magic finger rings, arm rings, seals, figures, mirrors, bells, medals and many other things possessing great magical powers, of which very little is publicly known, because our art has been neglected, and the majority of men do not even know it exists.'

—*Paracelsus*

He who demands obedience

Chapter Twelve

'So this is the famous Kit Skevy,' Lady Elody says to Mariner, looking over Kit appraisingly as he leans against her shoulder. On the slow, painstaking walk from Billingsgate to Lime Street, Kit seems to have recovered more of his mind, refusing to speak or walk beside Lazarus Isherwood, but Mariner notices that with returning wit comes failing energy. He's managed to stand whilst servants have fetched tools and freed him from his manacles, but Mariner has to nudge him to respond.

'Yes, milady,' he mumbles.

'Yes, thank you again, my Lady Blackwater,' Mariner rushes to add deferentially and Kit twists his head, slightly lethargically, to give her a piercing look. Mariner knows what he's thinking. *Who the fuck is this woman to you?* Mariner blushes, looking away. Even if she could speak freely at this moment, she has not even considered how to explain.

'I am Lazarus Isherwood, Lady Blackwater. It is a pleasure to finally make your acquaintance. I am grateful for your hospitality in exchange for what I have sold.' Lazarus is bowing in front of her, every inch of him a courtier and Mariner feels suddenly ten times coarser and dirtier. 'I am interested in what my fellows in the Lime Street ward have to offer.'

'We are happy to have bought from you, Lazarus.' Lady Elody bows back. 'And more than happy to host you here in Hart House along with Master Skevy.'

'You are?' Kit mutters and Mariner winces. She has not had time to explain. Lady Elody smiles at him.

'It is for your safety. Your friend has stolen you away from a man who would hunt you back down.'

Mariner feels Kit shudder beside her and wonders what terrible things have been done to him. He looks wearily up into Mariner's face.

'Well then.' She watches as his eyes close and open so heavily. 'To Dover?'

She sees a plan in his eyes. The London ferry, Dover by morning, then a ship to Calais. She does not want to be the one to tell him it's not possible.

'I think you underestimate Lord Isherwood,' Lady Elody says before Mariner can open her mouth. 'An ocean or even another country is not an obstacle for a man of his resources and motivation.'

'So the solution is to stay here in the city, right under his nose, with his son?' Kit glares at Lazarus who has turned to the servant at his right hand and is casually eating the dried figs he offers.

'Lord Isherwood will not come to Lime street unless he is invited by her ladyship. He is the most respectful of men.' Lazarus pops a fig into his mouth. Kit looks like he wants to hit him so hard in his jaw that he is forced to spit it right back out. Probably along with some teeth.

'Words are fragile things from your lips, like glass. Finely made and easily broken.' Kit's voice is slurred and his feet stumble as Mariner tries to steady him.

'He was raised on poetry.' Lazarus' voice is light, his manner entirely self-satisfied. 'It shows.'

'I have an apprenticeship to offer you, Master Skevy,' says the lady. 'You will stay here, an apprentice in Hart House, rather than return to the Grave Eorl.'

Kit goes still beside her; Mariner is unsure if he is frozen with the possibility of being free, or the fear of a new master.

'What kind of apprentice?' he asks, warily.

'An alchemist, if it suits you. I hear you have talent.'

He turns to stare at Mariner, and she shifts under his scrutiny, cheeks flaming with it.

'Do you?' he says flatly. 'I wonder how the fuck you heard that.'

Mariner grabs his arm and pulls him away from Lady Elody and Lazarus, mumbling insufficient apologies and tugging him into an alcove where he can lean, as grey as a dead man, against a tapestry of a ship on rocky waves.

'You must stay here,' she whispers urgently, trying to fight back the squirming feeling that she has let him down. 'Lord Isherwood is a Scottish Earl, he holds an ancient seat on the northern border, he's in the service of the King of Scotland and if he marches into the Silver Moon, Twentyman will not hesitate to sell you back to him!'

'Is he?' Kit's voice is vaguely curious. She watches him as he gives Lazarus Isherwood a sideways look. No matter what Kit says of loathing the man, his eyes still follow him. Then Kit's gaze flickers back to Mariner; hard, assessing. 'What have you told her?'

'Nothing!' Mariner exclaims and then grimaces when she feels Lady Elody and Lazarus staring at her. She pulls Kit closer so their words are mere hisses of hot air between their noses, nearly touching. All of her frustration over just how blindingly hard the last few days

121

have been spills out of her mouth. 'You don't understand, Kit, these people know what happened to you. They *know*.'

She did not think it was possible for him to pale further but he does, splaying his hands flat against the tapestry, then balling the fabric into fists.

'What do they know?'

'The fire, the witchcraft that the alchemists made you produce at Crossbones.' Kit flinches at the word, but Mariner doesn't know what else to call hellish fire emerging from fingertips, and still hurries to reassure him. 'I did not tell her, she found out on her own. I have kept your other secrets. She is only curious about Crossbones, I am sure. She does not know you cannot... feel.'

Kit takes an immense gasp of air, his throat stretched, muscles working, and then slumps, his head resting back against the wall, eyes lolling towards Lazarus Isherwood.

'He knows,' Kit murmurs, defeated. Mariner sighs internally, reaching to stroke Kit's face. It is an unfortunate secret to share with an enemy, but luckily not the worst one, nor the worst consequence they might face tonight. Mariner must go south of the river and deal with that for them both.

'I cannot stay here with him,' Kit whispers and Mariner is shocked, frightened even, to see a shimmer of tears in his eyes. There is a ripping inside her, between the need to comfort and the need to protect, as she always has done. This is the first time they have ever been in conflict.

'Kit, all the choices are still bad,' she mutters and his eyelids clench close, to stop tears falling. 'Stay, be safe. I will go back—'

'No.' Kit presses his hand over hers against his cheek, eyes opening with unexpected ferocity. 'Every single thing we saved is in our hiding place. Tell Twentyman she bought your apprenticeship also and then come here. You cannot leave me alone with them.'

Mariner stares at him, blinking. She had no idea it was enough, everything they had skimmed, but a buyout for one is much easier to reach than a buyout for two.

'I am no alchemist,' she whispers.

'Nor am I,' Kit snorts. 'At least she knows you. Go, go back to Twentyman before he finds you missed.'

She furtively glances at Lady Elody, talking quietly with Lazarus. She has already asked so much of this woman, how to ask for more? And will she even be wanted? Yet she finds herself nodding, watching Kit breathe out with gratitude and the grubby secret unfurls inside her that she has not said yes for his benefit, at least not entirely. Rather it is too tantalising, the possibility that tonight they can both be free and that freedom can be delivered by the slow, powerful smile and wealth of the dark-eyed woman who makes her cunt quiver. It is those eyes and the vague and tantalising promise inside them and not Kit that she keeps in her mind as she crosses over the misty bridge with Lady Elody's full purse.

'Where the fuck have you been?'

Twentyman is scowling pure thunder in the upstairs room of the Silver Moon and they unfortunately have an audience. Squire Kay and Ezra are both loitering nervously by the door and, surprisingly, Daisy is there. It's odd to see her out of the Hat, fully dressed in a yellow gown that was probably once fine but now has taken on the brownish colour of piss. It makes her skin appear sallower, and her beautiful blue eyes are ducked to the floor as she stands behind Twentyman.

'Don't look at her!' Twentyman snaps. 'I told Plenty to send word if you didn't turn up tonight and she sent Daisy down, and then I hear you've not only been plotting to spring Skevy, you've been sighted with him in the city! So speak up!'

Mariner catches Daisy's eye, knows that she has been the one to tell him about her plans for Kit. Daisy's fleeting, slightly shameful expression reminds her that there's nothing for her here. She's left what matters most to her on the other side of the river. So Mariner drops Lady Elody's purse on the many pages of accounts scattered over Twentyman's desk.

'Your payment from Lady Blackwater. She's sponsoring an apprenticeship for Kit in Lime Street.'

'Is she?' Twentyman weighs the purse in his hand and then spills it on the table, nodding for Ezra to come forward and count it.

'All of what we're owed,' says Ezra. 'And all in sovereigns.'

It is a mighty haul but Twentyman scowls and fingers the gold thoughtfully. The air stops moving with the breeze of the river from the window and the flicker of the flame in the grate hesitates. All the room waits to see what mood Twentyman will settle upon. Generally, he is displeased when he has lost control and the look he throws Mariner as he turns a sovereign in his palm is utterly filthy.

'He'll be back. No one at Lime Street will keep a branded brat like him for long, and you—' he points at her with the sovereign held between his first and middle finger '—you'll be going back down the Hat. Plenty has customers for you.'

He smiles nastily. She wonders if he spread the word around his lads: Mariner Elgin is on her back, come and teach her a thing or two.

'No.' Mariner feels the word in every inch of her gut before it crawls out of her mouth. Twentyman stares at her.

'No?'

She swallows down the sweet acidic bile of fear that lurches to the back of her throat. She feels Squire Kay and Daisy and Ezra's eyes fixed upon her as she moves forward, her shoes making the floorboards squeak loudly. She pulls the excruciatingly pilfered silver and gold out of her pocket and spreads it on Twentyman's desk. Irrationally, she panics that he will recognise it as stolen but how could he? Coin is coin.

'And what has that Lime Street witch bought now?' he sneers.

'Me.' Mariner tries not to let the lie sound false on her tongue. 'She's sponsoring me too.'

'Not with shillings and half-angels she isn't.' Twentyman snorts and pushes their stolen savings back. 'Go back to that lace-whore and tell her you're not for sale.'

He leans back, body slack with satisfaction, lip curled, foot tapping eagerly as he awaits her disappointment.

I am a game to him, she thinks. I will play no longer. She reaches into her pocket and pulls out her freedom. She has one good thing, one blessed thing left from her life with Elgin. Man lives on the word of God, Mariner, but a little coin does not hurt, Elgin whispered. One gold Spanish doubloon, heavier than a sovereign, the riches of the Spanish colonies that Drake plundered purer and truer than anything in Elizabeth's realm. A final keepsake of a lost future, set against the hope of a new one. She sets it on top of the pile of stolen takings. Twentyman's wide eyes fix on it, hand reaching forward, already grasping. Mariner slaps her palm over the top, absorbs his savage glare.

'Say we are settled, say it is enough and it is yours,' says she. 'I am done.'

'You are *done*?' As fluid as a snake striking, Twentyman suddenly turns the table, sending coins splattering noisily across the floorboards as he shoves Mariner back against the wall. 'You ungrateful little shitswine, you think you decide when you are done?'

His arm is pressing against her windpipe, choking her. Peripherally, she sees Ezra bending to pick up the doubloon, examining it carefully. 'You're nothing but a cockless boy and if I'd known you'd throw my favour back in my fucking face I'd have tied you to a bed in the Hat and broken you in myself!'

'Will! Will! Don't kill the lad!' Daisy is there, little fingers scrabbling at his shoulders, but Twentyman's elbow is sharp and suddenly her face is red with a bloody nose.

'She's not a fucking lad!' Twentyman bellows and leans closer as he presses his face forward, twisted with rage, spittle catching in her eyes. Her vision is tunnelling, black and orange, as Twentyman cuffs her around the head, jostling her teeth and starting a ringing in her eardrum. 'I've given you far too much slack, let you run like a lad too bloody long and it's time you learn your place!'

'Twentyman, let her go!' Squire Kay's voice is sharp. Shapes and people are fuzzy to Mariner, but she thinks Kay might be pressing a handkerchief to Daisy's face. 'It's not worth the trouble—'

'Don't talk to me about fucking trouble!' Distracted by looking over his shoulder, he lessens his grip enough that Mariner can at least get air down her windpipe. 'Griffin brought your fucking bastard back from your whoring in Antwerp and I've had nothing but trouble from the pair of them ever since!'

Mariner stares at Squire Kay in amazement. It's been a persistent rumour in the Silver Moon for as long as Mariner has been there, that the tale Griffin always told about Kit's providence was nothing more than pretty words to cover up a less savoury truth: that Griffin had fathered an ugly son off a now dead whore. Mariner has never been sure which version seems more absurd; that Griffin would take in a Flanders orphan out of the goodness of his heart or that Griffin could ever fuck a woman. Perhaps the truth is that Griffin's tales were merely cover for his sister's past mistakes. Squire Kay is blushing deeply, her eyes wet and Ezra's hand is suddenly on Twentyman's shoulder, insistent and calm.

'The gold is good,' he says. 'The Lady in Lime Street is a good client. Take the gold. Keep the client. It is good business.'

Twentyman flinches against Ezra's quiet reason, but nothing sways him like the chance at future gold. His panting breath is hot on her face, smelling of his dinner as she gasps for air, twitching and wishing she could reach her knife. She does not want the foul stench of ale and gravy to be the last thing she smells.

'They'll have you branded a whore and a thief in the city before the month is out.' Twentyman steps back and Mariner tries not to slump, fumbling to draw her knife too late, dizzy with the sudden influx of air in her lungs. 'I'll see you dance a merry gallows jig at Tyburn. I'll not pull your legs, Mariner Elgin. Not for twenty of your Spanish coins, and if I ever have the chance to fuck you sideways, I will.'

Mariner cannot speak, wishes she could say, the feeling is entirely mutual, but Squire Kay is pulling her upright, fumbling her out of the door, her head spinning.

'Go! Go!' she urges. 'Keep an eye on him.'

Mariner wonders who she is asking as: merely as the innkeeper who has kept Kit steady and alive all these years or is it possible that, all this time, Squire Kay has truly been Kit's mother? Before she can speak, Squire Kay has given her an encouraging push down the stairs. She stumbles the rest of the way, shoulder bumping sharply into the wall as she uses her own momentum to hurl herself out of the back door. Her heart is pounding, the fantastic relief of having got away with something actually aching in her throat. Plunging herself out into the night, legs staggering round to the stable, she rushes to the hole in the wall. Hidden by the crooked panel are their few precious items, she shoves them into a wooden box. We are never coming back, she thinks wildly. How much joy it gives her.

'You didn't tell me you had money.'

Mariner whips around, astonished to see Daisy standing at the top of the wooden ladder that leads up to the small overhang in the stable where extra hay is stored and Mariner and Kit have lived together for years.

'She pays in sovereigns for Kit but silver and half angels for you?' Daisy shakes her head.

'Would it have made a difference?' Mariner ties the box with a sharp tug, the rope burning her palm.

'Money changes everything.'

Daisy's voice is soft. Mariner looks at her properly. Her blue eyes, which have always reminded Mariner of the brightest ocean on the sunniest day, are now clouded. There is a melancholy to her Mariner has never seen before. She wonders, suddenly, if it was always there.

'Really?' Reprieve has made Mariner bold, and with all the stored up tenderness of a decade, she puts her palm against Daisy's smooth cheek. Those dainty nostrils, crusty with dried blood, flare. A fresh drip forms, a black stain in the moonlight, as if darkness is creeping out of her. Mariner could brush it away with her thumb, could kiss it, take Daisy onto her lips. Then Daisy quickly steps back, nearly losing her balance as she pushes herself out of the stretch of Mariner's desire. Her haste is a needle to Mariner's chest, slowly taking the air out of her lungs. She wonders if, later on, it might kill her. 'Not everything.'

'I didn't ever know you felt… as you do. About me. I never thought a lass would…' Daisy takes a sharp breath in and then strokes her hand against her stomacher, as if comforting herself.

'I did,' she says. There is no danger in admitting it now, with one foot already in Lime Street and knowing as she does that the truth changes nothing.

'You'll forget me, in the city, with that fine lady.' Daisy tosses her blonde tresses with a cold smile. Mariner's seen it before; it's the smile she uses for patrons in the Hat. 'You'll forget me by next week.'

Mariner instantly thinks of Lady Elody's bright-brown eyes.

'I hope so.' She pulls the rope of her box onto her shoulder and pushes past her, climbing down the ladder. Daisy looks down on her, face entirely shaded, a spectre or a haunting, no longer even a person. Mariner turns her back and sets her eyes towards the city.

ⲛⲽⲉⲡⲧⲩⲝ

He who promises

Chapter Thirteen

'I will come and tend to your well-being,' says Lazarus, once Mariner has left and the aloof lady of the house has directed the servants to lead Kit and Lazarus upstairs to their beds.

'You will go and fuck yourself.'

'She did not sponsor your apprenticeship for nothing.' Lazarus' voice is nothing but a murmur in his ear, making him shiver. 'She is an alchemist too and you are an alchemist's prize. Think on that.'

Fuck you, Kit thinks. You can make me feel small in this fine house with your fine manners, but in a dark lane on a dark night I would kick you to China.

As they climb the stairs, he barely has the mind for it, to negotiate these new bonds with this unknown lady alchemist who may or may not have a fish cellar to hang him in, but he knows that cutting ties with Twentyman is the road to freedom, if such a road exists. Mariner is right, all the choices are bad: to return to the Silver Moon is to risk Isherwood again and to stay here is to remain in the presence of Lazarus and every vile thing he makes Kit feel. He has chosen discomfort over potential imprisonment but it does not mean he is happy about it. For if Mariner is right and Lady Blackwater knows, just as Isherwood did, that some sort of fire was conjured by his unwilling hand, what will be her approach to investigate it? He could hope her femininity would deny some of the harsher tactics he's been exposed to this last week, but he once saw Mariner bite a man's cock in a fight. Femininity and violence are not mutually exclusive.

'Here is your chamber, Master Skevy,' says the servant.

That's a first. Not only the respectful moniker, but Kit has slept all of his life on a shared shelf above horses. This chamber is very small — only space enough for a stool, a box as a nightstand, a plate of bread and wine and a candle atop it — but the sight of the bed almost makes him weep. Before he can happily collapse, Lazarus is grabbing his wrist, eyebrows furrowed, but Kit has had enough of being manhandled. He smacks Lazarus around the head, a cheering clobber of the skull, sending him sprawling to the floor with a grunt.

'If you want to touch, you ask permission.'

'Forgive me, Skevy.' Lazarus pulls himself wearily back to his knees, eyes irritatingly amused. 'Might I have leave to attend to your hands so they do not become putrid, and kill you?'

Kit looks down at the white, peeling skin. He has no idea if he is in danger of putrefaction or not, but Mariner, on her way back to face Twentyman's wrath, will be annoyed if he dies. They are a team or he is nothing. He sits heavily on the fresh straw mattress. Warily, he extends his hands towards Lazarus who reaches once more inside his doublet, retrieving strips of bandages and a small vial. Kit is beginning to think that Lazarus Isherwood must wear clothing three times his size in order to accommodate all his trinkets. He is surprised he does not clink when he walks. Lazarus withdraws a pipette, dropping an orange-coloured oil onto Kit's palms.

'This is spiced oil, the warmth will heat the blood and skin again.' Lazarus unrolls a bandage and glances at the bread. 'Eat something.'

'No.'

'You must.' Lazarus gives him an odd look. 'He did not feed you.'

He honestly has not noticed. Lazarus starts to rub the surface of his hands, gently pressing in the oil. Kit stiffens. For a second, he is in the cellar once more, Lord Isherwood stripping him, calling him *it*. Pulsing through him is the identical feeling of his body, bare and stretched and trapped on the air, the scent of moulding straw in his nostrils. Lazarus looks at him.

'It hurts you?'

'No.'

'Then why do you flinch?'

'Because it is *you*.'

Lazarus says nothing. His thumbs make circles at the joints of Kit's wrists.

'These will blister, likely.'

Kit shrugs; after all, no one dies of blisters. Lazarus shoots him a curious look.

'You must be the devil to keep alive.'

'Before the alchemy, I was doing well enough. You, with your poisons, your father with his games, and before, Griffin, choked on a puffer's trick that nearly choked me too.'

Lazarus finishes wrapping his hands.

'Keep them dry. Your new mistress will want you functioning if you are to be of any use to her.'

'I don't know why she would think I could be.'

'We are at war.' Lazarus shakes his head as if Kit is being deliberately obtuse. 'There are Spanish ships making their way towards us. I told you, we are all striving for the pinnacle, and the gifts of the higher arts are all a prince wants. The alchemist who brings Greek Fire or the philosopher's stone is the alchemist who can defeat the armies of Europe.'

Kit ruminates on what Mariner said about Lazarus' status. The armies of Europe matter little to Kit unless they march down Bankside and run him through with a bayonet, but clearly they mean more to Lazarus. Kit had assumed, based on his limited observations (the house, the English bible, the son, the alchemy), that Isherwood was more like Sir Thomas Walsingham; a self-made man in Elizabeth's England, the kind of man whose Lordship speaks more to money and the Queen's gratitude than to lineage or prestige. It gives Kit pause. For if Lord Isherwood has an ancient name, why would he make his only heir a mere spirit in the European machinations of Cecil and Walsingham, a man who has learned how to make salves and set bones, like any common physician? The heir to an Earldom, he should be prancing at court and charming ladies or tilting his arse for the King of Scotland, not slumming about Europe with the likes of Griffin and Marlowe. Unless it is possible that a few drops of truth leaked into the chalice of lies Lazarus presented him with – that his father is truly ashamed of him. If he is, then what does Lazarus Isherwood have to gain from caring about his father's alchemical arms race?

'What has that to do with me?' he asks. 'Or you?'

'I bought your freedom here on the basis of my formulas and your talent,' Lazarus says steadily. 'You are the closest I have seen to an alchemical weapon of war. The alchemist who brings the Queen such a weapon will be rewarded. Lady Blackwater is an alchemist who needs to be rewarded. She is a woman alone, after all.'

Kit glares at him, curiosity sinking under fury. Lazarus can couch what he has done in terms of Kit's freedom and Lady Blackwater's needs as much as he likes, but the heady mist of victory is rising off him, he can clearly barely contain it. Lazarus has won everything he bargained for and done so at Kit's cost.

'Then she will be as disappointed as your father. I have no fire under my skin to give her.' Kit snatches his hands back.

'You do not know what you have within you, not even the smallest inkling of your truest self. I can guide you to know the nature of your being, what power you can achieve.' Lazarus moves closer. His breath smells of wine and figs, rich and cloying. 'Have you never wondered why you are this way? The secret of it could change your life. I would help you keep it.'

Kit snorts with laughter. Lazarus' face does not move.

'I am sorry, I thought for a second that you suggested you would keep a secret of mine.' Kit shoves Lazarus firmly in the chest, toppling him over on his behind. 'Arsehole.'

'You deny yourself and your possibilities.' Lazarus' legs are splayed on the floor in front of him and he crosses them at the ankle, as if he always meant to rest there, an infuriating smirk on his lips. 'It is cowardly and boring and, most importantly, will never work.'

'You think because you sold me from your father to this woman, you know me? You think I will be grateful and seek your council now, that you are redeemed in some way? Not even all the blood of Christ spilled atop your damned head would be enough.' Kit aims a kick at his foot and Lazarus quickly withdraws it, scrambling to his feet in a gratifyingly undignified manner. 'I would run to Egypt; I would make myself a pair of fucking wings and fly to the sun and it would not be far enough away from you!'

'Watch out of the window,' Lazarus demands, pointing to the small, coloured, diamond panes looking out over the street. 'In mere hours, someone will be lingering. My father will be sated by his experiments in your blood, as I hoped, but he will not forget you. You think this is over, that I am your only enemy, but you are in this, Skevy; it cannot be forgotten or outflown.'

Kit swallows with a gummy mouth, sour saliva and a slow gnawing of anxiety, low in his gut. Lazarus seems to read his expression because there is that maddening, knowing tweak of his lips.

'So fashion all the wings you like, Icarus, I am going nowhere,' says he, opening Kit's chamber door. 'And neither are you.'

'Fuck off!' Kit throws the bread at his head (he would be a fool to waste the wine) but Lazarus only catches it and deftly throws it back.

'Eat, Skevy,' he says, closing the door sharply behind him. Kit takes a rough, angry bite of the loaf, chewing noisily through a dry mouth, masticating fury more than anything else. Above all he hates about Lazarus Isherwood, he does not think someone so repulsive and duplicitous should be so God-damned conversational. Kit has often been made fun of for the way he speaks. Growing up fed daily on a diet of poetry from Griffin, his speech is too high for Southwark, too low for the city. Yet here is Lazarus, turning every phrase and every word back upon him; a twisted sword with a charming smile.

It does not matter, Kit realises, if he cannot seem to ignore Lazarus. With any luck, by daybreak Mariner will be back and she will be a free woman. Kit will be bound by an apprenticeship it is true, but running out on a Master who isn't the Lord of Southwark is a different game altogether. Lazarus thinks all of this cannot be escaped, but people like the Isherwoods do not realise how anonymising poverty can be. There are gutters in cities all over the country he can slink into and ships to be stowed away on, far lands to be lost in, if he can be quick. All he needs is Mariner and a plan, a chance to vanish, and he can put the coiling smoke and questing fire out of his mind and into his nightmares. Lazarus' question irks him – have you never wondered why you are this way? – but Kit does not have the heart for further wonderings. He does not know who he is anymore. When he lies his weary self down on the soft mattress and closes his eyes, he can still feel it. The henbane has retreated and now there is nothing to distract him. The pressure between his thighs, the sensation of intrusion like he has never felt before. Kit groans and rolls onto his side, curling himself into a ball so the ghostly fingers can no longer touch him.

Kit dreams. He dreams of Griffin and the first time he had ever spoken to him about the deepest secret of himself.

'Why am I not tall? The other lads are tall,' Kit asks him, sitting on his bed in his rooms that he shares with Marlowe, watching as Griffin washes and dresses. Kit is twelve years old or there about and in love with the theatre, so flush with first devotion that when Marlowe is away on his travels and Griffin is in Southwark, he lets Kit stay in his rooms and shadow him at the Rose. Griffin snores worse than Mariner but there is something about lying near a grown man that makes him sleep deeper.

'Well, lads grow at different rates, Young Kit,' Griffin says, washing himself. Kit stares at his form, as hairy and thick as drawings in books or statues in churches.

'Do other parts grow differently?' Kit asks, pulling the blanket up over his hairless chest. 'Other lads are… bigger than I am. When will I close, too? The lasses talk of bleeding through their openings but I have not bled in mine, so when does it close?'

Griffin's hands slow in his ministrations, then he dries himself vigorously and throws on a shirt, covering his nakedness. He sits on the bed beside Kit and looks at him steadily.

'You have an opening like a woman?' he asks.

'I do now.' Kit frowns. 'But it will close, will it not? So I am like other lads?'

Griffin sighs and looks up at the ceiling, at the patch of damp there, which, to Kit, always looks like a star.

'I suppose they could not have known this about you until you grew into manhood or womanhood, and your form is so male to look at, they would not know unless they checked.'

'Unless who checked?'

'It is nothing.' Griffin gives him a taut smile. 'I do not know how you will grow, Kit. You are different.'

Kit stares at Griffin, at his Adam's apple and his auburn chest hair tufting at the opening of his shirt that has still not appeared for Kit. He thinks of Mariner, smelling like a butcher's shop once a month, rubbing her lower back to ease the pain there. He begins, slowly, to have an inkling of the truth, creeping up on him; a spider's web, invisible in the dark then illuminated silver in the firelight.

'Other lads do not have openings,' he says. 'Only lasses do. I... am like a lass and a lad.'

'You are Kit Skevy,' Griffin said, cupping his cheek fondly. 'You can be anything you want to be.'

She who sees us with equality

Chapter Fourteen

'He is out of the city?' Mariner hears Lady Elody ask as she is led by a servant through the dark hallway of Hart House.

'Aye, but he'll know soon enough.' That is Lazarus' voice. 'A man might have already been sent to him in Richmond. We will have been seen. We need to move fast.'

Hair rises behind Mariner's ears, a chill spreading down her arms. She imagines faces lingering out in the darkness of Lime Street, watching them, hands reaching through the delicately patterned casements to take Kit away again. In the parlour, Lady Elody is seated in the window, wrapped in a cloak lined with fur over her nightdress, her pale toes peeking out from underneath it. Mariner blushes to see them; nails a little yellow, second toe slightly too long.

'Forgive me,' Mariner says awkwardly. Lazarus leaves, without so much as looking at her. Such a pompous man would be very satisfying to rob.

'The Grave Eorl sent you back?' Lady Elody tucks her knees up under a cloak like a child, gesturing for Mariner to join her.

'I bought myself out.' Lady Elody's smile of approval warms her deeply, starting in the pit of her stomach and rising like steam. Mariner cannot help smiling back. 'I had hoped to prevail upon you for the same grace you have extended to Kit. For an apprentice-ship.'

The words tumble out of her, made rougher by the late hour and the soreness of her windpipe from Twentyman's grasp.

'I am afraid with the arrival of Lazarus Isherwood I have no need of another alchemist in the house. I do have another offer for you, if it interests you?'

Mariner nods gratefully.

'I am for Queen's progress tomorrow. It is tedious but the only way to get gold from the treasury is to follow the treasurer. I have a mind to take a companion with me, a man from my lower born family, a country cousin perhaps. You would do.'

'Me?' Mariner wonders if it is a joke but Lady Elody nods calmly, as if she has not suggested something utterly mad.

'A widow is limited. If she has children they can be used for advancement. Even a daughter can be married off to gain a son-in-law, perhaps a privy councillor or a duke, someone near the Queen. I could do with a young gentleman and you, well, you make a wonderful man.' She smiles, and Mariner knows she is not joking.

'But milady, I am… common,' Mariner stumbles over the word.

'We will say you are from Devon or Cornwall or some other backwater.' Lady Elody waves her hand dismissively. It seems absurd, but there is temptation in it, too. The chance to begin again, a new name, far away from Twentyman and Daisy and the past and those cruel threats. To follow this beautiful woman wher-ever she leads. 'You are broad enough of shoulder and will cut a dashing figure at court. Although I cannot promise I will not hoard your company.'

She leans down and picks something off Mariner's knee, a minuscule touch that has Mariner's breath catching behind her teeth. In her mind's eye, she sees Daisy stepping back from her, fearing her and the desires inside of her, yet Lady Elody's hand sits upon Mariner's knee, heavy and delightful.

'Though you must be used to that. Has there not been a Southwark boy who liked your company? No girl?'

The night is dark, the room is quiet, the fire and the glass listening closely to these words that veer towards the things she never says. She clamps her own hand over Lady Elody's to stop the sinful movement of her hand against the crease of her bent knee but Elody's fingers are gently pushing up under the cuff of her shirt, a lazy intimacy that seems to crawl under her skin, a tic burrowing towards her heart and groin.

'No, milady—'

'Elody.'

'Elody, please, do not make fun of me.'

The fingers stop moving.

'My dear, I would never.'

She tugs Mariner's hand and she tips forward, as inevitable as a sinking ship, until their lips meet. So warm. Elody reaches a hand into her hair, opens her mouth, and suddenly Mariner is aflame, set on fire just as Kit was, burning in her skin. Fornication leaves a stain upon the body, such as is not impressed on it by other sins. Perhaps it is because it is the sin that transforms us. Knowledge grows her, fleshes her out, painted fresh by Elody's touch.

'Will you come to bed?' Elody pulls back, her lips shiny with Mariner's mouth.

'Yes, I mean, yes, I would like to.' Mariner tries to pull her mind back from where it is burning and melting into itself. 'I must see Kit. May I...?'

She lets her words linger. Dare I ask for more? Elody smiles at her, as if she sees the progress of these thoughts and kisses Mariner's palm.

'You are a free woman now,' she says softly. 'You can choose your own pleasure.'

When Mariner opens the door to Kit's room, he doesn't wake. She quietly strips down and pulls on a clean nightshirt before climbing under the blankets with him. She shuffles close to his back as she has done every night of their life together and, usually, Kit does not even wake for she doubts he even feels it. Tonight, however, as soon as they touch, he jerks awake.

'No!' He is up, squirming away, eyes wide with fright that Mariner has never seen before. At least not on him. 'Do not touch me! Get away!'

'Kit, Kit, it is only me,' she hushes, pulling back, giving him space as he curls into a ball and shivers. She has never seen Kit Skevy shiver. He has never felt the cold deep in his bones. She tentatively strokes a hand up and down Kit's bare back, gently avoiding the parts of his flogging scars that are still scabbed over. He is naked, his disgusting clothes left in a pile on the floor, and the bowl of water left on the nightstand for him is grimy with ruddy dirt. He has washed and yet he still smells of blood.

'Mariner?' She has only heard him whimper so in nightmares.

'I am here.' Hesitant as she has never been, she gently moulds herself against his childlike form, a ballast of warm flesh to protect what is cold and shockingly frail. Slowly, the trembling in his bones lessens, but it still jerks through his legs, a dog twitching in a dream.

'What did they do?'

Kit lets out a long sigh, his breath becoming more even, and he presses himself back against her and she holds him even tighter, feeling the air empty from his lungs.

'Do you remember when Twentyman had that mare, Mercy, and she wouldn't foal?'

'Aye.'

'Do you remember how they kept Mercy laid down and the lads had to hold her steady and the barber surgeon took those forceps to hold her open so he could—?'

'Aye, I remember.' Mariner finds she is breathing heavily. 'Kit?'

'Well.' Kit's voice is heavy. 'Now I know why Mercy kicked so hard.'

Mariner feels sick, nausea rushing through her in waves. These are the secrets of Kit's body that they've never spoken, but she knows Kit has never been fucked like a woman, he has never been touched there. The invasion of what he's describing, the terror of it, it is a sickening tremor that runs from her own clenched muscles between her legs down to the soles of her feet. They may never have hurt him physically but she can tell that just like Griffin's death, what has happened to Kit has hurt him in a way he has never felt before. There seems to be nothing she can possibly say that will make anything better but she feels like she must try.

'It matters not what's between your legs if you can cut off what's between theirs, remember?' she says. 'You told me that.'

Kit snorts softly and pulls her arm around his waist, nestling closer.

'So will the lady of the house let you stay?' His voice shakes like his body, a leafy tremble, but she follows his lead and ignores it.

'She will if I dress as a gentleman and go to court with her as her country cousin.'

Kit laughs, a bark of a sound.

'You will have to be from the back end of Yorkshire to pass for a country cousin with your manners.'

'She says I will be a mute. And from Cornwall.'

'That should solve it.' Kit laughs weakly. 'So you are for court and I am for alchemy lessons. With my luck, Lazarus will linger and then my unhappiness will be complete.'

'When the two of you...'

'He took nothing from me, I gave it, and I am angry because I liked it.' Kit breathes out hard. 'I thought I had him and I let myself like him. I didn't think, not for a moment, he might be using me. I made an absolute fucking *fool* of myself. Worse than Griffin.'

For all Kit sells his affection cheaply around Southwark, he has never felt that strong obsessional connection with another person that he has always derided. To be caught out in misjudged affection is a particular humiliation for someone as guarded as Kit Skevy. Mariner does not know what she can possibly do to make it better.

'I kissed Elody. I mean, Lady Elody. I... well, I lust for her,' Mariner stammers.

'You do?' Kit twists to look at her, his ordinary broad smile returning for a moment. 'Thank bleeding Christ for that! I could not figure out why you esteemed her so much.'

'I only tell you so you know you are not the only fool in the bed.'

Kit laughs softly, his shoulders dropping and then, he rolls over to rest his head against her breast, breathing out slowly. Mariner can't help but relax into the mattress, feeling the marvellous relief of a familiarity that, for a worrying few days, a part deep inside her had feared was lost. Even if she cannot stand to bear the world, here is one place she is a little safe.

'I wish we could go back to how it was.' His voice is young again, fearful.

She knows what he means. Time has shifted everything from its natural place, as if the tilt of the world that the scholars say is there has tipped too far, and now they find themselves tumbled into a different reality with different people; one life vanishing to make space for another. Mariner thinks she might like this one better.

'It will be well, I promise,' she says, stroking his hair comfortingly. 'All you must do is stay out of trouble, grind some powders and look at some star charts. It is just chemicals.'

'Just chemicals.'

Kit's voice has a soft ridicule to it she doesn't understand but his breath is evening out. He is starting to fall asleep, but she still has other things she must say, news she must bring from Southwark. She's heard Kit named as Griffin's bastard but this is the first time Squire Kay's name has been tossed into the mix. Twentyman threw the accusation at her so casually, hints of an argument that has repeated over and over down the years.

'Kit?' He stirs, still clinging onto consciousness. 'Do you remember a lady? On the ship when you came to London? Or before?'

'Hmm, there was snow,' Kit mutters. 'Came through the window. Tasted cold.'

He burrows his nose into her neck and snores. Kit has never before mentioned any memories of life before the ship, the day he met Griffin and left Antwerp. Mariner has never questioned it; after all, how could she? Her own memories burned away with her eye and drowned with the bodies of her parents. She has always thought that perhaps, just like her, Kit's memories are lost because better ones came along. After all, why would she remember the fear and the terror of a fire at sea, of the arms of her mother holding her close, of being separated in cold water amongst screaming voices? Now she wonders if anything is truly ever lost inside a person. Perhaps, in the dark ocean of Kit's mind, there is a long-sunk anchor that might be raised and with it: a memory of a mother. Red-haired, secretive Squire Kay. The woman they have left behind in Southwark, with no intention of returning to.

In the morning I will think on it, she tells herself. I will find a way to tell him and in the morning we will find our way through. We always do. She twists her head to blow out the candle and clings close to Kit, trying to find sleep, but it evades her. Always, just as she is on the precipice of slumber, she feels it again the sensation that brings her gasping back to consciousness, heart pounding. The feeling of eyes, waiting out in the darkness. Watching.

ノレダノレ乙

He who loves knowledge

Chapter Fifteen

Kit thinks Mariner looks like someone who deserves to be robbed. She's been trussed up in a flocked black and purple doublet, her hose tight and a frankly obscene codpiece peeking underneath. Her short hair is tucked under a courtier's cap, a tall swan feather erect and quivering, dyed a lurid purple and she stands awkwardly next to him in the hallway of Hart House, waiting for Lady Elody's carriage to be drawn around. The August dew is already burning away in the pre-dawn warmth, the sun unrisen on the blue horizon.

'This was waiting for me this morning.' She hands Kit a folded note. It's torn off a ledger and in Ezra's steady but elegant hand: *Men came to the Moon. Gave gold to anyone willing to tell when you cross the river. Stay North. God be with you. Ezra and S. Kay.*

'Stay inside if you can,' Mariner says. He nods but Kit wishes she was not leaving. Even when whipped near death, his body did not feel this out of sorts; the discomforting throbbing pulse between his legs, the hair on the back of his neck raised. He is a fox with a limp, constantly twisting his head, sniffing the air for coming hounds.

'Come, cousin.' Lady Elody sweeps past, out of the door and into the carriage. The ruse has begun and Mariner jumps awkwardly to follow, giving Kit a helpless look.

'Well,' he says, standing in the doorway, 'say little and bow much.'

Mariner nods, hoisting herself into the carriage in an ungainly fashion, squatting froggishly with her knees up against her chest on the narrow bench. Kit tries not to laugh.

'Enjoy your learning, apprentice.' Lady Elody's eyes rake over him, a plough in hard soil, catching his skin uncomfortably. She looks resplendent today but there is something chilling about the movement of all that black and purple fabric. He thinks of a corvid dragging a broken wing. 'I leave you in Lazarus' capable hands.'

Capable for what? Kit thinks, his gaze flickering to Mariner, but the carriage setting off down Lime Street on its slow procession into the misting dawn and Kit is without her again. It feels as if he barely had her back.

'Our turn, Skevy.' Kit jumps as Lazarus appears next to him, nodding to two horses that have been brought around, saddled with packs on them, as if for a journey.

'Where are we going?' Kit's eyes dart up and down the empty alley, checking the buildings for open shutters, for peepholes. 'I am to learn here and Mariner—'

'Is on Queen's progress and will not return to Hart House for eight weeks, at least. So your new mistress commands us North, to Manchester—'

'Manchester?' Kit has been no further North than the Curtain in Shoreditch. He thinks of the three or four days of road ahead. 'But... you said we were being watched.'

'Lord Isherwood is tethered to the crown and her court. You will be safe in the North for now.' Lazarus' eyes glint in the cold light of dawn. 'Must I put you back in irons, Skevy?'

Kit wonders if Mariner knows this, thinks, did she leave me here with him? Instinctively, he looks over his shoulder, down past Lime Street, to the Silver Moon and the Cardinal's Hat and the Rose and all the London world that he has known. He considers bolting, but where would he go? He cannot chase Mariner to court, and Ezra's words are sharp in his mind: stay north. So he mounts the horse, but when they trot out under Bishopsgate and take Shoreditch street out into the countryside, Kit can still feel it upon his back: the glare of London, unblinking, following.

The world changes in the North. The horizons are wilder, August colder with a bitter wind, the great hills standing behind one another in the colours of a two-day-old bruise. When they enter Lancashire three days after leaving London, Lazarus flies a strange, flapping flag of deepest purple marked with a raven on his horse. Wherever they go, they are met with nods and genuflections that no one seems to hide. The North is Catholic, everyone knows that, but gestures that would get you arrested in London are not hidden here. Farmers give them cheese and bread, old dams give them poppets and other trinkets. Bless our Lady Raven, they all say.

The house, when they reach it, is not like Lime Street; no fashionable black and white paint and diamond windows. It is cold, dark stone with turrets on the frontage; clearly an older part of what was once a castle now built up in a hulking, monstrous way with wooden additions and bulging aspects of red brick. Once inside the hall their single candles barely touch the cavernous heart of dark wood. As the door closes, Kit has the uncomfortable sense of darkness closing around him, just like it did in the cell.

'It is known as Blackwater Hall officially,' but the locals give it another name.'

Lazarus lifts his candle and Kit can make out the painted coat of arms hanging above the staircase. Black ravens on a field of purple, their beaks painted bloody crimson as they pierce a languishing hare. Behind his back, Kit hears the sound of the servant locking the door with a heavy click.

'Welcome to Raven's Roost, gentlemen,' says he. 'I am Pyncher, the housekeeper.'

Pyncher gives Kit a look which takes the welcome right back. He is dark haired, around sixty years old, tall and wiry with a long, hangdog expression and anxious nostrils that flare in displeasure. 'My lady wrote of what was needed. Come, if you please.'

They follow. Their boots echo on the flagstones and against the wood-panelled walls until Pyncher turns another key on his chain in a solid door. It is Kit's first time in an alchemy chamber and the walls are watching him. Roughly painted in the mural on the chimney breast, a body hewn in two, half male and female faces, shouting out of fire. All around him, pickled and mounted, are preserved and taxidermy creatures with their distorted floating noses and missing ears. Then more poppets, lined up in a hideous audience, pin and apple seed eyes never closing.

'Bless our Lady Raven,' Kit repeats, not wanting to step into the field of vision of these many dead things. 'What does she do for these blessings?'

'Whatever they need.' Lazarus shrugs. 'There has always been a witch at Pendle.'

Kit stares at him. There is a word to be burnt for. Lazarus Isherwood is a physician, a Scottish Lutheran, a rational man, or so Kit thought, but this a room bursting its shelves with every kind of uncommon, superstitious and catholic remedy he can imagine. He

149

wonders if Mariner knows what kind of woman she has kissed, how close to the pyre she dances.

'You said you were alchemists.'

'And in a hundred years more they may call us saints. Or lunatics,' Lazarus says. 'What do you think they will call *you* when they know what a fascinating miracle you are?'

Fascinating. The word pierces Kit's lungs, steals his breath, pours rage into his heart, and before his mind can catch up to his feet, he has grabbed a small, dull paring knife from the cluttered table and set it to Lazarus' throat. Lazarus stiffens but does not yelp or squeal, only looks at Kit with entirely apathetic eyes.

'What is the gain?' says he.

'What?'

'You stick me, I bleed out here, what do you gain? A dead body on the floor in a strange house with servants who will sell you out to escape the noose. So what is the gain?'

'And if I say pleasure?' Kit lets the tip of the knife catch Lazarus' skin, nick it, just a little. Lazarus does not even bother to flinch.

'Try to be more significant, Skevy.'

The thousand eyes press down upon him, Lazarus' included, in their ceaseless observation. Suddenly, Kit can smell nothing but the rotted straw of Isherwood's cellar. He swallows his own sticky saliva; his stomach is forcing the bread he ate on the road back up his throat. He violently wants to be anywhere but here, away from this place and this cruel sensation of slipping back through time, but he is hundreds of miles from everything he has ever called home and there is only one way back to Mariner. He drops the knife.

'Rationality perseveres,' says Lazarus. 'You cannot say you are not curious.'

Kit despises his sly tone. He will kill his own curiosity with his bare hands rather than ever admit this man to be right.

'Rationality says I get as far away from you and your henbane as possible.'

This is what he has been telling himself, night after night. It was all chemical. Just henbane.

'She will not protect a dullard apprentice,' warns Lazarus. 'You have little time.'

'There are other ways to learn.'

Kit picks up a book and slams his way out of the alchemy chamber but he imagines he can feel it; the inevitable tick of an invisible clock, pulling him through time, back towards the cellar and its darkness.

The North does not know it is summer. The rain is heavy and grey against the diamond glass windows and hiding the peaks up in the sky. Since to go outside is to drown in a flood of biblical proportions, Kit takes to hiding in odd places to read. His muscles soften and his breath eases when he can find a linen closet or even the abandoned, slightly horrifying priest hole he uncovers on the second floor, away from Lazarus or Pyncher. The housekeeper is a shadow, a phantom conjured by the house, so unexpected are his appearances that Kit has started to believe there must be a tunnel system in the old castle. He reads Agrippa's *De Occulta Philisophia* and the *Rosarium Philosophorum*. He learns that alchemists believe all physical elements hide spiritual secrets inside them and that the study and control of each layer of creation takes them closer to their creator. To ascend to a level of being where one can turn water to wine is a fantastical story, more absurd than *Doctor Faustus*, and yet some of it appeals. The practicality of Paracelsus, of all life on earth condensed down to different variations of mercury, sulphur and salt, Kit likes that. There is poetry in it, as Paracelsus says: *what is a human body but a constellation of the same powers that formed the stars?* When he lies down to sleep at night without Mariner, he looks at them through the window and thinks, you and me. We are one and the same.

A week passes, then another, and the books take over his thoughts, tire his mind. They begin to eat away at his pattern of staring out of windows for riders with Isherwood's voice inside his mind chanting: I will make such use of you.

At the end of the second week, the summer thunderstorms start. Kit is quietly reading Euclid behind a tapestry in the hallway when he is jerked out of his thoughts by a cacophony of hammering on the front door. He slams the book closed, churning with panicky nausea. This must be it then, the moment when Isherwood finds him again. Yet when Kit peeks out of the tapestry, he sees no liveried riders crowding into the house with wet boots and sharp, unforgiving faces. There is only Lazarus, and a farmer wrapped in a cloak, a bundle in his arms, sobbing tears and dripping rain from his cap all over the hallway rushes.

'… Some good to come of it,' the man is sniffling as Lazarus nods and reaches into his purse. The man's reddened face is slack with grief. He does not even count the coins as he pockets them roughly, rubbing his damp sleeve over his nose. He tenderly hands the wrapped bundle over to Lazarus.

'What are you doing?' Kit asks. Lazarus does not even look surprised as he shows the farmer back out into the downpour and closes the door behind him.

'Curious, Skevy? Answers are earned.'

It would be foolish to deny how intrigued he is, and perhaps it is only because he is steeped in relief that he is not being dragged back to London by Isherwood's men, but he follows Lazarus back towards the alchemy chamber. After all, the bundle looks far too big to be a poppet, and what farmer weeps over a delivery of cheese?

'At what cost?'

Lazarus' face half shadowed in the doorway, half lit eerily with orange light.

'If you see with your own eyes what you deem impossible for yourself, if you witness your own power as I have told you and it cannot be denied, you will give yourself to me.'

He remembers the taste of Lazarus' mouth, souring wine and honey, so vividly.

'I mean give yourself to me as my Initiate.' Lazarus' eyes are full of knowing and Kit coils inside himself against the embarrassment of it. 'You will be taught by me alone.'

'And what is my gain?'

Kit tries to sneer, but his throat trepidatiously thickens. The shadows in the hallway are too long, the turbulent night outside with its thrashing, singing trees are casting their leaping and dancing impressions, and the bundle in Lazarus' arms looks queerly heavy.

'What better gain is there than power?'

The confinement of the cellar crushes against his mind, the most powerless moment of his life. He has always thought that being impervious to pain was enough power for him, but then he met Isherwood. Now here, in this dark fortress in the wildest part of England, something else is being offered.

'No henbane this time,' says Lazarus, holding the door open.

Kit follows him inside. The fire has burned low and the strange greyish-blue light of the storm outside casts a luminous damp sheen, the wall of eyes glittering. Lazarus carefully unwraps his prize. Kit stares at the lumpy, misshapen thing, pearly white and flecked with blood. Then he sees a tiny fist, balled up. Hair.

'Stillborn en caul, a mermaid child,' Lazarus says, his voice almost fond with reverence. Kit stares at the child, born too early, still in sac. All around him, a thousand mouths stretch in their tiny screams.

'The parents gave it to you?'

'They have said prayers and they will bury the child when I am done, but the caul is valuable.'

Lazarus is opening his leather folio filled with blades, their blue smiles gleaming. Kit's instinct is to warn Lazarus not to cut the babe, but then remembers, the thing is already dead. Liquid with a faint odour, almost seminal, spills over the scalpel and Lazarus works the translucent membrane carefully, winkling the purple body out, a cockle slipped out of its shell. A thoughtful, silent birth. It is a boy.

'Wrap him back in the blanket,' Lazarus commands, and Kit does, flinching against the tiny, stiff limbs. Without meaning to, he strokes his little head, hair damp and matted. Then his fingers find a shocking dent at the back of the skull, strange, flaccid skin that wiggles when pressed, only filled with fluid inside. The child has no brain but his lips, perfect and mauve, are pursed open with all the look of speech, or first breath. For a second, Kit cannot move, split between tearful tenderness and twisting revulsion. Then he is rushing to re-wrap the babe's face, fingers clumsy and unkind, breathing hard through his nose but desperate to get back to Lazarus' side. He still feels the dead boy's presence behind him.

'What do you do with it?' Kit asks, watching Lazarus stretch the caul onto a board, wiping off the dried blood and strange, clumpy white residue. He cuts a piece the size of an angel, using tweezers to douse it in a solution he has ready in a silver bowl.

'Ground up it can cure fevers from beyond Spain, terrible sweating fevers. I have plans for it to be a wound sealant; so far, however the caul is too delicate to stitch in.'

Lazarus moves fast, plunging the scalpel quick and sharp into Kit's palm, pinning his wrist to the table before Kit can yelp or pull away. Then he drapes the wet piece of caul over the bloody spot.

'Wait,' he commands, but Kit does not need to wait. That same pressing, dragging sensation from Crossbones and the henbane, but only in his hand, and this time, coming from the caul. It is nothing but a wrinkled little patch, yet he can only describe the feeling as sucking, similar to the way a calf sucks a finger for milk. Then the edges of the caul creep. It is dead, it must be dead, the babe is dead after all, but now it is stretching. With a precipitous lurch, Kit feels sure it has a will, a desire, that it is seeking to wriggle up his fingers. He turns his palm, trying to shake it off, desperate not to have to touch it, but it has become stringy underneath and hangs like a clump of spiderweb, swaying. Kit wildly imagines tiny teeth clinging on; digging down into the grooves of his knuckles, the shroud of a dead child eating him from the outside in.

'Yes.' There is such rich, thick triumph in Lazarus' voice. 'It has become adhesive, as I hoped. You are an alchemical child. Your skin is a conduit for power. You touch a formula and it is perfected. Pinnacle indeed.'

Kit barely cares; he is scratching the gluey substance off his skin, picking it out of his fingernails and flicking the precious material to the floor, resisting the urge to stamp on it, to snuff out whatever is inside of it.

'It's impossible,' he says, because it damn well should be.

'Paracelsus says nothing is impossible if consistent with natural law. Is it inconsistent for you to be this? Fifty years ago no one believed the sun centred the universe, to be at the forefront of change is to court improbability.' Lazarus' grabs Kit's hand and digs a fingernail into Kit's wound. 'I know you are an atheist like your Griffin; you believe in no one God and I've seen how fearful you are, skulking around this house—'

'Liar,' says Kit, voice a breathless croak, because Griffin always told him this is the only rebuke to this one dangerous truth. Lazarus ignores him, eyes burrowing into Kit's.

'You have no prayers or divine will to strengthen or save you, only yourself. So I ask again, Kit Skevy, what better possible gain is there than power?'

Kit is raw, prised open, cold limbs pulled out of gentle encasing by the fury in Lazarus' words. He does not lie, Kit is numb with it: undiluted fear, stilling him, pinning him down naked to that damp straw, holding him in place. He looks at the worrisome beasts mounted on the walls, caught, kept, classified. How unending must their humiliation have been, and how it clenches a silent scream inside him. Slow, measured animalisation, torn apart in the darkness. Again and again. It will not be him. Inside his mind, he closes the door on the cellar. I am not there, he tells himself, I am never going back. I am going to be made of more than that one, aching hopeless moment, more than Kit Skevy, Southwark thief and brawler, more than anyone expected. If there is power to be had then I want it.

'Teach me then,' Kit says.

Victory has taken over Lazarus' facial muscles. He quickly slices the scalpel across his own palm, blood dripping down his wrist and staining his lace cuff. He grasps Kit's hand firmly, rubbing that mingled cut together. Then, when separated, he brings his ruddy hand to his mouth and licks it. It is the daintiest of movements, an apologetic check of flavour, but Kit is mesmerised by the tongue, pink and ludicrously shiny. Cautiously, Kit lifts his own hand to his mouth. A slimy, herbal and vinegary taste, then a burst of coppery blood. Lazarus nods, approvingly.

'Initiate,' says he.

She who silently watches

Chapter Sixteen

Whilst Her Majesty is staying at Havering Palace in Essex, Elody has taken quarters in the magistrate's house in the village of Havering-atte-Bower. It is two rooms, adjoined by a small closet that will serve as a dining room. It is not as grand as Hart House, but it is practical and warm.

'This will be your room,' Elody says.

'Mine alone?' Mariner turns to her in surprise. Elody looks beautiful today in deep purple, but not as alluring as she looked before, in the soft firelight of her drawing room, the silky fur of her collar so close to her vulnerable skin. Elody smiles and presses a gloved hand against Mariner's cheek. The leather smells like dirt and dust from the road.

'You are my young cousin, you may be heir to my fortune,' Elody says, rubbing her thumb against Mariner's cheek. 'There can be no hints of impropriety so we will be cautious. You will have to live up to your name, Mariner Patience.'

Mariner is chastened, immediately feels a fool but also feels a pang of longing for Hart House and the kiss last night which is now beginning to seem so distant. Elody smiles softly, in that way that gives Mariner the unnerving sensation she is reading her thoughts, and leans closer, pressing their foreheads together.

'Beautiful boy.'

Her kiss is dry on Mariner's cheek. Her chin so smooth, the warmth of her flesh so close. The clamouring miracle of this permitted touch makes Mariner's breath shudder, her body moving closer in a daze of excitement, her hand drifting to Elody's hip — then there is a sudden knock at the door and Elody quickly retreats.

'My lady?' One of the Blackwater servants peers in as Mariner pretends to be fascinated with the stained glass. 'Lady Catherine.'

'Thank you.' Elody pulls off her gloves. 'I will leave you, cousin.'

She moves through into her own private bedroom. Mariner steps curiously into the small adjoining closet. There are two chairs and a small table and a leaded window with dusky glass, even a bunch of red and white roses set out in a clay pot, their heady fragrance battling with the smells of the village floating through the open window. The magistrate clearly wants his gentle guests to feel welcome. Mariner does not mean to overhear, but the servants in their unpacking and shuffling between rooms have left the door to Elody's own bedroom ajar.

'I thought you would never come back to court, Mama said I must come to you,' a sweet, melodious voice is saying, urgently. Through the gap in the door, Mariner catches a glimpse of a young woman. She has a soft, heart-shaped face with cheeks as pale as a foxglove and pearls hanging daintily from her earrings. She is nervously wringing her hands and Mariner looks away, staring down onto the village square outside, hidden from view.

'She was right, Catherine, do not fret—'

'But I do not know what to do and I fear I am too late, *Venefica*.'

Mariner jolts at the word. *Venefica*. It is a word she has heard in her younger days, travelling with Italian strangers who used it to describe the Sorceress Circe when they told the stories of Odysseus' voyages.

'I received your letter. All will be well.' Mariner hears the sound of a hinge creaking and risks another glance. Elody s opening a wooden box that she brought from Hart House, made of walnut and locked with a key she withdraws from her bosom. Mariner darts her eyes away, watching a travelling tinker sell his wares, automatically calculating how much coin he might have on him. Elody's voice goes on. 'You must drink it all on a day when everyone is away. Tell your servants you are having a heavy course and wish to be left alone. You must not let your maid see and you must burn everything. Do you understand?'

There are sobs. Mariner dares not turn her head. She imagines tears rolling down the cheeks of the beautiful girl, sparkling like diamonds on petals.

'It is natural to be afraid, but do not let it stop you.' Elody's voice is calm but horrifically practical. 'God willing, you will be well.'

'This sin is on my head,' Lady Catherine says.

'No.' Elody's voice is the most ardent that Mariner has ever heard. 'It is on his.'

In Southwark, there are Cunning Women whom every girl knows. Some are apothecary's wives and some are old Mothers and dams who live alone on the country roads out south. It is hard to imagine someone as high born as Lady Elody Blackwater could be peddling the same potions and remedies as those women, ladies who bring babies into the world and sell poppets to cure illness. They are always only one dead patient, one bad bout of gossip away from the noose. Mariner stares at the tinker in the street, counts his pockets, one, two, three, four and tries not to think about why the woman who has kissed her so softly and taken her away might be giving a young girl potions to stop a forming child. Or why she might be called a witch. She hears the sound of a door closing and then feels Elody's hands on her shoulders.

'Your guest is gone?' Together they watch as the wealthy young woman steps out of the magistrate's house onto the square, the pearls on her hood catching the pink dusky sun. 'She is young.'

'They always are.' Elody's thumbs brush against the back of her neck, where lace ruff meets skin. Mariner tries not to shiver. 'Come, we dine at the palace tonight.'

She can taste nothing at dinner but fear. She stares at the dead, milky eyes of the re-stuffed swan with its beak painted gold, sweat beginning under her arms. She dares not engage anyone in conversation, a lace sleeve trailing in rabbit sauce. She imagines what might be said if everyone knew that there was a common thief under this cap, a woman thief too. Yet nothing happens. Courses are served, endless and cold, and too sugary to taste of anything substantial; first to the empty throne and then to everyone dining in front of it as if it is normal for plates of food to sit uneaten by an absent queen, before it is tossed out later for the dogs to fight over.

Elody talks constantly but in a way that requires Mariner to say nothing. She sends glasses of wine to those she favours, receives dainty dishes from gentlemen happy to see her at court again and makes frequent introductions, always speaking of Mariner the same way – Matthew Blackwater, my country cousin on my husband's side, not an outspoken lad, forgive his quietness, a stammer, never been to court before! Oh, the scar, a hunting accident – Each time, Mariner is amazed by the unsuspecting embrace in their eyes.

As they ride back to the magistrate's house after the towers of spun sugar and hours of dancing, Elody says, 'You did well.'

Mariner finds herself checking over her shoulder as they ride in the darkness. The air is strange in the forests of Essex. Close and hazy under thick trees and over flat fields yellow with rapeseed, too quiet without the river. She has lived so long on the banks of the Thames now; the cry of the gulls and the shouts of the wherrymen is the orchestration of her daily life.

'I did nothing.'

'Precisely. Did you see the Earl of Northumberland sent a dish to me? Harry Percy has excellent connections; he gets all the best manuscripts out of Bohemia.' She is flushed with victory and wine, lips purplish and plump. 'There will be hunting next week.'

'I've never shot an arrow.'

'The Court chase harts on horseback with dogs. It is very civilised.'

Mariner nods and under the cover of the woodland they ride through, risks reaching across to touch Elody's hand on her bridle. *Venefica,* Mariner thinks, puzzling again over that perilous word. Gloved fingers squeeze hers, lift her hand to kiss the heel of her palm, lips so beautifully warm.

'I am so pleased with you,' Elody says, her kisses tracing Mariner's veins.

There is nothing civilised about court hunting. Mariner watches hounds rip rabbits and foxes to pieces on the quests for great stags and thinks of the fucking waste. They have ridden most of the day in the company of some Privy Councillors, Mariner's silent presence giving Elody permission to ask: will you educate young Matthew on the goings-on at Court, milord? Mariner learns that these great men do love to drone on and Elody flirts until she has gained promises from at least three of them to dine at Hart House at summer's end. When the light is fading beneath the close trees of Waltham Forest, they fall into pace with a group of ladies, all gossiping about everything from the war with Spain to the new ruff of Sir Thomas Walsingham.

'Did you hear Lady Catherine is to be married, despite it all?'
One of the ladies raises her pencilled eyebrows. Mariner cannot
stop herself from stiffening but Elody merely strokes the neck of
her mare. Mariner thinks of the sobbing young woman, crying
of her sin in Elody's chamber. The hazardous instructions she was
given. Does she lie abed as they hunt, stifling her screams in her
pillow lest her maids hear her and her sin is known? Or has she
been too afraid to try and hoping she can pass an early babe off
as her new husband's?

'Oh, well it is the best thing for her,' the first lady says. 'A flirtation
with an ambassador never served a girl. Especially not a Spanish
one.'

Her eyes dart to Mariner and then away. There have been
comments about her darker skin, always lighthearted, delivered with
sugar-blackened smiles. Oh, but your young cousin is so dark, Lady
Blackwater! Her Majesty will have to send him to King Philip's court,
he will suit the purpose nicely. Elody has batted them all away: a
great rider and hunter, yes, he wears the sun so well at this time of
year. Mariner does not know what she will say when snow comes
and she is as brown as ever.

'She is fourteen, ripe for breeding. No doubt she would benefit
from your knowledge, Lady Blackwater.' The second lady gives Elody
a passing look, sharp and venomous. 'Such a devoted, god-fearing
woman too.'

'Yes, as god fearing as the Pope,' the other mutters.

Mariner sucks in her breath. Mariner cannot ask Elody if Lady
Catherine is Catholic, because then she will know if Elody is Catholic
too. To be a Catholic is to never be allowed more than five miles
from your own home, but worse for Mariner, is to be everything
Elgin ever taught her was hell bound. She may be an unnatural
woman in so many ways, but she has heard the true gospel, at least.

162

She does not know what sin is greater, but she knows which feels worse.

'And we hear another learned friend will soon return to court,' the second lady goes on. 'His lordship Isherwood? He has been much busy in the city.'

Mariner grips her reins too tightly. The horse beneath her shifts, shakes his head, absorbing her worry.

'Delightful,' Elody says, her voice unchanged. 'But these ladies' trifles are not for gentlemen's ears. Come ahead, dear Matthew, let us find you better conversation.'

As Mariner and Elody ride side by side in silence, Mariner longs to ask who else knows these things about Elody, the secrets she keeps in the walnut box, and can they be trusted. Will they come for you, one day, with pointed fingers? Will they come for me? Are you the most dangerous thing for a woman to be? Then there is Isherwood, who has been busy in the city, the city where Kit is supposed to be safe. Am I keeping him safe? Mariner asks herself. With my frolicking and lying, am I helping him or abandoning him?

'Keep smiling, my dear,' Elody says pleasantly, as if they are discussing nothing but the weather. Mariner wonders if she has guessed the turn of her frantic thoughts. 'Someone is always watching.'

Two evenings later, lying abed alone and woozy on the taste of Elody's lips, pressed against hers just before she retired, and too much fine, syrupy wine, Mariner is startled out of bed by the sound of hammering in the next room. She rises, feet bare on the floor to creak open the door. The little ante-closet between their two rooms is unlit, but Elody's door is open.

'I can't do it, I cannot,' a voice is sobbing, 'It has purged everything from me, it is killing me—'

'Be brave, girl, and go home!' Elody's voice is a brittle hiss.

'I cannot!'

Mariner watches, hidden in the shadow of her own dark bedroom as she sees Lady Catherine fall to the floor, weeping and clutching herself. She is wearing only a nightdress under her cloak and Mariner can see that slight swell of her belly where she digs her fingernails into it.

'A chamber pot!' Lady Catherine gasps. 'Please!'

Elody has a red glass bottle in her hand and stands in front of the young woman, blocking her crumpled, clammy face and straining body from Mariner's view.

'Hush, hush, drink this for the pain—'

Lady Catherine's voice becomes animal; huffs and grunts and half-sobs, and then Elody is scrabbling at her, ripping off the cloak, dragging at her nightdress so that for a moment, Mariner sees her as a long-nailed, devouring beast, tearing the young desperate girl apart. Then Elody is gathering the girl's clothes and quickly dropping the bundle into the room between their chambers.

'Burn everything,' she says urgently and Mariner jumps, for she had no idea her presence was known. Mariner nods as Elody strides back in and drags the girl to the bed. Mariner can't help but flinch at the terrible youth of her flesh, her narrow hips and her gangly legs, stained with ruddy smears, and turns her attention to the stinking pile of cotton. She doesn't want to lift it, for the smell of faeces and meat is overwhelming, clinging to the back of her throat, making her gag. So she gingerly nudges it towards the fireplace in her chamber with her foot, trying to ignore the dark streak it leaves behind. The embers have burned low and she piles on kindling and logs until it roars healthily into life. Then, using the fire tongs she carefully manoeuvres the bundle of fine clothing. The unusual weight of it is repulsive and she quickly leverages it onto the flame. At first she worries the burden will douse it, but the cloth catches on the edges, the heavier interior smoking slowly and then, as she adds more dried parchment, catching the centre of it. The smell is a combination of smoked meat and something sweet and uncanny, and Mariner stumbles to the window, fumbling with the latch and forcing her head out to suck in great lungfuls of cold night air. It tastes of mud and mouldy vegetables, but it is better, so much better than the smell inside.

'She is sleeping.' She turns to see Elody closing the door, the hem of her own nightdress tinged brown. 'She is over the worst of it now.'

'Are you a Cunning Woman?' Mariner whispers. 'A witch?'

'I told you, I am an alchemist.' Elody pokes at the fire, thrusting up sparks.

'Alchemy is gold and tricks and the elixir of life!' Mariner's voice is a fierce hiss, too afraid of being overheard. 'It is not poisons that keep a child from forming and take a babe away—'

'In alchemy I explore the body, how to heal it, to improve it. It is not witchcraft to treat women that others would turn away, that *men* turn away; it is not spell craft to give them what their bodies require.' Elody is turning back Mariner's bedcovers. 'Aquae vitae will make you sick if you drink too much of it, it will poison your liver and close your eyes forever, and yet it is the building block of any alchemical quest. What poisons one, strengthens another.'

'It is medicine?'

'It is salvation.' Elody's voice is suddenly furious. 'The girl is not fifteen, do you think she had any choice in how she was seeded? The least she can do is have a choice in how she survives it. You would ask for the same.'

Mariner cannot speak but of course she would. The knowledge that she would be no different from Lady Catherine does not stop the visceral dread.

'It is not witchcraft?' she whispers, thinking: You will not burn for this?

'If I were a man, you would not ask it; if I were Lord Isherwood you would not dare to.' Elody shakes her head. 'Soon Lady Catherine will be dancing at her wedding and the stain of the man before will be wiped away by holy matrimony. If it is witchcraft to give her a sanctified union and children inside wedlock then, yes, very well. Call me one.'

Mariner will not. Inside her mind she hears the voices of the men as they dragged her out of her bunk below decks: woman, woman aboard! Is it not the same thing, one word too much like the other? Mariner wants to speak, to say whatever secret reputation Elody carries she will not be part of it, she already knows the weight of these branding words upon her nightmares, but she cannot. She is captured by the sight of Lady Elody Blackwater, gently pulling her soiled nightdress off her naked body.

Mariner has seen so many naked women; carved on ships, with their tits out in sailor's taverns, and Daisy, most glorious Daisy, spread out perfectly on her tattered bed linen in the Cardinal's Hat. Elody's skin is slacker around her hips, there is darker hair at her groin and armpits and the loose flesh of her breasts and belly is marked with pink indents from her stomacher, as if her body has been pressed between the pages of a book. Every fear, every objection in Mariner's treacherous heart is silenced by her; bare, unashamed, miraculous.

'You cannot tell anyone, not even Master Skevy.' Elody has set one knee against the bed covers, a hand outstretched to Mariner. 'You must promise me, Mariner.'

It is the first time she has used Mariner's real name since they left Lime Street. Mariner scrambles forward to kiss her, ungainly and sinking into the mattress, gathering all of this wondrous woman close in handfuls, knowing she must be quick for this

166

might be all she has. Mariner has not once kept a secret from Kit before, but she has never had a woman above her, undoing her in every way, and Kit soon fades. She is tugged and ripped out of all of her clothes. Her trepidatious limbs shake in the cold breeze from the window; she is all hypnotised, clumsy hands and urgent, bumping nose.

'Promise.' Elody's hair is draped like a veil across Mariner's stomach.

'Very well, *Venefica*,' says she.

She feels Elody's triumphant smile curve against the crease of her thigh. Moths are like sinners, Elgin used to say. They are lured by the warmth and do not realise until it is too late that they are damned. I will burn my wings for this, Mariner thinks. To feel this wanted and this alive.

He who has them in his hands

Chapter Seventeen

'So now we have overfed this damn silkworm and it has killed its mate, what is next?'

Kit pokes the silkworm which apparently will hold the secrets of making pure gold inside of it. To him, it seems that alchemy is utter madness. In the last few weeks there has been less of the strangeness of having fire and air pour out of his fingertips and more bizarre animal husbandry that involves letting two silkworms fight to the death.

'Now we feed it the mulberry leaves dipped in the nut milk. When it has consumed them all, we heat it until it is dead and crush it. Then the residue will let base metals become gold.'

Kit gives Lazarus a sidelong look. They have tested many recipes and formulas in the last three weeks, but this one just seems plain unlikely to Kit, on top of being a thorough chore. Since the day of the caul, Kit has not again felt the creeping, lurking sense of power rising through his skin. Lazarus has theories about how exactly Kit's gift is brought forth, but Kit thinks this simply proves that some alchemist recipes have as much fact in them as Twentyman's book-keeping.

'What type of holy science is this? According to the three natures of Agrippa?' Lazarus asks.

'Natural.'

Lazarus hits him around the head with a slim volume on anatomy.

'Answers in complete sentences, Skevy.'

Every second of a day in his Instructor's company is a possible moment of pontification; the bread they eat at breakfast is a lesson in the alchemy of fermentation, a discovered beehive is a lecture in mathematical plane figures. August passed in a march of authors, most of them thrown at Kit's head. Since Lazarus knows he feels no pain, Kit knows he only does it because of how irritating it is to be treated like a fucking child.

'Natural, rather than celestial or super celestial.'

'Definitions?' Lazarus' fingers tap impatiently upon a hefty translation of Aristotle.

'A student of the elemental world is a healer, like you, learned in natural substances and the elemental sympathies between them, which is unlikely to get you hanged unless you accidentally poison a king. Then there is the celestial magician who interprets the influence exercised by the stars on the lower world, an astrologer, like Dee, which may get you banished, as he was during the reign of Queen Mary. Lastly, there is the student of the super-celestial world, who utilises ceremonial arts and alchemy to summon the aid of angelic spirits and achieve great feats of making gold and elixirs of life, as Kelley did. Which is probably why he is imprisoned in Prague.'

'And then there is you,' Lazarus snaps. 'Who will have a book to the face if he does not cease his insolence and feed his fucking worm.'

Kit holds his satisfaction at Lazarus' annoyance inside and begins to dip mulberry leaves in the almond milk. Tear shaped with a brown, grainy skin, Lady Elody has spent a fortune importing the nuts from the Far East. In the last week Kit has pounded and ground hundreds, soaked and distilled them to this perfect milk and now, Kit watches the wrinkly, white silkworm nibble on the dripping mulberry leaf. Then, suddenly it stops eating, curls up in on itself.

'Is it supposed to do that?' Kit prods it with a sceptical finger. It feels papery and cold.

'No, it is dead.' Lazarus picks up the dead body, tossing it into the fire. Kit feels a pang of mournfulness for the lost days of work gone into the tiny beast. 'Tell me what you have learned.'

'How to make a poison.'

'How else do you imagine such things are made?' Lazarus carefully pours the nut milk into a new bottle. There is a knock on the door of the alchemy chamber and Lazarus chivvies him with a flap of a hand to open it. Pyncher has the air of a man who loathes waiting, his anxious nostrils flaring. He pushes past Kit to enter, even as Lazarus is closing books, tucking the formula inside his cloak, all small gestures of obscurity. Still, Pyncher's calculating eyes rove over the table as he thrusts a small pile of letters at Lazarus.

'My mistress writes,' says he. Kit waits by the door, watching as Lazarus peruses, spies a small additional crease between those perpetually furrowed brows.

'Does she wish us to produce a unicorn?' he asks.

'She wishes for us to produce,' Lazarus says brusquely. He feeds the letter into the brazier. 'Thank you, Pyncher.'

Pyncher's nod is barely respectful and as he brushes out of the room, Kit hears his hissing whisper: 'Untrustworthy wretch.'

Kit does not immediately know to whom he refers. Is it Kit, with his low born blood, encroaching on Pyncher's world of nobility? Or is it Lazarus, with his secrets and letters that he burns before Kit can lay eyes upon them? Kit makes a show of locking the door, his back partially turned but not so far that he cannot see Lazarus surreptitiously slide the second letter inside his doublet. A crimson seal, as crimson as the herald of roses painted above the doors in Isherwood House. A coincidence, perhaps, but Kit is too alone and too cynical for coincidences. When he turns his back on the locked door, he wishes to be on the other side of it.

More often now, Kit dreams of the cold drifting through an open window and his fingers turning blue. He dreams of a man behind his shoulder, seated at a desk and bent over a grand ledger, the swan feather of his quill as pure as the driven snow that piles and melts against the window seat, turning it dark.

'Are his fingers dead yet?'

'Not yet.' A woman's voice, regretful. A hand on his shoulder that Kit knows is there for one purpose, to keep him in the room but also, deep down, to tell him that he is not alone with the man and his ledgers. He does not want to be alone.

'Fascinating.'

The touch on his shoulder becomes a grip, the bright room full of snow around him abruptly disappears into darkness. A pair of silver eyes above him, unblinking. Quick as a heartbeat, Kit is in the cellar. Its decaying stink is all around him and the touch on his shoulder is no longer light but heavy, suffocating, pushing him down whilst he is opened up.

'Away!' Kit kicks Lord Isherwood and his abysmal surgeon back, catching flesh, hearing a grunt of pain. His eyes open and he is in his small bedroom at Raven's Roost. There is a lumpy shape on the floor, a familiar sharp voice cursing under its breath. 'Laz! What are you doing?'

'Waking you,' Lazarus clambers to his feet. He is wearing a warm cloak over a nightshirt and breeches. 'Come.'

Kit groans, rising and pulling on clothes, shaking the sleep and cold edges of his dream away. He is used to this now, rising at odd hours for birthing animals, for moments in the moon cycles, to examine the stars in the sheltered garden. It is nearly mid-September and the North has remembered to have summer, such as it is. The constant rain has softened into sputtering mist. Outside, the night-time air is sweet and damp as Lazarus leads them, carrying a crate of equipment, down over the brook, swollen in its banks, and up the muddy slope to the graveyard. The small parish church with its neglected, crumbling steeple is set vivid and black against the bloated full moon. Kit pauses in the comforting darkness of the shadow under the trees, hesitant to step into the creamy exposure.

'Why here?' Kit asks.

'Because tonight we deal in the natural sciences,' Lazarus says. 'Do not jitter, Skevy, it is the dead of night, the church warden has been paid. You cannot skulk in Raven's Roost forever.'

Kit glares at Lazarus. Mostly, their interactions in the last month since Kit was initiated have been bearable, but when Lazarus turns his commentary to Kit's own person, he is overwhelmed with the urge to beat him all the way to Yorkshire. Lazarus strides to a flat tombstone and reaches down to the grass beside it, blocked from Kit's sight by the mossy marble. Then he lifts a wrapped bundle onto it, worryingly long and heavier than a dead animal or babe. Kit cannot stop himself drawing closer. Unwrapped, the sacking reveals grubby naked limbs, a distended neck, purpled and blue. Lazarus lifts heavy specimen jars out of the crate and Kit watches, a foreboding taste of bitter dandelion building at the back of his tongue, as Lazarus unrolls the leather pouch of sharpest knives and scalpels.

'You mean to cut her up?' Kit nervously eyes the door to the church, its silent, black windows, checking for a shift of a cloak or a flash of a face.

'Purest mercury can highlight different changes in the body, particularly to reveal the structure of the lung. As you can appreciate, it is not the kind of thing I can test on a live subject.'

Lazarus selects a scalpel, fingers dancing before he chooses. Kit looks down at her stretched neck.

'Who was she?'

'A poor thief, died by the noose this afternoon. Criminals are the only bodies physicians are given. I heard tell from the village she had no family.'

He can feel Lazarus' eyes on him, absorbing his obvious hesitancy but he cannot hide it. He knows it is legal, he has probably done worse and yet he cannot stop staring at the brand, almost identical to his, burned into her cheek. She is dead but still a criminal.

'When we met you were pilfering a dead man's coffin and now you are squeamish?' Lazarus says.

'A man needs to survive. You don't need to examine her insides for anything other than your own amusement.'

'My own amusement?' Lazarus sets the blade at the young woman's shoulder and draws a curved line with it. Kit waits for a rush of blood but then realises his own foolishness. 'I must have something to tell my father of.'

'Your father?' Kit doesn't understand the flabbergasted disappointment inside of him, how it steals his breath. He remembers Pyncher's words; a warning then, not a jibe, a reminder that nothing is safe. Sometimes, you don't know how much you trust a person until you realise you should not. Kit feels it then, the smallest increment of returned assurance he has been entertaining that being Lazarus' Initiative allows him some protection, and now he curses his naivete. 'You write to him?'

'I send him notes, nothing revelatory. Enough to keep him content. I do the same with your mistress.' Kit does not breathe as Lazarus, unfazed, curves the blade down between the woman's spread breasts. 'Both believe you have produced nothing noteworthy, but that you are progressing satisfactorily for a man who barely reads.'

Kit stares at him, his mind turning over this colossal confession: Lazarus is dancing carefully between the two most powerful alchemists in London, loyal to both, lying to both. He does not know why he is not repulsed or terrified but mostly, he feels a grudging respect.

'I read very well,' is all he can say. A small smile plays on Lazarus' lips. Kit feels a tinge of humiliation for his evident bruised pride, but pushes on. 'Neither suspect you?'

'Of course they do. They find their ways to watch, to listen.' Kit thinks of not only the letters, but Pyncher's loitering, of the darting eyes of the men who deliver packages. 'Trust is not a virtue for an alchemist.'

'So I should not trust you?'

Lazarus raises his eyes from the blade that has reached the woman's inverted belly button.

'Trust me to do what I have promised; you are my Initiate, I am your Instructor, I will help you reach your fullest potential. That is all that interests me. There is a saw in the crate, get it.'

Lazarus has peeled back the skin of the woman's chest, the fatty tissue of her breasts with it, opening her up, a fleshy book. Kit did not expect the inside of a human to be so muddy, so unclear, Lazarus wiping away dried blood to reveal the bone. The scent is of lamb offal on market stalls and mechanically, Kit picks the small wood handled saw out of the crate.

'Cut through each rib on that side, I will do the right,' Lazarus instructs. Kit pauses. His eyes keep being drawn back to the brand on her cheek, so much like his own. 'You do not believe it possible she will frown from heaven and curse you, so why do you care?'

Kit glowers at the taunts. Lazarus' corpse will one day rest in peace in a family plot, tucked away from the likes of them. The law will protect the bloated dead body of Lazarus Isherwood as it will never protect Kit Skevy's and can he be this man? One who takes a saw to the flesh of his own kind, as uncaring for her life as Lord Isherwood was of his?

'An alchemist cannot only look at a body in a book,' Lazarus says, irritably. 'He must learn to break bones if he is to mend them.'

It's a minuscule reassurance, a purpose at least. It is enough for Kit to pick up the saw. The ribs cut quicker than he anticipated; they bend with a surprising spring.

'She has twelve sets of ribs,' he says.

'Yes. Eve may have had one less but her feminine ancestors grew theirs back.'

Kit snorts. For all Lazarus is vexing, smugly intelligent and has no patience whatsoever, there is a dryness to him that Kit finds undeniably humorous.

'You seem to hold less stock in the gospel than your father.'

'I hold plenty of stock in it. Christ was a mighty alchemist.'

'And was dead by thirty three.'

All it takes is one person, one rumour, someone who can testify to witchcraft. This is you, staying out of trouble? Mariner chides inside Kit's mind, but he hasn't seen her in over a month and her warnings dilute with time.

The ribs are severed and Lazarus, with a few rehearsed flicks of the scalpel, pulls free the breast bone with a nasty squelch. There it is, the lumpy purple red flesh of the heart and the wide, greyish pink slabs of the lungs.

'Her lungs are smaller than expected.' Lazarus frowns. 'She is a woman, there is often a difference, but they will still be suitable.'

Kit wonders if his own lungs are smaller than average. He wonders if, at the start of creation, how many ribs he would have.

'Why did you choose to be male?'

'What?'

Kit's thoughts are pulled away from trying to measure his own lung capacity through breath to Lazarus' face.

'I can see you are curious. Why would you not be, as an alchemical child?' Kit scowls at him as he watches Lazarus casually clip the stem of the heart. 'You have always been in-between. So why did you choose to be male?'

Kit vividly imagines what Mariner's expression would be, her curdling disdainful sneer. That is the question of a person who does not know fear, she says. A man's question.

'That is like asking why you choose to be rich.'

'Do not be obnoxious, Skevy.'

The heart looks fragile and small in Lazarus' bloody, uncaring hands and slides so easily into the jar. It bobs, reminding him of boiled trotters bubbling in the kitchen of the Silver Moon, before its floating descent.

'Your entire question is built on an obnoxious premise.'

'Is it?'

Lazarus clicks his fingers for Kit to dig one hand under the silky, spongy lung nearest him.

'You would not say she chose the weight of her heart or the size of her lungs.'

'What has that to do with it?'

'Your question suggests I am split. You suspect someone held out breeches or petticoats and made me choose, it didn't happen. I cannot distinguish between the parts of me that are male or female any more than you can distinguish between the blood in your heart and the blood in your foot.' Kit's hands are shaking as he follows Lazarus' gestures and helps him lift these slippery organs and plop them, with a slight roll of the water, into the specimen jar. 'I am only myself, I am Kit Skevy, I always have been.'

Kit wipes his hands on his shirt and stares into the empty cavity of her chest. How curiously hollow it looks. He has the urge to fill it with earth, with water, anything to cover that yawning lack. A mouth without teeth, or a socket with no eye.

'We are not done.' Lazarus is taking the saw up to her temple and, so far, Kit has managed not to look at her face as a whole. The odd, single hairs between her eyebrows, the little black spots on her nose. She was so young and in her features Kit thinks he sees Mariner, sees a dozen Southwark thieves, sees himself. He wants to tell Lazarus to stop, to let her be, but he has begun, a soft grinding sound, moving quickly around the scalp, and then, with a shocking looseness, tips it off. Kit stares at grey and pinkish bulbous matter that makes up the mind and thinks, that looks like a fucking mess.

'When I woke you dreaming tonight, your voice was young. A child.' Lazarus is dipping a hand into the skull, lifting the rubbery flesh. He has the look of a fisherman resting a trout on his hand to be filleted. Kit has to shake himself a little before answering. He had not been aware his nightmares were being listened to.

'So?'

'Just because you cannot recall those memories does not mean they are non-existent. We can pursue alchemical avenues to retrieve them.'

'And take a saw to my head?'

'Less invasive.' Lazarus seals the jars. The young woman, it seems, will not be resealed, simply buried cut open and raw. 'But you would know yourself. There is power in that. What have you to fear from knowing?'

Kit watches Lazarus tip the mind of the young thief into the liquid. It does not float, and even though he knows it is impossible, he imagines it heavy with memories; her first grab, the heat of her brand, the final gasp of her death. All unreachable now, tucked away in a jar to gather dust at Raven's Roost. Kit realises he is breathing heavily. A remembered feeling, his body following a rhythm to a song he cannot hear.

'Nothing,' says he.

$\Omega\angle\mathcal{B}TTO\exists$

They who visit those in Heaven

Chapter Eighteen

L ady Catherine has disappeared sickly to the country to get
married. Elody says all is well and Mariner tries not to fret at
night that the poor girl will die without all the blood that soaked
her clothes and linen. In September the court moves to Theobalds
Palace, the home of Lord Burghley. Mariner does not understand
how it is appropriate for a man who isn't a king to live like one, but
Theobalds is beautiful and large enough to fit the entire court inside
it. The closeness of simpering ambassadors is oppressive, the extra
weight of those courtier eyes following her everywhere; in the
orchards, hunting parks and dining rooms. Yet the constant exhausting
vigilance does not deplete the enchantment that here she and Elody
have entirely adjoining rooms. Each night, when the servants are
abed, she can creep through the door that Elody pretends locks and
slide into the warmth of her lover. It is a tenderness beyond bodies,
an intimacy she never thought possible: sharing a bed, exchanging
whispered words before sleep, the daily minutiae of washing and
undressing. How beguiling it is, to watch a woman pick knots out
of her hair, to know she need not hide her gaze or affection.

'I danced with the Earl of Northumberland tonight,' Elody says as Mariner wraps strands of her dark hair around her finger. Coarse, thick, like horse hair and rope.

'I saw.' The Queen's birthday has been celebrated with the arrival of the Danish Ambassador, plate and furnishings sent from the Tower to accommodate him properly, and much hunting and dancing. Mariner presses a kiss against the back of Elody's shoulder, the brown, bobbly mole that sits there, and then marvels that she can.

'He is eager to hear of my new apprentice. He says he will tell the Queen.'

Mariner feels a clench of disquiet. She thinks painfully of Kit, left standing alone at the door of Hart House, bleeding into his breeches. It was over a month ago but somehow, the time has stretched out, become impossibly long so that Kit seems young in her memories now; a childhood whisper of himself.

'What will he tell the Queen?'

'That Lady Blackwater works for the good of the country and her alchemy deserves investment. That her Majesty's trees felled in the New Forest will be protected by me when they are formed for ships.'

In her mind, Mariner sees the fire again; bursting, writhing, spilling from Kit's hands, burning her skin and hair. She supposes it was too much to ask a woman like Elody, clawing her relevance in society back by her fingertips, not to make use of a potential asset like Kit. Unsettled, she reaches under her pillow, feels something crumpling roughly against her fingers. She unfolds it. It is a rough drawing of a woman tied to the stake, burning. Mariner recognises the crest of the Blackwater estate on her smouldering dress.

'What is this?' Mariner asks her.

'Oh. Someone will have paid a servant to deliver it.' Elody clucks her tongue dismissively. 'Burn it.'

'Do you not wonder who sent it?' Mariner folds the paper back up, hiding the disgustingly rendered open mouth scream of the woman tied to the stake with Elody's coat of arms on her flaming breast.

'That is easy.' Elody presses a kiss to Mariner's bare throat. 'Someone who hates me.'

'And there are so many?' Mariner's mouth is dry. She thinks of the walnut box on the windowsill, the ladies who still sidle up to Elody during the hunt, whispered pleas unheard under barking hounds. She thinks of the sidelong glances of wives who see Elody dancing with their husbands, a widow, yes, but a woman unmarried, a woman said to be learned, an alchemist, a witch prancing prettily in the Queen's court. Do they look and think to cut her down? Is it Lady Catherine, turned furious against her saviour? Are there other girls, poor women who have bled in Elody's rooms and emptied wombs and perhaps grown resentful? Mariner's racing thoughts screech through her brain, her heart pounding so loud she can barely hear the owl's musical hooting beyond the window. 'Who would want you dead?'

Elody laughs. For the first time, it sounds completely derisive.

'To be a courtier is to wish everyone dead,' she says, scornfully. Mariner shrinks away, made small and stupid in her fear. Elody shakes her head and sighs, cupping Mariner's face as if she is a troubled child. 'Burn it and think of it no more, dear Matthew.'

Elody rolls over in the darkness. Mariner folds the paper carefully and slips it back under her pillow. She already knows she will not burn it, this sharp reminder that however sweet the pears are here in Hertfordshire, however lazy the hares that frolic over the lawns, there are vipers in Eden. As Elody's even breathing begins to fill the room, Mariner is alone with her thoughts. Inside her mind, crudely rendered flames eat up the drawing of her lover, consuming her inky flesh to nothing. When she dreams, it is of hell, of the fire that is never quenched, of being unable to snatch Elody from a smoky death or Kit from pools of sulphur. She wakes, gasping, breathing hard through her nose. Save me from this, she prays wildly, save me from this, but as sweat cools and her mind catches up, she wonders what she needs to be saved from. Here she lies, in a shirt she did not make, with a woman she barely knows, at the heart of all the world, the court of the Queen of England. She can hear its low, droning beat all around her in the imagined breathing of the sleeping occupants of Theobalds; all the way from the wiry Queen herself down to the dozing rats in the cellars. It presses against her, the weight of the masquerade she has committed, the heaviness of each lie a cuff tying her to the bed; to be wealthy, to be a Blackwater, to be a man. There is nauseous despair in her throat, tasting too sweet as it rises behind her tongue. The realisation that the only thing standing between her and the flames drawn so simply under her pillow is the woman sleeping beside her. She has gambled a future, an entire salvation on Elody Blackwater, on her promises and kisses and the intoxicating feeling of been seen for fucking once, and now there is no way back. So she rolls over, moulds her body against Elody's and changes her prayer: Christ Jesus, I love her. Let this love not be the end of me.

*

Rain comes in mid-September, as does news of the Spanish fleet that the Earl of Essex is so busy trying to intercept at sea. Sideways glances at Mariner take on a sharper quality now the sun is hidden behind stormy clouds. Every room she enters she becomes the subject and Elody spends a good portion of every conversation finding excuses for Mariner's skin. She even takes to suggesting that Matthew Blackwater's dead parents might have had some Moorish blood in them, for anything is better than being associated with the Spanish, and Mariner's mind spins as she tries desperately to cling on to whatever tale Elody is telling. Then, thankfully, a distraction comes. Some say it is the news from Essex or her frailty, but the Queen takes to her bed, feverish, and the court is suddenly full of loud, reassuring voices. Only a cold, says Sir Robert Cecil as he stamps about, Her Majesty is strong, Her Majesty has the constitution of an English King. It would mean more if the last English King had not died of weakness before he reached majority. Still court dines, still court dances, still court hunts, as if they believe the mechanics of the thing, their stuffing and twirling and killing, will maintain their monarch. Mariner is dead on her feet from all this frantic gorging and frivolity, but at least, for now, she is no longer the subject of searing, judgemental stares.

'See how they flock back, flies buzzing around a carcass,' Elody says as they stand and watch a clutch of Privy Councillors and Knights of the Garter, all massed at the end of the room closest to the door that leads to the presence chamber. The Queen's motto is carved above the frame: *semper edeam*. 'It happens every time she takes abed. There they stand, useless, praying in equal parts she will not die but if she does, she will leave her crown to someone they favour. See, there is Cecil, he hopes for King James in Scotland, half a Tudor. There is Somerset, he hopes for Arabella Stuart, half a Tudor, and the Marquess of Dorset, he hopes for his wife's sake, another half a Tudor. Not with all their half Tudors can they make a whole one.'

'Are they the only claims?'

'A York can always be dug up, some poor boy dressed up in Sheffield to suit the cause.' Elody sips her wine. 'The Gaunts, their claim predates the Lancasters, predates the Yorks, and their heir is the Spanish Infanta, Isabella.'

Mariner understands. If the Queen does not name an English half Tudor or even a Scottish one, then England is ripe for a Spanish plucking. Mariner tries to imagine it, monasteries rebuilt, English bibles stacked onto pyres in Tyburn. She wonders how Elody feels about that. Everyone here would call it a disaster; would she?

'And here is another one who pushes Scotland's claim,' Elody says, looking at a man who breaks away from the Privy Councillors. He is tall with grey hair and a greying beard but vivid, dark eyebrows. The effect is powerful, as if his eyes are jumping out of his head.

'Lady Blackwater,' he says, bowing in front of them.

'Lord Isherwood,' says she. 'May I present my cousin, Matthew Blackwater?'

Mariner looks at him, this man who held Kit down like an animal to discover his secrets. His doublet is crimson and expensive, embroidered with gold roses, his shoes are polished and clean. His beard is neat. He does not look like the kind of man to open up a lad, but then Mariner wonders if she would know what one should look like. His eyes slide over her and then away and she's relieved not to be the focus of that particularly piercing gaze.

'The Queen is struck with an ague, I hear,' he says. 'I am surprised she has not called you up to tend her.'

'If the Queen desired it, I would happily serve her any remedy she asked. Where is your fine son, the physician? Still not fit for court?' she asks, her voice sweet even if her words are intended to deliver the sharpest blow.

'It seems ill health follows some of us more than others, and that is God's will alone. Just look at Lady Catherine, rising from her sickbed.' Out of the corner of her eye, Mariner sees the young Lady Catherine. A quick ceremony, the court heard, and now here she stands, a fourteen-year-old Countess with pearls the size of hailstones around her neck. 'Her husband wrote to me before their wedding, feared at the time she was struck low yet I warned him, 'tis nothing to worry about, only… women's work.'

Lord Isherwood smiles thinly and Mariner thinks; he knows about the walnut box.

'I hear you have a new apprentice,' says he. How his eyes are steel, how polite his voice, yet she is chilled to hear him speak. 'An interesting choice, by all accounts.'

'I hear you work with new ingredients,' Elody says, matching him, her own eyes unblinking. 'How fascinating.'

Kit and Kit's blood, in so many terms. Mariner's stomach clenches at the idea of him cut and parcelled up for purpose. The lute players start and Lord Isherwood offers his hand to Elody.

'Then let me tell you of it,' says he. Mariner wants to slap his arm away, but Elody merely inclines her head and allows him to lead her out amongst the dancers. Mariner knows she has a role to play here too and is pleased when Lady Catherine accepts her invitation to join upon the floor, leaving her husband to his wine and worrying. Mariner half listens to the young girl's chatterings of court gossip, her eyes fixed on Elody and their enemy, straining her ears for any soft, whispered words.

'It is strange to see them together, I'll warrant,' says Lady Catherine, nodding to Elody and Lord Isherwood where they dance in front. 'Mama says they have not stood up together since the day he gave her away to Lord Blackwater, and she never saw such a sour-faced bride. Although I suppose it was a fine day for the Blackwaters, an Isherwood bought in marriage, even from a discarded first one.' Her free hand touches across the ropes of woven silver hung with pearls around her waist; a protective gesture over her narrow abdomen. 'But we all must make the best of what we have.'

Mariner finds her words are lost entirely, all her genteel ones at least. She stares at the back of Lord Isherwood's head to notice the similarity in Elody's, tries not to see it, tries to tell herself that Lady Catherine is a liar amongst all her other secrets. She cannot do it. Her hand is numb, her mouth is dry. She wants to stop dancing, surely she must run, get out of this stuffy, hideous box of perfumed knaves and find some fresh, sea air to breathe but someone is always watching. So dance she does, on and on, as bound to the turning wheels of court as all these others. All she can see in front of her eyes is that scribbled drawing she has been carrying in her pocket; a woman on a pyre, the inescapable scream.

ΩχϤℓℬℒℰƲ

He who precedes understanding

Chapter Nineteen

'I am taking you to Manchester College,' says Lazarus.

'Why?' Kit looks up from where he is painstakingly injecting mercury into their harvested lungs to reveal the small, wobbly vessels illuminated in the flesh.

'Doctor Dee has an electrum mirror. We will borrow it to scry your past.'

Kit can only offer him a sceptical look. Scrying, sorcery, anything that involves the process of communicating with celestial beings feels even more like horseshit to him than the recipes involving making damned silkworms fight to the death.

'You'll find no angels in me, Silver.'

'Scrying does not always reveal angels like it does for Dee. I saw none.'

'You have done it?' He cannot quite imagine Lazarus, the man who is so interested in chemicals and powders he can heat and transform, being the same as the babblers who sit outside the city gates and swear they can talk to angels for a penny.

'Yes. I saw memories.' For a moment, his face seems aged, the lines and shadows sharper, so that in them, Kit sees his father. 'I remembered the day I was born and how bringing me forth killed my mother. I was born blue, and my father breathed life into me with his own lips. I could remember the feeling of it, as if I had carried it deep in the crevices of my mind all of my life forgotten; the twist of my spine, the terror of my first breath.'

These dreadful words seem implausible, from the lips of a man leaning against the table, ankle and arms crossed, his dark hair shining in the September sunshine. The day is too bright, light sparkling through the raindrops clinging to the windows, to bear such ugly darkness.

'He raised you from the dead,' Kit says. Lazarus nods.

'It is how I am named.'

Kit examines the way he pushes his tongue against his bottom teeth, jutting his jaw forwards and thinks: I know nothing of pain. For surely, this should be painful to recall for any man and yet Lazarus is as calm as if he were testing Kit on the lessons of Paphunitia the Virgin.

'To learn how the heart beats, we cut it open,' Lazarus says. 'The truth to unlocking the rhythm of your abilities lies in your memories of your own making.'

Kit stares at the bubbling mercury popping silver against the Venetian glass bowl and imagines it thickening, turning white, a blanket over a frozen wasteland in his dreams. He tastes snow upon his tongue. Kit does not know exactly what Lazarus has in mind with this visit, but the snowy dreams continue to plague him, night upon night. He has scoured his own memories of Southwark, trying to piece together winters he remembers with that high window in a fine house, but nothing fits. Lazarus intends to unlock his potential, a notion Kit has no recourse to interfere with since potential could amount to power, but Kit does not feel easy about the snow. Or leaving Raven's Roost. He glances out of the window, the harmless sunshine, a golden day. Still it condenses inside him, uncertainty pooling in the bottom of a vial.

'We will not be followed,' Lazarus says quietly, watching the dart of Kit's eyes. 'Besides, you look about as far from the city ragamuffin you used to be as a gravedigger does from Sir Walter Raleigh.'

Kit snorts with laughter, immediately clamping his lips to hold it back. They shouldn't do, but Lazarus' words comfort him, and he nods. Lazarus hands him an alchemist's robe to wear, heavy and black.

'You should know.' Lazarus pauses thoughtfully. Dee writes to him also. They were great friends. Discretion is paramount.'

Kit looks at Lazarus as he pulls on his black riding gloves, fits them over his fingers. Untrustworthy wretch, or so says Pyncher, but Lazarus could have said nothing. You should know, he said, instead. In those words lies the decision to include Kit, to inform him, to trust him, at least with this. Kit can say none of it back, cannot find the correct words for this confusing smudge of honesty in his association with a man made of contradictions. So he merely pulls on the scholarly robe. He likes the weight of it against his legs, a costume of another life. Without thinking, he spreads his arms wide, turning around, wordlessly asking for approval and then feeling childish for wanting it.

Lazarus smiles. 'You are suited to it.'

Kit keeps his hood up as they stride through the dark and drafty cloisters of Manchester College. He is an imposter; he is sure at any moment he will be caught out by these lucky so-called 'charity scholars' who learn all day and are fed for free. He is surprised by his resentment towards their youthful faces, their running footsteps squelching in cloister mud, their windy laughter. What I could have been, he thinks to himself, what I could have known. Before Lazarus can knock on a heavy oak door, a fluffy orange cat wriggles out of the wooden cat hole at the bottom of the door with a scrawny yowl. The door is flung open. There stands a hunched, white-haired, pale-skinned man in a black skull cap and a yellowing, wilted ruff. Doctor John Dee, astrologer to the Queen and polymath, his gown four inches too short, showing off skinny, veined ankles.

'Isherwood.' He looks over their shoulders with a frown of bushy eyebrows, darker on the edges. Perhaps he's caught them alight on the wings of angels he scries for. 'The damned cat keeps climbing into my ink.'

'I have brought my friend to see you, John.'

Kit whips around to stare at Lazarus. He knows it is likely just a front but it leaves a strange, sharp taste in his mouth to hear himself described as Lazarus' friend.

'Well.' Kit tries to look uninterested as Dee peruses him. Kit imagines letters being written behind his eyes, riding down to London. Tell him I look well, Kit thinks fiercely, tell him I do not look like a boy he had cranked open. 'Don't let the cat in.'

Dee's chamber is far more chaotic than the alchemy chamber at Raven's Roost. Although the chairs are beautifully carved and the glass in the window is clear revealing the tumultuous sky over the cathedral, the disorganisation is astonishing. He looks at Dee's feet shuffling around piles of books and would not trust him to distil anything carefully.

'I thought to take loan of your mirror, if you'd be so kind,' says Lazarus.

'I see.' Dee looks between them, the dark eyes suddenly much less good-natured and more calculated. Kit remembers he is supposed to be practically illiterate, insignificant, so he sets a disinterested look upon his face and bends down to pet the cat that has sneaked back inside. 'Why loan it, Isherwood? Use it here. I have all that is needed and the scholars are all at matins.'

'Very well.' Lazarus nods, surprising Kit as he sheds his alchemist robe and pulls out a heavy purse. 'For your time.'

'Bonny King James' coin is as good as any.' Dee scrambles up to weigh the purse in his hands and looks at the clock on his wall. 'I will make preparations.'

Dee opens a small door up a staircase, the cat following the trail of his grubby robes up the stairs. When the door is closed, Kit rounds on Lazarus.

'You expect me to spill secrets in front of the man who writes to your father?' Kit stumbles over his words as Lazarus' hands move to untie the ruff around his neck. 'Are you warm?'

'No, this is John's preference for scrying. All I expect is for you to follow my instruction.' Lazarus nods to his other purse laid down by his cloak and robe. 'The nosegay. Slit it and pour the contents into that wine.'

Kit opens it, fumbles amongst the gold angels for the small, cotton pouch, sewn together and sweet smelling. He picks up a knife left lying on a cheese plate, shooing away a mouse who has sneaked out from under the raised edge of a book. He pierces the cotton and shakes it into the dregs at the bottom of Dee's glass; a dusty brown powder settling on top of the purple.

'Stir it in.' Lazarus is shrugging off his doublet now, standing only in his Venetians and shirt. 'Pour more, two more glasses, but do not forget which one is yours.'

'Mine?' Kit stirs the clumpy residue until it is gloopy and grainy. 'I'm not drinking it.'

'Initiate.' Lazarus' voice is poignant; tinged with a power Kit has not heard since the night of the babe born en caul. 'Pour the glasses.'

It is on his tongue, quicker than the acidity of bile before vomit:

the taste of Lazarus' blood, mingled with his own, licked from his palm. Copper and command. Kit gathers two more glasses, pours the wine. When he looks up, Lazarus is lighting a bundle of herbs and then setting it in a small dish by the fireplace. The smoke from it is thick, strangely scented; like bay leaves and the persistent musty tang of catswort. No wonder the bloody cat can't wait to get in, Kit thinks.

Lazarus gestures for the untainted glasses, his eyes flitting to the door and the corresponding thump of footsteps that are undoubtedly coming down to them. 'Hold that one.'

'What is in it? Henbane?'

'Trust me, Skevy, just hold the damned glass.' The words are nearly formed on Kit's lips to remind Lazarus that he is the very person who told him alchemists are not to be trusted, but Lazarus is unpicking the cotton laces at his throat and revealing that triangle of skin that Kit remembers tastes so salty. He shakes his head. It is the damned burned herbs, he is sure of it.

'Ah, Isherwood. You will not let your apprentice go first?' Dee says, stepping back into the room in a grubby nightshirt. With his white cap and beard, he has the look of a saint approaching the pyre, those long, yellow toenails clicking on the stone. When he catches Kit looking, he says, somewhat stiffly, 'One must approach the celestial in a humble fashion.'

'I will demonstrate first,' says Lazarus, unbuttoning his breeches and stepping out. A flash of the palest flesh of the top of his thigh, white and flecked with dark hairs, before the linen shirt falls down to cover it. Kit swallows and looks away. Dee is moving to the table in the corner, tugging away a hessian cover from a mirror unlike any Kit has ever seen. It is space, it is blackest night, it is the gap between stars. Polished obsidian, the flicker of flames trembles within it and all he wants to do is look and look, even though, he notices with a strange thrill, the flames are the only thing it reflects in the room.

'Drink first, John?' Lazarus offers him one of the glasses of wine. Dee looks at the two glasses and then the one by Kit's elbow. He reaches for it.

'To your health,' he says. Lazarus sets the offered glass aside and does not hand it to Kit, Dee smirks knowingly and drinks. Kit holds his breath. He imagines the bittiness will not bother him, the wine in the jug had cloves floating in it, but he worries for the taste. Dee drinks deeply and Kit hopes he is not watching a man swallow his death but then, eyes closed, Dee raises his hands. He begins to mutter:

'Our Father of Spirits, Lord of all elements and divine wisdom the truest embodiment of whom is the word made fesh, that made God, Christ most wise and perfect, send unto us your celestial guides; we beseech thee for their names most holy, Michael, Gabriel, Raphael, Urial, Madimi…'

Kit has read Enochian, Dee's own language taught to him by Lazarus, but has never heard it used like this. Uncanny, a dreadful drone at the back of the throat, blending with a sudden, fierce drum of fresh rain outside and Kit wants it to stop, this croaking teem of unknown words that ties knots in his belly. Then Dee's crinkled knees buckle. The drone stops, his head hits the table, the wine goblet misses the beaten, faded rug and splinters in the fireplace.

'Christ, Laz, is he dead?' Kit bends to roll Dee over. The man takes a breath, thank fucking God, and with it, a hefty snore.

'It was only powdered mandrake, and now he will hear nothing we do not want him to. Though that is unfortunate.' Lazarus gestures to Dee's head, the nick and dribble of blood as he pulls his breeches back on. Kit looks at Dee's slack face, the way his chest rises and falls so slowly that, in between, it is possible to think he is dead. Kit has never killed a man, and any man who might have died as a result of his beatings in the ring, well, it was self-defence every time and he cannot be strung up for that. Witches are burned. He looks at Lazarus, a man who undoubtedly would be able to talk himself out of any dock with his moneyed connections, and suddenly hates him.

'No, it would be *unfortunate* to burn,' Kit snaps. 'It takes a fucking age.'

'Six minutes in the right wind.' Lazarus rolls Dee onto his side and stands up. 'Do not worry, Skevy, you have not killed someone with alchemy. *Yet.*'

Kit stares up at Lazarus, his sleeves still loose, sipping his wine, lips berry stained. He has killed before, Kit thinks. What is a physician truly, but a person so learned in all the ways a heart can stop beating?

'Time wastes.' Lazarus nods to the mirror. 'Will you look?'

Kit glances at the mirror again. Through the lingering haze of the catswort smoke, it still absorbs all the light in the room, a spot cut out of the fabric of the world, waiting to be observed. There is a throbbing in his throat, a bitter, penny taste by his tonsils. Lazarus' grubby little word, *yet,* how it chafes against him, but the only promise was more power, no assurances of what the power would make him. You are Kit Skevy, said Griffin. You can be anything you want to be.

'So I should look for wings?' Kit asks, rising and standing in front of the mirror.

'Let your mind wander and speak as you see.'

Lazarus puts his hands on his shoulders, standing behind him. It must be a trick of the obsidian that before he could see nothing but flame but now he sees himself more clearly than he ever has done in the reflection of water or in the back of a spoon. He sees the full of himself for the first time. Lazarus does not pray or chant, simply stands behind him, taller, wider, and in seeing those smooth dark locks and neat beard, Kit notices in full the difference of his own tight, fluffy red hair and his childish face, splattered as it is with those intense, dark freckles. In Lazarus' hands, in Lazarus' nose and jaw, he sees hints of his father, perhaps of his dead mother, of the bodies that blended together to make him; a man, a woman. Kit has, before, faced his own absurdity, skin of one man mismatched with the eyes of another. Yet as he stares, his eyes become black holes of obsidian, and he stops seeing Lazarus completely

Kit sees himself: small and cold, fingers blue, standing in a room he remembers with the large windows open and the snow on the floor. How grand it truly is, as grand as Hart House with its wall hangings and servants moving softly around. The man is there. Kit sees his long black robe, so familiar now, sees his unidentifiable form bent over his ledger. It is not just one book, but a wall of them, set between vials and flasks and jars of potions and poisons in a way that he intimately recognises. An alchemist. Then there is a girl, about twelve years old, pearls in her hood and a rosary at her waist. She is circling him, looking at his bare feet in the snow, his blue fingers, her own tucked away in her mink.

'It truly feels no pain?' she asks the man writing in his ledger. 'You say its mother did not survive?'

'They never do.' Kit feels the fierce, lonely thoughts of his little mind. This is mine, this ice is mine, I will make it as warm as my blood, and then it is melting, fingers reddening with heat from nothing. 'It seems to survive anything, though. I am unsure if it is healing itself or simply too stubborn to die.'

Too stubborn to die, those remembered words are the bitterest well that is a tunnel of obsidian. Kit tumbles through it. Flashes of small, vivid moments. A sharp nail, rusted on the edges, pushed again and again into a small, clean hand. Ankles tied too tight, the skin pudgy and red, resisting the rope burns that appear. Hot wax, dropped against the inside of a pale knee, the skin blistering and pink every time. He does not want to do it, not because it hurts but because he does not want to; no, don't make me, leave me alone. Someone was supposed to be here with him, a mother, he is sure of it, and he feels the missing of her for the first time in his life. Just as heavy and pressing as the night of Griffin's death, that cata-strophic chasm inside him that is somehow unbearably familiar. I have felt this before, this losing. This shirt with a button missing, this babe with no breath, this chest hollowed out of heart; I have felt it here. There it is, living inside me, Griffin dead, and before him, long ago, someone important, snatched away. Pain. Pain. Pain.

ᛒᛁᛒᚷᚹᛚᚳᚷ

She who only obeys

Chapter Twenty

Mariner forces herself to wait. She endures the everlasting chatter of Lady Catherine, the unending dances, the lengthy masque and the jarring cackling laughter of the court. She says nothing, the question building inside of her, squashed into silence by the presence of so many damned people; their sweaty bodies and false smiles engulfing her and Elody. Finally, eventually, they retire for the night. Usually she stays back in her bedchamber until after all the lamps and fires have dimmed to sneak into Elody's chamber but tonight she follows her into the room, letting the door slam. Elody raises her eyebrows but dismisses her maid with a flick of her fingers.

'You are in an evil temper,' Elody comments. 'You've worn nothing but a frown all night.'

Mariner is amazed that her lover cannot imagine what could have upset her with the arrival of this man, of her father, at court. Elody sighs into her furious silence.

'You need not worry about Isherwood,' she says. 'That he is here means he is not off bothering Lazarus and Master Skevy.'

'Lady Catherine says he is your father.' She had not known until the words leave her lips that they were coming, but now she is begun, she cannot turn back. Speaking them brings rage, and her voice trembles. 'Is it true?'

'Oh, is that all? Yes. Did you not know?'

Elody removes the pearls from her ears and Mariner stares at the small, oddly intimate holes they leave, mere dents in flesh that she knows the taste of. Mariner shakes her head, for of course she did not know, and she would bargain the shirt on her back Kit does not know either.

'Does Lazarus know?' she bites out. 'Does Kit?'

'How much do kept children know of their father's deserted progeny?' Elody muses, lips quirked sardonically. 'I imagine he does. We have not discussed it. So I have no notion of what he might have shared with the apprentice.'

'But *you* didn't tell Kit. Or me.'

'I had no notion I needed to.'

Her sanguinity is baffling. Mariner has the urge to walk out of the room and come back in, to begin again, so that at least some contrition might be found.

'He tortured my friend!' Mariner exclaims, throwing a wild gesture of an arm towards the closed door, to the implied monstrous Isherwood that lurks somewhere beyond it. 'If I had known—'

Mariner bites away the words. Elody pauses in removing the piles of glittering stones from around her throat.

'If you knew he was my father you would not have trusted me?' Elody shakes her head. 'You trusted Lazarus and you knew his parentage.'

Mariner stares at Elody. Everything inside her is screaming that it is not even comparable because she only trusts Lazarus because Elody seems to, but there Elody sits, unmoved, disinterested in the seismic shift of knowledge that has taken place inside her. Mariner cannot help it, her thoughts begin to curdle at the edges, uncertainty creeping in, but she pushes on.

'I did not trust him,' she says. 'And all evidence points to him fair hating his father.'

'Is that why you are so worried?' Elody lets out a breathy laugh and rubs a hand against her bare throat, the skin reddened from the weight of the pearls and jewels. 'No one can hate him more than me. We have no familial bond between us. He discarded me when he discarded my mother for a younger, more fruitful girl.'

'Lazarus' mother?' Mariner guesses.

'Yes. My marriage into the Blackwaters was a convenience for him, a way to secure dowry money and release the lingering burden of me elsewhere.'

Elody unhooks the chains from around her waist. When the metal pools on the cherry wood surface, there is a soft hissing sound, a serpent of gold. She wonders; am I only outraged because I did not know? The vastness of court intrigue, the weight of all these unknown connections, it stifles her. Her anger is shrinking, a flush of humiliation climbing in her cheeks and she is made little by it, struggling to recover and climb back into a normal conversation where she might be taken seriously.

'So you do not ... speak to him?' Mariner struggles to form her true question. You do not care about him, you do not trust him? You will not betray us to him?

'We speak as we must at court.'

'But you have Lazarus in your house. He is your brother.'

'We have the same father, but we have never been acquainted, not until he arrived at Hart House.'

She has never had a brother or sister, none living, unless she counts Kit, but Mariner doesn't understand how this could be true. There is a befuddling unreality to the lives of nobility, as masked as players on stages, so perhaps this is expected? Elody smiles at her knowingly.

'My mother and I were confined to a nunnery in France when I was a little child; excluded, unwanted. Lazarus' life has been very different from mine.'

Mariner hears bitterness in her voice, latches onto it, something fathomable and firm to grasp.

'That is why you did not tell me? It was... painful?'

Elody stiffens at the word and Mariner feels a flush of triumph – yes, there, that's something – but then Elody's suave smile slips back into place.

'Must lovers share everything?' She rises to stand in front of Mariner, to take her cap from her head and drop it onto the pile of dirty linen on the floor. 'To love you, dearest, is not to know every haunting of your past, every name you have been known by.'

Elody kisses Mariner's jaw and the wings of victory soar within her because she is loved, thank Christ above, loved by a woman and not as a friend and not for pity. She flies so eagerly out of her anger that she even starts to forget why she was so hurt to begin with.

'Truly?'

'Of course. It is because I love you that I do not share everything.' Elody's mouth tastes like sherry and spices, earthy and good and sweet. 'Dearest Matthew.'

Mariner winces. She hates this name, hates how sometimes, with Mariner's fingers inside her, this is the name Elody whispers rather than her own. It is brutal, the drift of her joy followed so abruptly by the tumble of her solace, and she pulls away, delight spoiling to bitter bile inside her.

'Mariner,' she corrects. 'You know my name.'

'Dear, do not sulk. What's in a name?' Elody's eyes are less dreamy and more impatient now as she sits on the end of the bed, tugging off her heeled shoes and wincing. There are painful tears in Mariner's eyes, the sudden exhaustion of rolling between doubt and delight making her tremulous and the way Elody is simply preceding, undressing like it is any other night is a rebuke, an urge towards silence. She speaks as if it is nothing, this previous name she once had, tossed out of the carriage on the ride to court, smushed into mud in the streets of London. Mariner cannot make herself silent.

'I am in it, I, who love you.' Her worst words are wrenched out of her mouth, unstoppable. 'I have never loved as I love you, yet you keep such secrets from me. Do you lie now? Do you wish, deeply, that I were truly Matthew? Would you…' How bitter it is to speak it, how her heart cries not to, yet here it is; the question at every turn of her life, from Elgin to the men she sailed with to Daisy, to everyone on God's wide earth but Kit: 'Would you rather I were a man?'

'Who does not wish to be a man, given what being a man brings a woman?' Elody's words are careless, her eyes on the laces of her bodice, not noticing the slow rip of Mariner's heart. In her mind, she sees Daisy stepping back from her, overwhelmed and dismayed by her desire, seen for nothing but sinful.

'So you do,' says she.

'No, I do not. Men are not pleasing to me in the same way you are.' Elody releases the sleeves of her gown and Mariner wonders how many there have been; other girls with pliant bodies and gasping mouths, keen to please and greedy to learn. 'I do not wish you a man's form, but is it not better this way? To be man in name? My dear, as Mariner Elgin you are no one. As Matthew Blackwater you can go anywhere.'

But I am only Matthew Blackwater as long as I am with you, she thinks. She does not know why the thought suddenly chafes when it never did before. When she does not speak, Elody looks up, a hunting glance in her features.

'Come here.'

Even sore, even partly wishing to run somewhere cold and dark and weep until she cannot breathe, Mariner obeys. Elody tugs her forward, setting her fingers to the points of Mariner's doublet, unhooking her from her sleeves.

'Are you not free?' Elody slips her out of her doublet and hose. 'Are you not able to follow your desires? Matthew or Mariner, have I not given you all that I promised?'

Mariner shivers and closes her eyes as Elody's chilled fingers seek her warm skin. They say that the world turns around the sun, that the God-given earth is not the centre of the wide ocean of the universe. More that mankind is one mere vessel, tossed in wild waters. Mariner feels it, her own smallness, her own untethered nature. Kit was her tether; the Silver Moon was her anchor. She desperately hopes Elody is another, but if she is Matthew Blackwater, is anything she builds truly her own? I do not know what is mine, Mariner thinks dismally, as Elody traces her collarbone, sternum, nipple. I do not know anymore, but this is all I have.

'Yes, my love.' Mariner keeps her eyes closed against the weight of it once more, the pressing stone of secrets and lurking doubt that threatens to crush the life out of her. 'Yes.'

ⴽⴱⵃⵞⵯⵟⵯⵟⵞ

He who solidifies the past

Chapter Twenty-One

'Kit. Stop now.'

Someone is touching his face. Kit blinks. The mirror is blank, flames flickering against its surface, his reflection swallowed up inside it. The room is dark, the fire burned low, the rolling thunder of a storm clattering sharply against the windows. Lazarus is standing close, dressed once more, his dark brows furrowed.

'You weep.'

Kit sticks out a tongue to catch the salty residue on his upper lip. He takes a step back from the mirror but his legs are as wobbly as the day he was whipped. Lazarus' arm is there, guiding him to the floor. Kit sits beside the still prone Dee, and watches a rat, gradually pulling a rotted apple core into its hole in the brickwork of the fireplace. He wonders if it is possible that the fresh mourning inside him, the dell of grief he has stumbled into, is inside such small animals too? As sun is to stars, as skin is to breath, so the alchemists say all matter connects but is this sorrow only mine?

'Drink.' Lazarus pushes a glass of wine in front of his nose. With a burst of warm cloves and ginger on his tongue, he begins to wonder if he truly saw anything or imagined it, but Lazarus has a notebook in his hand. He sees the scrawled pages of haphazard notes and he is staggeringly relieved for here is proof, here are the words outside of his own mind.

'Speak.' His voice is hoarse.

'You recall being kept by an alchemist, being tested, much torturous assessments that you did not feel.' Lazarus glances up at the mural of the pelican above them on the chimney breast, feeding its young blood from its beak, the alchemical representation of creation. 'You do not remember how you were made but you remember the loss of your mother. The woman who did not survive.'

Kit says nothing. The woman who did not survive what? The winter, the birth of him? Something worse? He tries to reach for that chasm of grief inside him that produced these tears but cannot find it; it is a tide receding from him, pulling back like the Thames. He wants to ask Lazarus, is this how pain works? Does it have an ebb and flow that no one has told me of? Sometimes deep enough to drown in and, other times, impossible to imagine it was ever above my head? He opens his mouth but Dee is stirring, moaning softly, and Lazarus is pulling Kit to his feet.

'We must go,' he says.

Kit casts one final look at the mirror as they draw on their cloaks. The embers give it a golden hue on its left side and he has the clearest sense from it, words forming inside his mind like remembered lines of poetry; there is more to find. More to see. There is more inside you, still.

*

'My lady has written.' Pyncher thrusts a letter, the raven Blackwater seal broken, under Lazarus' nose when he and Kit are in the nascent stages of creating the Arbor Diana, two days after they return from

204

Manchester College. 'You are to ride back to London tomorrow and we are to shut up here. She requests me to remove to Hart House also.'

Pyncher shoots Lazarus a thoroughly self-satisfied smile at his own elevation and then pins Kit with a vicious glare.

'There is much to be done.'

Kit takes that to mean that he best get out of the fucking way before Pyncher has him wrapped in sheets and thrown in a cart with the candlesticks. Whilst Lazarus oversees the packing down of the alchemy chamber, Kit retreats to the orchard for the rest of the afternoon. Apples cover the ground around him, red and shiny, pleasant to hold in a hand, crunchy to bite. Kit tries to commit the taste of it to memory; the crispy flesh, the cold, wet air, fresh and moist. In two days September will be over and he will be in London with a mouth full of city smoke and within arm's reach of both Twentyman and Isherwood once again. He is surprised by how little the first affects him, unsurprised by how intensely the second still does. Kit has skills he did not have two months ago. He can write in code, he can blend herbs and melt beeswax into healing balms, he knows the course of the planets and has tricks too, tricks worthy of the stage. He still does not know the rhyme or reason of which formulas seem to accelerate under his touch, but it doesn't matter to him in the same way it frustrates Lazarus. The new skills he has acquired are saleable, a touch of a little power, the knowledge that he can at least live out of his own pockets without selling himself to a fight master, and these are facts that make Twentyman negotiable where before he had been unmovable. Lord Isherwood cannot be negotiated. Even the self-knowledge he gained in Dee's mirror only lengthens his spectre. Kit recalls the sickening worship in Lazarus' father's eyes. How much more would it grow to learn that Kit was once kept by another alchemist, his abilities already tested, that someone else found him fascinating too? It makes Kit shiver.

'You will catch your death out here without a cloak.'

Lazarus sits beside him, stretching his legs out long, tipping his throat to the weak sun. Then, he pulls from inside his doublet the small notebook he used in Dee's room. Kit eyes it warily, for they have not yet spoken of all that he said in that room. Kit supposes it is because it is not safe to talk of such things within potential earshot of Pyncher, but just to see those scribbled notes on the page carves a rawness inside him, his mind left open for Lazarus' inspection.

'You melted the ice on your fingertips,' Lazarus says quietly. 'You did not say how.'

Kit closes his eyes and sees the moment again in his mind; nails turned from greyish blue to stinging pink. The apple under his tongue is chunky and floury, watery suddenly, turning to snow.

'I thought about how the ice was inside me. I believed it was inside me, that it could be warmed by my blood and... it was.'

'Hmm.' Lazarus reaches down for an apple on the ground. He thoughtfully rubs it against his white shirt, suddenly a boy sneaking a treat in the garden. 'Faith is an essential alchemical component.'

'You called me an atheist.'

'I did not say it was necessary to have faith in God. The alchemist must have faith that the potential of the universe is infinite and we have it inside of us to uncover it. It is a unique type of arrogance.'

'Dee said it was better to be humble.'

'Humble before the heavens, certainly.' Lazarus bites his apple. A dribble of juice creeps down his chin, his words are slovenly with fruit. 'But a student of the celestial arts must petition the angels for the skill to control the elements. You do not need petition for what has already been gifted to your skin and hands.'

'So you wish me to be more arrogant?'

'I thought it not possible, but yes.'

Kit snorts on his bite of apple, coughing suddenly where it clogs his windpipe. Lazarus thumps him hard on the back.

'It is an arrogance, however, that is best kept from Lady Blackwater. When we return to London we will need to curate our findings for her,' says he. 'And by extension, her newly minted cousin.'

Kit swallows a lump, raises an eyebrow.

'I have never kept a secret from Mariner before.'

'You were not my Initiate before.' Lazarus speaks the word so easily, but it lifts the hairs behind Kit's ears. 'You have seen what I will do to protect your secrets. I will not put them in jeopardy now.'

Twentyman often says it, what I will do for my lads, I'd take the noose for any one of you and expect you to do the same, but Lazarus has proven that he will teach Kit and poison for him and is asking nothing more than he continue to learn about himself. It is a different type of loyalty indeed. The end of September sun is orange and full as it dips down to the orchard wall. The glow of it turns the world a ruddy colour, the dry stone wall made fiery red, the ground glistening with bulbous fruit, and Lazarus' hair is streaked with auburn, his eyes cloaked in a burnished shine. Kit allows himself to catalogue it all, to stare at the way Lazarus' bitten nails catch the copper light. Then he remembers that time is passing, and tomorrow they will be riding back to the capital, with all these new secrets to carry with them. A watched sensation returns, a prey animal who knows that somewhere they have been caught in the scent.

'You did not get the answer you wanted. I did not recall my making. It is possible still that I was born naturally, somewhere, perhaps corrupted after birth.' He feels the edges of it then, the tide coming back in, waves of ancient misery he has no map to navigate. 'I feel nothing. I am unnaturally made. Perhaps I was a monstrous mistake.'

'People have told me all my life that my form dictates my character, that I am a monster born from sin, destined only for tragedy,' Lazarus says flatly. 'Being born ordinary or the intentions of your makers do not change how extraordinary you are now. Besides, you do not feel *nothing*.'

It is unfortunate, how those words catch something inside Kit's chest; more unfortunate still how when he flicks his eyes up to Lazarus' face, Lazarus is watching him, so calmly, and he must immediately pick a worm out of his apple to avoid it. Lazarus goes on.

'However he was made, an alchemist with elemental control would not need to wait forty days to flower an Arbor Diana; with his will alone he could transform base metal into a growing thing. With elemental control, such an alchemist could urge it only with a touch. If he was willing.'

His hand is still on Kit's back. For the first time since they came to Raven's Roost, Kit doesn't feel like he wants to move it. Lazarus Isherwood has lied to him before, has deceived and manipulated him, but here he is, speaking so casually, calling him extraordinary, outlining impossible potentials which, at every turn, have become unreasonably possible. The caul grew, the mirror spoke and here, in the wild and stormy North, in the company of this man who steps so high in the world he has no fear of tripping on the long arm of the law, it is very hard to believe that extraordinary means the same terrible, deadly things it has always meant in Southwark. But it does, whispers a small voice inside him. Unbidden, a noose forms in his mind, then a pyre, then fierce flame, coming as quickly as those flashing memories within the mirror. Kit ignores them.

'He is willing,' says he. Lazarus shoots him a small, wry smile; Kit is sure there is approval in it.

'Then we will work wonders,' says Lazarus.

Kit nods. He sits with the warmth of Lazarus' hand on his spine and tries to pretend the safety he feels in this moment is not a fragile, terrible thing.

ΙƷ&Ω⚥ↄᒧⱯ

He who destroys speech

Chapter Twenty-Two

The Queen is well enough to travel to Richmond Palace and Mariner is free. The Royal progress is ended and not even the terrible weather, the end of September crashing in with torrential rain, can sully her relief. She thinks longingly of Hart House, where no courtiers will crowd around her with their piercing eyes and whispered speculations, and for the first time in many weeks feels rising hope, for it is over, thank God. Then, on the morning of their departure from Theobalds, in the scramble of coaches dragged through mud and puddles, Lord Isherwood catches them as Mariner is pulling their coach door closed.

'I hear Lord Burghley has approved your demonstration,' he says, one large hand in a leather glove taking up nearly all of the small windowsill. 'Third Sunday in October, he says. I hope you will be ready.'

'Of course we will.' Elody smiles, and Mariner does not understand what has happened, her stomach twisting with dread.

'We spoke of it when we danced,' Elody explains eyes glittering with triumph as he strides away. 'His desire to see me fail will be the means by which I succeed.'

Mariner does not want to be seen by Lord Isherwood under any circumstances, failing or succeeding. She is horrified to imagine his presence circling Hart House again, hunting Kit like a trapped stag, but when she voices this to Elody, she is shocked to hear Kit is not there. He is on his way back from Manchester, where he and Lazarus have been the entire time.

'You did not tell me,' she says.

'You did not ask,' says Elody.

Mariner feels the heavy arbitrariness of this, a protest inside her against another secret kept by the woman she loves. She wonders what she could have asked, if a magic combination of words actually exists that would winkle out the truth. Then Elody begins to tell her of the dinners she will host, elaborate sugar balls, the great men of court who will carry on their dancing and feasting on Elody's coin, and Mariner feels her insides quailing. It is not over, she was a fool to imagine so, and now she cannot see the end.

*

Kit arrives back on the evening of the first of October. Mariner is standing on the upper landing when they stamp in and rather than skidding downstairs to catch Kit, she finds herself leaning on the carved banister, watching him.

'Is there any shitting city worse to ride through than London?'

He is pulling off his cloak and, underneath, is transformed. Dressed like a scholar, black and lawyerly, fine tailoring making her assess him as she has never done before. Kit has never been tall or pretty, but standing straight backed in dark cotton with a delicate ruff around his neck that brings out the fey pinch of his chin, he is arresting. He looks grown.

'There is no city worse to ride through with you. You nearly had that orange seller over.'

Lazarus is knocking dried mud off his boots and Mariner watches Kit copy him. Or maybe he does not copy him. Maybe he simply knows what to do now.

'If I had, I would have had his wares. Lucky me.'

'You are a reckless horseman.'

'For that, I will not share my oranges.'

She is hesitant to approach them, with their quick, sarcastic rapport. When she left Kit, he hated Lazarus at least as much as Twentyman but now there is an ease in his shoulders. He may not trust Lazarus Isherwood completely but he no longer believes he is menacing, that much is sure. Mariner hates that she does not know why.

'I wonder where Mariner is?' he asks, looking around with such eager eyes that she cannot deny him.

'Here.'

Mariner walks down the stairs, aware of Lazarus' eyes on her, no doubt assessing how she has passed as Master Blackwater at court, but she has not reached the bottom step before she has her arms full of Kit. He says nothing, his familiar grip too tight and crushing the breath out of her. He smells of the road and some kind of perfume on his collar, herbal and sweet, but the scent of his sweat is the same. A musky odour that she has slept beside for years and why it suddenly hurts her she does not know, but there is a clenching in her chest that makes her breathless.

'Kit,' she mumbles. She lifts her arms to grip him back, to tell him how she has missed him, how the things she has seen and done and witnessed have amazed and terrified her and how she is different, in ways she is not sure can ever be undone, but this is the same, thank blessed Christ. Kit, who loves her, Kit is the same.

'Matthew,' a soft voice says. Elody, coming down the stairs behind her with her eyes full of all the secrets Mariner promised to keep, fixing her gaze upon Kit's back. 'Decorum.'

She steps back, because she is not Mariner now, she is Matthew. Kit looks at her curiously, waiting for her to speak.

'You are welcome, Master Skevy,' says she. There is a humour in Kit's eyes, joyous bafflement, waiting for the joke, and it fades the longer she says or does nothing else, transforms into revelation and calculation. He bows.

'I thank you, Master Blackwater.' Kit walks back down the stairs. To Lazarus. Her eyes sting and she is abruptly full of horror at herself, at him, at how wrong it all is. Nothing is the same anymore.

Lazarus and Kit's return is followed by the arrival of Pyncher, a sour-faced cruel housekeeper who also appears to be the Blackwater steward. He despises Mariner. He does not question his mistress' assertion that Mariner is a relative he knows she cannot possibly be, but she finds herself often speared on the most pointed of glares. She also begins to notice strange men loitering near the house, their eyes fixed on the door. She checks their bed daily for more death threats and takes to carrying the original drawing of Elody's death around in her pocket, worrying it soft and floppy under her fingers, a talisman against worse coming. Elody is dismissive.

'All alchemists have spies,' says she, and Mariner wants to tell her that not all alchemists are women who many would like to burn for a witch. Mariner wishes she could talk to Kit, but she never sees him. He and Lazarus are planets in a different orbit, preparing for the demonstration in three weeks, barely sighted but for the passing tail of an alchemist's cloak. Resentment fills her slowly at his purpose and her aching redundancy, every silent day away from him piling upon another until every time she sees him through the window in the garden or going up the stairs as she goes down she thinks: you are not my Kit. You are someone I do not even want to know.

A week later and there is a cold snap in London. The roads are covered in ice and chunks of it float in the Thames, always a hint of sharper weather to come. Elody is having a private dinner with the Earl of Northumberland, Lazarus has gone to Gray's Inn in search of books and Pyncher has a plate of cheese, pickled onions and bread sent to Kit's room for supper. The message is clear. If Mariner wants to eat, she will have to eat with the apprentice, the only one of the two of them with a true place in this house. She knocks on the door.

'*Entre.*'

That imperialist tone, how it vexes, she kicks open the door with a little too much force. Kit is sat on his small bed, shoes kicked off and knees pulled up to his chest under his night shirt, a great book resting upon them with a pen in hand and a half eaten lump of cheese in the other.

'Oh,' he says, his tone telling her he expected Lazarus. Again, the sensation of being no longer wanted, it grates inside her.

'Food,' says she. He looks at the plate, bread untouched, what is left of the cheese.

'Yes.'

He draws his knees up closer, an invitation to sit. She does, taking the plate. She eats in silence as he writes, stares at the fine hose he is wearing, pale yellow, how they have discoloured at the toes, one bruised, purple nail starting to push through. She has been wearing hose just like it for months now but how strange it is to see them on his feet. She pokes his toe, experimentally. He does not look up and she can't help but smile to herself. This is the same, at least; he does not feel it. She presses a little harder and he raises his eyes, wordlessly reaches for the glass of wine. Hands it over. It calms her, these old codes and physical habits; they thaw the icy rankling inside of her, just a touch.

213

'Is Lady Blackwater Catholic?' Kit asks as Mariner drinks. His words makes the wine catch in her throat, as she coughs maniacally through her panic.

'Why?'

'Because her tenants are, her house is,' Kit says, so uncaringly. He is already turning the page, writing notes at an annoyingly fast speed. He's always been quicker than most with ink on his fingers, but not like this, writing and talking and barely noticing the curl of her hand into a fist. 'Lazarus says—'

'Oh, Lazarus says? Why would you listen to him?' Mariner hears the tremble in her own sneer. 'His father tried to have you jointed and salted and hung up for drying. You said he was a bad choice.'

It is not jealousy, she tells herself, it is simply that Elody is the one of the three Isherwood's to be trusted. This fury is reasonable, in the wake of Kit's casual mentions of Catholicism and all its terrors. He does not know as I do, what a rickety ship made of a walnut box we all sail in, she thinks.

'He is different now,' says he. Still he writes, the maddening scratch, scratch, scratch of a pen against paper. He does not even look at her; he does not even sound as if he cares.

'That is what Daisy says about Twentyman,' she scorns.

'You would know.'

She seizes it all from him, pen, book, paper, and throws it across his small room. It clatters and thumps irrationally loudly, catching a stool that topples over, a smash in the roaring silence and Mariner forces herself not to wince. They say nothing. Outside, she hears a servant climbing the stairs, a blackbird singing on the windowsill.

'Ridiculous.' Kit rises slowly, as if he cares not. '*Matthew.*'

It burns up from her stomach, this one word rejection of everything she has forced herself to be these last eight weeks, a thunderous thump of her pulse under her jaw, painful as a canker.

'He hasn't forgotten who you are, just because you've read a few books and you flirt with him.'

'No, he knows exactly who I am.' Kit picks up his book, dusting off the jacket with several quick leathery slaps. His face is reddening under his freckles, a sure sign he is irked.

'What, a chancer? A brawler?'

Kit's mouth flattens with anger.

'I am good at this.' He lifts his page of notes and tucks it into the book jacket. The ink is smeared. 'Lazarus thinks I could be made for it. No one knows my provenance. It could be in my blood.'

'He thinks you come from some grand line of alchemists?' She laughs wildly but Kit merely folds the book against his chest with a flick of his curls.

'Why not?' he says. 'I'm not like you. My parents aren't dead nobodies.'

It's true and cruel. She is furious, she is fearful, the same fear she felt when Kit decided that he wanted to steal from Twentyman, that he is choosing a different path. Resentment boils at his appalling transformation, for whilst Kit seems to be finding a sharper, more distinguished version of himself, she feels as if she is becoming more trapped inside the skin of Matthew Blackwater. Damn him, for his fucking hope, she finds herself thinking bitterly, always wanting to be more than he is. The urge to crumple it is irresistible.

'Unless Squire Kay has an alchemist in her family, I think you're out of luck, Skevy,' she says. 'The night I left Southwark, Twentyman said she was your mother. You're right, you're no orphan. You're a bastard, through and through.'

Kit's silence is complete, his expression stunned. Mariner knows that inside his mind, memories must be illuminating, brilliant as stained glass. Squire Kay, washing his back after his flogging, chiding them when they were younger for skating too long, and Mariner is viciously glad of his stupefaction. Perhaps now he will feel a fraction of the unsteadiness she feels. The world listing under her feet like a sinking ship, she will not feel pity for him, not one ounce.

'No,' Kit says eventually. 'My mother is dead.'

The edges of her anger relight. Of course Kit prefers his version of reality to what truly is.

'Your mother is Squire fucking Kay who likely got you in her belly before she was wed and left you in Antwerp until her brother earned enough to scoop you back up! You're a strange, freakish boy, Kit, but you're no alchemical genius, you're nothing special.'

She knows it is the worst thing she could say, the cruellest thing, and Kit has a fight in his eyes.

'You saw the fire. At Crossbones. It came out of my hands, not out of a formula, out of me.' His voice is contemptuous. 'Explain it.'

She doesn't want to; she doesn't want to consider that moment when hell opened to her and she eagerly ran away from her friend, so she leans into the apoplectic despair inside her, the gnawing beast of it.

'I can explain it – you opened the fucking coffin! When I told you not to!'

'And you made me get in the fucking boat!' He is suddenly shouting. 'I wanted to leave the country!'

It is beyond provoking that the same person who has been merrily learning alchemy and claiming some great heritage of power for himself for the last two months would now complain about it. Kit Skevy, she thinks darkly, always lands on his fucking feet.

'And miss out on your alchemy lessons with Lazarus Isherwood? On the chance to flirt and read and play scholar?' Mariner finds herself scoffing. 'Look at you! Fiddling in formulas and brews. Did you learn nothing from Griffin, choked to death on his own fucking hubris?'

'I learned the world is wide and I am more than Griffin ever thought to be; I do not make the thing, I *am* the thing!' Kit's eyes are gleaming as he stretches out a hand, littered with new scars, evidence, Mariner realises, of other tricks of nature. 'And one day I will be too powerful to burn.'

'What kind of puffers nonsense did he feed you in the North?' Mariner tries to put scorn in her voice but she can't stop looking at Kit's outstretched hand, the beginning of a spell or a blessing, a priest or a witch. 'What hellish heresy did you *do*, Kit?'

Kit doesn't answer and Mariner knows then, from the way the tips of his fingers tremble, that unspeakable things have happened to him, too. She remembers Lady Catherine, screaming that she would die, the fire consuming her clothes and the meaty mess inside it. He lowers his hand and she's relieved, hates herself for it.

'What kind of heresy have you been up to in her bed?'

He only uses this word to hurt her, a word made of all of her grotesque thoughts about the love she has found and the well of despair within her bubbles to screaming rage.

'So I am a hypocrite, at least I can *feel* my shame! My uncle will despair of me and God will shun me, but I cannot force myself to want a man, I only love her! But you fuck women, Kit!'

'I do not choose to be as I am.' Kit's mouth has swallowed its lips, a white line of words held forcibly back. 'I am wife and husband, to love me is to love both, who wants both?'

Mariner will not hear it, the sorrow inside those three words, because it is not fair that he has come back from the North a stronger man and she is coiling inside herself, weakness eating her bones from the inside out, and her self-loathing spills out of her mouth in a wave of bitter darkness.

'You could take a wife and live in peace and have all that I cannot but you toss it all away, call it dreary and dance in the flames! Is it not love to tell you when you're being so *fucking* stupid?'

Her words should not echo, but somehow they do, bouncing against Kit, standing there in his night shirt, one of his hose fallen down and, his freckled, knobbly knee, a knee that she has kissed the blood away from after a knock countless times, on display.

'If this is your love then it is small.' He shakes his head with infuriating distress, eyes glassy. 'I suppose I cannot complain, for now you have as little care for me as for yourself.'

That will burn later, but she forces herself to shrug it off.

'It is enough for her.'

Kit gives her a nasty look, one that she knows will accompany a barb so well chosen it will bury its way into her flesh and fester.

'You are her Daisy, that is all.'

Mariner sucks in her breath. He has always been able to do this, ruin her with a few words, comments sharper than jabbing fists, and she will not cry in front of him. She marches to the door, bumping Kit's shoulder and ignoring the sharp ache of it, thinking she has never hated anyone as she hates Kit fucking Skevy. Then she thinks of the perfect response.

'He lied to you. He's not only Isherwood's son, he's Elody's sister. He brought you from one Isherwood alchemist to another.' Mariner sees his eyes widen and knows her wild shot has landed. He did not know and this is her victory now. 'He will fuck you and use you, he will chew you up and spit you out and then you'll truly be Griffin. Just like you always wanted.'

She lets the door clap behind her and walks blindly to Elody's chamber, heartbeat violent and nauseous in her face and ears. She climbs fully clothed into the frozen bed, not caring to build up the dead fire, despite the sleet falling against the windows. She presses her cold hands between her thighs and remembers the day she'd asked Elgin why all men are not saved. Because the gospel is not for all men, but for God's elect Church, Elgin had said, smiling softly. God loves the sinners too, even despite their nature. Mariner had understood one thing then: not even the love of God is enough to save a person. Love can hide within it destruction, a future of pain. You are her Daisy, he said, you are the thing she does not love but will use until you are worn out and your heart is husky. She remembers the curdling disdain she had for Daisy's love of Twentyman, how pathetically naive it seemed, how wretchedly hopeful when there was nothing left to hope for. Mariner lets out a hacking sob; it starts from her chest, leaves her like a cough and slowly, the pillow dampens and the feathers wilt. She tries to warm herself under the blankets but it does no good; Kit's words keep her cold.

He who is the protector of man

Chapter Twenty-Three

Kit ducks into the dark city with the expertise of a thief who knows every quick escape, Mariner's words bellowing in his mind: your mother is Squire fucking Kay; you're a bastard through and through; he lied to you. He knows it's unwise to set out into the city where Isherwood's men spy, he knows Lazarus would lambaste him but Lazarus is a liar. Perhaps Kit's entire life is a tapestry of lies. As he walks, a cascade of memories tumble inside of him: Squire Kay brushing his hair, stroking his forehead in fever, making him drink ale in the summer. A woman who has always mothered him now transformed into this, a mother by birth. Yet he cannot deny the sensation inside him that he has been carrying since the mirror; the surety of his tangled despair that his mother has been dead all of his life and he has mourned her. Is it possible the mirror lied? He would ask Lazarus but does he even know who Lazarus is? Untrustworthy wretch, so said Pyncher, and without Lazarus there is only Mariner, but she thinks him selfish and stupid. She does not care that his entire world has become a fragile, uncertain place he barely understands. So Kit goes back to what he does understand.

On the south side of the river the familiar scents crowd in on him. Sweaty horses, ripe and sticky on his tongue, over-brewed ale, tangy and hoppy, and there is a lump rising in his throat as he stands in the back alley of the Silver Moon in the grey sleet of the night. His urgent conviction wavers and he chides his own recklessness – fucking idiot, Skevy, what is the bloody gain? He turns to go back, but here is Squire Kay herself. She is tucking her serving rag into her waist, stepping out of the door and when Kit looks at her he realises he does not remember the first time he saw her. Not like Griffin, whose shirt he remembers tucking his face into whilst the swollen sails of the ship flapped high and majestic above them.

'Kit!' Squire Kay catches sight of him, pales dramatically. Then she steps out into the orange darkness of the alley, lit in shards by the candlelight of the inn. 'You shouldn't be south of the river—'

Ezra appears behind her.

'Young Kit!' There's a name Kit has not heard in what feels like years and in two steps of his long legs, Ezra has embraced him. 'My, but you're looking so well.'

Ezra's eyes are skimming over the black alchemist robe he's become accustomed to wearing. He'd always thought Ezra a well-dressed man, but now Kit feels the softness of the finest cotton against his skin, the luxury of his black damask. Ezra has a shoddy, tired look to him that wasn't there before.

'What was the name of the brothel I was born in?' Kit asks Squire Kay. She is still for a moment, nervous fingers silenced. When she speaks, her voice is round with studied apathy.

'I don't recall. Griffin told me but it was so long ago.' She wrings her serving cloth between her hands and her eyes skitter away up the alley. 'If Twentyman—'

'Did Griffin say anything about who birthed me? He must have told you who she was… why I was there.'

He hopes for an easy denial; yes, he confessed she was a whore, they told us you were a foundling child. He will accept it; anything that removes him from this crazed unfamiliar world where this woman could be the mother whose abandonment lives in each of his bones.

'No, he never said. Why does it matter?'

Something ugly is trying to crawl up from Kit's guts, a dark creature clambering into his throat. It matters, he thinks, because Griffin said I was motherless and fatherless. It matters because if Mariner is right, I had a mother and an uncle and neither of you chose to claim me. The answer might be unbearable but still the question comes, vomited out of his lips, fast and breathy:

'Are you my mother? Did you birth me and leave me and then send Griffin to get me and never tell me?'

'What?' Her blue eyes seem to soften even as her mouth hardens. 'Of course not, boy! Do you look like Ezra Prophet is your father?'

Beside him, Ezra puts a comforting hand on his shoulder.

'Folks have always said such things about the two of you; it's the red hair,' says he. 'There's no truth in it.'

Kit is not sated by this denial, if anything, it makes it worse, tangling him further, desperate for a thread.

'But then why did Twentyman say so, and how did you and Griffin both know I do not feel as others do?' Unlike Mariner by the Pike Ponds, he doesn't remember a time when Griffin and his sister didn't know. 'I remember things now.'

Her eyes narrow.

'What do you remember?'

'Snow. A man who took notes and wrote in a ledger, my fingers so cold in a fine house, being... hurt.' Kit wants to say that he remembers his mother, but he can't. It would be a lie. 'I dream about it—'

'Christ's wounds, you are wasting time over dreams?' She shakes her rag at him. 'It happened just as Griff said! He found you in a whorehouse—'

'He didn't fuck women!'

Kit has forgotten how much silence Squire Kay has held her whole life about Griffin. Her body is still, letting Kit's words bounce around her, impervious to them, unhearing, eyes glassy. He wants to have pity but Kit's insides are raw, split and sliced and shredded with the memory of a mother lost. These are questions that require answers, the questions of his whole, poor, sad, strange life in Southwark. The oddest boy, the one who will not stay down, with something in his blood that pushes through his fingers and transforms the elements. How can he ever be better, be more, if he does not know who he is transforming from?

'There is a queerness to me. The things I am, the things I can do, you know it. I am made strangely, too.' She flinches at his words. Perhaps she's looked away from him, from the fumbles with lasses and lads alike, the same way she looked away from Griffin. 'Where does it come from and how can you not know?'

She grabs the shoulder of his robe, pulling him close by the scruff, just as she did when he was a child. Her breath is sour on his cheek; stale ale and maybe something stronger.

'You listen to me, you keep going forward and you never look back, not even to us, you don't stop for anyone. You always wanted shot of this life and look at you now!' She shakes him. The red veins in the whites of her eyes stand out. 'Apprentice as you are! A better future he could not have imagined for you, so you be fucking happy, else he saved you all those years ago for nothing at all. You hear me?'

She pushes him back and is gone, disappearing back into the Silver Moon with a drunken stumble.

'She misses him.' Ezra smooths Kit's ruff, fingers pinching the lace, assessing it. 'Kit Skevy. A grown man, your own way to make.'

Kit can't find his voice, can't force himself to say, I do not feel grown, I do not know my way, they say I am not even properly a man either now, but under Ezra's warm, soft eyes, he cannot deny him. So he nods.

'Get away now, lad.' Ezra rubs a thumb against Kit's cheek, a paternal gesture that for the first time in his life feels soiled. 'It's not safe for you on this side of the river anymore.'

It is the kindest of rejections, the implications speeding Kit's steps mindlessly back down the alley. You don't belong here, the press of Ezra's soft thumb says, this is no longer your life. He ducks his way through the streets that used to be his and wonders at this; how a home can become alien so quickly, how people who have been family can tell you to move on from them, cast them aside, and in telling you, can make you feel so easily discarded.

He pauses in a lane near Battle Bridge and leans against the crumbling paint of an alehouse because his vision is blurring so he rests for a second, palms pressed back against the timbers, catching ragged splinters. He hopes bizarrely that those tiny pieces of Southwark will needle their way into his skin and blood and never retract, that he'll get to keep this, at least, just this. Then, he has the sensation he is not alone.

He turns his head to the right, sees two men stepping into the lane behind him, forms blended of dark shadows and heavy mud, armed with a piece of wood and a bottle. He tenses, thinks this is the moment, here it finally is. Isherwood's men who have chased him up and down the country, now catching him in the dark of the night in Southwark. He's been foolish, he thinks, to trot back south and into his grasp. but then he recognises them. One is a jarkman, known for his forgeries, and one an angler, built like the side of a house and is said to know the richest windows in London to pilfer from. A familiar voice calls out from the left.

'So you're back,' says Twentyman. Kit doesn't know why he's surprised; Twentyman has all the qualities of Mephistopheles; just to step foot on Southwark soil is to conjure him.

'No, I'm not,' says Kit. He's looking Kit up and down like he's made of coins, a sneer on those thin lips.

'You look a twat.'

Kit snorts with laughter, these words no longer capable of knocking him down. Twentyman's hold on him has only ever been as strong as the bonds around him; Griffin's honour to protect, Ezra and Squire Kay's business to guard, Mariner to keep safe from the Hat. Now Kit is light and untethered, and all Twentyman can threaten is a beating. He's holding a poker, his favourite weapon of choice. Twentyman likes to leave marks, but Kit knows now: there are worse ways to be marked.

'Thanks, *Twenny*.'

His smile is feral, swishing the poker ominously through the sleeting air.

'This is what he imagined, I suppose, foolish old Griff,' he says. 'He plucked you out of Antwerp, tells us all you're an orphan when your hair is as red as his sister's and your face twice as ugly! Perhaps he thought he'd trick some lass into wedding him and pretend you were his, but then he met the poet.'

Kit says nothing. It's funny, that after all his pleading with Squire Kay, Twentyman is here, giving him the story she denied him.

'Griffin wouldn't throw over the chance at such a grand lover, would he? So what could he do with the child? Where could he turn?'

'Not you,' Kit says.

'Yes, me!' Twentyman's teeth are bared. 'Come to his sister, doesn't he, and asks for your keep in her house, the house I own most of? Always asking for more than deserved, always thinking himself higher because he got abroad and sold secrets and lifted his arse for rich buggers, thinking himself *better,* but he couldn't keep you, could he? I'm the one who made you a fighter, and you threw it away!' He gestures the poker over Kit's robe. 'We hear you're an alchemist now.'

'Where do you hear it?'

'Let's just say you find yourself worth a lot of fucking money for once.' Twentyman steps forward. Kit knows it will be Isherwood.

'Try me then,' says Kit. He is itching for it, suddenly, the sensation of a bone breaking, a nose or a jaw or the first chip of teeth, under his knuckles again. Twentyman just smiles knowingly.

'No need, no need. See, I reckon there's something owed for all that time I gave you, Skevy, all that learning how to be a man.' Behind him, with all the peripheral awareness of a rabbit, he can see the jarkman and frater approaching. 'Do you have secrets, pockets full of gold? Best turn them out for us.'

Isherwood is a fool to rely on a man like Twentyman to bring home a prize. Rather than truss Kit up and march him down to Whitehall for a reward, Twentyman reckons there is better recompense in shaking down an alchemist himself. Southwark folk don't walk a fat calf home for a pretty penny. They kill it.

'You're going to need more than that,' Kit says, looking at the poker and the meagre weapons of the other two.

'Oh, we've got more.' The taller jarkman grins, pulling out a short axe from the back of his breeches and taking a swig from his bottle before tossing it against the wall. It smashes, brown glass glittering the mud. Kit has never fought a man with an axe. He supposes there is a first time for everything.

'Turn him upside down and shake him,' Twentyman says, hitting the poker against the wall, beating time. A dance, then, a familiar thumping in Kit's blood. First, the jarkman lunges. Kit ducks and twists away from the blows of the angler but his alchemist's robes are ungainly and usually, he has Mariner to back him up. Mariner who thinks him unholy, a sinner going to hell. With a tug on those same robes, the jarkman has him pressed against the wall. The axe handle is forced chokingly under his chin whilst the angler slams the wood plank against his knees. Their effectiveness is in their speed and force, brutality that allows Twentyman to swoop in and claim his prize.

'What of love? What of loyalty?' Twentyman sneers as he fumbles Kit's pockets. His breath smells and tastes like rotten fish and there's something about this combination of scents that sends Kit back; he is pinned down against wet straw and struggling, feeling the crushing vulnerability of inevitable humiliation. Just for a second, familiar despair rises all over again, and he stops fighting.

'Floppy as a fish.' Twentyman laughs. 'Is this how you were for Griffin? No wonder he kept you. I'll have those boots and fine shirt and all. Strip him, lads.'

Kit wrestles but it is no good, what good can there be? The stars above are wide and shining and he is being robbed at home in Southwark, when a voice suddenly bellows out:

'Get off him!'

Something wet passes close to Kit's face and Twentyman screams, such a high pitched, animal sound Kit thinks of piglets, screeching and whining when caught. He's is clawing at his face, staggering away, and Lazarus is there, an empty vial in his gloved hands and a determined expression. The jarkman and the angler are open mouthed, staring at this young aristocrat with a rapier hung at his hip and yet somehow, having ruined a man with a bottle of water. Their astonishment is enough time for Kit to deliver a sound kick to the jarkman's balls, grabbing the axe whilst Lazarus distracts the skinny angler by throwing rocks at him.

227

'Back!' Lazarus is fumbling under his robe for a second vial, hurrying to uncork it, looking at the approaching angler with the same kind of fear he'd worn the day Kit nearly strangled him. Kit raises the axe, aiming at the angler's back, but is thrown to the ground. A blow to the back of his head, his eyes blurring, the brickwork beside him spinning dizzyingly upwards. The jarkman has picked up Twentyman's poker and is squaring up, a nasty grimace on his face. He can hear very little, aside from a ringing in his ears and the distant screams of Lazarus – for the love of God, Laz, stop screaming – as he wrestles the metal bar from the jarkman. He has it, beats his own rhythm against scalp and skull – one, two, three, four – until stillness takes the body. When Kit looks up, blinking blood out of his eyelashes, the angler is kicking Lazarus to shit. Quick pace, a time kept with screams, and Kit swings the poker to join it. The man is a house, however, barely listing with the impact. He turns to Kit with a nasty, black-toothed grin.

'Come on then,' he says, raising his plank of wood, grimly bloody on the edge. A different rhythm now, a slower, ominous crashing of sounds. Crunching wood to the shoulder bone. Thunking head smashed against brick. This catastrophic pattern of broken bones will pummel Kit to dust if he cannot bring the fucker down. Knees, knees, knees, thinks Kit. A wild swing of his poker, cracking a knee cap, but even when this man is halfway down he is Kit's height. He throws himself entirely at him. Body to body, sweat and blood and mouthfuls of mud, rolling and tumbling until Kit can scramble himself up over his wide chest and slam the poker across his throat. This is what Ezra taught him when Twentyman first put him in the ring: a man cannot fight if he cannot breathe. It's working, thank God, it is nearly over, but the angler's reach is long. He crawls pudgy fingers up to clamp around Kit's own windpipe. A race for air. His own heartbeat is so rapid and panicked in his ears; Kit feels it on his tongue. He knows he is in trouble.

'Laz,' he tries to choke out, glimpsing Lazarus lying prone nearby, thinking; do not be dead, you lying cunt, but it is useless. He thinks of the lungs in the jar, floating and soupy; are his simply not large enough? The darkness is beginning to creep in, and Kit realises he will not make it. The angler's blue lips form a victorious smile as Kit's hands soften on the poker, damp from the icy mush of a frozen churned up puddle the head is crushed against. Wet, Kit thinks, that will feel wet. As ice to water, water to ice, if only I could drown him in mud, push him under the earth and let it swallow him—

Then it happens.

ᘯᘓᘔᘓᒪᗢᒪᘿ

He who destroys and creates

Chapter Twenty-Four

The ice begins to melt, expand, water running away from Kit's
fingers. The angler's face is submerged in muddy liquid, his
legs begin to flail with desperation against this shallow drowning,
almost unseating Kit, but then there is a weight behind him. In the
corner of his vision, he sees Lazarus' boots, Lazarus' body, Lazarus
who has dragged himself over the angler's legs to pin him down
and finally, blessedly, the fingers slacken around Kit's own throat.
Kit breathes, how sweet it tastes, mud and blood and the scent of
piss as the angler enters his death throes. Kit stares at his watery,
dirty face, his eyes replaced with floating trails of mud, bubbles
stopping, stillness coming. Done. Then, with the relief of life comes
the terror of the consequences. To kill a man in self-defence is no
hanging offence, but this is a man drowned in water he made from
ice right here in the alleys of Southwark, where anyone could see.
Hatefully, he remembers the sure but ominous word Lazarus had
used in Dee's workroom: You have not killed someone with alchemy.
Yet.

'Fuck.' Kit staggers off the dead man, thinking, I must run.

'Are the others dead?' Lazarus croaks. His chest is heaving; there is blood matting his dark hair. He looks a horrible state.

Kit checks the jarkman. The back of his head looks hideous but he is breathing, though perhaps for not much longer. Twentyman's face looks bloody awful; yellowing and red, split open and weeping, but his chest is rising and falling. He has passed out, it seems, from the pain of having one side of his face melted away with acid.

'No, just him, just the one I—' Kit tastes bile in the back of his throat, forces it down, turning his face towards the wall, just in case it rushes up.

'No one will know.' Lazarus rises painfully to his feet, lopsided and limping, to grab the dead man's arm and pull it wincing over his shoulder. Kit sees his plan, two men carrying a third in what looks like a drunken stupor through Southwark at this time of night will not even raise an eyebrow. Kit looks up and down the lane. At the end of the Battle Bridge stream is a small wharf. Sometimes, farmers tie wherries there when visiting Horsleydown, usually unattended. Kit throws the dead man's other arm around his shoulder and the face is launched out of the water, mud leaking out of his mouth.

'This way,' Kit says. They stagger down the lane. He hopes that both Twentyman and the jarkman die before they are found, that everyone in Southwark assumes the jarkman finally had enough of Twentyman's fifteen per cent cuts into his excellent work. Thankfully, the tiny wharf, nothing more than a muddy shelf and unlit, has a small wherry tied, bobbing in the dark Thames.

'We are stealing it?' Lazarus says.

'Well, we can hardly fucking march back up to Overie Stairs and ask for a twopenny ride.' Kit drops the angler into the boat with a hefty thud. It sways precariously. 'Get the fuck in, Silver.'

231

Lazarus does, groaning, and Kit grabs the oars, steering out into the current.

'Down towards Deptford.' Lazarus' voice is tight with pain. 'It will be quieter.'

Kit happily obliges, cutting away from the flow of wherries crossing the river and downstream past the great, moored ships at Billingsgate, their huge sails furled. The shadow of the Tower looms over them with its watery black entrance, and Kit imagines sailing into its beastly belly, knowing he would never come out. Mariner's question haunts him: What hellish heresy did you *do*, Kit? In the North Kit read and learned much that Mariner would call heresy, but it is at home, in Southwark, where he has killed a man with his own bare hands. How to make sense of it? It cannot be reasoned with a dead man's still warm chest pressed awkwardly against his shins, so he pushes his thoughts to focus on the rhythm of the oars; he keeps his eyes fixed on the lights of London, inches of relief creeping up inside him for their dimming. Finally, when they are floating down by Redriff Marsh, Lazarus nods.

'Ever done this before?' Kit asks. Lazarus shakes his head. Kit has never dumped a body in the Thames either, but he knows how to do it. It's something everyone who runs under Twentyman learns by word of mouth at some point. He looks down at the giant dead angler and thinks that it will be a good day for Twentyman's other anglers indeed. 'Help me, then.'

Together, they tip him over the side. For so much effort, it is sickeningly easy, the casual flop of a heavy load under the soft, flowing water. He is weighty enough to sink but Kit prods him with the oars to make sure he goes down. Then it is done, Kit sits back down and finds Lazarus watching him closely. There is blood in his eyebrows. How did it feel for you? Kit wants to ask. The first time you took a life and knew you could be tried for witchcraft? Were you afraid of yourself too? Am I monstrous yet? Instead, he says:

'Is she your sister?'

Lazarus frowns for a moment.

'Yes. Did you not know? Is that why I came back from Gray's to find you gone? Even though Lord Isherwood's men spy at Lime Street?'

Kit hears the rebuke, the implied worry, but does not care.

'Why would I know?'

He does not ask the truer question: Why did you not tell me?

'Everyone does. It was the scandal of my childhood, how he set aside Lady Blackwater's mother and called his own daughter a bastard in pursuit of a male heir only to lose his second wife in bringing a crookback son into the world.' Lazarus stares out over the sparkling black water. This far away from the city founders and blacksmiths, the sleet is more snow. It falls thick and grey and is swallowed by the river, landing in Lazarus' hair, white feathers melting into nothing. 'I never met her before you did. After their divorce, she was cast off from our father like her mother in France, and then became Lady Blackwater when I was still a child. I was raised in Coldstream and then sent away to Flanders. I never thought of her, not until I heard she was set up in Lime Street and paying for corpses.'

'You don't speak like she's your sister, like...' Kit struggles for the words that accurately represent most how he feels about Mariner. 'Like she annoys you so much you could kill her.'

'That's because I share as much kin with her as I do any of his bastards that might be washing pots somewhere.'

Kit wonders if any of Lord Isherwood's children love him, because the legitimate ones certainly do not. He supposes Lazarus could be lying. He cannot tell if the strange taste in his mouth is the blood of the angler or the bitterness of his disgruntlement, and is it there

233

because Lazarus kept a secret from him, or simply because Mariner knew it first? Kit watches, fascinated, as Lazarus tries to pull his torn alchemist's robe over his shoulder, stifling an involuntary sound with flared nostrils. There is something about pain that is much like pleasure. The way it changes the body, seemingly without its volition.

'It hurts?'

'More so for being beaten.'

He has an urge to touch it. He reaches out a tentative hand and Lazarus goes still, watching him cautiously, as he gently sets a hand on Lazarus' sloped shoulder. His robe has fallen back off it, the collar of the doublet is ripped open; Kit can see a patch of bare skin that seems to be moulded higher than the other. Despite bedding him, Lazarus never removed his shirt. Kit runs a thumb, with a firm pressure against it, and Lazarus grunts softly, an exhalation of sound. Kit looks at him in astonishment.

'That was a good sound.' He frowns. 'You said it hurt.'

'It does, but there is bad pain and good pain.' Lazarus smiles and, for a moment, it almost looks fond. 'The muscles are tense from overworking, they struggle to compensate. With a firm touch in the right place, there is pain but there is also release.'

Kit stares at him. No one has ever spoken about pain in this way to him before; less of a fact and more an element, capable of trans-mutation into other properties.

'How does one become another?'

'It depends on many things. Pressure, constitution.' Kit keeps rubbing his thumb against the firm, taut skin until Lazarus' hand catches his wrist, right at the pulse point. 'The person.'

Their eyes meet. Pain is truly so much like pleasure then, that it can be worked towards and away from. Maybe other people need to feel the edge of pain, just as the edge of pleasure, maybe Lazarus is one of those people and here they are, drifting on the water with the shadows of the marshland trees sending them into ceep darkness. Perhaps it is just that feeling of soaring downwards through excitement after a fight, the colossal, elated relief of it, but Kit hovers his outstretched hand over Lazarus' bare throat. Lazarus does not resist as Kit's thumb presses on the corner of his jawbone, as his fingers rest on the other side and Lazarus' chin sits on Kit's purlicue. A dainty head on a platter of flesh. If he flattens his palm down, he will cover Lazarus' throat, just as the jarkman's stubby fingers wrestled around his own, but he does not. Instead, Kit urges Lazarus' chin to lift, an elegant stretch, and marvels briefly at the delicacy of it all. A test or an invitation, what it is he doesn't know, only that Lazarus is allowing it. His lips will taste of blood, Kit is sure.

'I drowned a man on land,' says he. 'I transformed ice.'

'You did.'

Lazarus squeezes his wrist, pleasantly, too tight. Kit knows that, for many people, the way a person touches them gives them all the indications they need of intent. He cannot tell if Lazarus' touch is gentle, kind, or if it is brusque and unaffected, but he can tell that he is noticing it, whatever kind of touch it is. Kit feels Lazarus' smile in the muscle of his neck, the lift of sinew as he speaks:

'You must learn how to do it again.'

IGNIS

PART III

'Human beings may come into existence without natural parents. That is to say, such beings grow without being developed and born by female organism; by the art of an experienced spagyricus (alchemist).'

—De Natura Rerum, vol.1., *Paracelsus*

ᔑ ᒲ ᒲ

He who has the saving water

Chapter Twenty-Five

'Here.' Lazarus reaches into a bowl and produces a large shard of grey muddy ice that he has clearly chopped out of the pond. The cold snap continues into the following week, the whole of London skidding to a halt with the frozen river. He sets it into Kit's hands. 'I intend to test your self-belief. Make water.'

'From ice?'

They are in Lazarus' bedroom in Hart House after supper. The room is bigger than Kit's, the bed not a cot but a four-poster carved beauty with dark-purple hanging curtains that Kit is strangely relieved are closed.

'Ice melts naturally. It becomes air naturally. You know both are not only feasible but inevitable. You already accelerated it in order to achieve your ends.'

'That's an interesting way to say I killed a man.'

For the last few nights, Kit's dreams of snow have been replaced by that moment, when the angler's last breath bubbled in the muddy water.

'You made a puddle and he happened to drown in it.' Lazarus' hands are as cold as the ice he holds but his words make Kit smile.

'You do not think we were seen?' he asks.

'No, but he will know we were there. I imagine the Grave Eorl will have a story to tell.' Kit nods but feels a familiar sense of enclosure, imagines Twentyman's melted face and furious words, Isherwood's eager, hungry expression. Lazarus pinches his wrist, nail digging in.

'Forget him, this is all that matters,' Lazarus commands. He steps back. 'Accelerate it again.'

He sees Lazarus is not joking, so he stands, gritty ice melting into his palms and dripping through his fingers onto his boots for hours whilst Lazarus reads letters. Kit spies the seal of the King of Scotland, thinks of Doctor Dee, praising Bonny King James' gold.

'You are still in King James' service?' Kit asks.

'Where is there more power than the crown?'

'He is only King of Scotland.'

'For now.'

This is treason. It catches Kit's breath, to talk of the death of the Queen and the throne and kingdom her cousin could inherit, if she does not bequeath it to someone else. In that case, it is to talk of war. Yet it comes so easily from Lazarus' lips, not even twenty-five years old, a Scot on foreign soil not two miles from the Tower, reading a king's letter with such concentration. Kit feels an appetent respect for the long vision of the future that he has.

'So you will go back there one day?' he asks.

'It is my home.' Lazarus tosses the letter into the fire and looks up at Kit. 'Focus, Skevy.'

Kit tries, but he cannot. If home is a place or a country, then he does not have one. He is Belgian, supposedly, though no one can tell him how, and he has been cast off from the Silver Moon and all inside her. Oddly, it irks him, that Lazarus has a home to return to. That for him, the current tumult of their lives, the bond of Instructor and Initiate is only a temporary tempest. He has a normality that will resume one day. What will happen to Kit when it does? The ice melts, but only because time passes, and when Kit is brought to Lazarus' chamber the next night, Lazarus has their Arbor Diana out on the table by the fire. Kit has not seen it since Raven's Roost, as it needs a dark, cold space to flourish. Lazarus has been keeping it in a cupboard.

'It flourishes?' Kit bends eagerly to look at it. It was only a drop of mercury and silver in a bowl before, and the diagrams in books show perfect, miniature trees, steely and shining. What he is looking at reminds him more of old pieces of coral from the deep ocean Mariner has shown him or a particularly spiky caterpillar he once ate on a dare. Kit feels a tugging inside him, that same wondrous urge he had to touch the liquid iron in the blacksmiths, and he presses a fingertip against it. Immediately, it splinters, a tendril reaching upward, seeking food or light, metal and living, all at once.

'You see?' Lazarus bends quietly beside him, tugging Kit's wrist back and replacing the glass dome over the odd, unfurling thing. 'Your touch is an echo of everything you are, how you could have been made. As you were brought to life, you give life.'

'But this is animation, this is not life.' Kit looks at the stretching tendrils.

'It is the beginning of life,' Lazarus corrects. 'If the Almighty can bring forth Christ in the virgin's womb, someone could make Kit Skevy in a jar.'

Kit laughs, but then he sees Lazarus' slightly nonplussed expression. He is serious. Kit stares back down at the Arbor Diana, still slowly twitching, mimicking life or, perhaps, if Lazarus is to be believed, starting to live. Kit is given his lump of ice and stands as he has done, trying again, but tonight all he can think of is the specimen jars at Raven's Roost. Is it possible to have such undignified origins and for it not to be a cautionary tale, a macabre death preserved for inspection, but instead, a beginning? Still, the ice turns his fingers red and chilled and his doublet soggy, but nothing happens.

On the third night, the ice is stuck with leaves and smooth on the edges. They are in Kit's tiny room in Hart House after supper. Lazarus has never been in here before and Kit is very conscious of the plate of apple cores and strewn, dirty clothes at the end of the bed, emitting the musty smell of feet.

'From the birdbath,' Lazarus says. 'The frost is waning, I think. So this is your last night with ice. Believe it, Skevy.'

'You believe it.'

'I do.' Lazarus' eyes are exactly the colour of the frozen lump of silvery brown ice in Kit's hands. 'But I am not an alchemical child; my belief is not directed towards myself, it is directed towards my Initiate.'

If he could, he thinks he would see the force of Lazarus' own will bending towards his; believe me, it whispers, believe yourself. Lazarus stokes the small fire in Kit's room and then seats himself on a stool in front of it, beginning to read Paracelsus:

'He who knows what iron is, knows the attributes of Mars, He who knows Mars knows the qualities of iron. What would become of your heart if the sun were not the centre of the universe?'

'Very little, I should think.'

'Speak less and do more,' Lazarus says. *'To grasp the invisible elements; to attract them by their material correspondences...'*

Kit stares in frustration at the ice in his hands. His own possibility is a cramped, irritating thing, no longer fearful and vast, the potential under his skin infuriating him instead of worrying him. How the fuck do I get you out? he thinks to his own, wet hands. Then, distracted, he wonders at Lazarus' hand as he holds the spine of the book, the long fingers, the dark hair on the mid digits, and how to hold this ice for so long would cause his brow to wrinkle, his jaw to tighten. For Kit it is nothing but water, like sweat is water, like the small, pinpricks of sweat upon Lazarus' brow. Sweat that would make his neck salty to taste, if Kit were to perhaps lick a tongue against it, as blood is a little salty, actually. As blood is warm.

'To control, purify and transform them by the living power of the Spirit – this is true Alchemy...'

He wonders that blood is warm whilst ice is cold; the grimy water sliding between his cupped fingers feels the same to him as the blood that flew in his eyes when he beat the angler in Southwark, the same as his own blood when it slipped down his legs in Isherwood's cellar. He cannot tell them apart, not when he closes his eyes, like now. They are the same feeling, both liquid, maybe one a little colder, but the same, as all matter is the same or interchangeable at the very least—

'Kit, Kit, look.'

He opens his eyes to see that Lazarus is scrambling up, book tumbling to the floor with a clunk, eyes wide as he stares at Kit's hands, and the ice that is melting to nothing, splashing onto the rug.

'Your fingers are hot, your palms are warm—' He grabs Kit's wet hands, turning them over, staring at the red, chilblained thumbs. 'Are you in pain?'

'What do you think?'

'Of course not!' Lazarus' laugh is so bright suddenly, so unexpected, the whoop of a child catching a ball or leaping off a bridge with friends. Kit can't help but laugh with him, because to amaze Lazarus Isherwood is a rare, shining thing. 'You did it, holy God in heaven you did it.'

Lazarus turns Kit's fingers over and kisses them, as naturally as he pounds powders and turns pages. A reverent, unwavering consumption, warm and penitent against the skin, offering his lips to every nail and knuckle in turn.

Kit cannot speak. All he finds is a stuttering breath. It might be a word: yes, now, please.

When their lips meet, Lazarus makes a tiny sound. A clicking moan, a door or gate opening somewhere out of reach. A painful sound, Kit thinks, a good kind of pain.

Clothes are quickly lost, shoes kicked off, arms tangled over one another in haste to shed collars and belts, and he's never done this before. Fucking in a stable or a cellar generally prefers as many clothes on as possible. For what else is lust but the power to bring a person helplessly to their knees so abruptly they do not care if their skirt is over their head or their breeches around their ankles? But Lazarus has him in hand now and Kit does not have words for this catastrophe of wanting. A destruction, perhaps, to be devoured or ruined or ruinous. To take this person, inch by inch, finger and wrist and shoulder and toe, to be tasted and known and mindless, but how to ask for what is needed to sate him?

'Laz, Silver.' Lazarus is fighting to release himself from his hose, bunched around his knees as he puts one pale foot on the excess fabric, trapping it to the sheets, in order to spring the other free. If he asks, Kit will fight his way back to control, but he needs to be told. 'Tell me to be gentle.'

Lazarus presses lips and tongue to the brand on Kit's cheek, his words a whisper that slides from skin to ear.

'No,' says he.

After, Kit lies on his side whilst Lazarus draws lazy constellations in his freckles. He stares at the puddle still on the floor and thinks, did that truly happen? Then his mind moves to Lazarus, to the mirror, to Mariner and Raven's Roost and the cellar. Are all things capable of such fast and astonishing change?

'*Cepheus.*' Lazarus' finger presses at the top of Kit's spine. 'The King constellation.'

'Mariner thinks you will fuck me and use me and chew me up

244

and spit me out,' Kit says. Lazarus' finger pauses in its track. 'That I will be Griffin to your Marlowe.'

Lazarus resumes slowly. Outside the rain has begun again, becoming the loud clatter of sleet. Kit imagines it, far away in the sky, hard bullets of snow that tumble to earth and by the time they reach it, are nothing but rain in mud.

'Surely you would be Marlowe. You know more poetry than me. *Eridanus*. The river.'

'You have more power,' says Kit.

'I did not transform ice with my hands.'

'You have more power over me.' Lazarus' finger moves to the top of Kit's right shoulder and then stops. 'Than I have. Over you.'

He knows Lazarus can feel the beat of his heart, its slow increase in speed. For though there may be watching eyes beyond the window and somewhere in the city there is a man who would like him butchered for ingredients, these facts cannot crawl under their door and into their bed tonight. Let Twentyman tell whatever tales he likes. He may not have Mariner or Squire Kay or Ezra or a home in Southwark anymore but perhaps this is something worth keeping.

'I do not,' says Lazarus. 'My heart, your sun, Skevy.'

Kit pulls Lazarus' hand around his body, close to his chest. He has always liked being held this way. Mariner sometimes finds it sticky, she complains of the heat and the sweat – Kit, by God, you are like a forge on a hot day! – but he has always enjoyed the heaviness of a leg tossed over his, being held in place. It is quite a force, to be designated the centre of someone's universe, the destruction and life around which they orbit, but he likes the burden of this, too. The curled pressure of another pair of legs against his. Another ribcage, another beating heart.

$$\mathcal{LV\bar{d}\!\!\not z\bar{J}\bar{d}\bar{J}}$$

She who is half darkness

Chapter Twenty-Six

'Ah, Matthew, this is Captain Larkin, she is handling some of my nautical affairs.' Elody sounds irritated to be interrupted, though Mariner was sent to St Paul's for ink for her sake. The city outside the Lime Street ward has become an even more hostile place to walk with dark skin. Some booksellers threw her dirty looks, some beggar children threw rocks. Filthy Spaniard, they shout, pebbles and insults catching the edge of her cloak as she pulls it close around her. Now, returned to Lime Street with shaking hands and her hard-won goods, Elody is busy entertaining yet another guest. The person turns to face her and Mariner stares. Skirts over her legs, a doublet over her chest with a knitted shawl protecting her and a felt sailor's cap, which her hair, long and honey coloured, is braided away under.

'A pleasure, Master Blackwater,' the Captain says, and she doffs her cap rather than curtseys. There is an amused creasing around her flat mouth and blue eyes as Mariner simply stares back.

'Matthew,' Elody prompts, her voice sharp.

'Aye, a pleasure too, Captain Larkin,' Mariner stammers out, taking off her own cap and holding it to her chest as she bows, just as she was taught to do for the quarter master.

'Ah, you have a sailor's heart then.' Captain Larkin laughs with a musical, Irish lilt and Mariner knows she has done wrong. That is not how a lordly young man of court receives those in service to him.

'Forgive my cousin, he has quite a romance with all things nautical,' Elody says, rolling up a map on her desk. 'Matthew, let the Captain be on her way.'

Mariner watches the Captain sweep the felt cap off her head in a farewell and tries to find her voice.

'Your vessel, Captain?' she asks. 'Its name?'

The Captain looks at her as if she is a callow youth and Mariner can feel Elody's displeasure, but Mariner has to know.

'*The Seahorse*, we are at Billingsgate,' she says. 'Farewell.'

Then she is gone.

'My ink,' Elody says. Mariner dazedly steps forward and sets it on the desk but turns to listen to the sound of the front door closing. *The Seahorse*, at Billingsgate, she thinks.

'Gentlemen are rarely sailors,' says Elody. Mariner knows it is a warning, that the cracks in her façade are splitting open with her blatant hunger, but she does not care. Captain Larkin is a mirage, a miracle, and she cannot let it slip through her fingers so soon.

*

Mariner generally tries to avoid Billingsgate. The London dock is filled with the great tall ships bringing lumber and wool and cotton and wine in from Denmark and Spain and the Indies, but also stuffed to the gills with sailors. Mariner always worries about seeing someone she sailed with, but nevertheless, three days later, she finds herself walking the dock, staring at the painted names and dodging sailors, searching for *The Seahorse*. She knows she looks out of place, a young lordly gentleman out for a stroll when he should be comfortably tucked away in the city, but then she hears a familiar voice.

'Master Blackwater!'

Captain Larkin is standing by a gangplank lank as barrels are rolled off a vessel. She looks much the same as she did three days ago, wrapped in a warm cloak and hair tidily tucked away. She raises a hand in greeting.

'Does your cousin have a message for me?'

'No.' Mariner stares up at the ship. She is not like *The Golden Hinde* with her blackened pitch hull, her red-and golden-painted decor, the Tudor roses carved into the stern. *The Seahorse* is a plain dark-wooded Caravel, the paint of her name flaking, but she is beautiful. 'What man has the ownership of her?'

'None,' Captain Larkin says, smiling as if Mariner is simple.

'But you are a woman?' Mariner's voice becomes desperate. 'It is not a costume?'

'If so, a good one!' Captain Larkin laughs. 'Your cousin Blackwater buys a flock of sheep, a new house, my time, no one asks if she is a woman.'

'She does not herd the sheep nor build the house nor plot a course to the Azures.' Mariner's hands are shaking and she wraps her cloak around her shoulders, against stinging wind and the heavy sky threatening snow. 'Are you a piratess? Like the ones from the Indies?'

'I sailed under one. Grace O' Malley. Fought the English for her. A good lady.'

Mariner has no presence of mind to consider that a young English gentleman would take this as fair warning not to probe the Irish sea captain but Mariner has lost the thread of Matthew Blackwater, for the first time in months. She is Mariner Elgin of *The Golden Riall* and *The Foresight*, she is a sailor and a woman again and she has to know.

'I don't understand, who let you do this? Who gave a woman a commission?'

'I need no commission, like your cousin I have my funds and how I spend them is my choosing.' Captain Larkin looks up at *The Seahorse* with a deep tenderness that Mariner feels burrowing through her, from her throat to the soles of her feet. 'That I bought a vessel and hired men with mine is my own business.'

Mariner tries to speak but words are impossible. Money, she thinks, this is what money can buy a woman. True and complete freedom.

'Will I show you aboard?' Captain Larkin jerks her head. 'You look like a lad who would enjoy the view.'

Mariner shakes her head, not daring herself to speak, terrified that if she steps foot aboard something inside her will break entirely. She will strap herself to the mast, Odysseus before the siren, and die there, happily.

'Then I hope I have satisfied your curiosity, Master Blackwater.' Captain Larkin tips her hat. 'Good day to you.'

'Wait.' Mariner cannot stop herself from grabbing Captain Larkin's sleeve as she tries to move away. In a flash, her wrist is clamped over with Captain Larkin's other hand, squeezing painfully tight, a warning to let go but Mariner can't not yet. Her chest is heaving with the effort of forcing out the words. 'Are you not afraid?'

'Of you?' Captain Larkin raises a sceptical eyebrow. Mariner shakes her head, tries to force her questions past her lips but they will not come: are you not afraid to be caught? Are you not afraid to be shamed? Are you not afraid of what will happen to you if you step so far away from the feminine role intended by God?

'Are you not afraid?' she repeats. The Captain's long, assessing glare has all the severity of the hard-eyed preacher. Mariner guesses she has used it to send many men squealing and bumbling backwards, spitting apologies, but Mariner will not be cowed. She has to know. Then the Captain slowly lifts their cumbrous bundle of hands and wrists towards her face. For a second the breeze stills and Mariner thinks the Captain is going to kiss the back of her hand, but instead, she feels the nip of sharp, angry teeth and a slobbery lick, like a dog. She lets go of the Captain's wrist with a hiss of surprise.

'Set that against your fear, Master Blackwater, I am of a rougher breed than you think.' The Captain laughs, rubbing the back of her hand against her mouth. 'I'll take good care of you and your cousin, when time comes.'

Captain Larkin climbs aboard and Mariner watches her go. There is a woman, commanding a ship, who can set her blue eyes to the horizon and feel salt against her cheeks and go anywhere and Mariner is no one. She is less than no one to be noticed, she has become Matthew Blackwater, his skin grows over her own and there is no horizon in sight. Envy and desperation are so heavy in her stomach she wonders if she will turn and vomit into the harbour. She walks numbly away, the songs of sailors and melodies of gulls pulling memories of Elgin quoting his favourite scripture to her mind: *For what thing is your life? It is even a vapour that appeareth for a little time and vanisheth away.* I am vanishing, Mariner thinks. She is an amorphous indent of shadow, eyeless and faceless. She does not know how to get herself back.

'What if we married?' Mariner whispers that night as she lies in bed, untouched beside Elody. 'Many ladies marry their cousins, even Queens do it. Then we could be together.'

'We are together.' Elody does not even roll over to look at her. 'If we were married my estate would be yours.'

'But if I had it, it would be yours, and maybe they would watch less if you were married.'

The death threat in her pocket is greying, the creases cut deep. She thinks of the shouts of 'Spanish fucker' called out to her on the streets of London, of the sidelong glances and gossip of court around Elody that follow them still. If she is married to Elody, she will be an English Lord and Elody will no longer be a woman alone. There is safety in those lies.

'Lord Isherwood will always be watching and if I married again, the court would watch more. They will expect heirs. I will not endure it again, the years of sliding looks, the comments on my womb and its contents. You are young and virile; they would call me barren.' Elody's voice is threaded with such bitterness that it shimmers. Mariner imagines it floating above their heads, silver embroidering the damask bed curtains.

'If we were married, I could serve you better as your husband,' Mariner whispers. 'Handle your business.'

'What do you know of business?'

'Sea ports. Sailing. Your business with Captain Larkin.'

It is such a deep longing now; if she were hung drawn and quartered it would be baked into every part of her, visible like rings on a tree. The open water, the chance to feel the rocking deck beneath her feet. Perhaps there is a way to be both Matthew Blackwater and be happy. Elody kisses Mariner's neck, breathing in deeply.

'What would be the point of sending my love away?' Her whispers make Mariner's skin pucker. 'As it will not make us safer, what need have we of matrimony?'

Mariner doesn't answer. She doesn't say she needs it because it would make her happy, because she is not sure that happiness should feel this fraught, but she does need the lie to be sealed. Lady Blackwater would have a husband and he could not be so lightly tossed aside. She will inhabit his skin, she will live in his life until she believes it more than the bible and maybe she could sail and maybe, just maybe, it would be enough. But Matthew Blackwater is no sailor and she surrenders to Elody's kisses, responds frantically, hoping her own passion will rise up and drown out her doubts. Still she dreams of open oceans and golden-braided hair and a lilting Irish laugh. When she wakes, gasping, not from nightmares but full of longing, she wishes it was Kit's arms she was folding back into. That they were in their little stable room under their cold stars and she could mumble her dreams without shame. But Kit is tucked away with Lazarus night after night, the two of them laughing and sharing a bed once more and his cruellest words cut her, over and over: you are her Daisy, that is all. So instead, she finds herself wishing not for him but for the past; for Mariner Elgin of Southwark, who would have robbed Matthew Blackwater for all he had.

The next day, Mariner thinks her wishes have gone awry when Pyncher tells her, face unusually disgusted, that she has a caller in the hall. Daisy is standing there, gazing at a portrait of Elody and Lord Blackwater. She looks so out of place, her best dress so tatty and too obviously revealing, and her blonde hair so uncombed and ragged down her back.

'Jesus Christ,' Daisy blurts out, looking up as Mariner enters, her eyes wide. 'Sailor—'

'How good to see you,' she says quickly, seizing Daisy's hand and pulling her into the study. 'I am Matthew Blackwater, Lady Elody's cousin.'

'Matthew Blackwater,' Daisy repeats. Mariner nods and leans against the door, palms flat, as Daisy looks her slowly up and down. Mariner can feel every inch of the expensive, dark-purple fabric that has become so normal to her, the gilded feather in her cap. 'Well, Matthew. I see I was right.'

Daisy's bitter smile is knowing; at least victorious in this, that Mariner did forget her, mostly, just as she promised to do. When she tries to test the range of her feelings for Daisy, it is like poking a bruise through a thick cloak. She knows there should be more pain, but she cannot quite feel it.

'Why have you come?' she asks.

Daisy's eyes fill with glistening tears. She always was a beautiful weeper.

'I heard you are alchemists now. Will says Kit is. His face, it's been horrible to heal.' Daisy shakes her head. 'He says he'd kill Kit Skevy for ambushing him like that if he didn't have such a powerful Mistress.'

Mariner can infer that Kit has gone to Southwark, like a fucking idiot, and had a brawl with Twentyman. She opens her mouth but she doesn't want to ask, doesn't want to admit to Daisy how far apart she has drifted from her closest friend. There is a tug, deep inside her, a sea anchor weighing down her soul: the loss of Kit in her life. She swallows hard, tries to hide it by folding her arms and nodding thoughtfully.

'I doubt Kit will give cures for Twentyman,' she says.

'It's not for Will.'

Daisy's hand drifts unconsciously to her stomach. Mariner sees the hint of the bump there, the way that the bodice of Daisy's gowns always flowed flat from her stomacher, but now her roundness is showing, a shelf on which her skirts sit. There is a tedious weariness to this realisation – how many other women has she seen this happen to? – yet this is different; a vinegary satisfaction barely distinguishable from spiteful disappointment.

'You're with child.'

'And I cannot be. If I go to the Cunning Woman Mother Plenty uses, he'll find out, he'll beat me dead for it, but I cannot have his child.' Daisy's eyes are a sparkling, watery blue. 'He'll not want me anymore and he'll have the babe for an urchin. I'll be nothing or worse…'

Mariner does not say it is not true. The Grave Eorl has homegrown many bastard thieves in the city. The women who bear them often don't last a year, destitute and impoverished, no longer fit for work at the Hat, which prides itself on selling the youngest, tightest flesh south of the river. Other stews pay pittance, not enough to feed two hungry mouths.

'It is dangerous,' Mariner says, hating how cold her own voice has become. In her mind, she hears Lady Catherine's ungodly, bovine roar. 'It can be deadly.'

'I don't care!' Those familiar blue eyes are the most panicked Mariner has ever seen. 'Please help me, please, he'll kill me either way.'

Daisy grips the fabric across her stomach as if she wishes she could wrench out what grows there. It's that digging in of her fingernails, so firm and desperate, that cracks something open inside of Mariner. She turns away from the tears, moving behind Elody's desk to the drawer where the walnut box sits. What is the point of living under *Venefica's* shadow if she cannot do this? She lifts the box up, holding it carefully, just as the door opens.

'Excuse me, I did not know we had visitors.'

Mariner's ribs tighten with the feeling of being caught, intention obvious, as Elody stands in the doorway, looking every inch the courtier. Mariner does not believe she did not know. Pyncher has clearly told her.

'Milady,' Daisy mumbles, dropping into a terrible curtsey. Mariner cringes at Daisy's clumsiness, her common voice and terrified, deferential eyes.

'Cousin, this is Daisy,' Mariner says.

'You are welcome to our home,' Elody says, and Daisy blushes. Mariner suddenly sees her through Daisy's eyes, as rich and fine as imported Spanish purple satin, smooth and unblemished and gentle. She wonders when exactly she stopped being able to see Elody this way. She cannot call it back, the same pure admiration she had when first they met, too bemired now by other things.

'Daisy, can you wait outside?' Mariner asks. Daisy nods obediently, eyes fixed on Elody's golden skirt hem as she backs out. Mariner stares at Elody, who folds her arms and leans against the door. Despite the casual posture, Mariner sees the slight, furious pursing of her bottom lip.

'Daisy,' Elody repeats slowly. 'Pretty girl.'

'She needs help.' Mariner sets a hand on the walnut box, the implied contents inside. Elody raises her eyebrows.

'There are Cunning Women she can go to south of the river for cures. Let her seek their remedies. Mine are expensive.'

'Please, I am only asking for this just once. For my friend, a childhood friend, someone who matters to me. I have kept all of your secrets; I just ask for you to keep this one of mine.' Mariner is surprised by how much she can feel her heart in her throat, a moment of simple theft turned into a test of affection. 'If you love me. Please.'

Mariner breathes heavily. Love me, she finds herself chanting wildly inside her mind. Love me as I need to be loved, love me enough to make it all worth it. Elody stares at her and then moves forward, cupping Mariner's face, pressing her thumbs too hard under the hinge of Mariner's jaw.

'*If* I love you,' she says. 'You are a liar.'

'What?' Mariner is baffled, chest tight for air.

'When you came to me you said there was no girl,' Elody's voice has become a low hiss against her lips. 'Do not deny it, the eyes you have for her. Like you wish she would do this.'

Her kiss is ravenous, a shipwreck. The pressure of her thumbs increases against Mariner's soft windpipe; a caught, squashed swallow.

'Did you love her?' Elody demands.

'No.' Mariner tries to shake her head, but Elody's grip is too strong. 'I admired her, yes, but she never wanted me, never saw me as you do, it is only you. I only love you.'

There is blood on her bottom lip from the ferocity of Elody's kiss but it does not hurt her; it is a balm. How she loves me, Mariner thinks, her mind ablaze with it. Enough to be jealous, enough to want to keep me, it must be enough. Elody kisses her again, sucks the blood from her, and though Mariner can barely breathe, she doesn't want it to stop.

'The blue bottle with the opal set in the stopper.'

Suddenly, the pressure is off her neck, Elody is walking away from her, and Mariner is a jumble of airy relief and the sharp sting of rejection. She does not know whether to be grateful she has not been struck or desolate she is being left. Here they come, the creeping doubts that start to wriggle back in whenever they are not touching.

'Thank you.'

Elody pauses at the door, her fingers drumming an impatient beat on the wood.

'It is no crime until she is quickened, for there is no soul.' Elody's jaw is rigid, pushing her chin pointedly forward. 'Do not ask if she has quickened.'

It is such a kindness, an unexpected way to save her conscience from the worst of it, that Mariner's feet are numb with gratitude. She blinks furiously against the sting in her eyelids. Being loved by

Elody is a tumultuous thing and, right now, Mariner has a flash of a traitorous thought: I am not sure I will survive it.

She sends Daisy on her way with the glass bottle tucked inside her palm and puts herself to bed for the next two days. Pulling the blankets up over her head helps her hide from her sin, from the watchful many eyes of God above. Elody tells everyone in the household it is merely the change in the weather, bringing her dear cousin low. She certainly feels brought low, pressed low by shame, and when the blankets no longer seem like enough protection from the eternal reproach, she takes refuge under the bed itself, slotting herself neatly between the dusty boards with their mouse droppings and the slats above her. Not quickened, she tells herself. No soul.

'Get up,' Elody says on the third day. She reaches under the bed like a snake charmer and pulls Mariner out by her bare ankle. 'Your whore is dead.'

Mariner sits in a pile of limbs, her cold feet rucked up against the rug on the floor and burns under the sting of heaven's glare. She imagines Daisy like Lady Catherine, drinking down the medicine, bleeding and screaming and beastly groaning but with no one to cling to, no one to burn her clothes. She begins to shake.

'I killed her,' Mariner whispers.

'Yes, you did.' Elody throws an embroidered cushion at her, the firm nobbles of French knotted roses catching her eyelid, making it sting. 'She died instantly, they found the bottle in her hand! It's all over Southwark that there's a poisoner on the loose, that a Cunning Woman has gone too far. The constables are rounding some of them up on the Long Southwark road. I told you to give her the blue opal bottle.'

'No, you told me the blue bottle with the opal!' Mariner wonders if hearts can shrink with shame. Hers certainly is, the back of her neck sweating, the fires of damnation warming her, just out of sight. She clutches the little pillow to her chest as panic rises, wanting it not to be true, and with it come useless prayers: God, let it not be true. 'Why did you not tell me there were two opal bottles?'

'I thought you could follow instruction!' Elody grips both of her hands across the back of her own neck, elbows wide, revealing the dark stain of her underarms to the ceiling as she looks up, taking in a deep breath of frustration. Mariner waits, looks tentatively around at what else might be thrown. Then Elody sighs, huffing air out of her nose. 'Well, she is dead. At least she can tell no one.'

The cruelty of these words washes over Mariner until the simple rolling force of them gently pushes her back under the bed. She lies in the darkness and lets the tears come, silent and pooling in the shells of her ears. She remembers the first time she met Daisy, how the wind whipped her wispy blonde hair across her face, catching in the perfect corner of her rosy lips. My name is Daisy Gale, she had said, and Mariner had thought it was the most perfect name for this tempest of a girl, whirling through her life with a smile. Mariner's chest feels as if it will cave in and she cannot stop the sobs. She tries to eat the noise of them, bites her lips raw, stuffs the firm stitched corner of the pillow into her mouth but it is no good. Her mouth is stretched wide, her eyes tightly closed, her tears dampening her hair and drowning her.

'I am sure I told you it was the blue opal bottle,' Elody says, over the sound. Mariner rolls on her side, wishing that Elody would crawl under the bed with her, lie by her side and give her a breast and a ribcage to scream into, scream for Daisy Gale who will now never be forgotten. Elody stands in the same spot, unmoved. So Mariner stares at her shoes through her tears, a finely embroidered pair with an Edenic scene stitched on them: Adam, Eve, the apple, the first sin. No, you did not, Mariner thinks, too afraid to pray. God help me, you did not.

ⵛⵍⴻⵅⴰⵏⴻⵛ

He who slays

Chapter Twenty-Seven

'Who will be there?' Kit asks as he pulls one of Lazarus' embroidered shirts over his head in his bed on the morning of their demonstration at Richmond Palace. October is waning, the cold snap is over and the river flowing with an icy breeze, and today, Kit will go to court.

'Privy Councillors, all manner of illustrious men.' Lazarus bends and presses a kiss to Kit's pale inner thigh. 'All that matters is that Cecil is there.'

Lazarus has explained that the Lord High Treasurer and Secretary of State, Lord Burghley, is old and ailing, so his ambitious son, the acting Secretary and leader of the Privy council, will be the one they must impress. Kit feels no trepidation at the prospect. For the first time since their return, he no longer glances out of the windows of Hart House, fearfully watching for an Isherwood coat of arms. Trusting Lazarus is the sturdiest armour, turning all blades of worry. Occasionally, deep in the slumber of the night, he awakes and hears Mariner's cruel words again – He will fuck you and use you, he will chew you up and spit you out – but Lazarus is there, a heavy arm in the dark, wrapped around him, drawing him back into the safety of his orbit.

'But still, we will be cautious. You are the apprentice, you need speak to no one,' Lazarus says, leaning naked against the pillows, watching Kit dress with lazy appreciation. 'We will show only what has been asked for.'

Kit understands. For the last week, he and Lazarus have been testing the limits of his transformative abilities of the four base elements. So far, he can only accelerate the melting of ice. He cannot seem to evaporate anything into gas and transmutation of earth seems unfeasible. No matter how much Lazarus tells him that all materials are much like one another on the basest levels, he cannot force himself to believe it is therefore possible for him to squeeze a lump of coal into a diamond. Fire, too, is elusive and troublesome. Whilst formulas made for flames of different colours always flourish under his touch, to keep flame burning in his hand with nothing but will and a belief it should be possible is a task too high.

'The fastest Arbor Diana,' he says. The formula they have developed allows it to bud and bloom in as little as thirty minutes. It involves a surreptitious touch from Kit, but it will do it. 'The flame that doesn't burn the wood. Though what military applications that has are beyond me, it will burn no ships.'

'It is not about equipping an army, just saying we could—' Lazarus' hand grabs his, kisses Kit's fingertips with that same soft veneration that shoots desire into Kit's belly '—for then the crown will give Lady Blackwater what she needs to fund her work.'

'To fund our fun,' says Kit.

'To fund your vigorous education,' Lazarus responds, pulling him down onto the sheets with that rare, golden laugh.

*

'So this is Richmond Palace.' Kit looks up at the white brick, the twisting towers and pointed cupolas with their gilded crosses and flying flags as they walk inside. 'Could be bigger.'

Lazarus throws him an annoyed look, but his eyes are humorous. Lady Blackwater is wrapped up in sables, close to the skin, to protect her from the stiff breeze off the river. Mariner is draped in them too, looking very lordly, and made more so by the potently sombre expression on her face. The news of Daisy's death is only a few days old but Mariner has settled into grief as well as a husband of a fifty-year marriage and he does not quite understand the nature of her melancholy. After all, Daisy Gale of the Silver Moon only ever knocked her back. Mariner has a lover living, a woman so compelling that she would eagerly bury her friendship with Kit. Yet as they walk inside, Kit senses Mariner's stiffness, her darting eyes. He had expected to see joviality at the heart of court; laughter, lavish men in buckled shoes prancing and showing their calves to twirling ladies with ropes of diamond in their cleavages. As they walk through vast wood-panelled rooms that smell of sweat and rosewater, the faces are fidgety and anxious. He sees how glances follow Mariner, how brows furrow, how lips turn to sneer and voices to gossip. He looks at Lazarus, questioning.

'Spain,' Lazarus speaks under their footsteps. 'The ships of the Spanish Armada have been spotted off Scilly. Lord Burghley commands all gentlemen back to their houses to rouse their tenants. Particularly those with coastal seats.'

'Truly? A land defence?'

No wonder they're all looking at Mariner like she's about to take a pike to them. He feels a swell of offence on Mariner's behalf before he remembers it is no longer his business to come to Mariner's defence. That is Lady Blackwater's job now.

They are taken up to the quarters away from the royal household where the Privy Councillors can have a quiet, discreet meeting. Kit is left alone to unpack the crate on the long table and light the brazier with small faggots from the fire, the perfect servant and apprentice, whilst Lady Blackwater, Lazarus and Mariner perform the part of courtiers in the room beyond. Kit hears the door open and expects it to be Lazarus, coming to check on him.

'Nearly done,' Kit says.

'Blessed of Hermes. Here you are.'

It is strange to see Lord Isherwood in the true light of day, no longer lit by candles. He is shorter than he seemed, hung from the ceiling, Kit can see how his pillowy eyes sag, that his hairline seems more receded. Yet the voice, it takes him quickly back to that dank, dark place. Every hair on his body rises. He knows his instinct should be to run, but with all the gold around him, the beautiful jewels of stained glass, politeness is being imposed from the brocade and carved wood.

'We were not expecting you, my Lord.' He tries to concentrate on watching the brazier burn but there is a faint ringing in his ears.

'I think you will find we were.' Lord Isherwood closes the door behind him. Kit hears the horrifying creak of the cellar's metal lock. 'I am told you are well.'

Kit knows the implications of those words, that Lord Isherwood wants him to believe Lazarus is speaking about him, betraying him, but Kit pushes that feeling away. He watches closely as the man steps forward, curiously perusing the items at the other end of the workbench, his hands clasped behind his back in the same way he would intone the gospels. Kit gently moves his fingers from the brazier to rest lightly against the bottle of aqua vitae. They use it for their blue fire, but Lazarus tells him it stings when thrown in the face. Isherwood gives him an interested look, eyes flickering to the bottle. Let him think it is acid and will slide his brows off.

'I am not hanging from the ceiling now,' Kit says.

'No, you are flourishing, by all accounts.' Kit imagines the report from Doctor Dee, the furious testament of Will Twentyman. Seemingly neither have deterred Lord Ishwerwood, who tilts his head slightly to one side, examining Kit from all angles, with the look of a man buying a diamond, or a horse. 'I am not surprised. You are both precious and holy. Your blood has proven to be a powerful, an astonishing ingredient.'

'If left corked it will be better in a year,' Kit says but his words, his jokes, they have never meant anything to this man. Kit glances urgently at the door. It cannot be locked. Did no one see him come in, did not Lazarus?

'Now you know more of our art, would you not consider how you could serve greatness?' He is still sliding slowly towards Kit along the length of the table. 'If you came back to Isherwood House. With me.'

Kit wishes it was acid in the bottle. He imagines the egoistic, expectant face bubbling and curdling like Twentyman's did; eyes popping, mouth drooling.

'I have all I need at Hart House.'

'Lazarus cannot teach you, cannot serve you as I can.'

Kit smiles. Some things are better than a splash of acid to the face.

'Oh Lazarus serves me very well,' he says. 'On his knees, mainly.'

The fury boils in Isherwood's eyes; the sorrow and resentment of a father scorned.

'You have the mind of a whore. My son serves only his country, he serves only me!' Isherwood seizes Kit's collar, shaking him, his other fist smashing Kit's hand with the vial into the bench. It cracks, it leaks against Kit's hand and though he knows his nostrils should be full of the vigorous scent of alcohol, all Kit can smell is damp straw. The wooden carvings of pomegranates above him are turning into a cellar ceiling. He wants to pull back, but how can he, feet manacled as they are? He struggles, his elbow catches the twisted metal stem of the brazier, spilling the burning coals inside it over the table with a crash.

'Kit!'

He's aware of Lazarus' voice but the crumbled, smouldering faggots meet the spilled aqua vitae and it alights, blue and roaring, just as they planned to demonstrate. It forces Isherwood back from the table with a curse, but the flame is fast, and Kit's hands are drenched. Blue fire chases his fingertips, meets his flesh, and there it is, running up and down his thumb, his first finger, his second, third and fourth and he knows it will continue to climb if he does not stop it, so Kit begins to think, panicking, of all he has learned about himself – I am flame, I am flesh, this fire is mine and in my blood, cease, come back to me, dammit – but it does nothing, only that the tips of the flames seem to be evaporating upwards into a spiralling wind. He had thought he could not do it, but here he is, turning flame to air somehow, and Isherwood looks as shocked as he feels. There is a roaring inside of him, that same gruelling pressing clamouring through his bones and the glowing faggots are whipped up in sparks; fluttering in small twisting hurricanes and if he cannot stop it soon, he might not stand. Then Lazarus is in front of him, throwing the edge of his cloak over Kit's flaming hand, the air full of the stink of burnt flesh, crisp and meaty. Kit can breathe again, staggering against Lazarus with relief. The expression on Lord Isherwood's face is turning from hateful to awed.

'Look at you.' His eyes move from Kit to his son, deep venom settling in the bow of his lips. 'You knew.'

'Cecil is on his way.' Lazarus pats damask against Kit's hands with a pinched expression, checking as the smoke disseminates.

'Yes, we might all do well to remember it.' Lady Blackwater is standing in the doorway with Mariner, Pyncher behind them, with glasses of wine on a platter. Mariner's face is a picture of astonishment, Lady Blackwater's is unreadable as she stares at the secrets they have kept from her. Kit can't stop his burnt fingers curling tightly around Lazarus' fingers through the cloak. Do we need to run? He wonders and surprises himself with how quickly he will go anywhere Lazarus tells him to if necessary. Her eyes are moving to the door. 'Please tidy up, Master Skevy. Matthew, get Lord Isherwood a glass of wine. He has clear need of it.'

It is her quick assertion of normality onto the situation, a lute player striking up a tune for a dance, that forces Kit into control of his heavy feet. Mariner is picking up a glass of wine to offer to Lord Isherwood, Kit is setting the brazier back, thoughtlessly scooping still smouldering charcoal off the table and into his hands until Lazarus knocks it away, stamping it into smoke under his shoes.

'Do not.' Lazarus jerks the burnt hand towards him, voice low, using his body to block the gesture from the Privy Councillors behind him, filling the room with their bored expressions and the rosy scent of their perfumed hair. Lord Isherwood is sipping a glass of wine but has not moved away, his finger thoughtfully tracing through the ashy remains on the tabletop. 'You will not feel it, Kit, I have to check it—'

'We are about to begin.' Kit closes his eyes sharply and forces them open again. He will not collapse or give in to the exhaustion seeping out of his bones. 'She will hate us more if we—'

'It feels no pain?' Lord Isherwood is close again, lips stained bloody. Lazarus twitches but does not look at his father. 'Lazarus, does it speak true? Does it sweat? Does it freeze?'

'Now, gentlemen, we must let Master Skevy finish his preparations, he has much to do.' Lady Blackwater steps elegantly forward, sliding her hand into Lord Isherwood's sleeve and smiling, all sweetness and ease.

'You speak false, Lazarus, it screamed! Over and over, it cannot be... I have never seen another, not one other, in all this time.' Isherwood's voice is becoming odd, his face is flushing deeply as he stares at Kit's hand. Remarkably, he grips Lady Blackwater tightly. 'Ella, did you know?'

The name is so paternal, so delicate, that Kit expects Lady Blackwater to change under it, to suddenly look more girlish, but her expression is a placid mask. Kit looks at Lazarus, searching for knowledge, but there's nothing. Just Lazarus' hand on Kit's burnt wrist and his eyes upon his father.

'You seem passionate, Lord Isherwood,' Lady Blackwater says. 'Come and stand with me, Lazarus will present our findings. I am sure you will be most intrigued.'

The door opens and a man walks in, the waters parting for him. It must be Sir Robert Cecil. He is dressed as a clerk, all black, but the finest lace and silk. He does not speak, but stands, arms folded, and nods at Lady Blackwater, who speaks.

'My Lord Privy Councillors, I hope you will appreciate what the alchemists of London bring you today: a demonstration of the true development of our art, worthy of the input of Her Majesty's treasury, for the betterment of England.'

She nods at Lazarus as the audience clap politely and Kit lurches familiarly at the sound. Here is the stage, he is simply in the wings, making the magic happen. He can do that, he can ignore the way Lord Isherwood's eyes fix upon him, mouthing something unintelligible. This is just a show.

They who know the secrets of truth

Chapter Twenty-Eight

'Did you know?' Elody hisses at Mariner, as Lazarus begins his presentation to the Privy Councillors. He speaks very eloquently, but Mariner hears none of it, unable to take her eyes from Kit.

'Know what?' Mariner whispers back. Elody nods to Kit significantly. On her other side, Lord Isherwood seems to have been so overwhelmed by Kit's staggering display he is shaking, Elody holding him steady in a show of daughterly care that Mariner does not know what to do with. Mariner shakes her head.

'Did you not know?' she asks. Elody doesn't answer. The way she looks at Lazarus Isherwood, the man who clearly did know, will be construed by those around them as merely interested, but Mariner remembers this look. It was the look Elody had on her face the night of Lady Catherine's terrible abortion. Calculating and savage, the eyes of a dragon hoarding secrets and preparing to spit fire to defend them.

'Whilst the Arbor Diana can bloom in forty days under any alchemical means, ours can bloom in a mere twenty minutes—' Lazarus says. Mariner keeps her eyes on Kit's burnt hands, watching the silver creation, as lumpy and strange as coral from the ocean floor, spread its roots. How much of it has come from his touch? Kit does not look up at her, but why would he? She called him hell bound and here he is, capable of making fire whip up like Elijah on Mount Carmel. Mariner's favourite bible stories were always the ones with ships in. Jonah and the whale, Paul and his voyages, those astonished fishermen turned disciples. Elgin, however, favoured stories of the transformative flame of God, perhaps because he needed to imagine that those they had lost to the burning ship and the deep water would be transformed too. Mariner looks at her best friend, the person once dearest to her heart and thinks: How can I not know what you have become?

'*Verveloekt huit!*' Lord Isherwood blurts out, his words garbled. He is staggering towards the table, the other Privy Councillors looking between him and Lazarus as if this is all part of the demonstration. '*Verveloekt, infans solaris—*'

He drops his glass of wine with a loud clang, splattering dark liquid over the floor. He is looking for something to hold him up, staggering, grasping Kit's shoulder. Kit is paler under his freckles than usual, Mariner wonders wildly if something about this wicked process is hurting him, feels a cramp of terrible worry that perhaps she has misjudged the association between him and Lazarus. Is Lazarus much more like his father than she measured? Is he causing Kit pain somehow with these majestic feats of inexplicable alchemy? Kit is stumbling, unable to hold the man up.

'Lord Isherwood is clearly unwell. Cousin, if you would be so kind as to help the apprentice see to him? Please carry on, Lazarus,' Elody says, and she pushes Mariner forward to help. Kit is slumped to his knees, Lord Isherwood draped across him like a pieta.

'Did you do something?' Mariner whispers frantically to him as

Lazarus talks above them. Kit throws her a disgusted, vehement look.

'Only you would look at him attacking me and think I did something,' he mutters, but now Lord Isherwood is thrashing, rattling the table and all of the instruments in a musical cacophony as his body convulses. Mariner throws herself across him, terrified the shaking will bring the shelves of carefully stacked acids and other toxins down on top of them. Then, blessedly, the body stops moving. Relief, followed quickly by terrible panic. She's aware that Lazarus has stopped speaking, that there is a chorus of lusty caterwauling around them. Privy Councillors calling for physicians, for surgeons, and then Lazarus is swooping down to set his ear to his father's chest, brows furrowed. He slaps the sallow cheeks softly, then firmly.

'He has been poisoned!' someone calls out. 'Send extra guards to the royal quarters!'

There is the sound of running footsteps, doors opening, male voices shouting, so many men, and Mariner is struck for the first time by the sensation of court shrinking around her. There are so many rooms, so many doors, so many guards between them and the river now, they are in the heart of it, right in the centre, with a dead man.

'Fetch bellows!' Lazarus shouts, and they are brought. Kit opens Isherwood's lips as Lazarus sets the sooty nozzle between his teeth and pumps. A pale, grey drizzling foam leaks out of the dead man's mouth. Lazarus stops and sets the bellows aside. If he grieves his father he does not show it. Kit is reaching for the goblet under the table, sniffing it suspiciously, his eyes widening.

'Almonds,' he says.

'Quiet, Kit.'

Lazarus' words are so soft Mariner almost doesn't hear them, but in the shock in Kit's eyes she understands. There is something in

Lord Isherwood's glass that killed him. Kit knows what it is. Kit might have made it, and now, Lazarus is silencing him. The look Kit gives her is undiluted terror, the same look from when they were mere sprouts and got into a terrible brawl on the frozen Thames and Mariner fell through the ice. How fearful he had looked then, thinking her lost, how furtive and flushed, horrified it was his own fault. This is beyond sin, worse than petty crimes that can be confessed in prayer and purified with the sacrament; this is treason, to bring poison into the palace, and as she holds Kit's gaze the realisation shimmers between them. They will kill him, Mariner thinks wildly. They will burn him at Smithfields.

'He is dead,' Lazarus announces. 'Natural causes.'

Now she sees the plan in the son of Lord Isherwood, the chance to be rid of a father he hated, to have the golden apprentice all for himself. Kit's eyes are darting between Lazarus and the body, his burnt, reddened fingers quivering. Does he blame himself? Around her she hears the rumblings of dissatisfaction, the sound of guards assembling outside the door, imagines she hears cries of 'Witch! Witch!' in the air. Will they come for Elody, she thinks madly, will they come for me?

'Now, now, gentlemen, let us not panic.' Elody's voice is smooth cream cutting through the riotous male bellows. 'If it were poison, it would be in the chalice, would it not? For he and I drank of the same and I am well.'

She swoops down and plucks the cup from Kit. Lazarus seems to have stiffened and Mariner notices how, behind the cover of Isherwood's dead body, he has furtively snuck his hand over to cover Kit's, their fingers so dangerously intertwined as they both stare at the corpse. They do not know if Elody will save them, Mariner realises. She stares up at her lover, sniffing the vial with a frown. Do not condemn them, she thinks wildly, please.

'It does smell tainted,' says Elody. There is an outbreak of wild yelling, and Mariner glances at Sir Robert Cecil, silent and staring at the dead Lord Isherwood with an impenetrable gaze.

'Arrest the server!' someone bellows, and guards in royal red surround Pyncher, who flinches wildly.

'Not I! Not I!' he cries. 'But I saw who did it, God help me, I did not think—'

'Who?' Elody approaches him with menace and the Privy Councillors watch this woman, a lady standing not ten feet from her dead father, so close to being called his murderer.

'Forgive me, my lady, I did not know the depth of his deception towards you.' Pyncher is weeping now, and Mariner impulsively reaches for Kit's hand. She does not know how she will do it, but if Lazarus goes to the Tower for this, she will make sure Kit does not go too.

'Speak!' Elody advances. 'You untrustworthy wretch. Tell me who has killed the man I called father.'

Mariner jerks as if slapped. You did not call him father, she thinks, staring at Elody. Something worse than doubt begins to creep up her spine. Such a lie, so easily given. What other lies could there be?

'Your cousin, Matthew Blackwater. He poured the poison from a vial in his doublet, it is there still, check if you do not believe me. Forgive me, my lady, I have only been a faithful servant,' Pyncher hiccups.

Mariner wants to look over her shoulder, to find the Matthew Blackwater he speaks of, perhaps the real one who actually exists somewhere and not the one whose skin she is living in. All eyes in the room are upon her and she wants to shout, but I am not him! The words do not come out and someone calls:

'Check him, then! He cannot be armed!'

The guards advance and Mariner has nowhere to run but why

should she? Pyncher is lying to save himself, obviously they will find nothing, but their hands are groping and tussling her. In a moment of memory, she is back in her hammock, bleeding, wrenched upwards. A woman, the sailors scream. A woman aboard!

'Milord, look.' The guard holds a small vial out to Sir Robert Cecil, who has the goblet in his hand. He sniffs one, then slowly, sniffs the other. Then he nods. How ruinous it is, this nod from the most powerful man at Court, from the hand of the Queen herself.

'It is not mine,' Mariner whispers. 'I did not put it there, I—'

Her words vanish when the light catches the glass of the vial, held in the Lord Chancellor's hand. It is blue, with an opal stopper, a mirror of the one she gave to Daisy, the accidentally poisoned chalice. She looks wildly at Elody, trying to understand how this unfortunate event has happened, but sees nothing but coldness.

'You are a liar,' Elody says, just as she said on the day Daisy came to Hart House. Knowledge crashes through her so painfully she doubles over, hanging between the guards like a woman in the stocks. Elody killed Daisy, perhaps out of jealousy. Elody has killed her father, for whatever reason she liked, perhaps with Lazarus and Kit's help, perhaps not, but now she is making it Mariner's fault. Wildly, she thinks it could be a test, that Elody might still save her if she can show enough love and so she gasps out:

'I am yours, Elody, only yours!'

'It is worse!' Pyncher shouts, his face a sharp vision of hatred and resentment. 'It is the same bottle used to kill a whore in Southwark! Matthew Blackwater is the Southwark poisoner! Matthew Blackwater is a murderer!'

She sees a flurry of movement in her peripheral vision, of Kit fighting against Lazarus to get to her side and knows it is useless. Run, you fucking idiot, she thinks. Run from these people, run back to Southwark, abandon all of this and get out, if you still can.

'Matthew Blackwater, you will be taken hence forth to a place of imprisonment,' a low, stately voice says, but she cannot see the speaker, only the door opening and the wide, watching court beyond. Faces peering, mouths jeering, no one to help her or save her, and suddenly they are sailors; glaring, hating, letting her be taken away, ripping her out of her life.

'But I am not him! I am not Matthew Blackwater!' she finds herself shouting, the truth her only pitiful defence, hoping that this one terrible fact about her might give her some grace. 'I am a woman! I am a woman!'

ᴀʟᴄʀᴊʟ

He whose name is Annihilation

Chapter Twenty-Nine

'We need to go back for her,' Kit says as Lazarus pulls him through a back door, pushing him down a spiral staircase, down, down, into the basements of Richmond Palace.

'No, right now, we need to find a way out of here.' Lazarus has a clamped grip on his hand as they stumble through the packed tunnels, full of crates and baskets of food brought in for the kitchens. 'This comes out by the stables.'

In the careless, calculated tone of his voice, Kit feels a hint of the man who stood, silently, in the corner of the cellar. He twists and shoves Lazarus firmly up against the wall, to remind himself that it is not the same.

'That was our poison.'

'Kit, we have no time—'

'Do not lie to me, I will beat the fucking truth out of you, did you plan this? To poison your father? To blame Mariner?'

'No.' Lazarus pushes him away by the shoulders and he stumbles against a sack of potatoes. 'Not to blame her! My formulas, your skill, my silence, his death. It was not an agreement, as such, we didn't say when or where, but...'

'You planned to murder your father with your sister and get away with it.'

Lazarus nods firmly and looks back over his shoulder his fingers flickering nervously.

'Then why do it in a royal palace? Why make it treason?'

'I do not know!' Lazarus' voice is furiously low and Kit sees that he has been as much taken by surprise by his sister as Kit and Mariner have. 'We need to get away, either Mariner or Pyncher could change their story, blame us—'

'We are to blame!' Kit points back along the corridor, his voice bouncing against the stone. 'Mariner is the only one of us not guilty of this, and we're going to leave the country? We, the monstrous, she, the innocent?'

Lazarus grabs his collar, pushes him back against the wall, lips close enough to be a stolen kiss but instead it is a vicious spittle of words.

'Monstrous, maybe, but we will live.' Kit wonders if it possible to taste another's desperation through their words. 'You will live, Skevy, if I have to tie you up all the way to Scotland.'

'Scotland, Lazarus? You wound me.'

They both turn their heads to the sound of her voice. Lady Blackwater steps daintily over rolling potatoes and enters the tunnel. 'Kit Skevy is my apprentice. I have paid for him. He will come back to Hart House.'

Lazarus says nothing but continues to use his hand to hold Kit in place against the wall. For the first time, Kit thinks it is a protective gesture.

'Your apprentice, my Initiate.' Lazarus carefully pulls something out of his purse. The same odd-shaped thing he used to bring down the wall at Isherwood House. Kit stiffens. 'You have your desire. We will not hang for it. We are leaving.'

'Your Initiate?' Lady Blackwater looks at Kit, smiling pityingly. 'I suppose he bedded you and told you that you were remarkable, the only one? Drew out your true powers and hoarded them for himself?'

Lazarus lifts the ball of explosive but Elody's fingers move, a flicker of silver, faster than a wasp and Lazarus gasps, clamping a hand to his neck.

'Laz?' Kit scrabbles to pull back Lazarus' fingers, finds a silver needle wobbling against his throat.

'I would not touch that, Master Skevy. It is dipped with a sedative. Ladies do need to take measures to ensure they are protected, after all.' She lifts a ribbon at the line of her bodice, showing a row of silver needles with minuscule leather caps. 'Do not worry, dear Lazarus will still be able to hear us for now, but it is time you and I had a discussion, without interruptions.'

Lazarus slumps, Kit struggling to hold him as they both crumple to the floor. Lazarus' eyes are wide with panic and his breath slow, mouthing the word: run. Kit wants to obey him, but his legs are shaking too much to bear his weight.

'Lazarus has kept many of your skills hidden from me, or so he thinks, but the truth is, I knew your potential before you ever stepped into my house. Even since before you terrified my father and brother at Crossbones. I have known it about you since I saw you whipped at the Standard.'

'That day, you are the lady who watched me,' Kit stammers, trying to hold Lazarus' lolling head up against his knee. 'How did you—?'

'You would be amazed with all the things I know about you. Things I have known your whole life.' She is looking at Kit with a fondness he doesn't understand. Lazarus' grip on his sleeve becomes even tighter. 'I knew you when you were nothing more than a child with cold fingers.'

Kit stares at her, his heart thundering. He looks at Lazarus in his arms, who is fighting to keep his eyes open.

'Did you tell her about the mirror?' He shakes Lazarus but his head is loose on his neck, drooping.

'Why would he need to tell me what I remember?' Lacy Blackwater says, stepping closer. 'You do not recognise me. They called me Ella then. I was much younger when my father conducted his experiments in Antwerp and I would watch.'

'No.' Kit shakes his head violently. 'He didn't know me, you're lying.'

'Am I?' Lady Blackwater leans forward, a smile on her lips, her voice conspiratorial. 'We would leave the windows open and let the snow blow in.'

Kit sees her as she was, young and stern and cruel, always fascinated, always curious, wanting to pinch the inside of his forearm. Does this hurt? she would ask, over and over. Does this hurt now? He does not want to believe her, but why does he remember if it is not true? He looks at the girl called Ella, the woman called Elody, once his torturer now his mistress, and the past collides with the present. Is it trustworthy, he wonders, this surety inside me?

'You knew who I was?'

'Initiate,' Lazarus mumbles. Lazarus is fading quickly, and whatever answers Lady Blackwater might offer, are they worth it if they require Lazarus to die?

'You trust him so dearly,' says Elody softly. 'Yet you do not know who he is. He does not love you, Kit Skevy, he is his father's son through and through. Even now he works to advance his way with the King of Scotland and he would use you to get there.'

'No!' Lazarus' eyes open, a sluggish pull, the whites swivelling to his silver irises.

'No?' Elody echoes mockingly. 'He sent Griffin the stage crafter the tainted formula. He killed him.'

Lazarus' countenance is full of fear. In the terror, Kit knows it is true but he cannot believe it. Knowledge thundering in his heart is struggling to reach his brain. He scrambles away, letting Lazarus' head smack onto the stone. He is splayed out so similarly to Griffin, the man whose death sent Kit into a spiral of desperation to leave London, that sent him to Crossbones, that sent him to the cellar. Every terrible thing that has happened to him this year is a line of toppled trees and there, at the beginning, the force pushing them over, is the same man who told him that Kit was the centre of his universe. Lazarus is looking up at him with dreadful, exhaustive weariness, not a hint of denial.

'Say not,' Kit whispers.

'Kit…' Lazarus' breath is laboured, his body failing. 'Your sun…'

'Say it is not true.' There is betrayal like fire in Kit's body, faster and more vicious than the flames of Crossbones. Griffin is dead on the floor and there is smoke closing his throat. Kit is laid out by Isherwood's physician and Lazarus is watching and they are in bed and Lazarus' penitent lips are opening him so gently, erasing that violent act of intrusion with a soft tongue and whispered words – 'Say not! Say fucking not, you bastard, say not!'

He is kicking him, he cannot see him properly through a strange haze over his eyes, can barely make out Lazarus' crunched, curled form and suddenly Elody has pressed a knife into his hands.

'He will not stay with you now, he will only prove himself faithless. Better, is it not, to be the one with the most power?'

Kit presses the blade against Lazarus' throat, thinks yes, this is some kind of justice for all the ways he did not see Lazarus. Better to turn a coat than burn in it. How burned Kit is, how the despair inside of him is wide and uncrossable, a yawning ocean of emptiness, the space that he carved for Lazarus Isherwood inside of him. Lazarus' face is swollen, eyes bloody, but they do not close. They fix on Kit that same way they always have done, as if he is the most riveting thing in the room. What is the gain? Kit thinks, against his will. What is the fucking gain? The knife tips gently out of his hand and clatters down.

'I thought not,' Elody sighs. Her hand is on his neck and suddenly his legs give way under him, sending him toppling into Lazarus' body. Another pin, he realises, and Elody stands over them both, looking vaguely disappointed. 'It seems, Master Skevy, that there is nothing my brother can do that will quite make you regret him enough to displace him, so we will have to leave the onus upon Lazarus to break your heart in turn. There is no love strong enough in an Isherwood to allow them to stay against their better judgement. We are beasts of self-preservation. By the time you wake, he will be long gone.'

Here then is the answer to the question; what becomes of his heart if the sun is not the centre of the universe? It is gone forever, turned inward, sucking all light inside of it.

⼭⼂⼃ᗡⵣ⌐⌐

She who rises up in strength

Chapter Thirty

Mariner has often imagined what the inside of Bridewell prison would be like. No criminal in Southwark has not done so, they trade stories about it, but none told her of how they would strip her out of her shirt, to determine she was in fact a woman. Mariner feels herself fold in upon herself, like ancient drawings of ships taken by kraken and leviathans, bucking in the centre, masts cracking, to be pulled asunder. She says nothing as they unwrap her bindings in the small room the guards kept for their own meals and work. She makes no sound or movement as they poke the skin of her breasts experimentally and make comments that she is, in fact, a lovely size for such a short-haired unnatural thing. She does not fight when they lead her to the deepest part of the prison, low under the earth where there is nothing to smell but dank straw and people's waste and where sludge of the streets that pours through the high, barred, open windows when the rain comes. There is only one other prisoner there, buried under a pile of filthy straw, unmoving.

Spectators come, the guards let them down for a penny, to eye her fine breeches and shirt with its delicate embroidery and to speculate if she had been an imposter or perhaps a man had decided to cut her hair and dress her up to fuck her. They watch and wait for her to piss in the bucket to find out if she has a cock hidden. She thinks often of Kit, of the way Lazarus held his hand behind the dead body of his father, that earnest, protective gesture. Lazarus will persuade his lover to cut his losses, to flee to Prague or some other alchemist city and why should Kit not go? Mariner slumps against the slick straw and none of these thoughts hurt her. What spears her, over and over, is that Daisy Gale's last thoughts might not have been that she was losing her pregnancy but that Mariner had wanted her dead.

'You have a visitor!' the jailor calls through the door. Mariner blinks. She looks at the plate of bread in front of her, untouched, weevils crawling.

'What day is this?' she calls back.

'A day hence.' Then his voice drops to a lower register. 'It'll cost you to see her alone.'

Mariner realises he is talking to someone, that there truly is a visitor and not just more onlookers come to gape. Kit, she thinks, it must be Kit, thank God he has not fled – but when the door swings open and Elody sweeps in, holding her fine gown up above the straw, Mariner can do nothing but stare.

'Come on, you,' the jailor says, bustling into the room and diving a hand into the straw to heave out the woman. For a moment, she dodges him, wriggling around in the straw like a spaniel and it is bizarrely comical, this cruel man bending and floundering to catch her. Then he does, seizing her by the hair and wrenching her up. With a jerk of horror, Mariner realises she can't be more than twelve.

'Another witch,' the jailor says smugly, as the young girl hangs limply in his hands. 'Killed her stepfather.'

281

He drags her out easily, her filthy toes and knees bumping on the floor. Mariner cannot help but catch her eyes, sees the miasma of despair inside them, the solid, unmoving resignation. This is the way, her gaze seems to say. You cannot be quick, you cannot be smart, you cannot think your way from the blow that is coming so be dead now. Untether your soul and mind from this body that will burn or hang. Mariner looks away as the door slides shut and the bolt is dragged across with a screech. She and Elody are locked in together. She is wearing all dark colours today, garbed like a widow, face covered by a veil that she lifts to meet Mariner's eyes. She holds a small bottle in her black gloved hand; the glass dark green so Mariner cannot see what is inside. She sets it down on the straw and kicks it towards her.

'The human body can survive many things but not without fluid,' Elody says.

'Is it poison?'

'It could be poison, I suppose. We have never spoken of the many reactions a person may have to different toxins; after all, a woman can die from a bee sting.'

She is ashamed, suddenly, of the part of her that desperately hopes Elody is here to say that she is sorry, that none of this was her doing, that perhaps even Lazarus and Kit are the ones responsible and she only said what she said because of Pyncher's accusations, that she is working hard to save Mariner's life. Elody smiles. How easily this woman has always been able to read her every thought, and Mariner's shame deepens, her cheeks flushing painfully.

'Do you grieve me so, Mariner Elgin?' Elody's voice is so sweet it turns her stomach. Self-loathing rises, agonising helplessness. She blinks, hard and fast, tells herself; you must not cry in front of this woman. You must not beg. You are a fucking sailor.

'Was any of it real?' Mariner asks, willing her voice not to crack.

'I could ask you the same thing.' Elody's face, strangely, is tautly earnest. 'Did you love me, myself, or did you only love the freedom I gave you? The name and the chance to finally get what you needed, to live and fuck and love as a man?'

'I am a woman who only loves women.' Mariner rests her head wearily back against the slick, damp stone. She feels as if she has been fighting this battle all of her life. 'What other way is there to be that? Than to live as a man?'

'I know,' Elody says, but she does not know. How could she? Mariner thinks, with her own money for a house she can hide women in, buy ships in, be free in? No one in Southwark is coming to bash her head in for it. 'It was what I liked about you, truthfully. I intended to keep you, but you made it impossible.'

'How?' Mariner cannot get rid of the incredulity in her voice.

'You threatened to expose my secrets. You asked me for the life of that girl; you set our love against her need and found her more important.' Elody's eyes are incredulously shiny, suddenly. 'Before that moment, I was sure that you were mine, that nothing would compel you to act or speak against me, not even your Kit, but I was wrong. You tried to use your love to control me. That is all love is, really. For did not your Daisy do the same thing? Coming to my house to manipulate you with her love, and then you came to me to do the same. No love is without motive.'

'That is not true, Ella.' Mariner takes the childhood name she heard on Lord Isherwood's lips. Elody seems startled but quickly recovers.

'It is. No love is without condition.' Her eyes are distant. 'My mother loved me so much so that I would hate my father more. She taught me the beginnings of my art, of herbs and recipes, to follow God. Then she died when I was only nine years old. I was left alone with my hate and my faith and my art. My father loved me so I would be pliable and useful and to soften some of the hate my mother left inside me and then he sent me away too. He had power over me, he used my love and turned it to rage when he sold me in marriage. That is all love does, twist to rage and despair. The truest alchemy there is.'

It is so close to how Mariner is feeling at this moment, bitter and sorrowful, that she has to bite her lip.

'We could have been different,' she says, pressing her head back against the wall.

'How?' Elody's voice is softly derisive. 'You so happily slipped into the skin I gave you to wear, you tossed your old one aside without compulsion. What was there of you to love?'

'I took that name and skin for you!' Mariner protests. 'I thought you loved me as I was and that would be enough to endure it, but you saw nothing in me but opportunity.'

'Not true.' Elody's voice crumbles slightly. 'I cherished you, but... this is how things must be. How they are ordained to be.'

'Ordained?'

Elody nods, her face a strange rictus of excitement Mariner has never seen before.

'When the true church fell in England, my father could set aside my mother. Every terrible thing that has happened in this country happened because King Henry strayed from his true wife, and with the bastard daughter of a lute player on the throne, England will never be saved. Not until she bows to his Holiness once more. Kit is the alchemical child, he will tame the Red Lion, he will make the elixir of life and I will do as my father never could.' Elody's eyes take on a frantic gleam. 'With Kit's creations, his Holiness will live forever, and all the poor and sick of the world will flock to him to receive blessing and healing. Kit Skevy will be transformed, a saint for the true believers to pray to and turn to. The coffers of the

Vatican will never dry, we will supply armies to King Philip endlessly. This Armada will take Britain, a new heir will be named and the Spanish Infanta will take her rightful place as Queen. Every wife, every daughter cast aside by this terrible heresy of the English church will be restored.'

In her words, Mariner finally hears Elody Isherwood. She hears the young girl, cast aside by her father, mourning a mother, mourning a family. She sees the resentment that has grown there in place of grief, the thorny hatred that has blossomed into a woman who is not only ready to turn traitor, she believes herself a crusader.

'Why are you telling me this?' Mariner asks.

'So you will know it a mercy.' Elody's face is transformed with fervour. 'The alchemical child will bring the consecration of Emmanuel's sweet and holy blood to England. Better for a reformer like yourself not to see it. Better to hang than burn, dearest.'

Mariner had no idea that Elody even knew she was a reformer. How strange to be categorised this way, to have her death arranged because of it. If she is truly still a reformer, with her want of women, breeches and the open sea, then she is the poorest excuse for a disciple there has ever been.

Elody picks up the bottle from the floor, pressing it into Mariner's hands and Mariner could almost laugh to see the glitter of tears in her eyes. Does she believe her own distress? Is it possible?

'May God have mercy on your soul,' says Elody.

And yours, Mariner thinks, I loved you and I hate you and I hope you burn in hell as I will surely do, but she says nothing. She stares at the small bottle and does not look up to watch Elody leave. She knows she could drink it now, that she could be free, but there is Elgin inside her mind, a memory from the past when a sailor had thrown himself into the surf at night, holding a cannonball. He told her those who did such things were possessed by the devil.

'They will not be saved?' Mariner asked.

'The grace and mercy of our Lord is boundless, perhaps our understanding is limited compared to the power of Christ.' Elgin put his hand around her small shoulders. 'But perhaps the Lord God lets the devil take them down to hell to warn us of the sin of despair.'

Mariner presses the bottle to her forehead and weeps, because no matter how the world has shifted for her this year, her feet cannot be removed from what she believes to be true. If she is to die, then she will not lose the chance to see Elgin again. She throws the bottle across the room where it lands in the straw. If the young girl is brought back in and slowly pulls the vial inside her nest, Mariner does not care to notice.

'You're a woman.' There is a voice calling through the shutter, pulling her out of dark dreams. This one isn't cruel or angry, it is lilting and Irish. 'I must say, now you make a lot more sense.'

Mariner thinks she might be dreaming as the door opens and Captain Larkin, in her tall boots and felt cap, is let inside.

'Jesus!' Captain Larkin, pulls her scarf around her neck up over her chin and nose. 'Worse than a brig.'

Mariner rubs a hand over her eyes, just to check that it's really happening, but Captain Larkin does not move, nor does her face become any more impressed.

'Did she send you?' Mariner finally asks.

'Who? Your cousin?' Mariner does not bother to arrange her expression into anything less scornful. Something flies through Captain Larkin's blue eyes and then disappears. 'Not your cousin.'

'If so, we were ungodly in more ways than I anticipated.'

She expects revulsion, she expects guardedness, what she does not expect is a laugh, hoarse like a seagull, from behind Captain

Larkin's blue and grey woven scarf. The creases around her eyes deepen with it.

'You speak quite freely of it. This… cousinly love,' says she.

'Freely for a dead woman.' Mariner is too tired to lie. She won't bear the heaviness of them anymore. 'It is not as if they can kill me worse for wanting a wife.'

'I am not sure about that. You are not yet condemned. I would take that secret to God, Master Blackwater.' Captain Larkin walks carefully across the cell and looks up through the damp window, examining the pouring waterfall of overflow dripping through it. Mariner wonders what secrets Captain Larkin will take to God, when her time comes. Then the Captain turns back to face her. 'But that is not your name. Hardly feels right to call you the Southwark Poisoner.'

'I did not do it.'

It seems important to tell her, for some reason.

'Not my business—' Captain Larkin shrugs lightly '—but I'll have your name if you're giving it.'

'Mariner Patience Elgin.'

'Mariner.' The way she says it, the firmness of her lips around a smile, it sounds so pleasing. 'You sailed then?'

'Aye. *The Golden Riall, The Foresight.*'

'Captain Drake's ships.' Captain Larkin's blonde eyebrows disappear under her cap. 'How?'

'My uncle was a ship's surgeon. My parents and his wife and child died in a fire at sea. He took me in, took me with him on his travels.'

'You were playing a lad.'

'Until I was caught.' When Captain Larkin tilts her head curiously she says: 'First blood in a bunk.'

'Ah.' Captain Larkin nods. 'That is bad luck.'

If only it could be a defence in court, the horrendous bad luck of it. To have been born with a sailor's heart in a woman's body, to be born poor when riches could have freed her, to be born loving only women when it is so horribly sinful to do so. Such abominable fucking bad luck to be alive in a world that very much wants her in hell already.

'I have always thought so,' Mariner sniffs, swallowing back her tears. 'Will you come to my trial?'

'No, I will be sailing.' Her eyes dart away and Mariner quickly realises why. This is a voyage bought for Elody. The Spanish Armada is coming and she has everything she needs now; if she gets Kit to Lisbon or Rome. It will likely do no good, but speaking the truth aloud is suddenly important. This is who Elody is, it says, how it helps the cringing disbelief inside her that remembers the soft nights and tender kisses.

'She is intent on treason against the Crown, you know that.'

'I know that any treason to an English queen is likely music to Ireland's ears.' The Captain's voice is sharp. 'Besides, I do not turn down gold. I cannot afford to.'

Mariner thinks of Kit, stowed away in *The Seahorse*, headed for the Spanish Armada and beyond that, a shackled life as a performing alchemist for Elody Blackwater. Then she thinks of Lazarus' hand on his, so precariously barely hidden in a room full of England's most powerful men.

'There is a man with more gold,' she says. 'Lazarus Isherwood, the new Lord Isherwood. I'd wager he's still in London.'

Captain Larkin is unmoving, staring at the pouring water.

'Why?' she asks. 'It will not help you.'

'It will help someone I love. She has him, Kit Skevy. My...' She stumbles. Can she call him her friend, her family, her brother after what she has said to him? 'Please.'

'I'll promise nothing, but I'm not one to turn down a better deal.' She turns back to look at Mariner. 'So.'

Mariner can tell she does not want to say farewell – for how disingenuous would it seem? – and Mariner is not quite ready for the conversation to stop so she blurts out:

'Why did you come?'

Captain Larkin gives her a long look, as if considering her answer, and then lowers the scarf around her lips.

'To answer your question. Yes, I am afraid, always, of this—' She gestures to the cell around her. 'Of getting on the wrong side of an angry judge, of a pirate's noose or a traitor's badge, yes, I am afraid.'

Captain Larkin crouches right in front of her and cups her face. It is desperately tender, and Mariner cannot stop the tears that fall down her cheeks.

'But I am more afraid of being stranded on dry land, and at least in the heavenly realms there is the great glass sea to sail,' says she. 'Set it against your fear, if you can.'

Mariner gasps, tries not to weep but it is impossible, and she pushes her grubby hand into her face, wishing she could scratch out her own eyes.

'*Whist, whist, mairnéalach.*' There are warm fingers pulling her hand away and dry, chapped lips against her forehead. A benediction, a blessing, and Mariner feels the warm breath of the captain on her face. It is too much generosity, she doesn't want this much affection born of pity from such a woman. She would earn it, if she could, if there were time. So instead, she pulls away, lets Captain Larkin rise, her blue eyes greyer and more stormy than Daisy's ever were.

'See the horizon for both of us,' says Mariner.

'Aye.' Captain Larkin nods. 'Sailor.'

Mariner lets the word sink into her chest as the door opens and closes, holds it over her heart like a brand, and she squeezes her eyes tightly shut. There she sees a woman captain, standing by the mast with the world before her, chasing the wind over the glittering waves.

Chapter Thirty-One

Kit wakes in a small, cramped space. He cannot move his shoulders, a tunnel of darkness all around him. A coffin, he is sure, and so he screams, finds his screams muffled by something stuffed in his mouth. He tries to reach up and pull it out, but finds his hands are bound too. Suddenly there is light coming from his right side, leaving him blinking, and a voice is speaking.

'I am sorry, Kit, I did not know you were awake. The priest hole is not the easiest for communication.'

A priest hole, just like Raven's Roost. Not just a Catholic household, Kit thinks. He imagines that this time, if scripture is spoken during torture, it will be in Latin. Elody removes the gag from around his face and Kit coughs, the taste of bitter fabric on his tongue. She has hold of his shoulders, easing him out from under the wood ceiling to set his back against something firm. The world is tilting in a rhythmic motion, the room made of cramped wood with walls that lean and funnel up towards one another. It must be a Captain's cabin, he ascertains from the heavy trunk, the carved chair and table. He is leaning against the bed, built into the wall, he has been kept inside the wooden frame, his body squashed there and rolling with the water.

'Would you like something to drink?' Elody asks politely, pouring two cups of a tisane. The liquid tips inside the cups swaying side to side. 'I know you will not feel the need for fluids, but you should replenish yourself.'

'No,' Kit says, eyeing it warily. Elody sets a cup to her lips. She drinks whilst Kit watches, wondering if she will poison herself to prove a point, but nothing happens. She offers the second cup to Kit's lips. He hesitates, feels the dryness inside his mouth, and then leans forward to sip the tisane. It tastes of peppermint and chamomile. The smell is invigorating and he cannot help but breathe deeply, eagerly sipping more. He wonders if he can hit her, perhaps crunch his forehead against hers and run for it, but she has the hot tisane within reach and perhaps a knife hidden in her dress, he is not sure he will make it. Then he remembers he is at sea. There is nowhere to make it to.

'Do not swallow too fast, here, let me unbind you first.' He is surprised when she sets aside the clay cup and unbinds his wrists and feet. 'I would suggest you do not try to stand up. You have been asleep for nearly a day and a half. Your legs may not obey you.'

Kit believes her. He tries to wiggle his toes and nothing happens.

'Mandrake?' he croaks. She tuts and hands him the cup of tisane. His hands shake but he manages to press it against his lips, slurping noisily.

'I see Lazarus has taught you his herbs.'

Kit takes another sip, hoping it brings the feeling back to his toes.

'Did you kill him?' he asks, even though there is a pressure in the centre of his chest just to think of him.

'What need would I have for that?' Elody sits down beside him.

Kit is surprised to see her so informal, the way she slumps against the leg of the chair, hair loose around her shoulders and legs crossed childishly. He searches her appearance for signs of the woman who flicked a poisoned pin at Lazarus and begins to notice them, the sharp pricks of silver in the white lace at her bosom, hints of hidden needles. It is an echo of the feeling he had when he first realised how Lazarus had betrayed him in the cellar; that sensation of having missed all the signs of who a person is. 'I told you, if you kept him alive Lazarus would find a way to survive. He has already run back to James. I imagine him halfway to Scotland by now, to recover his position without your influence.'

Kit closes his eyes against the vision he has of Lazarus sitting in the orchard of Raven's Roost, the sun in his hair, apple juice dribbling down his chin, telling him they would work wonders.

'I have no influence.'

'Oh, Kit, you do not think he was teaching you alchemy for your benefit, do you?' Elody laughs, tipping her head back. In the line of her throat to her ear, she looks a little like Lazarus. 'Likely, King James will be disappointed that Lazarus must renege on his father's promises of the Red Lion elixir. That will be tricky but Lazarus will find another alchemist to sell James his dreams.'

Kit remembers Lazarus leaning over him, picking straw out of his hair and saying: Your rage, Skevy, is not from the fact that I chose to use you. It is that you did not have the chance to use me first. If Elody is speaking the truth, then Lazarus has used him in every possible way, as well as having lied abominably about being part of Griffin's death.

'If I am so valuable then he will come for me,' he says weakly, not even sure if he wants it. 'I am his Initiate.'

'Do you think so? You, who stood over him when he was helpless and beat him? Who held a knife to his throat?' Elody shakes her head. 'You will never forgive him and he knows when to cut his losses. Why would he return for you, Kit? You will never love him and now he knows it.'

Kit closes his eyes. Her words, so satin smooth and gentle yet filled with barbs that curl into his mind and tug loose melancholy, are too much for him to fight against. She is right, of course, he has never told Lazarus that he loves him, or could have loved him, because despite everything there is a weight in his chest with Lazarus' name on that he already knows will not shift. This is not a good pain, Kit thinks.

'What of Mariner? You betrayed her,' he asks, and Elody sips her brew.

'I would have kept her, if I could have trusted her,' she says. 'A shame that she stole poison from me and killed her old lover with it.'

Mariner has been pulled away from Kit, or perhaps he has pushed her, the old bonds between them stretched and fraying but this Kit knows to be true: nothing on the wide green earth would compel Mariner Patience Elgin to harm Daisy Gale. Too many years of yearning, too much terrified love. It is in this that he knows Elody, a little bit more. Here is a woman whose lies are mellifluous; songs of speech, easy to nod along.

'You're a liar,' says he.

'You think I lie about seeing you whipped at the Standard? About knowing you from your youth? You were fascinating to me, when I was young. The other subjects in my father's experiments, they wailed, they died of burns, there was nothing significant about a single one of them. But you, you could feel no pain. It was miraculous. Do you still think I'm a liar?'

Kit turns his face away. He doesn't know. Behind his closed eyelids, he sees the young girl he saw in the mirror. He cannot deny the similarity now that he is looking for it, her stern nose and flat mouth, the same superiority in her dark eyes.

'You knew me from a whipping but Isherwood did not know me from hanging in a cellar?'

'Like many very powerful men, my father never anticipated that he could be deceived. That the experiment he thought lost and gone could perhaps have been taken.'

Taken? Kit thinks. Immediately, he remembers Griffin; the softness of his shirt that Kit recalls pressing his face into when they sailed from Antwerp to England. Griffin, who was killed by Lazarus. He closes his eyes against the sensation that thought principates, a wave of rancour and howling despair.

'As for recognising you, that is because he barely looked up from recording your skills to notice your face in the years he had you,' Elody snorts. 'He barely saw mine until I was of marriageable age, and I'll warrant that Lazarus was careful never to show your true skills to him, that our father never knew you felt no pain. He would have known you then, Kit. In a heartbeat, as quickly as he did moments before his death.'

Kit thinks of Lord Isherwood's last words to Lazarus: It feels no pain? Lazarus, does it speak true? Then Kit wonders, does any of it matter? The outcome is much the same. I am her captive as much as I was his.

'Are you going to cut me up for parts?' Kit sneers, hiding his fear as best he can. 'Mix me into compounds? What do you want?'

'I want what I saw.' Elody's eyes fix upon his hands. 'Lazarus tried to keep it from me, proved his own betrayal, but you are more than a man with no sensation: your skin produces miracles. The Holy Father will pour riches into your every endeavour. We will raise armies under your standard and the holy troops of Spain will march across Europe. The secrets of alchemy, the philosopher's stone, the elixir of life, they will spin from your fingers. You will make gold for the mother church and she will never, ever be defeated. You will be a saint, Kit.'

Kit thinks of the triangle Lazarus drew in the dirt on the floor of the cellar many months ago. If this is truly what it means to be at the pinnacle of alchemy, then it is a fucking curse indeed.

'I will not. I have no control, I can perform no miracles. Lazarus has good formulas, sometimes they work. Not one of them yet produces gold.' He smiles at her, hoping this ruins her day. 'So you will offer the Pope a promise you cannot keep and then we'll both be locked up in his dungeon. Or priest hole, should he have one.'

'You only have no control because you have not been properly motivated.'

Elody rises and opens the door. A captain enters, a woman captain he guesses by the skirt, but the stranger appearance is Squire Kay, being shown into the cabin. She does not look healthy; pale and sallow with a large bruise blooming under her eye. It widens when she sees Kit and then she winces with the pain of it.

'Sit her down, Captain Larkin.'

Squire Kay is guided to sit gently in the chair at the small table. She seems discombobulated, her eyes rolling; Kit wonders if she is only drunk or has been subject to one of Elody's poisoned pins.

'Now we are all together, just as before.' Elody puts a hand on Squire Kay's shoulder and she flinches slowly, with a low groan. Kit thinks he knows where the bruise came from.

'As before?' Kit looks at the woman he has known all his life. She keeps her eyes on the table, her shoulders hunched, waiting for inevitable blows.

'She was your keeper; all of the experiments had one.' Elody is moving around the cabin as she speaks, drawing out a silver basin, setting it on the table. 'I had no idea when I was a young girl that the man who brought compounds and tinctures to our house in Antwerp to furnish my father's experiments was the brother of the maid who kept you safe. Even less notion that he was less a salesman and more a spy.'

Griffin, Kit thinks, unable to stop staring at Squire Kay as Elody pulls him up onto the narrow bed. The cabin is so close that his knees hit the table and now he is sat directly across from her, whose eyes still linger on the grain of the wood, her whole body swaying slowly with whatever suppressant is coursing through her blood.

'My father thought you dead, that you jumped out of a window and into the river. How desolate he was and how glad was I. I thought, perhaps foolishly, he would care more for me without his favourite pet but I was wrong. He sold me in marriage soon after.'

Elody sets Kit's hands inside the silver bowl.

'I thought of you, occasionally, as I began my own alchemical endeavours. The dead miracle. Then I saw you being whipped at the Standard, a young man surviving a deadly beating, unaware of his own skill. A coincidence, it must be. I would have turned away, but who should I see beside you but that same man who sold my father his powders? Same hair pulled back, same green cap.'

Squire Kay has closed her eyes, silent tears trickling down her cheeks.

'I saw him and I knew his sin. I could not fathom how it was done until I had him followed, saw his sister from afar. The maid and the alchemist. What a plan they cooked up, to steal my father's greatest treasure! It was almost admirable.'

'So you killed Griffin because you did not think of it first?' Kit asks. Squire Kay has eaten her own lips, pursed them inward, from the pressure of not weeping.

'It was Lazarus' formula sent to Griffin, not mine. For all your friend had the look of failure, I knew he was dangerous alive with all the secrets he knew about you. He'd performed his own marvel to disappear you, I didn't put it past him to do it again. Once he was dead, I put some thought into how to approach you, asked for stolen goods and for you to deliver but God had other plans. His plans are always perfect, for without Lazarus, perhaps you would not have progressed this far. Now—' she places a piece of lead into Kit's bound hands '—make gold.'

'I cannot.' Kit stares at the little chunk of metal. Elody doesn't answer but pulls one of Squire Kay's wrists up to rest on the table; stiff, a reluctant doll with resentment in her eyes. Then she draws a set of pins from her pocket. Kit stares at them, their bright vicious bodies catching the dappled sunlight through the round windows. They do not have leather caps on their tips. They may not be poisoned, but Kit doubts she intends to hem skirts with them.

'It occurred to me, when I saw you flinch from my father, when I saw you beat Lazarus bloody, that what drives you is fear.' Elody withdraws a pin from the set. 'What does a man who does not feel pain fear? I realised it must be this.'

With great delicacy, Elody presses the tip of a pin just below the dirty cuticle of Squire Kay's first finger, who whimpers softly, trying to force slowed limbs into movement against the grip Elody has on her wrist. The needle quivers, standing upright and attentive in a millimetre of skin.

'When we were young, I admired you. I thought, there is a child who feels no pain, will never feel a broken heart. Now I see how wrong I was. You love, Kit Skevy, and to love is to fear.'

Elody slams her empty clay mug down on the head of the pin. Squire Kay screams, the kind of scream that turns quickly to gasping sobs and when Elody pulls the mug away, Kit stares at it. The first finger, pinned to the table, a specimen caught on wood with blood spreading darkly behind it, a perfect backdrop. Frame it and hang it in Raven's Roost among the other oddities. Label it carefully, the perionychium, the germinal matrix.

'So if you love her, make gold,' says Elody.

'I cannot.'

'You will learn.' Elody reaches for another pin and Squire Kay's sobs become breathless with panic. 'You have nine more chances before I turn to more permanent motivations.'

Kit tries. He sits in the screams, the blood rolling down the tilt of the table to drip and pool onto his immovable legs. Squire Kay's full-throated despair, spittle raining on his face, becomes snotty, animal moans and groans and he tries to think through it. I am the sun, I am the stars, I am my blood and skin and I am this piece of lead and all matter can be something else, please, be something, for the love of fucking Christ stop screaming – the metal does nothing.

When all five digits of her right hand are pinned, splayed, ready for dissection, Kit thinks she might faint, please let her faint, but instead of moving to her second hand, Elody begins to wrench the fingers back out of the wood. The canine yelps, the freed blood spattering against his face, Kit closes his eyes against it and thinks with all his desperation, this blood is nothing, this blood is like my blood, all things are like this at their core, her blood is like my skin, like my hair, like my hands, this lead—

'Very good, Kit.'

He opens his eyes and looks down at his hands. They are wet. He lifts them and molten metal slides off his skin into the bowl. His hands shake, the bowl shakes, the whole world feels like it is shaking.

'That is a step. There will be time for others on our journey to Rome.' Elody nods approvingly and leaves Squire Kay cradling her hand to her chest, huffing and sniffing. The pins are still in her fingers, claws now, blood tipped. 'You have learned well, but now it is time to rest.'

Elody is pressing a cup to his lips. It smells different this time, harsher and sharper and Kit does not care if it poisons him. He will do anything to get away from the piteous wails across from him, from Squire Kay's frantic terror. He gulps it down readily and with his last thought before the shaking world is edged out by darkness, hopes he does not wake up.

ᚢᛚᛒᛗᛚᚷᚳ

He who burns up the past

Chapter Thirty-Two

Kit is woken by his teeth jostled inside a bouncing head, his forehead bumping against the wood of a carriage as it rolls over cobblestones.

'Just in time,' Elody says. She sits opposite him, resplendent in black and violet, clean and neat. He does not know how many days it has been since he was last fully awake; turbulent dreams of Lazarus and Griffin and choking on black smoke have been interspersed with tisanes, forced between his lips in the darkness. There must be a bleary question on his face, because Elody says, 'Four days since we left London. We made good time. His legs will still be unsteady. Help him.'

Beside her is Squire Kay, one hand wrapped in bandages stained brown with blood. Her eyes are flickering with nervous energy. She is more alert now, at least, but looks haggard; hair loosening out of her cap, stringy with sweat, a yellow stain on her bodice that smells of vomit. When Elody steps out of the carriage Kit looks into her face as she crouches to help him stagger to standing.

'Can we run?' he mutters to her.

'You cannot run anywhere.' Her words stink; herbs and sickness and perhaps an undercurrent of sherry. 'Just wait.'

Together, an uneven clatter of feet and leaning bodies, they slump down from the carriage onto the street into the misting October rain. It is a sudden assault of sounds, horseshoes on stone, the raw caw of wheeling gulls: a recipe for a particular feeling. His insides are turning, organs reshuffling and sliding past one another to re-assemble in an old remembered pattern. Staring up at the dark wood of the Antwerp house, its pointed roof and boarded windows, he feels the same apprehension he did when he stood before Doctor Dee's mirror; a gnawing anxiety that truth is coming to him, however unpalatable, and cannot be stopped.

'Where are we?' he asks Squire Kay.

'We are in Antwerp, Master Skevy, at *Vervloekte huit*. The Cursed House.' Elody turns a key in the door and uses her shoulder to push it open. 'This is where you were made.'

Inside, the house smells musty; spots where furniture once stood dark shadows on the floorboards, fireplaces empty. The floor is littered with rat droppings, illuminated only by the spare cold light of the city's grey sun piercing through the edges and holes in the boarded-up windows. Kit remembers none of it.

'Of course he would never sell, kept it like a shrine to you, Kit. Never once thought to change the locks. I am sure Lazarus will burn it to the ground.' Elody raises her skirts to climb the dusty stairs. 'Come, let us show Kit where he lived.'

His legs are heavy, one more alive than the other, dragging and bumping on every stair as Squire Kay puts his arm across her shoulders to help him up. Her sweat is a sour musk on his tongue.

'What am I waiting for?' he mumbles to her.

'Just listen to me,' she whispers. 'In my pocket, there's a bottle. When I tell you, you take it, aye?'

Kit does not understand. He has never known a time when he did not trust Squire Kay, but is the woman really in front of him the same woman who has cared for him all these years in London? The same woman who apparently saw Kit born and grew up here in the Cursed House, rather than a brothel, and never told him the truth?

'Promise me, Young Kit.' Her breath is heavy from the effort of moving him up three flights of stairs. The stains on her bandaged hand are darkening. 'Promise me—'

'In here.' Elody wrenches open a closed door. 'You'll remember soon, Kit, I'm sure, this was your little prison! More luxurious than your friend's hole at Bridewell.'

It is a wide space, dark and grey, and could very well be in Raven's Roost or Hart House for all Kit recognises it. Then Elody is opening the shutters, the pale light fills the room with the vision of grey sky over water, and she unlocks the narrow window. It's the sound of it, the creaking swing, the musical latch, the sudden rush of passing water and city bells: he is filled with ancient longing. As it grows he is shrinking, he is tiny, there is snow drifting through that open window and his hands are cold, so cold.

'Come and look.' Kit stumbles over and stares down at the cobbles below, the narrow street, the river Scheldt. He remembers its name, remembers how it felt to stare from here at the tumbling water and wish to be sailing away on it.

'That is where your shirt was found, flapping like a flag of surrender.' Elody points to a lantern on a pike by the river. Kit remembers how he would watch them be lit in the evenings, flickering away inside their tiny metal cages. 'Your little death. I suppose your Griffin climbed up and pulled you down.'

When he asked Griffin if he brought alchemical secrets back from Antwerp he said, only one. If it was truly him, he does not recall it.

Kit stares at the water. How strange to recall the cadence of its sound, so different from the Thames.

'I think my father may even have wept for you. Is that not strange? After everything he did to my mother I do not think he shed one tear for us. But you were his great victory.'

'Why are we here?' Kit asks. Elody's hand grips the edge of the window and she stares out over the river, at the boats passing.

'God has seen fit to blow back King Philip's ships. The Armada could not land.'

Kit is unreasonably satisfied to hear this. Not especially for the safety of his countrymen or himself – after all, Catholics have been just as dangerous to him as reformers in the last year – but because it is not what Elody wants. He badly wants her to be disappointed.

'It is His will,' Elody continues. 'The mystery of His will is beyond me, but it becomes even more urgent that you learn. Here will be the best place for you to do so. When you truly know what you are capable of, when you remember, I do not think I will have to spear more of her fingers for your power to flow. Nor will you fight it, when you understand your place.'

Kit can feel Squire Kay trembling against him. He wonders if it is fear or memories. He looks around but nothing more returns to him.

'Is this where I was born?' Kit asks.

'I knew you'd be curious.' Elody pulls the window closed. 'Let me show you where it was.'

The silence of the house wraps around them as they move back down the many stairs, wood creaking, dust parting under their feet. When they reach the ground floor Kit watches Elody open a smaller door, reinforced, with metal on the inside.

Elody passes Squire Kay a lit candle. 'Lead the way.'

The flame sputters as her hand wavers but she steps into the darkness, the candlelight illuminating narrow stone steps down under the house. Kit follows, hearing the sound of Elody locking the door from the inside behind him. He reaches the bottom step and tries to look around through the deep gloaming. The scent in his nostrils is of charcoal and wet stone under the earth and something else too, something metallic, that sits at the back of his tongue and makes his spine stiffen. Elody walks down the stairs behind him with absolute confidence, brushing past him in a waft of floral perfume, to take the candle and set it to a sconce on the wall. The cellar illuminates as the old pitch and tow flames into life. Kit doesn't know what he expected but it is not this. Painted all over the walls are the scenes from the *Rosarium philosophorum*, the king and queen of sun and moon, laid together and descended into fire to be reborn, anew. There is a fire pit dug into the floor, almost as wide as the walls. A grill sits atop it, iron bars close enough they can be walked upon and in the centre is the most absurd thing Kit has ever seen. As tall as a man, giant and gleaming, burnished in places and tarnished in others, flashes of gold catching and reflecting the dancing flame. The closest thing Kit imagines it to be like is an egg; but uneven and stained. He sees dark handprints, he thinks burnt by soot, until he moves closer and sees the dark grime of dried blood.

'Colossal, is it not?' Elody raps her knuckles against it, ringing hollow and deadly. 'What did Lazarus teach you such vessels are for?'

'The philosopher's stone, the compression stage of the Red Lion elixir.' Kit doesn't want to think about Lazarus but the answers are there, he can't help but speak them. When the right compounds are created; the purest mercury, the living Arbor Diana, when an alchemist has achieved these steps he sets his sight on the vessel.

'*Filius philosophorum* means philosopher's child. Some alchemists believe recipes for it give forth the precious stone or the elixir of life but for a time my father operated on a more literal interpretation. He considered that by putting a vessel for child bearing inside the process for the *filius philosophorum* could yield the results he wanted. The perfect child. Better at least than his own cursed children, a discarded daughter or a deformed son.' Elody walks around the hulking beast of it, a look of disgust and adoration on her face. 'It has been posited by the alchemical fathers that babes could be made outside of the womb, homunculi and such. My father's first experiments were not successful, seeded in horse dung and then kept in the vessel. It was no good. By the time I arrived here after my mother's death, he had begun creating his own seeding process. Do not ask me of it, records were all burnt, but he realised the scholars had been wrong. He could not get away from it. In the act of creation at least, a woman was needed.'

Elody strokes its surface but her eyes are distant.

'Needy whores. He placed his secret seeds inside them. Fed them arcane blood, grew them big on it, kept them in the vessel. Then cooked at the peaks of their labours. It barely worked. Until you.'

'I don't believe you.' He says it because he does not want to believe. He thinks of the lungs of the woman, jarred up in Raven's Roost. It is one thing to end up pickled, another thing to begin that way. To be born here, brought into distorted life by this grotesque vessel and the torture Elody so casually describes.

'All alchemy requires sacrifice.' She draws a finger along a metal seal, cracked, clumsy and silver, as if it has been reformed again and again. 'The specimens laboured inside with the fire lit beneath them. Whatever lived was cut out.'

He has walked forward, over the grate, the cold coals below, to place a hand against it, this nightmare he was born into. It is chilled, bumpy, rougher than he expected for the glittering, ominous sheen of it. He does not remember ever feeling it, he does not remember the dark inside of it, the slippery mercury to bathe his first breath with his mother's screams echoing against gold. Lazarus said he recalled his own birth. How Kit wishes he could pull it out of his own skull, cut and dig with Lazarus' knife until this particular memory could be found, held up to the light for examination, but there is nothing. Naught but a terrible story.

'Tell him, woman. You saw his birth.'

Kit twists around to stare at Squire Kay. She is standing by the back wall, the head of the faceless King behind her.

'I did not see her seeded nor put in,' Squire Kay whispers, staring at the terrible vessel. 'But I saw you come out.'

Her eyes flicker to Kit.

'It was so hot down here, so smoky, barely any ventilation.' She gestures to the small crevice of a blocked window that peeks out onto street level. 'The screams were the worst. She rattled that thing, how she battled to get out, they used long sticks to hold it in place and I knew she was fighting. They doused the flames, they emptied it, that accursed thing, she was dead inside. I never saw her face but I saw her arm, flopping out. Burned all over and pink. They fished you out of her blood and the mess and they thought you dead, for you did not scream, but there you were, so alive, and burned all over. They gave you to me.'

She cradles her wounded hand to her chest. Her eyes shine, catching the firelight, tears beginning to tremble past her nose.

'I was so scared to touch you, lad, for fear I'd hurt you.' When her voice cracks, Kit feels it, a fissure running through him, breaking open dry earth inside. 'I never could.'

'They called you *infans solaris*, the sun child, born of the flame,' Elody says, and was this not what Lord Isherwood shouted with his last breath? Not calling for his two children, there in the room, but for Kit. 'You were the painless one. You were the last they tried and the only success.'

Kit doesn't even turn to hear her, he doesn't care, all he cares for is Squire Kay. She stretches out her spare, unbloodied hand, fingers flexing desperately for him, grasping his doublet to pull him closer.

'Where did they bury her?' he whispers, his hands in her red hair, fisting it close. 'My mother?'

'You have no mother,' Elody says behind him.

'I wish I knew, I am sorry,' says Squire Kay, pulling him against her in a clutching hug. Kit can feel her pressing something in the pocket of her dress against his leg. The bottle. Her voice is nothing but a breathy sob in his ear. 'You are a natural coat maker.'

Kit douses the tears inside him, holds a sharp breath in his mouth. Those words, they can only belong to Lazarus. Instinctively, he surreptitiously slides a hand into her pocket and withdraws the bottle.

'You have no mother! The seed of man produces a child; a woman is but a vessel!' Elody slams her hand against the mottled surface of it. How the sound travels, strong enough to make the flames in the sconce flicker. 'You have no mother, no father, you only have a creator. My father made you!'

Her voice is savage, an almost inhuman wail.

'He chose you from seed, he watched you grow, he held you in his hands for your first breath, do you know he did not hold me after I was born? Too disappointed was he that I was female. He discarded me, disowned me, called me bastard, fruit of another man's seed! You were chosen, only you!'

She seizes Kit, yanks him back towards the vessel, their feet clattering so hard on the grate as to shake the entire thing down. She gives the top of the vessel an almighty shove and it cracks open, an egg sliced. The inside of it is ruddy with spilled blood, silver trails and grime dust left at the bottom. The remains of my mother, Kit thinks, the remains of me.

'You are what he wanted, not a daughter he hated or a crookbacked son he was ashamed of. A miraculous thing that would never feel the pain of his cruelty, nor the ache of his absence. So you do not weep or grieve for your whore's womb, *infans solaris*, you know nothing of pain. Let us put you back in and set you aflame, shall we? So you can truly remember what it is to be made?'

She grabs his neck and pushes his face down towards it as if she intends to tip him in then and there. The smell is metallic but still somehow, after all these years, sweet and animal with the lingering scent of decay. Six minutes with a good wind, a much quicker death in a metal egg heated with flames. Kit is a jumble of a hundred different things he cannot organise, but he is sure of one thing. Whoever he is, wherever he came from, he will not get back in the monstrous vessel ever again. He pulls out Lazarus' bottle and smashes it against the inside, glass splattering into the dust at the bottom, his hand bloody. It begins to spew forth a familiar black smoke and Kit imagines Lazarus bottling the formula, sending it to Griffin with instructions, watching from afar, near the Rose, as they all battled to save him. The thought cannot make him heavier; it cannot make his sorrow wider.

'What have you done?' Elody yanks him back, both of them staggering on the shaking metal grate. Kit launches himself forward out of her grip, shoving his bare hands into the vessel and the smoke, trusting what he knows will happen and it does, for Lazarus has never put a true formula in his hands that has not worked. He feels it press into his blood, crush through his veins, a crumpling of power inside of him, a house falling down. All people are this, Kit thinks, we are the same stuff as darkest night, a mere transmutation from oblivion. If he could give form to the endless despair inside of him, of Griffin's death, of Lazarus' betrayal, of this unkindness dredged in the deepest part of him that he is a killer with his first breath, stealing away the life of his mother, what might that look like? When he turns his hand upwards, what spills from his pores, from his arms and his skin, is obsidian, is stygian, is the end of creation.

'What are you doing?' Elody is coughing, scrabbling at him, nails cutting into his clothes, but he doesn't care. Lazarus means him to do his worst here, to kill Elody and end his own suffering with it, a final mercy from Instructor to Initiate: I will not let her have you, I will not let her take you back to another cellar that you fear so deeply. So he breathes the smoke in, thinks of his lungs filling with it, breathes it out. Lazarus was right, it was only a matter of belief and how can Kit not believe now? Hearing Squire Kay's story, standing here on this ugly spot where he was made a monster. The black smoke spins and soars, violent thunderclouds, there is the sound of a tremendous grinding and he thinks perhaps it is burrowing into the foundations but he is lost in it. He cannot see Elody, he cannot hear Squire Kay and he will die here, in the place he was made, and is it not fitting?

No one is waiting for me, Kit thinks; the shadow beyond is not really shadow at all, but a book closed, a curtain dropped, a theatre burned to the ground. All things are blended together, one natural twist away from something else. Flesh to fire, flame to water, bones to earth and memory to air. Everyone I love and have ever loved is here and now and always. I am leaving them.

ꝰᛞꝩᛣᛚᛖꞁ

He who knows pain

Chapter Thirty-Three

There are hands around his wrists, dragging him away. Then there is sweet, stale air and a repeated, horrible grinding sound. There is a light and a pair of steely silver eyes.

'Breathe,' they say.

Kit does. He stares at Lazarus Isherwood, his face bruised yellow and purple from Kit's boot, somehow inside the walls of the Cursed House, a torch lit and exposing a tunnel. You came back for me, you did not leave me, Kit wants to say, and I will despise you until my dying day for what you did, you lying fucker. All he does is breathe.

'Come,' says Lazarus. Squire Kay is coughing up grey vomit besides Kit; it stinks of bile and charcoal and she begins to stagger forward, her hand on the wall, as if she's walked this dank underground passage before. Lazarus has Kit on his feet, is propelling him forward before he can think to ask a question.

'The tunnel runs from this house to the end of the street, the founders. I paid them good coin for the use of it. The wall opens, it is split and can only be pushed from this side.'

310

'How did you know?' Kit's voice is a croak. His mouth tastes of ash.

'Your friend told me. This is how they smuggled you out of the Cursed House the first time.' Lazarus nods to Squire Kay, her red hair caught in the fire of the torch. 'I paid Captain Larkin for a stowaway from London. Elody had you under lock and key in the Captain's quarters but not Kay. They held her in the brig. It was easy to have a discussion.'

Kit's mind is full of smoke but through it, he sees hazy pictures. Lazarus, hiding on the ship he has been sailing on, Lazarus, speaking to Squire Kay, Lazarus, sending Kit the bottle.

'You did not intend to kill me.'

'Never.'

Kit is not sure it is a given, but he is not in a position to turn down salvation even from the hand of Lazarus Isherwood. They stagger, Kit's hand brushing and snagging against the cold chilled stone. Here he is, alive when he never expected to be.

'Did you see it?' he asks abruptly. 'The vessel? Did you hear what she said?'

Their footsteps are loud, shuffling stomps. Squire Kay's breath is wheezing. Beside him, against him, holding him up, Lazarus is silent.

'I did,' he says.

'It must give you comfort,' Kit says. 'To know how right you were.'

'It gives me no comfort to think of how you suffered, brought into the world this way.'

Kit lets out a bark of laughter. It bounces back to him, a plague of dogs, cheerless.

'Funny, I never suffered a minute in my life until you killed Griffin.'

'Unremembered suffering is still suffering, Skevy.'

It's almost relieving, this blend of hatred filled with irritation, the candescent rage against this man; always so smug, always so quick to be so frustratingly, utterly right.

'Fuck you.' Kit tries to push him away but he is too weak, more of a nudge of shoulders, and Lazarus only grips tighter. 'You killed the man who loved me most in this life.'

'That is not true.'

'So you did not kill him?'

'That's not what I meant.'

Kit closes his eyes wearily; he is emptier than he has ever been, all of his viscera crushed out and into Lazarus' black smoke. If this is what it is to be loved by Lazarus Isherwood, it is a treacherous thing indeed. They have reached the end of the tunnel. There is a stick leaning against the wall and Squire Kay is swinging it wildly in the air to catch a latch on the ceiling. There is a world above, a benediction of light leaving them blinking, and then rough, burnt founders hands to pull them up. As the founders are paid and the trapdoor closed again, Kit stares at it, trying to remember a childhood escape made this way, a dark tunnel into the hot, glowing hearth of a workshop, but there is nothing. All he can think of is that somewhere, under the ground, is the body of Elody Blackwater, first child and creation of Lord Isherwood, laid out in an alchemy chamber, dying Griffin's death.

'We must go home, Kit.'

Squire Kay's hand is on his shoulder. He would know her touch anywhere. It is not by her fingers or the pressure, things other less-created men might feel. It is the way she stands behind him. She has been watching him his entire life.

'Why?' Kit looks at her, this sooty-faced tremulous woman who stole him and made him family. 'Why did you care so much?'

'Oh Kit, I cannot say, but... only, your hair maybe.' She pets it softly, eyes dreamy. 'I'd always wanted a babe with hair the colour of my own.'

Kit wonders if that is all it takes to save someone. A person coming along and thinking, I see myself in you.

'You didn't tell me.'

'Who would?' she sniffs, gesturing to the trapdoor and the horrors beneath it with her bloody hand. 'I'd come over with Griffin, hoping to get out from under Twentyman for a bit. Ezra had not the money to marry me. I was only eighteen, had a reputation already.' Her chin juts forward, defiant. 'Griffin said I could get better wages here, save up. I always wondered if he just needed a way to get a connection into Isherwood's house, on Walsingham's ask. He was getting work playing, tutoring too and when I started working for Isherwood I recommended Griffin for sales of hard-to-get goods. He spied and I earned and I never thought I would...' she trails off. He can tell he is the unexpected thing, the unplanned want, the unforeseen love in a scheme that was all about gain. 'When I was dismissed I asked him to get you out. You'd never said a word to me, Kit, not in five years, but when you met Griffin... You were like a lost kitten, followed him everywhere, starting to repeat him, starting to chatter, forgetting so quickly. He named you for a joke but soon it was all you would respond to. When we landed in London you asked us where you came from and he said—'

'It matters not who you are born to but where you are made,' Kit finishes dully. She nods. Her face is full of fragile hope, eyes pleading for forgiveness.

'You were made in Southwark,' she says. 'Like us.'

All Kit can do is squeeze her hand. I was not, he thinks. I was made in the fire.

'Why Skevy?' he says.

'I do not know.' She shrugs helplessly. 'I think he got it from a book.'

Saved for my hair, named for a joke and a book. It is a new type of unbearable that it should all be so fucking meagre.

Aboard *The Seahorse*, if Captain Larkin is at all surprised that Lady Blackwater has not returned, she does not show it. She takes a heavy purse from Lazarus and says:

'To London again, then?' She looks at Kit as she says it. 'By the way, it was your lass in jail, Mariner Elgin, she were the one who told me to come to him. If you reckon yourself saved in anyway, it was by her hand.'

Kit takes this with him as he is shown beneath decks to a small but private cabin, straw mattresses below and a hammock above. He climbs into the hammock that smells of salted meat and thinks of Mariner, locked up in Bridewell, waiting for a death she doesn't deserve and still trying to defer his. He remembers the way she grabbed his hand beside Lord Isherwood's dead body, an instinctive gesture, one that has pulled his hand back from fire and nettles nearly all his life. He remembers wrestling with Lazarus as she was taken away. No last words to recall, just these ways their bodies betrayed them, even after so many terrible words and such distance. I love you in my flesh, I will protect you with my skin.

Hours pass, the wind rises, the smell of goat grilled on the cook box filters under the door as the day wastes across the channel and they sail into night. It rains on deck and there is a drip, sometimes splashing his face, sometimes his hand. He does not move. Then Lazarus is there, closing the door softly behind him, leaning against the door in the slightly battered borrowed garb of a sailor. He has more the look of pirate than alchemist, eyes purpled and jaw mottled with a yellow stain. Lazarus moves closer, looking down on him. Carefully, a hand that is somehow bruised too – did Kit stomp on it? He doesn't quite remember – reaches to touch his arm.

314

'I will never forgive you,' Kit says, quietly.

'I know.'

Lazarus's hand moves up his arm to his shoulder. The hammock sways, Kit swings into the touch and then away from it. He does not try to stop it. The hand reaches his neck and tangles in his hair, tugs with that pressure that Kit enjoys, that is probably too hard for everyone else but perfect for him.

'God's wounds, Silver.' Kit shakes his head, shakes the hand loose, tries to loosen this sensation of being trapped and safe in one breath. 'This is damnation indeed.'

Lazarus pushes down the fabric of the hammock, placing a knee in it with a wince and then, with a squashed groan, rolls in beside Kit. He thinks he could probably tip him out, should he want to, Lazarus is clearly too stiff to fight it. He doesn't.

'*This word damnation terrifies not him…*' Lazarus quotes.

'*For he confounds hell in Elysium*,' Kit finishes. '*Doctor Faustus*. Do you still find it far-fetched?'

'I am starting to find it quite reasonable, actually.'

Kit hates himself for smirking, but there it is, still unstoppable, the bubble of laughter behind his oesophagus.

'How can I trust a word out of your mouth?'

Lazarus says nothing. The hammock squeaks. The rain falling into the ocean is a second sea, crashing and meeting the first, and drips through the seams in the wood down on their faces.

'Initiate,' says Lazarus. Together, they silently allow that one soft word to unravel its thousands of meanings between them. You were not mine when I betrayed you, the word says, I said you could trust me to uncover the truth of yourself, not that you would like it. I promised to protect your secrets, not that I would give you mine.

'Why did you kill Griffin?' Kit asks.

Lazarus hesitates and Kit thinks, if you lie to me again, I will have no choice but to murder you. I will pull your heart out of your chest and eat it.

'Elody started writing to me two years ago, sending me formulas, books, notes. We had never known each other in childhood, never met, but everyone knows the story of the child made a bastard by divorce. I had no notion that whilst I was growing up in Scotland and my father worked in Antwerp she was kept there too. I thought she had stayed at the abbey after her mother's death until she was married. She never corrected me. She wrote to me about alchemy and she flattered me and I knew what she wanted: an ally against our father.'

Lazarus' voice is reflective. It sways with the hammock, soporific.

'You were always right about one thing: nothing I ever did would make him love me or value me, and without his love or value, I would never advance beyond a physician and a spirit. I was nothing but a tool in his hand to be utilised. I saw in her a route towards my father's end and my own freedom from him.'

'And what better gain is there than power?'

Lazarus clenches his fist and releases it. Kit sees in his palm the scar of his initiation, white and hard.

'All she wanted from me for an alliance was the death of one man and for it to look an accident. He was a man of no consequence who few would miss. His death for my life, my future. I saw no harm in it.'

'You saw no harm to you,' Kit corrects.

'And I was wrong.'

Your harm is my harm, Kit hears. He is not ready to accept it.

'She never told you she had found me?'

'No, and I would not have cared. I had what I wanted. She agreed that we would cultivate a situation where our father could be poisoned without implicating either of us. A natural death is an easy murder with the right tools.'

Kit twists to look at him, marvelling at his ruthlessness, no compunction or hesitation. He has seen Lazarus Isherwood naked, has watched him reset bones and brew formulas and blow up walls and there are still people in the world who see nothing but his hunched back. It is baffling to him.

'Then Lord Isherwood heard she was buying Kelley's body, I do not know how.'

Griffin's good marketing, Kit thinks sullenly, Twentyman's savvy selling.

'We discovered you. My priorities... shifted.'

'Is that what you call it?'

'I call it affection, Skevy.' His voice is sharp. It's quite something to be admonished with one word and embraced with the other four. He doesn't speak or move and Lazarus goes on. 'I knew of her Catholicism, her fervour. I knew I would have to keep you a secret from her to keep you safe as I had done with my father, at least until he was dead. Then I would be wealthy enough to buy you out, remove us home out of her grasp.'

Kit recalls Lazarus, only a few weeks ago, telling him that he would return home to Scotland. Kit had no idea he was included. Mere days ago it would have lit him up with pleasure. Not now.

'I calculated she was only interested in you as far as you advanced her in court and towards our father's death.' Lazarus pauses. 'I regret that.'

Those words on these lips, Kit would not believe them if he had not seen them. It is possible then, for this man to feel remorse.

'Regret because you did not anticipate it first?'

'Regret that I could not protect you, as I wished.'

A drip falls in Kit's eye. He blinks it away, blinks it out of both eyes, suddenly.

'How could you protect me from what I have always been?'

317

It is bitter to speak it, but true.

'You cannot blame yourself for your Griffin's death.'

'If I had died in that accursed vessel with my mother then Isherwood would not have kept me, Squire Kay would not have taken me to London, Elody would not have chased me! She would never have met Mariner, you would never have killed Griffin and both of them would be alive and well in Southwark!'

He is breathless with it, the relentless stream of his own culpability. Lazarus does not answer. The wood around them creaks musically. They sway and Kit's breath, gently, slows again to match the man beside him.

'He went in search of the alchemical child because he thought I was born broken,' he says. 'Because my sister was born female. Blame us for being unable to satisfy him.'

Kit shakes his head. Whatever they have done grown, for the fatherless children they were, he has nothing but scorching pity.

'Who made him that way? What speck of ore in his blood, what tilt in his temperament?' Lazarus' voice is shockingly tender, considering a man who saw him as nothing but a failure of form. 'Most would blame God, but since you have no God to blame, blame my father for your creation, if you must blame someone for being yourself.'

'Monstrous, made of man?'

'I do not think you will find it much different from being monstrous, made of God.' Lazarus' voice is very dry. 'All there is to do is live.'

But it is not only to live, Kit thinks, it is to live with himself. The ugliness, the sorrow, the remembered and unremembered pain of everything it means to live inside this alchemical form.

'How?' He asks it more to himself, not expecting an answer but Lazarus turns his head towards him, his eyes through their violet lids settling upon his face.

'Come to Scotland,' Lazarus says.

Kit shakes his head. The denial should feel easier.

'No. I'm going to Tyburn. For Mariner.' He looks at Lazarus. 'But you will go to Scotland?'

Slowly, Lazarus shakes his head. His hair, dark and greasy, falls away from his face and Kit stares at his jaw, the sallow bruises underneath beard.

'The planets, moon and stars cannot change their courses, not whilst the sun burns. They will follow.' Lazarus turns to look at him. 'I will follow.'

Kit stares at him. Is it love then, he wonders, to feel a person could unmake you with a word? To feel stripped, all the time, vulnerable and half-made? If so, the poets have not written it well at all.

'Is it a good pain or a bad pain?' Kit asks.

Lazarus' smile is crooked, one cheek too sore to dimple. He takes hold of Kit's hand in his.

'It remains to be seen.'

Lazarus squeezes his nails into Kit's palm; a brand, a warning, I will not let you go without me, not yet. Kit looks down at the row of half-moon shapes Lazarus' finger has left. The symbol for Luna. Imagination. Kit finds it impossible, even now, to imagine a world without the man beside him, as impossible as fathoming the endless night when the sun is finally extinguished. Here they lie, encased in wood, floating between the wicked waters and wild air and the world is wide and fucking lonely. Kit surrenders, sighs, and turns over his hand. He lets Lazarus' palm rest against his own and then tentatively, their fingers intertwine. The drips from above have made their skin wet, moisture caught between them, warm with blood under the skin, blending towards something else. Flesh to rain, hands to leaves. Slowly, beads of water on their joined flesh become steam, evaporating from them in strange patterns and Lazarus breathes in, sharply.

'Tell me how it feels,' he says. 'It has been theorised and postulated, this grasp of the invisible elements, to be able to attract them and control them, but no one has ever written what it would feel like.'

Kit sighs and rubs a thumb against the back of Lazarus' hand, through the steam still softly floating there.

'What is *feel* to a man who feels nothing? I know it is wet, but what is wet to me, truly? Different from dry, different from hot, but neither more pleasant nor unpleasant, so interchangeable. All things are this way, are they not? We are constellations, we have planets inside of us. I only think of these things, how all is the same, all the same and...'

He lets his words drift away from him. He releases Lazarus' hand and lifts his own, the steam follows and when he looks at it again, becomes rain, falling upwards from his fingers, flying back up to the wood to soak through, perhaps up and onwards, returning to rain-clouds. The same, always the same, but different.

'You feel something, Skevy.' Lazarus' fingers trail through the steam in wonderment. 'Belief.'

The cautious edge of a tiny smile, an echo, somewhere deep inside Kit of all the things he does and has felt for this man. Kit does not answer but links their hands again, giving into that tender pressure of another human, the awareness of their fragile bones, their soft flesh, the precious flimsiness of these bodies. He does not say what he has is not belief. Mariner has told him that faith is a certainty of things that are not seen. Kit has touched the vessel of his own creation. So how can it be faith to breathe each day, knowing the air will nourish you? What faith is required to simply accept all the horrible, wondrous things he is?

'I believe I can save Mariner,' he says. 'All I need is six minutes.'

LXXLLEL

He of fire and justice

Chapter Thirty-Four

She is tried on All Hallows' Eve. The guards scrounge up an overskirt for her to wear over her men's shirt when she appears in court. She's never worn one in her life, the fabric is strange and heavy against her knees and she tries not to stumble in it as she is brought in, shackled to the other prisoners. They stand in the dock, facing a row of twelve London merchants, her jurors. A line of male eyes, flicking over the open neck of her shirt, the exposed skin, her breasts which they have not let her wrap. Those eyes make her wonder if she should plead guilty – why should she suffer this vicious assessment? – but when it is finally her turn and she is shivering brutally in a cold courtroom with no shawl to fold across her shoulders, the words leave her lips:

'Not guilty, your honour.'

Pyncher is first. He is snivelling and red-faced, tells a sorrowful tale of a great lady deceived and betrayed, who took in a cousin she had never met out of the goodness of her heart. The fact that Elody is not here, gloating, tells Mariner that she has already sailed, leaving Pyncher to fend for himself. He protests his own innocence, he describes the horror of Lord Isherwood's death, and the jurors shake their heads and tut, these city men all imagining themselves resplendently titled, brought low by a jealous witch.

'She lied to my mistress, she lied to me,' Pyncher says. 'A murderess indeed.'

Mariner thinks that will be it, they will have heard enough. Then Twentyman is called to speak against her, in the suspicious death of Daisy Gale. Half of his face is yellowed and slippery, yet the repulsed looks on the faces of the jurors – the nosegays smushed against their nostrils when they glance at him – all melt away when he speaks of Daisy. Let it never be said that the Grave Eorl of Southwark cannot spin a yarn. All eyes are wet as Twentyman's voice breaks.

'I found her dead in our bed, that poison in her hand.' Tears streak down his cheeks and she hopes that they hurt his brutalised skin. 'All I have worked for, all I have built, was for this joy. To marry and raise a family with the lass I loved. All of it dashed in that moment I found her, and worst still, for her women friends told me she was with child. To lose them both… Forgive me.'

Twentyman weeps. How piteous they are for him, this self-made landlord out of Southwark; the women of the courtroom sob into their handkerchiefs. They don't know that Daisy never shared his bed except when he was fucking her at the Hat, that if he had known his babe lived in her flesh, he'd have tossed her out on her ear. When he steps down Mariner wonders if he will lunge for her. How satisfying it would feel to fight him back, to cut all the lies out of his throat, but her knife is probably in a guard's pocket by now.

'I swore I'd see justice done. You'll die, you witch, and heaven knows no one deserves it more.'

These words mean nothing, Mariner only hears the true taunt behind them, words that, if he could, he would be spitting at her: I swore I'd see the end of you, I swore I'd not pull your legs and look at you now. Even with gloating anticipation in his eyes, Mariner simply stares until, with a slight tic of displeasure, he is forced to walk away from her bewildering vacancy. If he sees defiance, let him, she thinks. Let him think he still has not hurt me when truly, he has brought me to my knees.

'Have you nothing to say in defence of yourself?' the judge asks, disinterested. He is already thinking of ending the day, of his wife at home, of his plate of roast duck and sauce. She is nothing to him; when he lies his head down tonight to snore he will not even remember her face. What can she say? I have loved a woman and she has betrayed me, cruelly, your honour. I was blinded by my lust for her and a need none in this room can possibly understand, to prove to myself that what I am is real. That my affections were true, not some corrupt product of my imagination, that it is possible for a woman to love a woman as you love your wife, your honour, as Adam loved Eve. I was a fool to fall in love but I am not a murderer. She could say it, but the words of Captain Larkin haunt her. Take this confession to God, for what is a woman who lusts for women but a witch? Hanging is quicker.

'As God is my witness, I am not guilty.'

The jurors do not even look at her. She was guilty when she walked in.

They tell her she is to die on the fifth of November. It is quite something, Mariner thinks, to leave the earth knowing the day of your death as you have known the day of your birth. To commit it to your short memory, to at least have that, just in case no one else exists to remember it. She thinks of Kit and Captain Larkin. She hopes that she has made the correct bet on Lazarus Isherwood, that he loves her Kit enough to save him, but perhaps he does not. Kit could be on his way to Rome in shackles, or maybe he is dead. She prays for him. She prays more than she has ever done in her life, but quickly wearies of it. What point is there now, in only speaking to God? She will meet him soon enough. She imagined that knowledge of one's own death would transform every moment of the remaining time, but it does not. The straw still stinks of the dead girl; she is still hungry, still thirsty, she still pisses and shits, her body utterly unaware that there is now little point any of it.

On All Hallows' Eve, children all over the city are going souling, knocking on doors for alms and prayers. In her half dreams, ghosts come. Daisy, as bare and beautiful as she used to be, lying in her bed at the Cardinal's Hat, flesh pink and mauve, her glowing belly taut as a full sail. Griffin, leaning against the wall in his indolent way, great grey circles under his eyes and black spittle staining his stubble.

'This is all your fault for dying,' she tells him. 'We were happy enough before.'

He says nothing, the kind bastard, only smiles at her as if to say; happiness and ignorance are not the same thing and could she have called herself happy? Full of longing and unfulfilled? Kit's words return to her, over and over, of how small her love has been. How little she has taken from the world, how little offered to herself. All Souls' Day dawns but the ghosts still return, night after night, and she is glad of their company.

On her last night alive, a ghostly woman appears before her, hair wet and tangled, face marked with barnacles and flame.

'Maria,' the woman whispers. Salty water flows out of her mouth.

'*Mamae*,' Mariner answers. This is the only word she has of the language etched deep inside of herself, in a place she does not dare to look. Her dead mother sits beside her, stinking of salt and the ocean floor, and Mariner confesses all. Her love of Elody, of the sea, of Kit, of the freedom bought with short hair and breeches and above all, her love of safety. To be unseen and unnoticed by the men of the world, to walk through it as one of them, safe forever from their eyes. Her mother offers no wisdom or blessing.

'*Maria, minha filhota*,' she says, again and again. A drowned name for a drowned child who was plucked from the sea and the fire by her uncle. What was once forgotten is fished out of her memory by these watery, dead hands. With it, too, come lullabies that her mother sings to her, voice bubbling under waves.

José embala o menino

Que a senhora logo vem.

Before the sun rises, Elgin comes. He holds rags in one hand and whisky in the other. His smile is pale blue, made of pre-dawn light.

'My son-shaped daughter,' says he. 'My niece-hearted nephew. A woman indeed.'

'Will I see you soon?' she asks. She fears he will say no, that her selfishness in her desires, for the skin of women and the freedom of men, has locked her out of the heavenly realms. All of her sorrow and regret and pain have been for nothing for she is neither loved in this world nor saved in the next. He does not answer.

'I am afraid,' she whispers. I am afraid I am not chosen, I am afraid I am not repentant. I am afraid my short, small time on this wild earth has been wasted entirely.

'*For what thing is your life? It is even a vapour that appeareth for a little time and vanisheth away*,' says he.

When pleasant sunrise strokes her face, she can feel herself vanishing.

*

London is beautiful on a Monday morning in November. The cold frost of the night has left the world glistening, every leaf sparkling and the mud tracks sprinkled with a hard crust of white glitter. The brown water of the Thames is thick and churning, teeming at its bank and as the carts roll to Tyburn Mariner turns her face to it, to the wherries and the ships with their high masts and bright sails, to the wheeling gulls with their unending shrieks and cries. Londoners jeer and shout as they roll down Chancery Lane, away from the city, but all the prisoners stood beside her are silent. Some see familiar faces and lift their shackled hands in stunned greetings that are made farewells in a moment. At Tyburn, the crowds have gathered around the gallows. The nooses are hanging ready, swaying in the breeze with the falling leaves of the elm trees, the colour of rust. It makes her think of Kit's hair against a pillow, lying in their cot in the stable, a nub of a candle casting a pitiful glow that illuminated the strands; golden, red, brown. How she has loved him, her friend, her brother. How she hopes he lives.

People jeer and scream as they are led up to the gallows, and Mariner stumbles against the damned skirt, falling to her knees, hands on the sun-dried wood. She is young again, skin still stretched and painful, recovering from her burns and set to scrubbing the deck. The holystone pushes grit up under her fingernails and the great gasping flap of the sails is above her. The clanking anchor lifts and voices surround her, rough and tuneful, singing:

Vayra, veyra, vayra, veyra,
Gentil, gallanntis veynde:

Twentyman is in the crowd: eyes eager, body taut, waiting and willing her to break, even now. How odd and small he seems from up here on the gallows. The raw sunlight bursts through the trees, rendering all the faces watching entirely the same; masked in shade, already gone.

I see him, veynde, I see him
Pourbossa, pourbossa.

The noose is dropped around her neck. She remembers Elgin, rubbing salve into her burns on that spot with his quick, clever fingers, then Kit, obediently cutting her hair to the right length at her neck. Their touch so close, every time, to the veins and life that flow beneath it. She looks at the rope above her. It is a chain and she is an anchor to be wrenched into the sky.

Hail all and ane, hail all and ane,
Hail him up til us, hail him up til us.

Mariner lets tears fall as she winces to stare up at these last stinging rays of sunshine, and thinks, in them I will be vanished in a moment. Sound is changed inside her; heartbeat so loud she can barely hear the joyous blackbird song on the morning air, or the man next to her muttering the words of the great English Creed:

'... and on the third day he rose again according to the Scriptures, and ascended into heaven, and sitteth of the right hand of the Father...'

Mariner wishes he would stop so she can listen, just listen a little harder, to hear past the blackbird's song and the rabble jeering to the tide of the Thames, the water of the world. That is what she wants last to hear.

'... and he shall come again, with glory, to judge—'

'Stop!' a voice cries. Mariner looks down from the blazing sunshine, the world all dark shapes but the voice is familiar, and a red-headed man is tussling with the guards, they are pushing him back. He is speaking in a low resonant tone; she cannot catch it but it sounds like Latin. Kit, no, she wants to shout, Kit, no, go away, but he is stretching out his hands, grabbing something out of the air. Suddenly, he is aflame. It balls into his hands, thick as the Sovereign's orb, arms wide, Christ on the cross, nailed and burning. There are great shrieks. The guards are frightened, falling back, cursing, and Kit closes his eyes as he chants, the fire spreads up his arms and down his legs, engulfing him.

'Stop him, stop the devil!' Someone is pushing forward. Mariner sees it is Twentyman; he is throwing a cloak, hoping to put Kit out and pull him down. Kit does not fall. He does not smother. His fire catches Twentyman's shirt, his breeches, and he screams. Mariner sees the cruel drawing sent to Hart House, a witch aflame. People are pulling away from him, scared to be caught, shouting for water, someone fetch water! Twentyman is falling, Twentyman is dying. Mother Plenty will be happy, Mariner thinks.

'Now, do it now!' one of the guards is shouting, pointing at the scaffold, but Kit is still chanting, voice mesmerising. His clothes are burning off him and turning to ash, his skin beginning to burn too, smelling like cooked bacon as he climbs the gallows. His fire catches the wood under his feet, only built this morning, not yet damp with dew. The prisoners yell and thrash in their nooses, the guards abandoning them. There are screams that he must be martyr or a devil, naked and fiery, whispering and crackling. He is the most ungodly thing she has ever seen and she is happy, so happy to see him again.

'Spare me, Lucifer! Spare me!' the man beside her wails.

'Kit?' She does not mean to sound so questioning but she does not know this being, this creature, with eyebrows melted to his face, fully baptised in fire without a scream. How awful he sounds and smells up close, popping and cooked. Yet the eyes are still the same, those endearingly odd eyes. You are still mine, she thinks. It is you I loved best, with the smallness of my heart.

'Forgive me, Mariner.' The blood on his lips hisses in the flame. At that moment, Mariner knows in her heart that Kit Skevý has decided to burn his way down to hell with her, if necessary. Mariner looks at his eyelashes, melting away, and feels nothing but an endless benevolence, the crushing joy of holy love. She opens her mouth to tell him all is forgiven, that he has been forgiven always, but the floor drops from underneath her feet and Mariner Elgin knows no more.

ᏳᎬᏚᏢᏆᏗᎬ

She who knows only herself

Chapter Thirty-Five

Someone is poking her cheek. It is rude, she thinks, to be poked awake when she is in her bunk and the rain is falling and the world swaying so softly inside the ship. She opens her eyes to tell whoever it is to bugger off, but sees no thick fingered sailor, only leaded windows with blue glass and droplets of rain. The air smells of burning. Suddenly, it returns to her, the scaffold, Kit scorched and flaming... she sits up, frantically, twisting her head to look for the source of the smell. It is only her hair, scorched close to her head.

'T'was the fire.' Ezra is sitting in a chair by the bed, his feet up on the blanket. 'You look more a lad than ever but you're alive.'

So she is. She tugs at her short, dry hair, frizzled and melted on the ends. Here it is, the world again, the air the same, the room unrecognisable.

'Where are we?'

'Mortlake.' Ezra looks around thoughtfully. 'Lord Isherwood has the loan of it from Doctor Dee.'

'How long have I slept?'

'This is only the third day,' Ezra says. 'Kay has gone back to the Moon. Left me here to fill you in.'

He hands her a glass of wine and, in looking down at it, she realises how violently scratchy her mouth and throat are. She drinks fast, gulping, tasting nothing but relief for the way it douses the itch in her throat. As she does, Ezra tells the tale of Squire Kay, stolen away in the night from the Silver Moon, gone for ten days, Ezra's frantic terror that she was dead. Of her return two days ago, bruised and beaten with only one working hand, Kit alive and hardened by the truth of his past, Lazarus Isherwood awkwardly out of place in Southwark but refusing to leave Kit's side. She hears of Elody, shut away in that dark hole of the Cursed House with the dreadful vessel, killed the same way she killed Griffin. She tries to ignore the stinging sorrow of that; the way it seems to leak out of the tissue of her lungs, unstoppable, some suppressed part of her that fears and mourns this woman who was so many firsts for her. With only the smallest flash in his eyes, Ezra recounts the death of Griffin at Lazarus' hands. It is little wonder then that Squire Kay has not come anywhere near Mortlake. Mariner is surprised she even stood to bear Lazarus saving her and Kit in Antwerp.

'She is glad to be home,' Ezra says flatly. 'But not healed.'

Then, Ezra tells of the plan. For Kit to burn, an unholy distraction, for Lazarus and Ezra to use acid to loosen the structures of the scaffolds, to line gunpowder underneath it. To pull Mariner and Kit from the wreckage and pray that in their deaths, they will somehow survive.

'Many died in the fire and the trampling,' Ezra says. 'It's the talk of the city. The playhouses have reopened and they are already setting it to stage.'

Mariner is not surprised. She remembers Kit, blazing like the great martyrs of Rome. What tales will Londoners tell in the coming years about the devil came forth, speaking Latin, the Prince of Hell at Tyburn?

'Where is he?' She instinctively looks at the bed beside her for hints of his red hair on the pillowcases. Then she remembers the way it had curled and burned, making the air taste bitter.

'I can take you to him.' Lazarus is standing in the doorway. He is not wearing his alchemist robes or doublet sleeves, his cream shirt cuffs pushed haphazardly up to his elbows. From the look of him, she imagines that caring for a practically cremated Kit has not been an easy task. She nods and Ezra helps her to steady her feet underneath her. Her bones ache, as if she has been pushed down many flights of stairs, but she is alive, at least.

'Captain Larkin?' she asks.

'Sailed away to Scotland.' Mariner buries her disappointment and nods. What reason had Captain Larkin to loiter, to see if she lived? None at all.

'These are for you.' Ezra nods at a pile of clothing; breeches and a fresh shirt and jerkin, a cloak for the cold and a wide hat to hide her face. 'You know you'll always be welcome back at the Silver Moon. After a time. Best to stay dead for now, if you can.'

She knows the time needed is however long it takes to forget a person entirely. Easier done in London than anywhere else. Ezra hugs her close, giving Mariner a final deep inhale of his soft, dusty scent with gentle murmuring farewells, before he makes his way back downriver to Southwark and his wife and their final, full ownership of the Silver Moon, free of Twentyman. Mariner follows Lazarus through the small house. With the sodden garden at the back and the high Thames at the front, it has the tranquil effect of a moored ship and Mariner is lulled into comforting silence. It is just as well, for she has little to say to Lazarus Isherwood; words lost under the weight of all the lies he and Elody told to her. Did you know? She wants to ask. What she intended for me?

'You are keeping no servants?' she asks instead.

'I do not anticipate us being here for long.'

Mariner knows that she is no part of the implied us. Lazarus Isherwood has only contributed to her salvation out of love for Kit Skevy, that much is clear. Downstairs, Kit's room is dark, the windows covered with black fabric and smelling strongly of mint. It has a steamy quality, as if someone has bathed and let the wet air sit. The candles flicker low, ominously, near the bed, wide enough for two. From the look of the crushed pillows, Kit has not been resting alone. Lazarus bends to the body on the bed, stiff and unmoving.

'Kit, Kit.' He heaps such mountains of tenderness inside the name of his lover. 'She's here. She's awake.'

There is a stirring under blankets, nothing more than a lumpen shadow in the close darkness. Lazarus rises, giving her a stern look.

'He is under many herbs. He may not be coherent, but it is the only way to keep him still long enough to heal.'

'If only you had been there that time he had a deadly fever,' says she. Lazarus' lips quirk in a squashed smile but she imagines there are hints of camaraderie in it. It is a unique and impossible task, keeping Kit Skevy alive. She moves cautiously to the bedside, heart hammering with what she might find.

Kit reminds her, oddly, of a joint of pork served at court, pink and glistening all over. His eyebrows and eyelashes have burned clean away, so have most of his ginger curls. His skin is raw all over and bloody in places, lips cracked red as if he has stained them with crushed beetles like the fine ladies of London.

'Do not trouble yourself over my hair, Lazarus says it will likely grow back,' Kit rasps out. She imagines the inside of his throat looks like the outside, rough and peeling but wet and bloody all at once and winces.

'Still, I think Master Henslowe will not be rushing to ask you to play Dido.'

The corners of his mouth lift in a wry smile, a trickle of blood starting from his cracked lips, suddenly a terrible, carnivorous beast. Do not tell jokes, she warns herself, and sits cautiously. She wants to hold his hands but they are bandaged, wrapped up in fresh white cloth. No doubt they bore the brunt of it.

'You took a terrible risk.'

'We timed it. It was no great alchemy, except for me to carve the fire into the ball shapes. It was an oil paper starter. Stage craft and the art of painlessness were the real tricks.'

Mariner remembers how easily Kit pulled fire out of seeming nothing; the orbs of it rolling in his hands. She wants to disagree but perhaps this is how Kit needs to think of himself now. A charlatan with an edge rather than a miracle and so she only nods.

'It was not a spell then?'

'A spell?' Kit's forehead wrinkles. Skin bunching and peeling. 'No, it was the conjuring of Mephistopheles. From *Doctor Faustus*.'

Mariner does not mean to laugh, but it is too funny, this idea of Kit scaring all of London with something they have seen dozens of times in the playhouses.

'You idiot,' she says, fondly.

'Nearly a dead idiot. Lazarus is furious, of course,' Kit says, his eyes sliding to the door and pulling back the blanket. His right leg is splinted. 'I broke it when we fell through the scaffold, but he thinks I am healing better than a normal man might.'

'Well, you are not a normal man.'

If Kit still had eyebrows, they would be rising.

'You believe me now?'

The story of the Cursed House in Antwerp is harrowing, even told through the measured, dispassionate voice of Ezra Prophet. *Happy are they that have not seen and yet believe*, Elgin whispers scripture to her, and what more does she need to see?

'I was afraid before,' she says, because it is too cruel now not to speak the truth. 'We have always been the same and I was afraid you had outgrown me. You, made of man and I...'

'Made in God's impeccable likeness?' Kit licks his bloody lips. 'We can be whatever we fucking want to be.'

His voice becomes weak at the end of the sentence, exhausted. What toilsome cost they have endured to simply be themselves. She stares down at his bulky, bandaged hands and tries not to weep. She sniffs firmly and glares at him.

'You let me believe I was dying.'

'Yes, I did. We are the monstrous dead.' Kit laughs and then coughs, coughs for too long and Mariner reaches for a glass of small ale. She holds it to his lips, watching his pink throat work to push it down. When he has finished, he gives her a slightly fearful look. 'Am I forgiven?'

'You did save my life.'

'Not for that.' Kit shakes his head, a slow turn, skin flaking onto the pillow. 'You were not her Daisy, not at all.'

It is not an apology but it is what she wants most to hear. They always know what the other needs most the hear.

'And you are not his Griffin,' she says. Kit sighs, his eyes closed. She understands the taste of his relief, now that the words that have been eating away at the back of the mind can be finally silenced, and only by the person who spoke them first.

'Come here.' His voice is starting to get slippery, his eyelids struggling to keep open. Mariner gently lowers herself to lie alongside him, safe in the knowledge that she can never hurt him, but not wanting to disrupt any of his fragile skin. He does not smell like himself anymore, now of spiced oils and chicken fat. She listens to his breath evening out and twists her head to look at his face. Was this what he looked like when he was born, pink and polished and pulled from a nightmare? What comfort can she give him?

'As far as the ocean is wide so I love you,' she whispers.

Kit smiles again, this time lips closed, a small tear in his eye. Mariner is not sure he has noticed it.

'Aye, so wide,' he breathes.

Mariner breathes through her nose, staring at the shadows and light that dance across his glistening face. This benediction, this recantation of past words spoken so cruelly, how it stings behind her eyes and tightens her throat, but she won't cry and wake him, drifting into precious restful sleep beside her. Instead she watches his eyeballs move behind his blistered eyelids and remembers the vastness of the love she had felt before the drop. It cannot have come from nowhere, so she thinks. There is love beyond, more love than she had ever anticipated.

Mariner leans close and presses a kiss to Kit's chapped, ripped lips, tasting copper. This is my blood, she thinks, given for you.

*

There is snow falling in Dover harbour. The end of the year fifteen ninety seven is brought in with a chill so cold the Thames freezes around the bridge and they have to catch the ferry from Deptford. Still the harbour is bustling, a ship is set to sail with snow on her carved seahorse figurehead and sails tightly coiled around her masts, waiting to be unfurled. Mariner stands on the dock, snow in her shorter curly hair, golden brown skin enough for passers-by to shake their heads and mutter under their breath: bloody Spaniards. To look at her, one would think her a queer traveller, standing with a hunched companion, all wrapped up in a cloak, face hidden, gloved hand on a walking stick. Kit has healed better than Lazarus hoped in the last two months in Mortlake. His eyebrows and eyelashes have not returned, the skin there still pink and shiny, but his freckles are coming back across his cheeks, paler than before. The broken leg is stubborn and he must walk with a stick for now. Mariner hopes he will use it properly and not beat children with it.

'Are you sure this woman will want you?' Kit asks.

'It is worth a try.'

Her heart is the lightest it has been since the noose dropped around her neck. Ezra has, in an act of sweetness beyond what Mariner expected, written to say he has heard Captain Larkin is coming into Dover.

'Do you have all you need?' Kit asks.

'Aye.'

Lazarus has fronted her enough money for her journey, given in a small purse without a word. Mariner did not thank him, since she is partly convinced he would pay more to get rid of her and he can easily afford it. The rest is the clothes on her back, the wits in her head and a new knife bought on the ferry down from a tin trader.

'I have something for you.' Kit fumbles, his hands clumsy in the thick gloves to protect the new skin from the cold, and withdraws some papers bound together. 'It is Ovid. It is how Griffin learned me my letters. You must learn to write to me. You must tell me where you are. Swear it.'

'I swear it.' She tucks it inside her doublet. He smiles. His lips still crack with the cold.

'What will you say to her?'

'That I grew up on the ships. I am a good sailor. That I dress this way because it is what I like and that I am a woman.'

'Be cautious of when you share the last.'

'I know.' Mariner leans forward and presses her face down against Kit's. She does not know how long it will be, and this last touch, this last sweet scent of him, still heavy with honey and healing thyme, it will have to be enough to sustain her. 'Brother mine.'

'Sister mine.' Kit whispers the claim against her forehead, lips pressed there in glorious beatitude. She blinks back her tears. She will not say she will miss him, for it would be like commenting that she would miss her heart, so she simply says,

'Where will I write to?'

'Address it to the Rose in Southwark and it will find me.'

She doesn't ask why he is not going to Scotland with Lazarus; she does not tell him that she is happy for him and relieved that he is choosing a path for himself rather than following a man who, far too much for her liking, reminds her of his sister. So she merely walks towards the ship. Aboard, she finds Captain Larkin, wrapped in a fur-lined cloak and staring at the cold water.

'So it's you, is it?' She folds her arms.

'Could you have use for me, Captain Larkin?' Mariner asks. 'I grew up on the ships, I am a hard worker. I am a woman looking for a place to sail, if you will have me.'

Have me, Mariner prays, let me live in the small slither of the world you occupy where a person can be both sailor and woman. Let me learn how to balance these parts of myself truly, share the little safety you have made for yourself with me. Captain Larkin looks her over steadily, thoughtfully.

'You're no English lass, are you?'

'No.' Mariner shakes her head. 'Father out of Scotland, mother of Portugal.'

'Well, anything is better than English.' Captain Larkin frowns. 'Will you fight against the English for me, if asked?'

'If you let me sail with you, I'll fight anyone.'

Captain Larkin laughs. How joyous that sound was in the dank prison of Bridewell, how sunny it is now, floating with the snow.

'Well enough, sailor,' she says. 'What do we call you?'

'Patience,' she says. She hopes it will trip off the tongue. Mariner Elgin is dead, like little Maria, the girl child lost in the waves and flame over twenty years ago. She has been a niece, a son, a sailor boy, a gentleman, a murderess and a witch, and now she is standing in front of a woman captain, with a future that is only hers to chart. Freedom is paid for, by someone's sacrifice or her own, never given. She can finally meet the cost, can meet it with the little love she has and the vastness she will find inside of herself because God does not look so fierce upon her anymore.

'Welcome aboard,' says Captain Larkin. They shake hands. There are snowflakes resting on Captain Larkin's braid and her hand is damp, warm, comforting. How easy it is now to touch this person, no longer Matthew Blackwater, no longer hidden in plain sight. How marvellous it is that Captain Larkin is talking quickly about pay and profit, saying they are sailing to Calais from there onto Cadiz and now the anchor is being raised, and she looks back to the dock. She raises her hand in farewell, unsure he will see it, but she swears, just for a moment, she sees a hint of fire in a raised hand, bright and gold. A miracle, but what are miracles to a woman twice dead, baptised to life in water and flame? The gulls are calling, circling, egging her on to whatever is next. She turns her face towards the wide ocean.

⌐⌐⌐⌐⌐⌐⌐

He whose name is Renewal

Chapter Thirty-Six

Kit arrives back at Mortlake, stamping snow off his feet. It has been a long day up and down the river to Dover and he is stiff in a way he is still getting used to. There is no sharpness of feeling, no indication that burning himself up like a lantern has made him any more susceptible to feeling pain, but there is simply more resistance in his joints. When he woke after the scaffold, eyes resisting opening on the way to Mortlake, it was Lazarus who put a hand firmly on his chest and said:

'You must not move. Not if you want to live.'

'So I am alive again?' His voice had been nothing but a whistle, a squeak of air through swollen flesh.

'Just.' Lazarus' voice had been tight with fury. 'Seven minutes, Skevy. You were fucking late.'

'Forgive me.'

Two words; so much effort to breathe them past stiff lips. Forgive me for loving Mariner more than I love you, forgive me for needing to save her. Forgive me for being the sun in your universe, holding you in my thrall. Then Kit had felt a hand in his hair, except there

339

was no hair left. A palm, tentative for the first time, against his skull.

'I will try.'

With eyes closed, Kit wondered if that was the best they could offer one another – attempts at absolution. In the last two months, long nights punctuated by a sleepy-eyed Lazarus administering healing draughts, the constant unwrapping down to his pink, shiny nakedness, balming and rewrapping, with gentle, wry comments upon his progress ('Less like flaked almonds and more like pork skin, today'; 'Are you healing me or preparing to eat me, Silver?') absolution has been slowly arriving. Now all sins are known, exoneration is spreading through the blood. Every hurt Lazarus has caused is held in the golden balance of the persistent attentiveness of his care and devotion, his crowding dedication to their mutual survival and the unfading fealty of his kiss.

'You made good time,' Lazarus comments, as Kit enters the small study and tosses his cloak onto the back of one of the two chairs by the fire. Lazarus has still not opened up any of the other rooms, bookshelves still shrouded with sheets, a clear indication that even after four weeks, Lazarus has no intention of staying. Every day, more and more correspondence piles up on the desk, the seals becoming increasingly difficult to ignore. Sir Thomas Walsingham, Sir Robert Cecil, Lord Burghley, and today, the seal of the King of Scotland is broken and resting on the edge of the armchair, Lazarus' eyebrows taut together as he reads.

'He wishes you to return to court?' Kit stretches his damp boots out in front of the fire and slowly removes his gloves, careful not to rush and rip the tender flesh, as Lazarus taught him. He clenches and unclenches his pink, shiny hands, feeling the stretch of the new skin, the fingertips with even less sensitivity. He is more prone to burning them than ever.

'No, he wishes me to come to Edinburgh.' Lazarus sets aside the letter. 'There is news from Prague. Edward Kelley is truly dead. He died of wounds, trying to escape.'

Kit has not thought of him in over half a year. How strange it is to think that in the time he has been learning how to be an alchemist, one of the greatest of their age has been languishing, dying, imprisoned by one of the fiercest monarchs in Europe because he claimed to make gold. It is a stark warning.

'What has Edward Kelley to do with you?'

'After him, my father had the loudest claim for a miracle. Emperor Rudolf has lost his conjuror, so has Queen Elizabeth, since Kelley was an Englishman. She will no longer look to Dee. King James, no doubt, wants to ensure my father's secrets are returned safely to their rightful inheritor.'

Kit imagines the courts of Europe as a stage, seen from above in the Gods, watching the monarchs in the wings pushing characters onto the boards. For all that alchemists jealously hoard their secrets, for the virtue of simply being born on soil that is English, Scottish, French, all they bring into being is already claimed for a crown. Kit does not want to be mastered by anyone, ever again.

'I suppose you will not come with me?'

'As what? Your friend? Your alchemist? Your lover?'

'My Initiate,' Lazarus says, leaning forward to take Kit's hand. 'But yes, the others also.'

Lazarus tells the truth now and that is better. Or perhaps it is simply now that Kit never expects the entire truth from him, and that is better. For does he really want to know all the reasons the King of Scotland might want Lazarus in Edinburgh? The embroilment of court, of plots and schemes, is something Kit intends to leave far behind.

'Come with me.' Lazarus leans towards him and kisses him, very slowly. Lazarus' tongue is softer against the inside of his mouth, but perhaps the skin is new there too.

Kit pulls away, shaking his head.

'You know I would care for you always,' Lazarus says factually. The words I love you are meant to contain the entire world, but from Lazarus' lips he hears the truth of what they do not say. All the things Lazarus is and will not stop being because he loves Kit.

'If I come with you, you will ask me to make gold.' Kit sighs and, as Lazarus opens his mouth, speaks over him. 'You will say now – I will never do that, your gift is your gift, all I want is your safety and to have you warm in my bed every night – but when the King of Scotland presses you to use your alchemy for his gain and you have so far to climb and others to beat, you will ask me to make it. You will ask me to unwrap every secret in the universe because there is only one way to protect an alchemist from other alchemists so… you will ask me to scale the pinnacle. I have no desire to be a saint or a sorcerer, and you cannot promise me that if I come to Scotland you will not give into the temptation to make me one.'

'You think you are too much temptation.' Lazarus strokes the back of his hand with a thumb.

'I think you are too much temptation,' Kit returns, pauses for a second. 'If I loved you less it might be easier.'

'But you do.' Lazarus leans forward, silvery eyes fixed upon him, hunting still, hunting after all this time. 'Love me.'

'Unfortunately,' Kit admits. 'For the both of us.'

Lazarus sighs, Kit does not know if it is in frustration of himself or in Kit for seeing him accurately, but he leans forward again, to trace his lips over the space where eyelashes once grew.

'There might come a day when it is less unfortunate. When I am strong enough to protect us both without asking you to press the truest bounds of your skill.' Lazarus' breath smells of grape against his cheek, the taste of their first, catastrophic kiss. Kit does not know how much of these words are lies, or simply wisps of hope. Only time will tell.

'There may come a day when gold comes from lead and dead men walk.'

'It will come quicker if you put your skill to it.'

'I cannot make gold if the formula is not good.' Despite all he has learned of himself, Kit does not believe, at his core, that lead can be so easily shifted into gold, as water to steam or ice to water. It will take more than an alchemical child, it will take an alchemist of unprecedented mind to achieve such atomus transformation. If Kit is limited by his capacity for imagination then here sits his limit.

'But the remnants of the living are not found beyond us.'

Kit thinks of the moment in the Cursed House when he thought he was dying; the quietness beyond.

'You say there is no heaven? So bold.' Lazarus smiles widely, as he always does when Kit veers towards the heretical.

'What is the human body but a constellation of the same powers that formed the stars in the sky?' Kit waves his hand, as if he will conjure a ghost from the fire and ash. 'To dust we return, Silver.'

'Not yet.' Lazarus rubs a thumb along the back of Kit's neck and pulls their noses together. Kit knows now, the timbre of a goodbye. If this one had been scripted, they are coming to its end, the lines running away from them.

'Try to be less significant in the future,' says Lazarus. 'If you possibly can.'

'I will not swear it.'

There is something beginning in his chest, perhaps a cousin to the sensation that has lived inside him his entire life since he was cast screaming and naked from the vessel, the knowledge of his mother's death somehow imprinted on his tiny, alchemical body.

There is good pain hidden inside the pain of parting, Kit thinks. Lost people are gone forever, but we carry them inside of us, always. It is an alchemy of its own majesty, to be at once gone and present.

'Your sun.' Lazarus presses a hand against Kit's heart. Kit hears the words for the promises they are; I will hold your heart in mine again and feel it beat. I will not leave this earth and become nothing more than a creature that lives forever inside your chest. Without your sun in the universe my heart will not survive and as I am the stars and you are the body, as the planets are to the plants, so we are connected now and always.

'Your sun,' Kit promises.

*

In the first week of fifteen ninety-eight, Lazarus rides north to Scotland. Kit takes the river east to London. On his journey through the city people generally respond to him as a wandering Merlin, most cross themselves, some ask for blessings. Only one lad tries to kick him, but Kit beats him soundly with his walking stick until he wails. At the Silver Moon, Squire Kay is, for once, not behind the bar. She sits on the bench outside, wrapped up against the frosty chill, enjoying the rare but violently gold January sunshine. When she sees him she jumps, knocking the ale beside her over.

'I'd not have known you.' She gazes at his short, patchy fuzz across his head, his hairless face. Kit sits beside her, tilts his raw skin to the sun's rays. Warm, he thinks; that will feel warm.

'On the deed for this place, now Twentyman is finally off it, your name, is it Squire Kay?'

'No.' If she is surprised by this line of questioning she does not show it. 'My birth name is Katherine Griffin and I am married. The deed is in our shared names, Ezra and Katherine Prophet.'

'I am needing a new name,' he says. 'I will not bother you for board, I promise, I will live in the city and I intend to travel, but if you would have a cousin or relative long lost—'

'Yes.' She grips his gloved hand so fiercely he feels it through the leather, the pinch of it. 'I will always have you.'

He holds her hand back, listening to her soft sniffling tears as she closes her eyes, blinking against the sunlight, and he lets it fill his vision with gold. Perhaps it will be easier for them to love one another now, without Griffin and the secrets. Perhaps it will be easier to say this is my family, what is left of it, what I have chosen to hold fast.

Later, Kit stands, unnoticed in the open doorway of the Rose, whilst Ned Alleyn screams at Mister Henslowe.

'We cannot do Faustus at Court, it is impossible! We have no stage craft!' Ned bellows. He is wearing Faustus' cap; they are clearly in the middle of the scene and the bored Mephistopheles is wearing a tremendous mask that looks too big for his head.

'The Queen has asked for Marlowe for the Twelfth Night, since he is so bloody fashionable,' Mister Henslowe says. 'Especially after that little shit of a martyr made himself a burning Icarus at Tyburn with Marlowe's damned words.'

'We cannot do justice to hell with this shit—' Ned aims a kick at Mephistopheles who curses and almost falls off the stage '—mumbling like a mummer behind a dog's breakfast!'

'I can rewrite it, if you like,' adds Will, clearly roped in to playing Valdes again.

'Oh, can you rewrite *hell is discovered* out of Doctor bloody Faustus?' Ned yells. 'Where will they go, instead? To fucking Verona?'

'I am an alchemist,' Kit says, raising a hand and his voice. 'I can help you with your stage craft.'

He pulls his hood back. He is keeping his mostly bald head wrapped these days, but he can do nothing about his lost eyebrows and pink scars across his throat and hands.

'Christ's bloody wounds!' Mephistopheles declares. 'He should be the Prince of Hell, not me!'

'Shut up.' Ned Alleyn turns to Kit. There is a moment when Kit wonders if he will put together this odd-eyed, bald and scarred man with the strange child who used to follow his last stage crafter around, but of course he does not. The city has been rife with ague; there are rumours the Queen is sick again and the Irish have won a great battle against the English at Carrickfergus, Southwark-born soldiers buried under Irish skies. The world turns on and once you are dead in London, you are dead. 'What have you got?'

Kit smiles and pulls one of Lazarus' bottles out of his cloak. He makes a show of twisting his fingers above it as he's seen Ned Alleyn himself do when playing Faustus, and then pours grey smoke out over his hands. It billows the same as it did the night they escaped Isherwood House and in the dancing grey plumes Kit sees horses riding north and ships sailing.

'God's nails, that is good,' Will says, eyes gleaming. 'It could be a tempest, or forest magic.'

'Could be fire out of hell, more's the point.' Ned folds his arms. Kit can tell he is trying to look unimpressed but his knee is jiggling in excitement. 'You're an ugly sod. Not on the run, are you? No hue and cry up for you?'

'No.' Kit shakes his head. Nothing follows a dead man.

'Then why are you here?' Ned glares. 'You could be selling tricks to fine folks on the Bridge.'

'Because here is the only place I ever wanted to be,' Kit says, letting himself grin. He knows it is unsettling. He finds this aspect of his new face incredibly useful. Mephistopheles steps back from his visage. 'I can give you such magic as you've never seen.'

He makes a show of withdrawing his other hand from his cloak, clicks his fingers to produce fire, willed from his blood and being and the small flash paper in his palm. It sits perfectly atop his fingertip. Ned Alleyn whistles and Mephistopheles claps so hard his mask falls off.

'Done,' Ned says with a clap, gesturing him forward. 'Now at Court you'll have to use all your tricks, there's no trapdoors available and little in the way of wings, no Gods to speak of, unless we send a lad up with some string…'

'Well done,' Will says, offering him a hand to shake. What do we call you, alchemist?'

'Christopher Prophet,' he says. 'Kit.'

He follows them up onto the boards. They creak familiarly under his feet. Kit holds his breath for a moment as he walks forward into that beloved space, takes in the comforting scent of the wood and the earth and the magic of it, of transformation and power. Of words made flesh, of dreams made real. For this is where Griffin lives and breathes still, if souls live anywhere at all, in paper and words and audience tears. Kit wants every stage in London, he wants to produce hell, overthrow Paris, burn Dido. Be better, said Griffin.

'We will work wonders,' says he, hearing Lazarus' voice speaking the same, always present, inside his mind. The words chase around the empty theatre, buffeting the wooden seats and then up to the cold sky, soaring on birds' wings before transforming, becoming nothing but air.

ᛒᛂᚷᛢᚾᛚᛂ

He of bright joy

Epilogue

1599

'Why the fuck are there so many fairies in this damned play?' Kempe grumbles from the wings of the New Globe in Southwark, waiting whilst the poor lads given the roles of the frolicking fairies caper about the stage to much delight and whooping from the audience. May Day is here and Burbage likes lovers in Spring. Kit carefully opens a vial of familiar grey smoke, setting it at the stage's edge to eke out small mistings of the coming magic, the future transformation.

'Shhh, go and find your ass ears,' Will says to Kempe, standing at Kit's left side. He is playing Oberon today, a long robe that ages him and a crown of ivy upon his head. 'This is the best magic you have done for me, Master Prophet.'

'Good, but not the best, I have the best of it for later.'

'Such tricks you have,' Will smirks. 'You have people in the audience tonight?'

'My sister, come from Ireland,' Kit says easily. Mariner sailed in two days ago. Her letters in the last sixteen months have been short and badly printed. Kit met her off *The Seahorse* in Billingsgate, a rapid embrace, smelling of salt and sweat.

'Your hair,' she said, ruffling the short, red fuzz that has refused to truly grow consistently.

'Yours,' he said, tugging at the long, dark wild curls over her shoulders. In her absurdly tall pirate boots, a sabre around her waist and ballooning men's breeches, she had all the look of a pirate queen, wearing her height with a power he had never seen before. They ate and drank at the Mermaid near St Paul's, next door to his new lodgings, whilst he told her of the theatres he has worked in the time they've been apart.

'Where do you sail next?'

'Flanders again.' She munched away, pie crust gathering on her upper lip, all semblances of the careful, conscious awareness she cultivated as a terrified woman living as a boy in Southwark entirely disappeared. 'Larkin has a good connection with some wool traders there. It is easy money.'

'Larkin? Not Captain?'

When she blushed, Kit knew that she was mended.

'You don't hear from him?' she asked. No need to say his name. Kit shook his head. He did not tell her of strange books, of packages of finest compounds and ingredients, that arrive at his door every few months with only the mark for sol, the sun, in wax or ink on the packing. As her only surviving male relative, the wealth of the Blackwater estate divulged to the young Lord Isherwood. He remembers the pierced monsters on the walls in those houses, the jars of organs and specimens. He half expects one day to open the door and find a cart of them waiting outside.

'I didn't know you had a sister,' Will says.

'She's a sailor,' he says.

'A woman sailor, a maiden voyager.' Will's eyes gleam in the way they always do when he is thinking of pillaging a person's life for poetry. 'Might I meet her?'

'She's not long in London.'

Kit knows she is too afraid of being remembered. Her name is a warning along the streets of rising above one's station, do not seek to lust after more than your lot or the devil will come to drag you down to hell, like he did the Southwark murderess.

'Tonight? I'll buy,' Will says eagerly.

'I will be busy tonight.'

He hopes he will be. A package arrived yesterday from the Lime Street ward, instructions in Enochian. There are Scottish Earls and Barons visiting the Queen at Greenwich. Kit imagines him quietly catching a wherry upriver to the city. He will slip back to court, Kit is sure, unless he is quick.

He places the bowl of new mixed powders at the edge of the wings and, carefully, using a pipette, drips three droplets of water upon it. Purple smoke erupts, glamorous and vibrant, and Kempe rushes off stage, hidden from view, to find his ass ears. The audience are gasping and shouting and Kit grins. The smoke is beginning to turn orange as Will leans around to give Kempe a shove back out onto the stage. The uproar is outstanding, there is laughter, there is amazement, and when Kit looks in their faces and eyes, he sees belief. A man turned into a donkey, a biblical miracle in the grubby theatres of London, and Kit made it happen. He imagines a man with silver eyes sitting in the back balcony on a comfortable cushion, a satisfied quirk on his lips.

'Magnificent,' says Will, waving smoke away from his face. 'I will have you make a ghost for me next, Prophet, if you could.'

Kit nods. Of course he could. He lives with the shadow of a missing person, a lost voice. As Will enters, calling out his line in the midst of the audience's dimming laughter, Kit takes a moment of his own silence to remove his gloves. It is not often that he urges the formulas with his own touch outside of his little chambers; the small bench against the window with his slowly acquired alchemical books and beakers and brazier. When he washes he sometimes freezes the water, just to remind himself it is all still true, but it all matters less without those eyes following, coaching, reprimanding and praising. They are out there tonight, he is sure of it. So he must make sure the show is significant.

'Skevy.'

He looks over his shoulder. Foolish, he thinks, to imagine such a man would be content with sitting so far away, unable to see his fingers move. Kit looks him over. Nearly a year and a half apart has changed him in some ways; finer clothes, Spanish silk, a pearl in the ear, longer hair, shorter beard but the same eyes, oh, still the same. So many questions could be asked: Are we strong enough, now, to merge these spheres of our lives? Are you cold too, so far from the sun in your universe, a planet drifting on the long course back to me? The one he asks is:

'Will you watch?'

'Yes,' says Lazarus Isherwood. He steps quietly closer, slotting between the wall and Kit's shoulder, a body assuming form in the space that has been waiting for him. A hand on the lower back, familiar breath against his ear, the presence of the second, beating heart, so close. Kit reaches out his bare hand to the dying orange smoke, feels that familiar pressing of power inside and out, the elements transforming and gathering energy, the magic of the Dream onstage puffing and rising to the rafters. Of course it works, it is perfectly mixed by familiar hands, salt, sulphur and mercury, the base of all things, transforming and finding air, and Kit hears Lazarus smile. That small exhalation of pleasure. There you are. I remember you.

351

'Again?' Lazarus' breath is in his ear. They stare together at the orange wisps of smoke that trail from his fingertips, half fire, half air, truth in their twisting shapes. A heart, a sun, a universe. Kit smiles. Titania has woken, Oberon's magic is cast and the air is full of alchemy and wonder. He spreads his hands wide. Begins.

THE END

Author's Note

Writing historical fiction in the digital age has both its challenges and benefits. In the virtual world, I am grateful to the Folger Shakespeare Library for their detailed Day-by-Day Court manuscripts for Elizabeth's reign. Also the creators of the Agas digital map of Early Modern London, without which I would have been, quite literally, lost.

In physical reality, I must thank the team at Chetham's Library in Manchester for their wonderful John Dee exhibition and for answering my inane questions. I am also indebted to Gladstone's Library for the many days I have spent writing and exploring their collection in order to make sense of the theological science that was alchemy.

I could perhaps write a treatise on all the stranger-than-fiction historical recipes and methods that medieval and enlightenment alchemists utilised. I took great delight sprinkling these nuggets of bizarre scientific history throughout the book, but my absolute favourite recipe for making gold is still the fighting silkworms.

Like many of my writing comrades, I am often most inspired by my fellows. We lost some precious wordsmiths in the time it took me to write this book: Hilary Mantel, who taught me everything I know about historical fiction; CJ Sansom, who brought the Tudors to life so viscerally, for so long; and Oliver Emmanuel, playwright and my teacher. I am grateful, respectively, for *Wolf Hall*, for *Dissolution*, and for every coffee bought and every lesson taught.

Glossary

Angels – Gold coins worth ten shillings.

Angler – An Angler (also called a hooker) is a thief who breaks into people's houses by using a long hooked stick to open windows and then hook out whatever he wants to steal; particularly clothes of value.

En Caul birth or en caul – a baby born inside the amniotic sac.

Enochian – John Dee's celestial and occult language gifted to him by angels. Examples of the Enochian script can be seen in the chapter headings, in the names of the Enochian Hierarchy.

Firecrackers – Thick rolls of paper filled with gunpowder that would produce a sparks and a bang.

Frater – A frater begs and steals from women at markets.

Jarkman – A jarkman is a forger.

Pilloried – A pillory is similar to a type of stocks, the aim being that the criminal is restrained in a public place and forced to endure public scorn. The pillory was often wooden boards, forming holes for the head and wrists and locked together, either free standing or on a pole. Sometimes, the ears would be nailed to the wood to make it especially uncomfortable.

Puffer – A Puffer was the slang, derogatory term for an alchemist. A charlatan, a hack.

Red Lion elixir – The *tincture physicorum,* possibly the elixir of life.

Scrying – Scrying in the sixteenth-century alchemical practice is different from the fortune-telling the word is sometimes associated with. John Dee and Edward Kelley, famous scryers, used the practice to communicate with the heavenly realms, particularly angels.

Spirit – a word used to describe a spy.

Sovereign – The most valuable gold coin in the Elizabethan currency, worth one pound and ten shillings.

Swevel – A swevel was a piece of wire fixed from the roof to the floor of the stage. A lit firecracker, set off at the top would shoot to the bottom and give the appearance of a bolt of lightning.

The philosopher's stone – a mythical alchemical substance, rock, or egg that can turn base metals into gold, possibly also the elixir of life.

Upright Man – An Upright Man has authority over all the other criminals in his area. He can also make his living thieving on highways. Will Twentyman is an Upright Man in the sense that the other criminals around him give him deference.

Winchester Geese – Prostitutes in Southwark not licensed by the City of London or Surrey authorities but by the owner of the land on which Southwark sits: the Bishop of Winchester.

Acknowledgements

Never-ending gratitude to my agent, Alice, for your encouragement during what has been an almost impossible twelve months, and to Laura and Jamie at Bedford Square, for their continued belief and support.

I'm indebted to my editor, Donna, who teaches me more Irish words with every book, and my early readers, Sam the Dramaturg and Rachael the Pedant, for your very necessary feedback. Also to my fellow colleagues in historical fiction for their invaluable insight – thank you to Nat Reeve, Mariner's biggest advocate and fellow Tudor obsessive, and Sophie Keetch, my guide through second-book syndrome. Every panic was less awful when shared with you.

Thanks to my parents for filling the house with books about the Tudors, and to Mr U-W for his faultless and formative introduction to *Doctor Faustus*.

It's nearly impossible to make this job work as a viable career without someone providing backup, emotional and financial, especially in the tangle of persistent chronic illness. J, my sun, without you, nothing happens, not even dinner. Thank you.

Photo courtesy of Emma Hinds

Emma Hinds is a queer novelist and playwright living in Manchester with a focus on telling untold feminist stories. Emma's debut novel, *The Knowing* (Bedford Square Publishers) published January 2024 and is an exploration of female trauma in the vivid and cruel world of the Victorian freak show. Emma has also written a few previous non-fiction books (in another life as a theologian) with an essay published, *Tarantino and Theology*; with Gray Matter Books and Emma's book, *Ineffable Love: Christian Themes in Good Omens*; published by Darton Longman Todd.

emmahinds.com

📷 *@elphreads*

**Bedford
Square
Publishers**

Bedford Square Publishers is an independent publisher of fiction and non-fiction, founded in 2022 in the historic streets of Bedford Square London and the sea mist shrouded green of Bedford Square Brighton.

Our goal is to discover irresistible stories and voices that illuminate our world.

We are passionate about connecting our authors to readers across the globe and our independence allows us to do this in original and nimble ways.

The team at Bedford Square Publishers has years of experience and we aim to use that knowledge and creative insight, alongside evolving technology, to reach the right readers for our books. From the ones who read a lot, to the ones who don't consider themselves readers, we aim to find those who will love our books and talk about them as much as we do.

We are hunting for vital new voices from all backgrounds – with books that take the reader to new places and transform perceptions of the world we live in.

Follow us on social media for the latest Bedford Square Publishers news.

@bedsqpublishers
facebook.com/bedfordsq.publishers/
@bedfordsq.publishers

https://bedfordsquarepublishers.co.uk/